# Praise for Brenda Minton and her novels

"Community, traditions and faith combine to create touching scenes."

—*RT Book Reviews* on *The Cowboy's Christmas Courtship*

"This heartwarming read shows that God's plans are always greater than we can envision."

—*RT Book Reviews* on *The Cowboy's Holiday Blessing*

"Familiar characters and timely issues—addiction and moving beyond past mistakes—combine with touching scenes to make this a very satisfying conclusion to the Cooper Creek series."

—*RT Book Reviews* on *Single Dad Cowboy*

# Praise for Virginia Carmichael and her novels

"Carmichael crafts strong, honorable characters who try to do what is right. The characters will educate readers and remind us all that we are not our mistakes."

—*RT Book Reviews* on *Season of Hope*

"Calista and Grant's relationship builds at an appropriate pace, and readers will especially connect with Calista as her character grows and learns to love."

—*RT Book Reviews* on *Season of Joy*

"Sabrina's commitment to her nieces is inspiring, and having a female mechanic as a heroine is a welcome twist. Prejudices and discrimination are handled deftly."

—*RT Book Reviews* on *A Home for Her Family*

**Brenda Minton** lives in the Ozarks with her husband, children, cats, dogs and strays. She is a pastor's wife, Sunday-school teacher, coffee addict and sleep deprived. Not in that order. Her dream to be an author for Harlequin started somewhere in the pages of a romance novel about a young American woman stranded in a Spanish castle. Her dreams came true, and twenty-plus books later, she is an author hoping to inspire young girls to dream.

**Virginia Carmichael** was born near the Rocky Mountains, and although she has traveled around the world, the wilds of Colorado run in her veins. A big fan of the wide-open sky and all four seasons, she believes in embracing the small moments of everyday life. As she's a home-schooling mom of six young children who rarely wear shoes, those moments usually involve a lot of noise, a lot of mess or a whole bunch of warm cookies. Virginia holds degrees in linguistics and religious studies from the University of Oregon. She lives with her habanero-eating husband, Crusberto, who is her polar opposite in all things except faith. They've learned to speak in shorthand code and look forward to the day they can actually finish a sentence. In the meantime, Virginia thanks God for the laughter and abundance of hugs that fill her day as she plots her next book.

# The Cowboy's Christmas Courtship

Brenda Minton

&

# Season of Hope

Virginia Carmichael

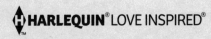
**HARLEQUIN**® LOVE INSPIRED®

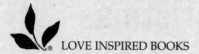 LOVE INSPIRED BOOKS

Recycling programs for this product may not exist in your area.

ISBN-13: 978-1-335-44814-9

The Cowboy's Christmas Courtship and Season of Hope

Copyright © 2018 by Harlequin Books S.A.

The publisher acknowledges the copyright holders of the individual works as follows:

The Cowboy's Christmas Courtship
Copyright © 2013 by Brenda Minton

Season of Hope
Copyright © 2013 by Virginia Munoz

www.Harlequin.com

Printed in U.S.A.

# CONTENTS

THE COWBOY'S CHRISTMAS COURTSHIP    7
Brenda Minton

SEASON OF HOPE    223
Virginia Carmichael

# THE COWBOY'S CHRISTMAS COURTSHIP

Brenda Minton

In memory of Ed Tonellato,
for all of his love and support.

Dedicated to Bonnie, Chloe and Lisa.

For to us a child is born, to us a son is given, and the government will be on his shoulders. And he will be called Wonderful Counselor, Mighty God, Everlasting Father, Prince of Peace.
—*Isaiah* 9:6

# Chapter One

Gage Cooper hit a curve in the road going too fast. His truck slid a little, warning him to slow down. For the first time in a long time, he was in a hurry to get home. Maybe he wasn't ready to face the music or his well-meaning family, but at least home sounded good.

He thought maybe it was the time of year. It was the end of November, and with the holidays coming, winter edging in, it made Dawson, Oklahoma, inviting to a guy who had been on the road a lot. Maybe it was just time to make things right. When a guy looked death in the face, in the form of a one-ton bull, it made him think about how he'd treated the people in his life.

As if the bull hadn't been enough, Granny Myrna Cooper had called him last week to let him know what she thought of him. She'd said he was nearly twenty-seven, and he needed to figure out who he was and what he wanted.

What *did* he want to do with his life, other than ride bulls?

As the eleventh kid in the Cooper clan, that wasn't so easy a decision. Being second to the last sometimes made him feel like the kid waiting to get picked for a dodgeball team in grade school gym class. The kid that always got picked last. Or second to last.

He topped a hill, George Strait on the radio, his thoughts closing in on the homecoming that would take place in less than five minutes. Suddenly he saw a woman standing on the shoulder of the road as rain poured down. He hit the brakes. The truck slid sideways and came to a shuddering halt as a couple of rangy-looking cows and a calf walked across the paved country road.

The rain-soaked woman brushed hair from her face, and glared at him from where she stood in the ditch. A black-and-white border collie at her side hightailed it toward the cattle. He could ease the truck into first gear and pass on by once the cattle moved out of the road. His attention refocused on the woman standing in the ditch, tiny and pale, big work gloves on small hands.

No, he wasn't going to drive on by. He was a Cooper. Cooper men weren't bred to leave a woman in distress. Man, sometimes he wished they were. The woman standing in that ditch had a bucketful of reasons to dislike him. Good reasons, too.

He parked his truck, sighing as he grabbed his jacket and shoved the door open, easing down, careful not to land on his left leg. Rain poured down. It was the kind of rain that chilled a man to the bone.

The cows scattered. The dog nipped at hooves and the woman, Layla Silver, called a command. She held wire cutters. A big chunk of fence had been cut and the barbed wire pulled back. Why didn't she just run the cattle to the nearest gate?

Gage moved to block the cows from running down

the road. Layla ignored him, except to flash him a brief, irritated look. Well deserved. He'd been driving too fast for this road, in this weather.

She moved a little as the dog brought the cattle around.

"Nice driving," she eventually said.

Gage stood his ground, keeping the cows from slipping past his truck. When the cattle moved, he got in behind them, pushing them back to the ditch, in the direction of the fence. He didn't respond to Layla's criticism. He had it coming, and for a lot more than driving so fast.

A heifer tried to break free and turned to run past him.

"Watch that one," Layla shouted, her long brown hair soaked and rain dripping down her face.

He shook his head to clear his thoughts and moved, helping the dog bring the cow back to the herd. The animals moved through the soggy ditch. Gage eased his right leg first because the brace on his left knee didn't have a lot of give, not for stomping through grassy ditches or rounding up cattle.

He was two weeks postsurgery. Maybe he should explain that to Layla, not that she would care. She stood back as the cows and the calf went through the break in the fence and then she grabbed the barbed wire and started making repairs, twisting with pliers held in her gloved hands.

"Let me do that." He reached for the pliers and she looked up, gray eyes big in a pretty face, her mouth twisted into a frown.

"I can do it myself, thank you." She held tight and fixed the fence as he stood there like the jerk he was.

"Why'd you cut the fence?"

"It was cut by someone other than me. I finished it off so I could go ahead and put them back in, then fix it."

"Who…"

"If I knew that, I'd put a stop to it. You can go now."

Yeah, he could, but that would make him a bigger jerk than he'd been years ago. At seventeen he'd been pretty full of himself. A few months short of twenty-seven, he should be making things right. Another fact about a bull headed straight at a guy, it made him want to fix things. His life had flashed before his eyes. Every wrong thing he'd done, and there'd been a lot.

"I'll give you a ride to your place," he offered.

"I can walk."

"Layla, it's pouring and it's cold, just get in the truck."

She shoved the pliers into the pocket of her jacket and stared up at him. Somewhere along the way she'd gotten real pretty. Not made up, overly polished kind of pretty. She was naturally pretty with big gray eyes, sooty lashes and a sweet smile. When she smiled.

"I'll walk."

"No, you won't. Don't make me have to pick you up and put you in that truck."

"Stop pretending to be a nice guy, Gage Cooper." Her voice broke a little. She turned and started to walk away.

Her house was back down the road and then up her long drive, unless she walked through the field. The rain had gone from steady to a downpour. He reached for her arm, lifted her up off the ground and trudged through the ditch with her. She smacked his back, kick-

ing him to get loose. Gage cringed, because this probably wasn't what his surgeon would call "taking it easy."

With what felt like a wildcat in his arms he climbed
the slight incline to his truck, yanked the door open and
deposited the soaking wet female on the seat. Man, this
was exactly why he didn't play the nice guy. Because
it didn't work for him. Women didn't fall over with
soft eyes and smiles. They fought him, and in general
thought he couldn't do a nice thing unless he was after
something in return.

He whistled and told the dog to get in the back
before he limped around the front of the truck and
climbed in behind the wheel. Layla sat in the passenger seat, shivering. He turned up the heat, shifted into
Drive and pulled back onto the road.

"Thank you for helping, Gage. I guess you're not
such a bad guy." He mimicked a female voice and saw
her lips turn just a little. He went a step further and
forced his voice a little deeper than reality. "Why,
you're welcome, Layla. And thank you for noticing."

He offered a flirty grin that usually worked. She
didn't smile back. She wasn't the kind of woman he
was used to.

"You're not a nice guy, but thank you for helping."

"Okay, you get the points for that one. I'm not a nice
guy. Where's your brother?" Because the kid had to be
a teenager now and old enough to help out.

"I'm not sure."

He let it go because the cool tone of her voice told
him it wasn't any of his business. He would drop her
off at her place and head on to Cooper Creek Ranch.
End of story. Yep, none of his business.

But for some reason those thoughts pulled a long

sigh from deep down in his chest. It had a lot to do with that moment on the ground before the bull tried to trample the life out of him. It had to do with facing the past. His past. And now, his past with Layla.

Because Layla was probably the person he'd hurt the most. And then life had hurt her even more. Another reason he was angry with God, he guessed. Layla and Reese, two people who didn't deserve the rotten hands they'd been dealt. Why did good people suffer while Gage walked through life without a care in the world?

Layla closed her eyes for a brief moment to gather her wits and push back the sting of tears. She was so tired. So completely exhausted. She'd been tired for seven years and it wasn't getting any easier. Seven years ago her little brother, Brandon, had been eight years old, and he'd needed her. Now he needed someone with a firmer hand than hers. But she was all he had. They were the last of the Silvers.

Their parents had died in a car accident just months past her nineteenth birthday. Somehow she'd convinced a judge to give her custody of her little brother. Her plans for college, dating, getting married, had ended the day she and Brandon walked through the doors of their house. He had needed her.

The truck slowed, then bounced and bumped up the long driveway to her house. She opened her eyes as they drew close to the little white house she'd been raised in. Her stomach churned, thinking about how hard it had been lately to hold on to it.

She'd lost a decent job in Grove and replaced it with an okay job at the feed store in Dawson. She'd had to take out a loan against the place to put the new roof on last summer and then to pay for the medical bills when Brandon broke his arm.

"You okay?"

Gage's voice cut into her thoughts. Why'd he have to sound like he cared? Oh, that's right, because he was good at pretending. For a second she'd almost fallen for it. Again. And that made her feel sixteen and naive. The way she'd been when he'd sat down next to her at lunch one day back in high school. He'd offered her a piece of his mom's pie and then told her he needed help with chemistry.

"I'm good," she answered. She'd fallen in love with him her junior year. He'd walked her to class. He'd taken her to the Mad Cow Café; he'd been sweet.

He stopped the truck in front of her house and before she could protest, he walked around to her side to open the door. The last thing she wanted from him was chivalry. She didn't want or need his kindness.

"I said I'm good." She hopped down from the truck. "I didn't get my knee busted up in the world finals or get a concussion that knocked me out for a day."

"But I won." He grinned and she held her breath, because that handsome, cowboy grin with those hazel green eyes of his could do a number on any girl, even one who wasn't interested.

He was scruffy, and sorely needed a shave and a haircut, because his brown hair was shaggy. That made her smile a little, because she liked the thought of the homecoming he'd get looking like something the dog dragged in on the carpet. Ripped jeans, threadbare T-shirt beneath a denim jacket and several days behind in shaving. His mom, Angie Cooper, wouldn't be happy.

"I'm going inside," she announced.

He glanced away from her, to the stack of wood at the side of the house and then up, at the thin stream of smoke coming from the chimney. "I'll grab some wood."

"Please don't."

He turned and looked at her. The rain had slowed to a steady drizzle, but drops of moisture dripped from his hat. She swiped at her face and headed to the porch. "Go home."

"I'm going to get you a stack of wood and make you a pot of coffee."

"I drink tea."

"I'll make you a cup of tea."

She stomped up to him. "I don't want you to do this. Your guilt is the last thing I need."

"It isn't…" He shrugged off the denial. "I'm going to get you a load of wood in and make you a cup of tea while you get warm."

"I would rather you not. I can get my own firewood and make my own tea."

For a second she thought he might leave. He looked down at her, emotions flickering through his eyes. And then he smiled. "Layla, I'm sorry. It was a long time ago, and I haven't done much to make things right. Let me get the wood. Please."

Contrition. She always fell for it. Every time her little brother said he'd help more or do better, she believed him. Gage had soft eyes that almost convinced her he meant what he said. Besides, she was older now. She could withstand that Cooper charm.

"Okay." She inclined her head to the woodpile. "Thank you."

As he trudged off, grabbing a wheelbarrow along

the way, she headed for the house. She'd managed to get a wreath on the front door and the other day she'd bought a pine-scented candle. That was as far as she'd gotten with Christmas cheer.

When she walked through the front door she shivered and wanted to keep her jacket on. But it was soaked through. She hung it on the coatrack by the door and did a quick search for her brother.

Brandon was nowhere to be seen. She thought maybe he'd taken off with friends while she'd been out in the barn. He was hard to keep hold of these days. And he was less help now than he'd been as a little boy.

She needed some warm clothes. The sound of wood thumping into a wheelbarrow meant Gage was still outside. She hurried upstairs to her room and pulled a warm sweatshirt over her T-shirt. Her hair was still wet so she ran a towel over her head, then dried her face. As she walked down the stairs, she heard clanking and banging from the living room. Wood smoke filled the air and she smiled.

Gage Cooper squatted in front of her cantankerous old fireplace insert, rattling the vents and coughing as smoke filled the room. She hurried forward and twisted the right lever. The smoke started up the chimney again. He looked up at her.

"Sorry, I couldn't get it to work."

She shrugged off the apology. "It takes skill."

"I have skill."

"Of course you do." She glanced at the pile of wood on the hearth. "Thank you for bringing that in. I could make you a cup of coffee but I don't have a coffeemaker. I only drink tea."

"I'm good." He shoved in another log. The embers

glowed brighter, sparked, and the fire came back to life. "There you go."

He pushed himself to his feet. Layla's hand went out to steady him, but she pulled back, unwilling to make contact. He smiled at her, as if he knew.

"I'll make tea." She walked away, leaving him to make the slow trail after her. "And then you should go."

She called back the last without looking at him.

He chuckled in response.

When he entered the kitchen she turned, watching as he sat at the rickety old table that had been in the house since before her birth. The wood had faded. The chairs wobbled. She'd tightened them dozens of times over the years but they were close to being firewood.

"So, how's..."

She cut him off. "Let's not make small talk and pretend to be friends."

The microwave beeped and she pulled out a cup of hot water, dropping a tea bag in before chastising herself for sounding like a shrew. But the stern lecture didn't last long. He deserved her anger.

She looked at him as she dunked the tea bag. He had settled on one of those wobbly chairs, his left leg straight in front of him. His hat was on the table and he'd folded his arms over his chest.

"I'm sorry that I hurt you."

"I think you've said that before." She put the second cup of water in the microwave and brought the finished cup of tea to Gage.

"I was a kid, Layla. I was spoiled and thought I could do no wrong. I didn't think about your feelings."

The words stunned her because he sounded so amazingly sincere. His face looked sincere. His eyes looked sincere. She was not a good judge of character. She was the person who kicked the dog out of the house for chewing up shoes and then let him back in, thinking he wouldn't do it again.

The few relationships she'd had in her teen years had been with the wild ones her mother had warned her to stay away from. But then, at sixteen her mom had told her to fall in love with a Cooper, a man who would treat her right.

Layla didn't want to think of all the reasons her mom had said that to her. The list had been long. Her mom's life had been hard. She hadn't wanted her daughter to follow in her footsteps. Layla's mom had wanted her to marry someone who would take care of her, who wouldn't hurt her.

"Layla, I mean it. I'm sorry."

"Right, I know. I'm no longer a naive kid, so thank you for the life lesson and now for the apology but…"

He grinned again. "But you'd rather hold the past over my head."

*I'd rather keep my heart safe.* "I'd rather you drink your tea and go."

Because if he sat there any longer, she'd remember how it felt when they studied chemistry together, and how she'd discovered chemistry of a different kind when he kissed her, a sweetly chaste kiss but one that had changed her life. And then she learned that he'd been using her to get to her best friend. At sixteen, it had felt like the worst thing that could ever happen. If only she'd known how much more life could hurt, she would have cried less over him.

As for her best friend, Cheryl, the friendship had ended. Not because of Gage, but because Cheryl had stayed in college when Layla had come home to raise Brandon. Cheryl married a man from Texas, and she had a baby now.

From outside she could hear the loud engine of a truck. She heard laughter and then doors slamming. Brandon was home. After a few minutes he tumbled into the kitchen, bringing cold air and the strong odor of alcohol.

"What's for supper, sis?" He glanced in Gage's direction, grinned and plopped into a chair that nearly collapsed. "What's he doing here? Got yourself a new man? One with money?"

Before she could stop him, Gage Cooper jumped out of his chair. He grabbed her little brother by the front of his shirt and pulled him to his feet. Gage's face went red and Brandon's went a few shades paler.

"Don't talk to your sister that way."

"Or you'll what?" Brandon slurred. "What'll you do, Gage Cooper?"

"I'll mop the floor with your sorry hide."

"Oh, right, because you always do the right thing."

Gage let him drop into his chair. Layla hurried to separate the two of them.

"Gage, you should go."

Gage looked long at her brother and then at her. "Layla, you deserve more respect than that. More than either of us has shown you."

"He's a kid. He's made mistakes."

"He needs someone to yank a knot in his tail."

"It won't be you. He's my brother and we're handling things."

"Of course you are." He looked around and she knew that he was seeing the ramshackle house for what it was. The kitchen appliances were on their last legs. The floors were sagging in spots. Insulation was non-existent. Wind blew in through the windows strong enough to move the curtains.

"We are." But she was barely holding it together at the moment. She knew how to be strong. But she didn't know how to accept his sympathy.

Gage leaned over Brandon again. "If I ever hear you talk to your sister like that again, you'll answer to me."

"Whatever." Her brother turned his head.

Gage let out a long sigh and pushed his cup in front of Brandon. "I'll take a rain check on the tea."

Layla nodded, too stunned to find the right words. She watched Gage shove his hat back on his head and walk slowly down the hall to the front door. A minute later his truck started, and she knew he was gone.

The fight left her in one fell swoop. She sat down at the table and reached for the steaming cup of green tea. Brandon leaned forward and lost his lunch all over the kitchen floor.

She was handling things.

She was handling being a single parent to a rebellious teenager. She was handling the bills that had to be paid. And somehow she would handle Gage Cooper being back in town.

## Chapter Two

Gage rolled up the drive to Cooper Creek. He breathed in and out slowly, trying to let go of the urge to go back and beat some sense into Brandon Silver. But that would put him smack-dab in the middle of Layla's life, and that obviously wasn't where he wanted to be. Layla was the kind of woman a man married. He made a habit of staying away from the marrying kind.

He parked next to his brother Jackson's truck and got out. For a minute he stood in the driveway looking up at the big old house where he'd grown up. In a week it would be hung with lights and trimmed with red bows. His mom sure loved Christmas. And she loved her family.

He took off his hat and scratched his head. He didn't know why that love had been feeling like a noose for the past year or so. Maybe because it had felt like he couldn't meet any of the expectations placed on him. As he walked up the steps, the front door opened. His mom stood in the doorway, her smile huge. She wasn't a big lady but sometimes she seemed like a giant. She had a way of being strong and in control, even with a bunch of men in the family towering over her.

"It's about time." She smiled, and he smiled back.

"I haven't been gone that long."

"Since summer." She grabbed him in a big hug. "I thought you'd be here an hour ago. I was starting to worry. I even called your cell phone."

"I left it in my truck."

"Weren't you in your truck?" She pulled him inside. "Where were you?"

"Helping Layla Silver put some cattle in."

His mom's smile dissolved. "She's had a rough time of it lately. Word around town is that Brandon has been pulling some capers."

Capers. That was his mom's way of saying the kid was in deep trouble.

"What kind of capers?"

"Stealing, setting hay on fire and vandalizing. But he hasn't been caught, so it's all just hearsay."

"Well, right now he's sitting in her kitchen drunk."

"I've heard that, too. And it's a shame. His daddy was a horrible alcoholic before that accident. They say he was drunk that night."

"I know." He didn't need to hear the story again. He didn't need to relive his own guilt again. "What's for dinner?"

Change of subject. His mom looked up at him, her smile fading into a frown. "I thought we were discussing Layla?"

"I know what we were doing. Now we're avoiding discussing Layla."

He'd like to avoid reliving his past and all of his mistakes in the first few hours of returning home. There wasn't a thing he could do about what he'd done. He couldn't do anything about the injustices in the world, when guys like him walked through life without a bump or bruise while the good guys took the hits.

Good guys, like his brother Reese, blinded after an explosion in Afghanistan. Gage was not on good terms with God right now, and Reese was the big reason why.

The last thing he wanted to think about was Layla, and how he'd become her friend because Cheryl Gayle wouldn't talk to him. Finally, after a few short dates with Cheryl, he'd realized his mistake. She'd been pretty—and pretty close to annoying.

And he'd missed Layla. He always thought she'd be married by now. If things had been different, she probably would have been.

"Gage, I'm glad you're home," Angie Cooper said, reading the look on his face.

"I'm glad I'm home, too." He walked with her through the big living room. In a few days they'd put up a tree. Not a real one. They'd changed to fake trees the year his brother Travis met Elizabeth. Her allergies had almost done her in that first Christmas.

Now the wagon ride they used to take to cut down a tree was just a wagon ride. They would all pile in the two wagons, take a ride through the field and then come home to hot cocoa and cookies. Family traditions. The Coopers did love them.

He wasn't crazy about them. He'd been living in Oklahoma City off and on. Had even spent some time down in Texas. Anything to avoid coming home.

"It was good to have Dad out there for the last night of the finals." It had been even better to wake up in the hospital and see his dad sitting next to the bed.

"He was thrilled that he could be there. And so proud of you. But I would have liked for you to come home and have the surgery here instead of in Texas." His mom touched his arm. "How is Dylan?"

Dylan was a year older than Gage, and the two brothers had always been close. Dylan had been living in Texas for about a year, avoiding the family. Mainly because he had known they wouldn't understand what he was doing. "Mom, he'll be home as soon as he can."

"Why is he doing this?"

"Because Casey is his friend, and she needs someone to help her while she goes through chemo. She doesn't have family."

"I know but it's a big responsibility for a young man."

"He's twenty-eight, and you've taught us all to help those in need."

"It's one lesson you've all learned." She hooked her arm through his. "Jackson is here."

"Good. I meant to tell him about a few bulls that are going up for sale."

"You boys and those bucking bulls." She shook her head. He didn't mind that she didn't get it. She got just about everything else that mattered. Before she walked away he hugged her again.

"I've missed you."

She smiled at that, "I've missed you, too. Sometimes I don't know if you know how much. Which reminds me. You missed Thanksgiving last Thursday. But you did not miss serving dinner tonight at the Back Street Community Center."

He nearly groaned. He hadn't timed this as well as

he'd thought. Each year they had a community dinner a week after Thanksgiving.

"How long do I have?"

She patted his back. "A few hours. Don't try to leave."

From the kitchen he heard Jackson laugh. Gage walked into the big open room that always smelled like something good was cooking, and usually was. He ignored Jackson and opened the oven door. Rolls. He inhaled the aroma and closed the door.

"Better stay out of there or Mom will have your hide." Jackson poured himself a cup of coffee and offered one to Gage.

"No, thanks."

"Did I hear you say something about Layla Silver?"

Gage shook his head.

Jackson took a sip of coffee and stared at him over the rim of the cup. Gage zeroed in on the pies lined up on the counter. He went for one but his mom slapped his hand away.

"Those are for the community center."

"I had restaurant food for Thanksgiving. Don't I rate at least a piece of pumpkin pie?"

"Not on your life, cowboy. You could have come home."

"I couldn't leave Dylan."

His mom went to the fridge and opened the door. "I have a coconut cream pie I made a couple of days ago. Knock yourself out."

"Thanks, Mom. That's why you're the best. Where's Dad?"

"He took a load of cattle to Tulsa. He's staying there tonight."

Gage grabbed a fork and headed for the table to finish off the pie. "So, you guys have fun at the community center."

He knew he wouldn't get away with skating out on helping. He thought it would be fun to try. He took a bite of pie, closing his eyes just briefly to savor the taste. His mom's pies were the best.

"You're going with me," his mom said from the kitchen as she opened the oven door and removed the homemade rolls. "Jackson, Madeline and Jade are helping, too."

"You know I can't stand for long periods of time." He grinned as he tried out his last excuse, pointing to the knee he'd had surgery on.

"We'll get you a chair to sit on."

He'd lost. He knew when to let it go.

Jackson sat down next to him. "Lucky for you, Layla Silver will be there, too."

"Thanks...that makes it all better." Gage finished off his pie. "I'm going to get cleaned up."

He made it upstairs to his room and collapsed on the bed that had the same bedspread he'd used as a teen. The posters on the walls were of bull riders he'd looked up to as a kid. Justin McBride, J. W. Hart and Chris Shivers. He crooked one arm behind his head and thought about how life had changed. He'd wanted to be them. Now he rode in some of the same events they'd ridden in. But he was still running from life.

Since he had time he flipped on the TV and searched for reruns of the finals. He didn't find them so he settled for a few minutes of a popular sitcom. A guy who had made mistakes and was trying to make amends to the people he'd hurt. Gage thought about how much he had in common with the guy in that show. Since his bull wreck at the finals, he'd been thinking a lot about his list of wrongs.

How did he make amends to the people he'd hurt? Where did he start? He sighed, because he knew that he needed to start with the person he'd hurt the most. The person who liked him the least.

How did he do that without giving her the wrong idea?

The parking lot at Back Street Community Center held about fifty cars. So far there were only a dozen or so. Layla parked her old truck and reached for the green bean casserole she'd brought. In the passenger seat, Brandon looked miserable and almost as green as the casserole.

"Come on. You can help serve." She handed him the dish. "Don't drop it."

"I think I can manage to carry a pan." He had that sullen, teen look on his face. She ignored it because she knew he wanted to get a rise of her.

"Let's go, then."

"Why can't I help the guys put together the buildings for the nativity?" He nodded in the direction of Bethlehem, or at least the Dawson version.

As they walked by, the star over the manger lit up briefly, flickered and went out again. Someone yelled that they'd found the short in the cord.

Brandon slowed, probably hoping she'd tell him to do what he wanted. She shook her head.

"You're going inside."

He groaned. "I thought helping out was a good thing, and you're telling me I can't."

"You're helping, just not where you want to help."

They walked through the light mist to the front of the church that Jeremy and Beth Hightree had turned into a community center. Brandon lagged, his face one of absolute misery. For a second she almost caved, nearly told him he could help with the nativity buildings. But then she remembered why she'd dragged him along.

Days like this made her wish for someone to lean on. An aunt or uncle, anyone. But the one uncle they had was just as bad an alcoholic as their father had been. An aunt who was married lived in Africa. She and her husband were missionaries and rarely came home.

She walked through the doors of the old church and paused for a moment, feeling a wonderful sense of calm. The sanctuary of the church had been turned into a dining room. Tables were spread with white cloths. Pretty centerpieces added color. Layla could smell the aroma seeping up the steps. Turkey, ham, all of the typical Thanksgiving foods for this community dinner.

Peace. She looked to the front of the church where the wooden cross still hung on the wall. For a brief moment she closed her eyes and drew on a strength that came from within. She didn't have family to turn to but she had God. She had a community that loved her.

"Are you going to stand here all night?" Brandon sulked behind her.

"No." She moved on, walking through the sanctuary to the stairs.

"I'm going to stay the night with Lance," Brandon informed her as they headed down the stairs.

"No, you're not." She took the dish from his hands. The friend he'd mentioned was off-limits. "You're going to help me and then we're going home. And you're going to stay home. You're grounded."

"Layla, you're five feet tall. How are you gonna make me?" He towered over her. She knew he had a point. And it made her mad. In the past year he'd started challenging her, making things difficult. It had been easy when he was little. Now he needed a dad.

Standing in the kitchen of the community center, they had an audience. He did that on purpose. He picked public places to argue because he thought she would give in.

"Brandon, you're staying home."

"Who's going to stop me if I decide to leave?"

"I guess I'll make you." She knew that voice.

Gage stepped out of the shadows. He'd shaved and changed into new jeans and a button-up shirt. He'd left behind the shadow of growth on his chin. The dark stubble distracted her. He was talking again and Brandon looked a little cornered.

"Brandon, if I have to, I'll drive you home and I'll make sure you stay there."

Brandon smirked. "Who gave you a suit of armor and a white horse?"

Layla's thoughts exactly. Brandon had probably heard her say that at some point. She'd repeated more than once that she didn't need help. She could handle things. But lately it had been getting a lot harder. Losing her job had been the last straw.

"I don't need a suit of armor, jack…" Gage closed his mouth and then smiled across the kitchen at his mother, who had cleared her throat to stop him from going too far.

"Well, I don't need you to play daddy to me. I'm doing just fine."

Gage got close to her brother. "You're going to serve turkey, smile and be polite to your sister. If not, we'll call the police and have a talk with them about you coming home drunk."

Layla wanted to scream. Gage Cooper had been home for one day and suddenly he thought he had to ride to her rescue. She could do this. She'd been doing this for a long time. Her eyes filled with tears as she thought about how to take control of the situation.

Angie Cooper appeared at her side, always warm and smiling, always generous. Layla wanted to sink into her arms, but she couldn't let herself be comforted right now. It was too risky because she was too close to falling apart.

"Let Gage do this." Angie slipped an arm around Layla. "You need to take a deep breath and let people help."

Layla nodded, but she couldn't speak. Her strength was a thin cord that was unraveling. Instead of objections she mumbled something like "thank you," and then she allowed Angie Cooper to lead her back to the kitchen, where they searched for serving spoons and talked about the weather forecast.

People were starting to file in. There were families who might not have had a Thanksgiving dinner and people from the community who wanted fellowship with neighbors, talk about the price of cattle and the drought, maybe catch up on other news.

All around her, people were talking, smiling and laughing. Layla was trying to find a way to hold her life together and keep her brother from ruining his.

She served her green bean casserole and kept an eye on Brandon, who had been given the job of serving drinks.

She avoided looking at Gage. He'd found a kitchen stool to sit on while he served potatoes. From time to time he'd stand and stretch. Typical bull rider with a broken body and too much confidence.

Once, he caught her staring. He winked and she knew she turned a few shades of red. She could feel the heat crawl from her neck to her face, and probably straight to her hairline. She turned back to the next person in line and served a spoonful of green beans, smiling as if everything was perfect. Wonderful.

But Gage Cooper smiling at her was anything but perfect.

When the meal ended and the kitchen was clean, Layla went in search of her brother. She found him upstairs helping Gage carry bags of trash to the Dumpster. The night was dark and cold. The stars were hidden by clouds and the weatherman had said something about snow flurries. It was early in the season for snow in Oklahoma.

"Time to go." She stood on the sidewalk as they tossed the bags into the receptacle.

Gage turned to Brandon. "Get in my truck."

"Gage, I can do this." Layla pulled her jacket tight against the wind and looked from him to her brother.

"I know that." Gage pointed to his truck, and Brandon hurried across the parking lot like an eager puppy. Layla felt the first bits of anger coming to life.

"What in the world?" She watched Brandon climb in the passenger's side of Gage's truck.

"He's going to help me at the ranch tomorrow."

"Why?"

"To keep him out of trouble." Gage tilted his hat back and walked toward her. "Layla, I'm trying to help. Maybe show you that I'm sorry."

"So this is your way of making things right? You pretended to need help in chemistry."

"I did need help in chemistry." He grinned that Cooper grin that went straight to a girl's heart. Not hers, though. She knew better.

"And now I'm just a charity case that makes you feel better about yourself?"

"You aren't charity," he started. "But you're right. I am trying to feel better about myself."

"Use someone else to soothe your guilty conscience."

He smiled again, and her heart ached. "There are plenty of people that I need to make amends to. I'll get to them."

"As soon as you're done with me?" She shook her head. "At least you're honest."

"Yeah, trying to be." His eyes softened, hazel-green and fringed with dark lashes. "You're too good for me, Layla."

She thought about it for a minute. "You're right. I am too good for you."

"Exactly. Now, if you don't mind, I'm about done in. I'm going to drive your brother home, and I'll pick him up bright and early tomorrow morning."

"I have to work at the feed store in the morning. You might have to wake him up."

"I can do that. And I'll bring him home when you get off work."

She bit down on her bottom lip and stared up at him, wondering if this was another game he was playing, a game she didn't have the rules for. He liked those games. She didn't. At the same time, she really needed help with her brother. Hadn't she whispered that prayer just hours earlier?

Across the way lights came on in Jeremy and Beth Hightree's home. The tree in the front window lit up, and a spotlight hit the manger in the yard. Christmas. It was a beautiful, wonderful time of hope and promise.

"I'm not sure." She looked from the Hightree's decorated house back to Gage.

"Layla, let me do this. The kid's in trouble and you need help with him."

She didn't want to admit it, but she did need help. She was worried about Brandon, about the guys he was hanging out with and the rumors about what they were doing. It had never been easy for her to accept help.

The first few years she'd worried that if she struggled, they'd take her brother away. It became a habit, doing things on her own.

"You can trust me."

She nodded and walked away, Gage's words following her to her truck. She doubted that she could trust him, but for a few minutes she had the very break she'd been praying for.

She would have to accept that it had been given to her by Gage Cooper. He was home, and she would have to face the past, and the way he'd hurt her all those years ago.

## Chapter Three

Gage pulled up to the Silver place the next morning. It was eight o'clock and he'd already been to the barn that morning. He'd fed horses, driven out to check on cattle grazing on the back part of the ranch and then he'd had a big breakfast. Jackson had showed up to work with some young bulls they were hoping to buck next spring.

He walked up to the square white house, just a box with wood siding, a fairly new metal roof and a front porch that could use a few new boards. The only sign of Christmas was the wreath on the front door. He guessed it was still early, barely December.

The house was silent. Gage knocked on the door twice. No one answered. He turned the doorknob. It was unlocked so he walked inside and walked from room to room. No sign of Brandon. He went back outside. Maybe the kid had actually gotten up early to feed for Layla. But Gage doubted it.

He walked out to the barn, his left leg stiff in the brace. It was going to be a long two months gimping around. The dog joined him. It wagged its tail, rolled over on its back for him to rub its belly. He obliged and then straightened to look around.

The few head of cattle were munching hay. He turned, scanning the horizon. That's when he spotted a lone figure heading across the field in the direction of town.

"Good grief." He shook his head and turned back to the truck. The dog followed. "Stay."

The border collie sat, tail wagging, brushing dirt back and forth. He smiled at the dog. "Okay, you can go."

The dog ran to his truck and jumped in the back. He doubted Layla would thank him for that. He'd call her later and let her know where the animal had gone. As he pulled down the drive he watched the figure getting smaller and smaller. Brandon had cut through the field and he was climbing the fence to get to the road. Gage hit the gas and took off, dust and gravel flying out behind his truck.

When he pulled up next to the kid, Brandon shot him a dirty look and kept walking. Gage rolled down his window.

"Get in."

"I can't. I told a friend I'd help him get some hay up today."

"There isn't anyone putting up hay at the end of November." Gage stopped the truck. "Get in, now. If you don't, I'll call the police and we'll see what they think about underage drinking."

"Like you've never done it." Brandon stopped. He stood at the side of the road, all anger and teenage rebellion.

"Right, well, I've done a lot I'm not proud of. But I never came home and puked on my mom's floor."

"She's my sister, not my mom." Brandon shot him a look and then looked back at the road ahead of him. "How'd you know?"

"I overheard Layla telling someone at the dinner last night. You know, she's given up just about everything to stay home and take care of you. The least you could do is man up a little and help her out. She only got one semester of college in before she had to be a full-time mom to you. I don't think she's had much of a social life. She sure isn't having a lot of fun."

Brandon walked toward the truck. "Aren't you the user who pretended you liked her back in high school?"

"I told you, I've done a lot I'm not proud of."

"So now you get to tell me how to live? Maybe we could both get right with Jesus on Sunday."

Gage whistled low. "You don't really play fair."

"No, I don't. I just figure you aren't really the best guy to be preaching at me."

Gage opened his truck door fast, and Brandon jumped back, no longer grinning. "Get in the truck."

Brandon's hands went up in surrender, and he put distance between himself and Gage by walking around the truck to get in on the passenger side. Gage climbed back behind the wheel and shifted into gear. Neither of them talked for a while. As they were pulling up the drive of Cooper Creek Ranch, Brandon glanced in the back of the truck.

"Is that my dog?"

Gage pulled up to the barn. "Yeah, I guess it is."

"What's she doing here?"

"She acted like she didn't want to be left at home alone today."

"That's crazy. Layla's going to be pretty ticked if she comes home and the dog is gone."

"I'll call and tell her I have you and the dog." He parked and got out of the truck. Brandon took his time joining him.

The side door of the barn opened, and Jackson walked out, his hat pulled low. He took off leather gloves and looked from Gage to Brandon before shaking his head. He shoved the gloves in his jacket pocket and waited.

"You two ready to work?" Jackson made strong eye contact with Brandon.

"Sure, why not." Brandon edged past Jackson into the barn.

"Nice kid." Jackson slapped Gage on the back. "The two of you can be surly together."

"I'm not surly." Gage strode past his brother, not much different from what Brandon had done. He watched him walk down the aisle between stalls, looking closely at the horses in the stalls.

"Nice horses." Brandon stopped in front of the stall that belonged to the champion quarter horse Jackson and Lucky had bought a year or so back.

"Yeah, he's nice all right. Don't let Jackson catch you messing around with him."

"Yeah, guess we could actually pay off the mortgage on the farm and then some with a horse like that."

Mortgage. Gage tried to pretend he hadn't heard the remark, but it settled in his mind, making him wonder what mortgage they could have on a nearly decrepit farmhouse and twenty acres of rough land.

Maybe that explained the dark circles under Layla's eyes? Not that a guy was supposed to notice those things. He'd learned that lesson from his sisters the hard way.

"Where do we start?" Brandon moved on past the stallion to the office.

Gage followed him inside and watched as the teen took a seat and kicked back, his booted feet on the desk.

"Get your feet down." Gage knocked Brandon's feet off the desk. "First, we have steers needing to be vaccinated. We'll drive them into a round pen on the twenty where they're pastured."

"Fine. Let's go."

Gage motioned him toward the door. The two of them headed for an old farm truck. Jackson was stowing supplies in the metal toolbox on the back of the truck. He turned as they approached.

"Ready to go?"

"We're ready," Gage opened the door and motioned Brandon in. He joined Jackson at the back of the truck. "Is there anything you need me to grab?"

"Nope, I have lunch in the cooler and coffee in the thermos. We're set to go."

"Let's do it then."

"Gage, why are you doing this?"

"Doing what?"

Jackson shot a look at the cab of the truck where Brandon waited, and then back to Gage. "Don't play stupid."

"I'm helping Layla get control of her little brother before he lands himself in trouble."

"Out of the goodness of your heart?"

"Yeah, why not?" Gage started to walk away but Jackson stopped him.

"When do you ever do anything just because it helps someone else?"

Anger flared but quickly evaporated because Jackson had a point. "So, I haven't been the most charitable Cooper ever. But sometimes a guy sees the right thing to do and he does it."

"And it has nothing to do with Layla Silver being downright pretty and available?"

"Layla's pretty?" He scrunched his eyebrows in thought and scratched his chin. "Yeah, I guess she is."

"She's also the girl you treated poorly back in high school."

"Well, maybe I've decided to make a few things right." He was itching to get away from Jackson and this conversation, but Jackson didn't appear to be letting go any more than a dog that had found a good bone.

"Making amends, are we?" Jackson headed for the driver's side door of the truck.

"Yeah, something like that."

"There's a lot more to it than just doing a few good deeds to make you feel better."

Gage whistled for Layla's dog and pointed to the back of the truck. Once the animal was in, he walked around the truck to climb in. He wished he could get in his truck and take off, no looking back.

But he'd made a commitment, and he was going to see it through. Besides, even though he didn't want to admit it, he didn't feel like running.

After work that evening, Layla drove up to Cooper Creek Ranch to get her little brother. She parked her old truck in front of the two-story garage, but she didn't get out right away. It felt too good to sit in the truck and relax. The silence felt almost as good as the sitting.

A scratching on the door of her truck caught her attention. She pushed the door open and Daisy jumped back, wagging her feathery black tail and panting ninety-to-nothing.

"Traitor," she said. Daisy didn't mind. Instead she licked Layla's hand and then ran off in the direction of the barn.

Layla started walking in the direction the dog had gone, her feet dragging. The barn made her poor old wood building look miserable by comparison. Her barn had been built by her grandfather in the early 1900s. This barn was a metal building, half stable and half arena. It even had an apartment attached.

The Coopers had a little of everything. Quarter horses, bucking bulls, cattle, not to mention the banks, oil and apartment complexes. They were wealthy, but they were also the kindest people she knew. They were generous and good to their neighbors. Not that they were without their own problems. Not that their children, most now grown, didn't occasionally do something wrong. She guessed she liked the Coopers because they were genuine and sometimes they messed up.

She walked to the barn but she didn't go in. Early evening had settled over the countryside, turning the sky dusky gray and pink. In the field cattle grazed. It was peaceful. She needed that moment of peace. It was too cold to stay outside, though, and she'd left her jacket in the truck. She shivered, reaching for the door as it opened. She jumped out of the way.

Jackson Cooper smiled as he stepped through the door. "Layla, long day?"

"Always." Every day for nearly eight years. She managed a smile. "Is Brandon making a nuisance of himself?"

"Not at all. We worked him hard today. He asked about pay and Gage said we're putting part of it in an account for college and giving the rest to you to decide what he gets."

"Really? That was Gage's plan?"

Jackson grinned. "He came home responsible or guilty. Whatever happened, he's trying to help you out."

"He doesn't owe me."

"He thinks he does."

"I should get Brandon and go. I'm sure you all have more to do than keeping my brother out of trouble."

"Go on in. They're in the arena. I'm heading home." Jackson patted her shoulder and walked away as she headed into the barn.

She could hear them in the arena. Her steps slowed as she neared the entrance that led from the stable to the arena. She listened carefully to the clank of metal, the pounding of hooves, shouts from someone other than Gage or Brandon.

Through the wide opening in the arena she saw her brother in a metal chute, settling on the back of a bull.

She yelled out, "No!" But it was too late. The gate opened and the bull came spinning out, her brother clamped down tight on its back. She walked fast around the metal enclosure, keeping a cautious eye on the bull and her brother.

The ride didn't last long. The bull spun fast and

Brandon went flying. He rolled out of the way as Travis Cooper moved between him and the animal. Gage headed her way, grinning, obviously proud of himself. Quickly, something obviously clued him in to the fact that she was as far from happy as a woman could get. His smile faded and he shot a worried glance in the direction of the arena, where her brother had gotten to his feet.

"How dare you!" She pushed past him to open the gate now that the bull had been penned up. "Brandon, let's go. We're going home."

"I'm not." Brandon said, but then he had the sense to look a little worried.

"I didn't give you permission to ride bulls. I don't have the money for hospital bills. And I can't…" She couldn't lose anyone else. She swallowed the lump that lodged in her throat and refused to look at Gage. He had a hand on her arm but she shook her head. She didn't want to see sympathy in his eyes.

She avoided those looks from people. Had made it a habit right after her parents died. Those looks had turned her into a sobbing mess, and she'd had to be strong. She didn't have time to fall apart. Brandon needed her to be strong.

"It was a steer," Gage offered. "I wouldn't let him get hurt. And I'm not going to start him out on our bulls. Come on, Layla, you know that."

"Right." She motioned Brandon through the gate. "We're going home. I have chores to do and I still have to cook dinner."

"I ate with the Coopers, and we did the chores at the house a couple hours ago." Brandon kept his eyes down, staring at his boots.

"Thank you." The anger seeped out, leaving her shaking and weak. "But I haven't eaten and I'm ready to go home."

"Layla, can we talk?" Gage maneuvered her away from Brandon and Travis. "We'll catch up with you guys at the house."

"Right." Travis gave Gage a long look before nodding. "Come on, Brandon, we'll see if there's any leftover pie."

Travis and her brother walked out of the arena, leaving her alone with Gage. He nodded toward the bleachers that served as seating when the Coopers held small events on the ranch. Layla didn't want to sit and talk. She wanted to go home and put her feet up. Most of all she wanted *not* to think about Gage Cooper or how her life was falling apart while he played at fixing his.

She sat down on the second row of seating, shivering as the cool metal bench seeped into her bones, chilling her. Gage didn't sit down. He shrugged out of his canvas jacket and placed it around her shoulders.

"Thank you." She looked up at him, wishing he could always be this person. But this Gage was the dangerous Gage. He was the person a girl could lose her heart to. Even when she knew better.

"Let me teach him to ride bulls."

Gage gave her an easy smile. Life was a big adventure for him. He traveled. He rode bulls. He lived for himself. She closed her eyes because she knew she wasn't being fair.

When she opened her eyes, he was watching her. Intent. Curious. Handsome in a way that made a girl's heart melt. It was his eyes, she thought, and shook her head.

"I do not want him to ride bulls, Gage. I want him to grow up, go to college, get married and have kids. I want…"

She couldn't say that she wanted him to be grown-up so she could stop worrying. That wasn't fair. She'd known when their parents died that her life had to be put on hold to raise her brother. She had worked hard to keep the authorities from placing him with strangers.

She'd put aside her dreams of college, a career, marriage and children. That wasn't Brandon's fault.

"I'll keep him on steers until I know he can handle bulls. I think if you'll listen to me, you'll understand why this is important."

She looked up, meeting those sincere hazel eyes of his. He'd been in the Southwest, so his skin was still golden-brown from the sun. "Tell me."

"He needs something to keep him busy and people who will keep him busy. He's in with a bad crowd right now, Layla. You can't be with him all of the time. So if he's here when he isn't at school, we can keep him out of trouble. I can help you with that."

"Right, so this is about you?"

He grinned again, white teeth flashing. "Could you stop being so mean?"

Layla closed her eyes and nodded. "I'm sorry. I'm not a mean person. I'm just tired."

The bleachers moved and creaked as he sat down next to her. His shoulder bumped hers, and she inhaled the scent of the outdoors. How could he smell that good when he'd been working all day?

"I know you're not mean." His voice was soft. "I was teasing."

Her heart tried to open up. She couldn't let it. "You hurt me."

"I know and I'm sorry."

She nodded, not looking at him because she couldn't look into his eyes right then, not when her emotions were worn thin and she needed someone to lean on. It couldn't be him.

"What is it you're doing, Gage? Are you trying to earn my forgiveness?"

"I don't know." He leaned back against the bleacher seat behind them and stretched his leg in front of him. "Maybe I'm trying to find my way back."

"God doesn't require you to make amends to be forgiven."

He didn't respond for a minute. She wondered if she'd hit the nail on the head. She looked up at him. He was staring at the arena, his strong jaw clenched. She focused, for whatever reason, on the pulse at the base of his throat.

Finally he sighed. "I have to do this."

"I forgave you a long time ago. When we're young everything feels like forever. I was a typical teenage girl who thought if you smiled at me, we'd probably get married. I know better now."

"Girls really think that?" He smiled at her.

"Maybe not that drastically. But when the teenage girl is already…" She didn't want to have this conversation, but it was too late. "When the girl isn't feeling loved, she is probably looking for someone to love her."

"I'm sorry that I wasn't the person to love you."

So was she. "Well, you did me a favor. You taught me to be more careful. We've all hurt people, Gage. It's part of life, part of growing up."

"I know. But somehow I've skated through life with almost no repercussions and other people have suffered…."

He had more to say, but she didn't want to hear it. They weren't friends. They didn't share secrets. She stood up and moved away from him, away from his story and his emotions.

"I should go."

He grinned and stood up. "Too much?"

"Yeah. I think if you need to confess, I'm not the person. But I'll take the help with my brother."

"Thank you."

She took off his coat and handed it back to him. His fingers brushed hers. Layla pulled back, surprised by the contact, by the way his eyes sought hers when they touched.

"Good night, Gage." She hurried away, leaving him standing in the arena alone.

## Chapter Four

Gage didn't plan on going to church with the family Sunday morning, so he woke up before sunrise and headed out, dressed for work in old jeans, a flannel shirt and work boots. Layla had a few fences that looked like a cow could walk right through them, and he knew she'd fight him if he offered. So he wasn't going to ask, he was just going to do it.

It was cold, so cold he could see his breath as he walked along the fence line after parking his truck at the end of Layla's drive. Talk about a mess. The fence posts leaned and the barbed wire was so loose a cow could walk between the strands.

He didn't know why kids had bothered cutting the fence. They could have pushed the fence posts over. But not after today. He planned on pounding the posts back into the ground and tightening the wire, maybe replacing some of it.

It would take all day. So he wouldn't have to sit across the Sunday table from Reese and fight his anger all over again. He wasn't angry with Reese, but with the hand he'd been dealt. Gage wouldn't have to go to church and face God with that anger.

He stopped at the corner post. The sun was coming up over the tree line, shooting beams of light into the hazy morning. It wouldn't take long for it to burn up the fog and melt the frost that covered the grass and trees. But it sure was beautiful.

As the sun rose, he pounded away at fence posts, working his way down the line. He eventually had to get his sunglasses, and then went back to work. He didn't know how Layla did it all. She was working, trying to keep her brother from becoming a juvenile delinquent and holding on to this farm. He shot a look toward the house, a good thousand feet to the east of where he stood. At that moment she walked out the back door, her tiny frame hidden inside a big coat, a knit cap pulled down tight on her head.

He didn't move on to the next post. Instead he watched as she leaned down to pet her dog and then walked to the barn. He watched as she walked through the doors and a minute later she opened a side door. The horse that ran into the corral took his breath away. Maybe it was the distance, maybe it was the rising sun catching the gold in the red-gold coat, but the animal was crazy beautiful.

Where'd she get a horse like that? How had he missed it last night when he and Brandon had fed the livestock? Right, he'd fed the cattle. Brandon had taken care of the horse, and Gage hadn't thought much about it.

The animal tossed its head and ran around the small enclosure. Layla stood on the outside of the corral, her arms rested on the top rail. The horse changed to a slow, gaited trot that was pretty showy.

Eventually Gage shook his head and went back to work, pounding the next post deeper into the ground. Five more to go. He was down to the second from the last post when Layla walked up to him, her arms crossed and that knit cap making her gray eyes look huge.

"What in the world are you doing?"

He finished the last post, pounding once, twice, three times. He tried to push it, but it was in tight. "Fixing your fence before the cattle realize they can walk right through."

"I can fix my own fences." She looked like a woman about to stomp her foot.

"I know you can. I'm being helpful."

"No, you're feeling guilty. And angry. And I don't know what else. But I am not your problem. You are your problem. Stop trying to fix your life by fixing mine."

He stepped back, stung by her words. She might have a point. "Whatever."

Yeah, that didn't sound much like a teenage girl. He let it go. He had fence to fix. He pulled the tools out of his jacket pocket and grabbed the fence.

"Stop."

He looked up from the wire he was holding and pushed his hat back so he could get a better look at her. He yanked off his sunglasses and shoved them in his pocket. "Why?"

"Because I've got to get ready for church, and if Brandon sees you out here, he isn't going to want to go."

"He'll go."

"Because you'll make him?" She nearly smiled. The edge of her mouth pulled up, and her eyes sparkled just briefly. It took him by surprise, that almost smile.

He shook off the strange urge to hug her and went back to work, ignoring her as she continued to yammer at him, telling him why he was about as low on the food chain as a guy could get.

Finally she did something that sounded a lot like a growl and then she punched him on the arm. He swallowed down a laugh and turned to look at her. She was madder than spit.

"Are you about finished abusing me?"

She yanked off her knit cap and shoved it into her pocket, setting her light brown hair free to drift across her face, set in motion by a light breeze. "No, I'm not done. If you don't get off my property, I'm calling the police."

"You're going to turn me in for fixing your fence?"

"Yes." She bit down on her bottom lip and the angry look in her eyes melted. "You make me so mad."

"Because I'm cute and hard to hate."

"Something like that." Her mouth opened like a landed trout. "I didn't mean the cute part."

"Of course you did."

"No, I didn't. You think you're cute. I don't."

"I could use a cup of coffee. And where did you get that horse?"

"I don't have coffee. And the horse is mine."

"I know he's yours."

"My old stallion died a few years ago. The filly is the last foal I got from him. Her mother was a pretty Arab that I bought at an auction."

"Seriously?"

"Yes, seriously. I had to sell the mare, but I kept the foal. She's three now."

They were walking toward the house at this point. Gage didn't know exactly how it happened. Maybe she started to walk away and he followed. Or maybe they both started walking as they talked about the mare. It didn't really matter; it just meant he was losing it. No big deal.

As they got closer to the house, he glanced toward the corral and the mare that now stood at the opposite side of the enclosure. He whistled and the horse turned, her ears twitching at the sound. She trotted across the enclosure, her legs coming high off the ground in the prettiest dance he'd ever seen. Her neck was arched and her black tail flagged behind her.

"Nice, isn't she?" Layla looked at the horse with obvious pride.

"What are you going to do with her?"

"I had planned to train her for Western pleasure, but then I realized she was a barrel racer." She shrugged slim shoulders beneath the oversize canvas coat. "I don't know... I might sell her."

"Why would you do that?"

She didn't look at him. He guessed if she did, he'd see tears in her eyes. He didn't know what he'd do if faced with those tears.

Layla hadn't meant to tell him that she planned on selling Pretty Girl. But the words had slipped out, her emotions were strung tight and she had confided in the last person on earth she should have been confiding in.

"Layla?"

She shrugged.

"I don't have the money to haul her around the country or the time to train her. She really deserves to be a national champion." She stumbled over all of the reasons she'd been telling herself. When she looked up, he was looking at the mare and not at her. She breathed a sigh of relief. She didn't need to see sympathy in his eyes.

"I'll buy her."

"No." She practically shouted the word and then felt silly.

This time he looked at her. "Really?"

"No, not really. I don't know. Maybe I won't have to get rid of her. Vera said I could work nights waiting tables at The Mad Cow."

The owner of the local diner had always been good to Layla. When the job opened, Layla had jumped on it. Yes, it added one more thing to her to-do list, but it would bring in a little extra money at Christmastime.

"When are you going to start working for Vera?"

She walked up to the corral and reached up to pet Pretty Girl's velvety nose. The mare nuzzled against her palm, her breath warm, her lips twitching and soft. The mare was her dream horse. But dreams changed.

A hand, strong and firm rested on Layla's back. She wanted to shift away from the touch, but she couldn't. Not even when the hand rested on her shoulder, his strong arm encircling her.

"Don't get rid of her, Layla."

Why did his voice have to be so soft, so sincere?

*Buck up, Layla.* She gave herself the stern lecture and moved from his embrace. "I need to get ready for church."

"I'm going to finish that fence." He reached for her arm and she stopped. "Layla, don't give up."

"I won't." She smiled and backed away from him. "And thank you, for the fence, for talking. I'll see you later."

He waved and then headed back to the fence he'd been working on. She watched him go before she hurried across the yard to the house to finish getting ready. As she headed to her room she yelled at Brandon to get up. He wasn't skipping church. She heard him mutter that he was awake.

She'd give him ten minutes.

Now she had to figure out what she would wear to church. She opened her closet and rummaged through the clothes. A stack of notebooks on the bottom of the closet caught her attention. She hadn't looked at them in years. She didn't plan on looking at them now. Who needed voices from the past to remind them how it felt to have a broken heart?

That girl of sixteen was long gone. She had work-callused hands, a heart that didn't have time for romance and bills to be paid at the first of the month.

At a quarter to ten she walked through the house, carrying the boots she would wear with her denim skirt and searching for her Bible and her brother. She found her Bible on the table next to the chair she'd fallen asleep in two nights ago. She didn't find Brandon.

She slipped her feet into her boots and grabbed a jacket off the hook next to the door. She knew where she'd find her brother. And she was right. He was down at the fence with Gage.

After tossing her purse and Bible in the truck, she walked down to where the two were working away, laughing and talking like old friends. She watched as Brandon pulled the wire tight and Gage clipped it to the metal post.

"It's time to go to church." Layla shivered in the cool morning air.

"I'm going to stay here and help Gage." Brandon didn't even look up. But Gage met her eyes and she glared, letting him know this was his fault.

"You're going to church." Layla cleared her throat and stood a little taller. "Come on."

"Layla, Gage doesn't go to church, so I'm not going."

She heard Gage groan. She shot him another disgusted look.

He sighed.

"Guess I'm going today," Gage grumbled, clipping the last strand of wire. "Come on, kid, before you get us both in trouble."

Brandon looked from Gage, whom he had obviously counted on to be his ally, to Layla. "Seriously, you're giving in to her. Just like that?"

"Just like that."

"I'm not dressed for church." Brandon tried the argument, and Layla knew it was because she always made him put on his best jeans and shirt for church.

Gage wasn't dressed for church, either. His jeans were faded and ripped at the knees. His boots were covered in mud. He obviously hadn't shaved in a couple of days.

"Don't look at me like that," Gage shot back at Layla, probably because of the once-over she'd given him. "We're going to church, and this is how we're going. Besides, I'm about ready to sit down."

"So church is a good place to get warm and put your leg up?"

He laughed, a rich, velvety laugh. "You said it. And I'm driving."

"We're not going to church together." Layla found herself walking next to him, and even feeling a little bit sorry for him because he walked slower than normal. When she glanced up, she saw his mouth tighten in pain.

"You're riding with me. And after church, I'm pretty sure my mom will insist on you all coming over for lunch."

"That should be a good reason for me to take my truck, so that you don't get stuck with us at lunch."

"Layla. Stop arguing for five minutes. Please?"

She stopped, because he looked as if he needed a break. When they reached his truck, he limped around to the passenger side and opened the door for her. Brandon climbed in the back without an argument. She wanted to be mad, but instead she felt a little jealous. After fighting with her brother the past couple of years about everything, he was suddenly compliant, and it had to do with Gage Cooper.

He had a way of bringing people to his side. She remembered back to high school, even in grade school. Gage had always had a crowd of friends. She'd seen him step between friends who were about to go at it, and somehow, with a few words and an easy smile, manage to settle things.

"You know this is going to start rumors, right?" she said as she reached for the seat belt while he got in behind the wheel.

"Oh, well." He turned to the backseat and Brandon. "Is there a pair of boots back there?"

Brandon handed him a pair of boots, beautiful deep brown leather with perfect stitching. Gage took them with a grumbled thank-you. While the truck warmed up, he jerked off his mud-covered boots, grimacing as he pulled the shoe off his left leg. Layla started to tell him he didn't need to fix fences, babysit her brother or drive them to church. He needed to slow down and get better.

But she let it go. If he worked off whatever he was going through, whatever he wanted to change in his life, he'd soon ride off into the sunset and leave her alone. Again. The sooner he was out of her life, the better she'd be.

She grabbed the mud-covered boots he'd taken off and handed them back to Brandon as Gage pulled on the other pair. He now looked like a cowboy who'd been riding range in his best boots. The image made her smile.

A few minutes later they were pulling into the parking lot of the Dawson Community Church. People turned to look at them. Layla resisted the urge to slump down in the seat.

"Are you trying to hide?" Gage pulled into a parking space. Killing the engine, he looked at her.

"I'm not." She sat up straight.

"Yeah, you are. Worried about how it will look, you showing up to church with someone like me?"

She shook her head and reached for the door handle. Brandon was already out and headed across the parking lot. Layla watched him go, focusing on his retreating back and not the man sitting next to her, smelling of the outdoors, soap and ranch.

"Layla, I get that I'm the last person you want to be seen with." He laughed a little. "Sometimes I'm the last person *I* want to be seen with. But you need a little help with your brother and with the farm. I know people have tried to help you over the years and you've said you could do it all yourself. Well, I'm not as willing to believe that as everyone else. Or maybe I'm just not as willing to be run off."

"I've noticed." She smiled and opened her door. "They're ringing the bell."

He wasn't willing to be run off. Yeah, she got it. But she was counting on the fact that eventually he'd get bored. Or the lure of the road would pull him away.

As she walked across the parking lot to the pretty country church that she'd attended most of her life, she thought that maybe he wasn't the worst thing that had happened to her. Brandon was in church this morning. He'd stayed home last night. And he'd talked about his plans for the week, about going to Cooper Creek Ranch after school and what he'd learned from Jackson Cooper about cattle.

It could be worse.

As she walked, Gage limped fast to catch up with her. He reached her side, shooting her a look that she didn't dwell on. They were going up the steps and Slade McKennon was at the door, the way he always was, handing out church bulletins. He handed her a bulletin, and then gave one to Gage. He looked from one to the other of them, his eyes narrowing.

"I was helping her fix some fences," Gage explained as they walked through the door.

"I don't need an explanation," Slade whispered as they walked into the church.

Gage took hold of her arm and pulled her to the Cooper family pew, sliding her in right next to Granny Myrna Cooper, the biggest matchmaker in the county.

Everyone knew that Myrna Cooper had taken it upon herself to give each of her grandchildren one of her heirloom rings. Mia Cooper and her fiancé, Slade McKennon, had been the latest recipients of one of Myrna's rings. Before that, Jesse Cooper and his new wife, Laura.

A person with a lick of sense wouldn't want to give Myrna any ideas about where her next ring might find a home.

But obviously Gage didn't have much sense.

## *Chapter Five*

He should have seen it coming. Nearly his entire family was standing on the sidewalk after church. Of course they invited Layla and Brandon to lunch, as he'd known they would. He'd counted on it, actually. But the curious looks from his family, and from people leaving the church, those he hadn't counted on.

Couldn't a guy just be nice and help someone out?

And then he heard his mom invite Layla and Brandon to join them on the wagon ride in the fields. Today?

"That isn't until next week." Gage jumped into the conversation, trying to stop this runaway train before it sped away from him.

His mom shot him a warning look. "The weather is supposed to get bad so we decided to go today."

His grandmother sidled up next to him, her smile making him more than a little nervous. That grin on Granny Myrna's face meant one thing. She'd taken to matchmaking again. Couldn't her own engagement be enough for her? And where was Winston, anyway?

"You're making this a lot easier than I thought you would," his grandmother whispered loudly. Like she thought no one would hear, but everyone did, and those standing closest to him laughed.

He opened his mouth to object, but he couldn't think how to stop his grandmother. And if he said too much, he'd hurt Layla. He didn't want to hurt her, but people needed to realize that Layla was the kind of woman a man married.

He normally stayed as far away from the marrying kind of women as he could. A waitress at a café in Texas, a secretary in Arizona—women who weren't interested in settling down.

He wasn't a terrible person; he just didn't want to lead anyone on. He'd done that in high school, to Layla. He'd been filled with regret ever since.

And as soon as his leg healed up, he planned on heading out of Dawson. He'd been thinking he might like to hang out in New Mexico for a while. A friend had some bucking bulls down there and he'd asked Gage to help him out, maybe stay at his ranch for a while.

"Your eyes are glazing over," Granny Myrna whispered close to his ear. "They're discussing having you drive one of the wagons."

"Good." He shifted the weight off his leg. When he glanced around he realized they'd lost Brandon. "Where'd the kid go?"

Layla answered him from where she stood, next to his sister Mia. "He went home with Lewis Marler's family."

"Lewis? Is that a good idea?" He looked from Layla to various members of his family, because no one seemed concerned by the news that Brandon had taken off with some kid named Lewis Marler.

"He's fine." Layla stiffened slim shoulders and turned away from him.

Next to him, his grandmother laughed a little and she might have whispered a warning, telling him to tread slowly. He ignored the laughter and the warning.

"You think?" he said. Layla shot him a warning look, the kind that if she'd been a cat would have been accompanied by a warning twitch of her tail.

"Yes, Gage, I think."

"So, I guess we should all head on out to the ranch." Jackson pushed his cowboy hat on his head, slipped an arm around his wife, Madeline, laughed and walked away.

Gage watched as the rest of his family dispersed, including his granny Myrna. They left him standing there with Layla Silver.

He pulled the keys out of his pocket and Layla didn't move. She had pulled a white knit cap down over her hair but strands still blew around cheeks that were now pink from the breeze. Her gray eyes sparkled with moisture and her lips were glossy from the balm she'd just pocketed in her red coat.

She was about the prettiest thing he'd ever seen.

"We should go." He inclined his head in the direction of his truck.

She nodded, and he took that as agreement that they'd be riding together. He guessed he'd hoped she would insist on either going home or riding with someone else. Instead she walked next to him back to his truck, both of them silent.

When they got to the truck he opened the passenger side door for her. She glanced down the road. He figured she was still thinking about Brandon. She brushed hair back from her face, giving Gage a close look at the worry in her eyes.

"He'll be fine," he offered, hoping to take away what looked like the weight of the world on her shoulders.

"That isn't what you thought a few minutes ago. Maybe I shouldn't have let him go."

"No, it isn't. I guess you can't hold a kid hostage."

She nodded and climbed into the truck. Gage stood in the door for a minute, wishing he knew what to say. He wasn't the Cooper who knew the right words to say. He'd never been the Cooper out rescuing damsels in distress, rushing to the aid of neighbors. His brothers had always been better at the white knight thing. He closed the truck door and a moment later got in behind the wheel.

"We can go find him, if you want," he said as he backed out of the parking spot.

"Maybe I should go home?" She bit down on her bottom lip, her gray eyes focused on the road ahead of them.

"Why would you do that? Do you have something you need to do?"

"I always have something that needs to be taken care of. I do need to put plastic over my windows. I need to work with my mare. I should be there to wait for Brandon."

"You can keep coming up with excuses, but I also think you need a break. When I take you home, if Brandon isn't there, we'll go look for him."

A Christmas song played on the radio. Layla listened and she didn't answer Gage for a long time. Finally she shrugged. "I don't feel right, showing up at your house for a family event. It's your family. It's a Christmas tradition that you all do together."

"I think my mom is more excited about you joining us than she is about me being there," he offered, smiling at her before turning his attention back to the road.

"Thank you, that's nice of you to say."

"I'm not just saying it. Another Cooper family tradition is that we love to include people. It wouldn't be Christmas if we didn't have a big crowd."

He turned onto the drive that led up to the Cooper house. Layla looked about ready to jump out of her skin. Yeah, he got it; this place probably did look a little overwhelming to someone who wasn't used to it. He remembered the look on Mia's face when she first joined their family. He'd only been a little kid but he had watched from the crowd as they gathered to greet their new sister.

Layla wasn't like Mia. His sister had never been quiet, not really. Once she'd gotten used to their family, she'd pushed her way through life. Layla did what she had to do with a quietness that he wasn't used to.

But, like Mia, she didn't seem to want people in her business. She wanted to do it all on her own.

"It has to get exhausting," he murmured, not really planning to say it out loud.

"What?"

He pulled in next to Jackson's truck. "Being you. It has to be exhausting. You've been a grown-up your whole life, haven't you?"

Her lips parted and she blinked. Oh, great, she was going to cry. He hadn't meant to make her cry. He ran a hand through his hair, trying to come up with something to lighten the mood.

"You've been carrying the load alone, not really letting people help." He groaned, because that wasn't any better.

"People help." She reached for the door handle, fumbling to find it. He leaned across, moved her hand and opened the door. She leaned back into her seat to avoid his arm.

He couldn't avoid her scent. Couldn't avoid meeting those serious eyes of hers. It took him back to that day in the cafeteria when he'd asked her to be his tutor in chemistry. She'd given him that serious look. He'd flirted, smiled, maybe winked, and finally she'd agreed.

Then he remembered the look in her eyes the day she'd walked around the corner of the hallway and saw him with her best friend. He'd just kissed Cheryl and looked up to see Layla, eyes wide with pain.

In that moment he'd realized what he'd done to her. It had been eating at him for years. Back then he'd tried to tell her she was too good for him. It had only been words at the time, but as time went on, he'd realized how right he'd been.

She was still too good for him. But that didn't stop him from wanting to kiss her. Once upon a time she'd tutored him in chemistry. He was thinking seriously about returning the favor.

Layla saw the look in his eyes change. He'd leaned over to help her with the door because she'd suddenly lost the ability to find a door handle. But something happened. The air got sucked out of the truck, everything stopped, and as he moved to sit back up, his gaze locked with hers.

Layla pushed the door open and fled the confines of the truck, nearly bumping into Travis Cooper and his wife, Elizabeth. Travis grabbed her arms to steady her.

"Whoa there." He grinned and let her go. "Trying to run will only make him chase faster. He's a lot like a dog after a rabbit that way. Better to freeze and hope he doesn't see you."

Elizabeth's mouth dropped and she gasped. "Travis, enough."

Layla couldn't agree more. She looked around, rethinking the desire to run, considering the advice Travis had given her, and then wishing she'd brought her own truck. Elizabeth put an arm around her waist. Layla moved from the touch but she smiled at the other woman, hoping she'd understand.

"They're like Labrador pups—they can be overwhelming, but they mean well." Elizabeth should know, she'd once been an only child growing up in St. Louis. Now she had a baby, a husband who could charm stars from the sky and an extended family that filled two pews at the Dawson Community Church.

"I know they mean well." Layla watched as Gage walked away with Travis, leaving her to walk with Elizabeth and the baby in her arms.

"Gage will push back if they push too hard," Elizabeth offered.

"That's good to know." Layla started to say Gage helping her would be a temporary hobby. He'd soon move on.

He'd get in his truck and take off, the way he sometimes did. She'd been at the Convenience Counts convenience store when he filled his truck with gas this summer, bought a few candy bars and a bottle of water before heading out.

Trish, the owner, had asked where he was going. He'd given her that easy smile and told her wherever the wind took him.

She'd been jealous, wondering what that would be like, to take off and leave problems and responsibilities behind. She'd tried, years ago. She'd gone to college, thinking she'd graduate and never come back to Dawson. But her parents' deaths had changed all of that. She'd come home, and she would never leave.

"Are you okay?" Elizabeth asked as they got closer to the house.

"I'm fine."

They walked up the steps. Gage had waited on the porch for them, pushed the front door open and held it, his gaze remaining on Layla. When they entered the house Elizabeth left her alone with Gage. Somewhere Christmas music played, and a voice joined in, a deep bass voice. Tim Cooper, maybe. She smiled, especially when others joined him.

"I'm sorry," Gage whispered close to her ear and she nodded. The smile disappeared.

"It's okay." She shrugged out of her coat and he took it, hanging it with the others on the hall tree at the door.

From the kitchen she heard the laughter and conversation of his big family. She could smell the roast that Angie Cooper had put in the Crock-Pot. Layla imagined there was more than one. With a family this size, would one roast feed them all?

"If you're sure." And then he kissed her cheek.

Her cheek?

He pulled back, and for some reason he looked at

her with a kindness that took her by surprise. His hand touched the cheek that he'd kissed and he smiled.

For a moment she wanted to be someone else, someone more exciting, maybe the type of person he could fall in love with. That woman would be free to take off at a moment's notice. She wouldn't have responsibilities or a job at the local feed store.

But Layla wasn't that person. She couldn't leave Dawson at a moment's notice, and she couldn't let herself fall in love with Gage Cooper.

"We should definitely join everyone before they send Granny Myrna to find us."

They both laughed, and Layla felt the tension ease away as she thought about Myrna, legendary matchmaker, and kindest soul in town. As they walked down the hall to join his family, she tried to hold on to that moment.

Lunch with the Coopers kept a person too busy to think. There had been laughter, conversation and too much food. Gage had sat next to her, not really participating in the conversation, but from time to time leaning to say something to Layla, a side note on whatever the family had been discussing.

Gage finally drove her back home that evening after sundown. She had containers of leftovers that Angie had sent along, so she wouldn't have to cook that night. She thought more likely that she wouldn't have to cook for days. She had memories of a perfect afternoon with a family that enjoyed being together, laughing and talking.

She also had memories of sitting next to Gage as he handled the pair of golden-coated draft horses that pulled the wagon. The rest of the family had piled in the back. She had been pushed onto the bench seat next to Gage, a blanket over her legs and a thermos of hot chocolate in her hands and two cups.

The ride had lasted two hours, with the family singing carols, until the sky started to turn gray and the temperature dropped. Layla had shivered in the seat next to Gage, and he'd slipped an arm behind her, pulling her close to his side.

Wonderful memories to cherish.

Now, several hours later, his truck pulled to a stop in front of her house. She saw lights on in the kitchen. She didn't think she'd left them on. Her gaze shot to the barn. She would still have to feed.

"I'll help you."

"What?" She looked at Gage in the dark cab of the truck, his face touched by the glow of the security light near the barn.

"It's cold and it's late. I'll help you take care of your animals."

"Brandon can do it."

"Let's check on Brandon and see how his day went."

He said it in a way that worried her. Why would he be concerned about Brandon's day?

They walked up to the front door. She heard the television and saw the flicker of light from the screen. Gage reached past her to push the door open. They stepped inside, and Layla stopped when she saw her brother stretched out on the floor.

"Brandon!" she called out in concern.

"He's passed out, not dead."

She kneeled next to her brother, feeling the pulse in his neck. He opened his eyes and grinned.

"You stink." She moved away from him.

"I got sick on the porch."

"Just when I think you're going to change."

Brandon frowned and closed his eyes. "I'm not going to change. Remember, I'm just like dad."

She'd said that to him. She sat back, still on the floor. Strong hands rested on her shoulders. She'd told her brother he had to change or he'd be like their father. The words had been harsh, fueled by her anger.

"I'm sorry." She whispered the apology.

But was it too late? She'd spoken this into existence. She'd planted the seed in her brother, hadn't she? She'd been so tired when she'd said it. She'd been worn down and she hadn't known what to do next. She had watched him stagger into the kitchen, just fifteen and drunk, and it had reminded her of their father coming home on a Friday night, his paycheck gone after a trip to the casino, where he'd known that he'd strike it rich.

He'd had many addictions, their father. Once he'd been a bull rider, then a drinker, and then he'd been a gambler.

Those were their family traditions. But she wanted something better and lasting for her and Brandon. Faith—that was the one thing she'd worked at giving her brother. A faith based on the greatest Christmas tradition of all.

"Gage." Coming out of her trance, she turned to him. "You should go."

She wanted to close the door, pull the blinds and pretend they weren't falling apart, the same way she'd pretended years ago. She'd gone to school, worked hard, smiled and pretended.

"I'm going to feed." Gage nudged Brandon with his boot. "Get up. You can help."

"I can't." Brandon covered his face with his arm.

"You will." Gage leaned and grabbed her brother's arm, pulling him to his feet. "You're going to get some fresh air, sober up and grow up."

"I'm only fifteen. I'm not supposed to be grown-up." He staggered a little as he got to his feet.

"Yeah, well, your sister has enough on her plate without you making it worse."

"Whatever, man." Brandon backed up a few steps, then propelled himself to the front door. Layla wanted to cry. She wanted to scream at him.

She stood and went after him, catching him at the front porch.

"Brandon, you don't have to be like him. Like Dad. You don't have to do this."

He glanced back on his way down the steps, his eyes blurry, his smile wavering. He was somewhere between being a boy and a man. What kind of man would he become?

"No, you were right. I'm just like him."

"But I don't want that for you." Layla looked past her brother to the other man standing on her front porch, his hazel eyes full of sympathy. She refocused on Brandon. "You should want more for yourself."

"I don't know, Layla. I'm just messed up." He tumbled down off the porch and would have fallen if Gage hadn't caught him.

She watched them head for the barn, her brother and the man who thought he owed her something. What did she do now?

# Chapter Six

She was sitting at the dining room table with a cup of hot tea when Gage walked through her back door thirty minutes later. Brandon had stomped through five minutes earlier. She had tried to talk to him. He'd waved her off and kept walking.

Gage stood in the doorway, his hat pushed back, his mouth a grim line of disgust, or anger. She didn't know which. She pointed to the cup of tea she'd made for him. It was the least she could do.

At this point she didn't think she was going to push him out of her life the way she'd planned a few days earlier. He seemed determined to make things right. Whatever that meant.

He didn't sit down, just stood there looking around the kitchen at everything but her. After a long minute he sighed and reached for the other chair. He pulled it close to hers and sat. Taking off his hat, he tossed it onto the table and ran a hand through his unruly brown hair.

"Why haven't you asked for help?" He leaned back

in the chair, watching her with those hazel eyes fringed with dark lashes, maybe seeing more than most people.

She looked up, blinking fast to clear moisture that skimmed her eyes, blurring her vision. What did she say to that question? Did she tell him about the bruises her mom had hidden, or about cleaning her dad up after a drunken night and not telling anyone? Maybe she should tell him about cleaning hotel rooms at fifteen to keep the lights on. But her family had never talked about those things, not even with each other.

When she took over as head of the family, she'd kept the tradition of keeping things to herself. People had often asked if she needed anything, if things were going okay, and she always smiled and said everything was fine.

And they'd allowed her that illusion, even though from time to time a bill was paid anonymously or meat was provided by a neighbor who said they had too much.

Now, with Gage looking at her so intently, she shut down.

"Plenty of people have helped us."

"Yeah, when you let them." His hand slipped through his hair again and he shook his head. "Brandon needs help, Layla."

"I know." She brushed at her eyes, felt moisture that she wouldn't let fall. "I know."

"Why don't you talk to Wyatt Johnson?"

The pastor of Dawson Community Church. She'd thought about it. First she had to admit that they had a problem. Her dad had tried a twelve-step program once, thinking he might get clean. The problem was she didn't want people knowing that she wasn't okay, that she wasn't handling this. She was hiding the same way an addict hid.

"I'll think about it." She glanced at the clock on the wall in front of her. "It's late. You should go."

He nodded and pushed himself up, using the rickety old table as leverage. It creaked beneath his weight. She stood, because she should follow him to the door. She needed to thank him for helping, even if it was about him more than it was about them.

They walked through the tiny living room, warm from the fire in the fireplace. She could hear Brandon in his room. At the door, Gage took her coat off the hook and handed it to her. She didn't ask; she just slipped it on. Without questioning him or herself, she followed Gage outside.

Cold air brushed her heated cheeks. Layla walked down off the porch and looked up at the clear sky. Christmas was coming.

Gage's hand closed over hers. He led her across the yard to his truck. She should pull her hand from his and go back to the house. Alone. But she was so tired of being alone, of shouldering everything on her own.

She was letting Gage make amends, because he needed it. She was letting him make amends because it had been so long since someone took part of the load from her shoulders.

At the back of her mind she remembered who he was. Gage hadn't ever been the responsible Cooper. But his hand was tight on hers, strong, warm. How did a girl pull away from a touch that made her feel safe?

Safe and Gage. The two didn't go together.

They neared his truck, snow flurries falling cold against the warm skin of her face. She felt hot and chilled all at once. She couldn't get sick, not now, not when she needed her job.

"If you want, I can talk to Wyatt." Gage's voice broke through the wild chain of thoughts rushing through her mind.

"What?" Oh, Brandon. "Yes. Let me think about it."

"Now is the time to get him help."

"Gage, thank you, but I'll take care of it."

"Right, of course. Because you like to keep the doors barred and people out of your life." His eyes narrowed. "I saw once, you know."

"Saw what?"

"A bruise on your cheek. You tried to hide it with makeup. And when our math teacher asked you about it, you said you tripped and hit your cheek on the table."

Shame heated her cheeks. She looked away from him, but his fingers touched her chin, turning her to face him.

"I need to go inside." She shivered in the cool, damp air.

"Not before I do this." He leaned in, and she didn't dare to breathe, even knowing she couldn't let him kiss her. She shook her head. He pulled her close and held her. She was tight against his chest, his strong arms around her, his hands on her back.

"Gage," she whispered into the warm flannel of his shirt. His heartbeat beneath her ear was steady. He was warm and solid.

She shouldn't have stayed in his arms, held against him, but she couldn't stop the need from rising up inside her, the need to be held. For those few moments she felt safe. Like someone was in this with her. Her heart didn't care if it was Gage.

"I'm going to help you, Layla. We're going to get things settled around here. I won't go anywhere until we have things fixed up, and Brandon on the right track." He whispered the words close to her ear, then brushed a kiss across her cheek.

*He wouldn't go anywhere, until...* She needed to pull back. His words were a reminder that he couldn't be the person she counted on. Just one more moment in his arms. He kissed the top of her head and then she drew back, leaving the warmth of his embrace.

"I should go."

He peered down at her. "Are you sick?"

"No, why?"

"You look pale."

"It's winter and I have fair skin. Of course I look pale."

He brushed a hand across her cheek. "You feel warm."

"I'm fine."

The snow fell harder and she pulled her light jacket tight to keep out the chill. It wouldn't snow long, just enough to be pretty. Gage had pushed his hat down low over his eyes.

"I really should go." He reached for the door of his truck. "If you need anything at all, call me."

She nodded, but she wouldn't call him. She didn't call people. He grinned and shook his head because he knew.

"Goodbye." She backed away from him.

"I mean it, about calling. I know you won't, but I mean it."

She nodded and then headed back to the house. The dog met her on the front porch, wanting inside.

She reached for the doorknob as Daisy jumped around her, barking at the closed door. Gage's headlights flashed across the porch as he backed out to turn around. The dog barked again, and Layla walked in the front door.

Brandon was asleep. She glanced at the clock and shook her head. It was too early, but she let it go. He had school in the morning. She had work.

She flipped on the hall light and headed for her room, the one bedroom upstairs. It was freezing cold. Sometimes it was so cold that a glass of water would freeze on her bedside table before morning. But she loved the room in the eaves. It had been a part of the original home, back when her ancestors had first settled in Indian Territory, taking advantage of government land, the railroad and the river.

It had been her sanctuary. It still was.

She changed quickly and then reached into the closet for her robe. Once again she spotted the notebooks that held her journals. She should read a book, not a journal from years ago. But she grabbed the one on top. Just a quick peek.

Big mistake. She shook her head as she read entries that detailed her crush on Gage Cooper. Yikes, she had doodled his name and hers. She had recorded prayers. Some for her family, friends and people in Dawson. And one for Gage, that he would love her.

The journal of Layla Silver, sappy teenager, delusional, hopeless romantic. Back when she'd once believed in fairy tales and happy-ever-afters.

She tossed the journal back into the dark depths of her closet and grabbed a romance novel off her bookcase. Much better to lose herself in fiction than get lost in the past.

When she walked downstairs, Brandon was in the kitchen rummaging through the fridge and pulling out Angie Cooper's leftovers.

He looked at her, his eyes somber and sheepish. He shrugged. "I'm a jerk."

"Yes, you can be." Why should she disagree? She took the leftovers and started dishing them up on two plates. "But I love you and I worry about you."

"I know." He looked down at the floor. He was a kid. A six-foot-tall kid in worn jeans and a hoodie. He still had acne and his hair always needed to be washed.

He probably needed hugs, too. When was the last time she'd hugged him? It had been years. She remembered him as a little boy needing their mom. She'd still needed her, too. But she'd done her best. She'd hugged him a lot back then. Mrs. Phelps, his babysitter when Layla worked, had hugged him, too.

She put her arms around him and held him tight for a long minute. He protested and squirmed.

"What are you doing?" He tried to move out of her arms.

"I think you need a hug."

He groaned but then he gave her a quick hug back before escaping. "There, are you happy? I hugged you. Just don't tell anyone."

She smiled and they both laughed a little. "I won't."

"Good, because that was weird."

"Brandon, I want you to talk to Pastor Johnson. Wyatt is a good man. He's been through a lot. Maybe we should both talk to him." She pulled a plate out of the microwave and stood there, looking at her little brother who now towered over her.

He shrugged and took the heated plate from her hands. On his way to the table he mumbled that he'd think about it.

They'd been falling apart for a long time. She wondered how Gage Cooper, a man who barely seemed in control of his own life, was the one forcing them to fix their broken lives.

She reminded herself that he'd used her before to get what he wanted. He no longer wanted to date her best friend, or help with chemistry, though.

He wanted to be a better person. She couldn't fault him for that. But she also couldn't let herself fall in love with him. Not this time.

Thoughts of Gage fled, because she noticed the pile of mail she'd dropped on the counter the day before, and then forgot about. She sifted through the envelopes, wishing that she hadn't. The day had been long enough without adding to the stress. She took one envelope from the pile and walked out of the room with it.

If Brandon wondered why, he didn't ask.

Gage walked through the barn at Cooper Creek on Monday morning. Limped, actually. His knee was swollen and sore. Too much time on his feet. The doctor had warned him to take it easy. He'd always had a hard time sitting still. Listening wasn't actually one of his best traits, either.

The door opened. He turned, smiling when he saw Reese walk through the door, his white cane swinging in front of him as he traversed the dark world he'd lived in since returning from Afghanistan.

"Anyone here?" Reese kept walking, smiling as he moved forward.

Reese never seemed to get angry. Or bitter. But Gage had been bitter enough for both of them. Why would God let this happen to Reese? Reese, who always helped others, unlike Gage, who skipped out.

Gage had a lot of anger, because if God was going to punish someone, it might as well be him and not his brother. He could admit to himself that he'd been taking a lot of chances for that very reason.

"Hello?" Reese called out again.

"I'm here." Gage turned away from his brother, the way he'd been doing for the past year. "I'm going to work that new gelding."

"Is he any good?"

"Good as most," Gage answered, walking down the aisle between the stalls and stopping in front of a dark chestnut gelding. The deep red of the horse's coat caught the sunlight from the open window. The animal moved to the stall door, shoving his head at Gage. He ran a hand down the sleek neck.

The horse made him think of the mare he'd seen at Layla's. She had a prize horse and he doubted many people knew it.

"You still here?" Reese walked up, his cane tapping the stall door.

"I'm still here."

"Good to have you back."

"Yeah." He snapped a lead rope to the horse's halter.

"Gage, it's time for us to talk. You've been mad long enough. I'm not sure if it's something I've done or if someone else made you mad. But I do know you can't keep running off every time someone says something that gets under your skin."

"I'm not running."

"Not this time?" Reese reached and the horse nuzzled his hand.

"Not for the time being. I'm going to put a few things right."

"Meaning?"

"There are people I've hurt, people I've done things to. It's time to make amends."

"Right, I'm not going to argue with you about that. But that doesn't tell me why you've avoided me like the plague." Reese stopped, a slow smile spreading across his face. "You afraid you'll catch blindness?"

"No." Two years ago, they probably would have been in a fight by now. He would have pushed Reese. Reese would have pushed back. They would have been rolling in the aisle of the stable until someone stopped them.

"You itching to hit me?" Reese asked.

"Probably so." Gage smiled a little as he said it.

"Then do it. Hit me."

"Right."

"Because you can't hit a blind guy?" Reese grinned and reached, pushing Gage just a little.

"Don't."

"Don't start it if you can't finish it, Gage. If you're going to be mad, I'll give you something to be mad about."

Gage pushed back and Reese took a step, then found his balance. He laughed, but Gage wasn't amused. Reese was baiting him—he knew, and he should let it go.

"It should have been me." He leaned in close and the

words came out gruff. Reese shook his head, clearly not getting it.

"What should have been you?" Reese stepped close, his smile gone.

"If someone should have gotten hurt, it should have been me. Not you."

Reese took off his sunglasses and shoved them in the pocket of his shirt. He stood there for a long minute, staring in Gage's direction, and then he shook his head.

"You've got to be kidding. All of this anger is over my blindness? What, you think God looked down one day and thought He ought to smite someone, so He picked me? But He messed up, because you would have been a better target?" Reese used his cane to find the bench next to the office. He sat down. "I don't know if I should laugh or knock you down."

"I don't think you can take me."

"I think I can. This isn't a punishment, Gage. It's life. It's a new path and a new challenge. It's opened doors for me to share my story, and my faith."

"Yeah, I get that." Gage sat down next to his brother, rubbing his knee. "I'm not an idiot."

"No, you just play one in the movies."

"Shut up. I know that God isn't looking for people to punish."

"You were angry because you thought I deserved better." Reese grinned and then laughed. "Because you think I'm that righteous. That's pretty good."

"Shut up."

"I will, if you'll tell me what's going on with Layla Silver."

"I'm helping her out. She needs the help."

"I think she's always done a decent job of holding things together."

"That's what everyone thinks." Gage leaned back, resting his head on the rough wall of the stable. Was he the only one who could see that she was barely holding on? "I didn't plan on helping her…it just happened."

"Gotcha. Well, if you're planning on skipping out of here anytime soon, just remember that she's a…"

"Nester."

"Yeah."

Gage knew that. He had no intentions of getting tied up with someone looking for a ring and a walk down the aisle. He had plans. In a few months he was heading to New Mexico. He'd stay and help his friend with his new bucking bulls. That might take six months. He might even buy a few bulls of his own to add to Jerry's herd.

He also planned on returning to bull riding as soon as the doctor gave him the okay. He was still young. He'd won the finals. Next time he'd win the world title.

"Gage, seriously, you have to get past the anger."

"I'm working on it."

"Right, okay." Reese stood and unfolded his cane. "I came out to find you and tell you I'm going to be a dad again."

"No way." Gage stood and clasped his brother's hand.

"Yeah, way. Listen, Gage, I'm not angry with God. Don't you be angry for me."

Gage knew he had to get past this. It wasn't that easy.

"I'm happy for you and Cheyenne."

"Thanks." Reese cocked his head to the side. "Still angry?"

"I'm working on that, so give me a break."

"Fine. Mom wanted you to know she's going to Tulsa with Dad. You're on your own for lunch and dinner."

"I think I can handle feeding myself."

"Don't tell her that. She'll think you don't need her."

Gage laughed and walked back to the gelding. "She knows we all need her. Lucky is knocking on the door of forty, and he still comes over for lunch." Their older brother, Lucky had been married since his junior year in college.

"Yeah, she wouldn't know what to do if he didn't." Reese headed for the door. "I have to find Cheyenne and get back to town. Could you try to stay out of trouble?"

"I'm trying."

Gage watched his brother go. It was hard, letting him walk away without offering to help. But Reese knew where he was going, what he was doing, and he knew how to make it through the world, even blind.

Gage had been in church the first time Reese spoke, telling everyone that blindness meant trusting. He had to trust the people in his life. He had to trust that there was nothing in his path when he walked through the house. He had to trust that obstacles would be moved. He had to trust the cane and his other senses. More than anything, he had to trust God.

He'd said that everyone should trust God as if they were blind.

Gage had been angry when he'd listened. He hadn't gotten it. He hadn't gotten how God could do this to his brother. How Reese could be so accepting. Now, watching his brother navigate a dark world, trusting his senses, trusting the cane, maybe now he did. Or at least he was starting to.

He guessed if he'd been Reese, he would have been fighting mad. He would have fought the darkness. He would have fought the cane. He would have hit a lot of walls and bumped into a lot of obstacles.

The irony of that hit him head-on. He *had* been hitting obstacles and bumping into walls.

# Chapter Seven

Layla left the feed store at five o'clock Monday afternoon and walked across the street to the Mad Cow Café. Vera had offered her a job a couple of nights a week. One of her waitresses was pregnant and on bed rest. The job wouldn't be permanent, but it would get her through the holidays.

Her feet ached as she made the block and a half trek to the restaurant in the concrete block building, painted with black-and-white spots like a Holstein cow. As she walked she inhaled the aroma of Vera's fried chicken. She watched as a few of the town council members strung lights and hung lighted candy canes from electric poles. Christmas was coming. It made her hopeful. But it also worried her because she never knew how she'd make the holiday a good one for her brother. Not that he'd ever really seemed to care. But she cared enough for both of them.

The parking lot was crowded. Older farmers were there early to make sure they got Vera's famous fried chicken before it was sold out.

When she walked through the doors of the only

diner in Dawson, several people turned to wave and call out a greeting. She returned the greeting and went in search of Vera. She found her in the kitchen, turning chicken that she fried in cast-iron skillets.

"Hey, girl, good of you to come over and help." Vera wiped her hands on a rag and straightened her hairnet. "We're swamped already."

Vera handed her tongs over to the other cook, and motioned for Layla to follow her.

"You're assuming I know how to wait tables." Layla followed Vera out the swinging doors and back into the dining area.

"Oh, honey, you've been here enough, you know the drill. The only thing you won't know is the abbreviations, so don't try. I'll have Breezy show you the ropes on the first couple of tables and then you'll be on your own."

Breezy Hernandez turned from the table she'd been waiting on. She was Mia Cooper's long-lost biological sister.

"Hey, Layla. I'm glad to see you." Breezy hurried past with an order to turn in.

Vera grinned. "That girl has more energy than ten of me. She's doing a great job with the music on Saturdays, too."

"So I've heard."

Vera handed Layla an apron, order pad and a pen. "Good luck."

She would need more than luck. Monday night at the Mad Cow was crazy. The tables filled, emptied and refilled. Layla took orders, stopped to talk when she could, made salads and then did it all over again.

"Layla, when did you start working here?" Slade

McKennon, in his police uniform, opened a menu. It was thirty minutes until closing time and the café had cleared out, leaving just a few tables to wait on.

"Vera needed a little help." She pulled out her order pad.

"That's great." He looked over the menu and then set it down. "She's out of chicken, right?"

"Sorry."

"No problem, I'll have a chef salad with ranch dressing. Coffee to drink."

Layla wrote down the order and started to walk away. Slade touched her arm. She saw he wasn't smiling.

She let out a long sigh. "Brandon?"

"Afraid so. Don't worry, this isn't official, but I wanted you to know that we had a report of some kids driving recklessly on Back Street yesterday afternoon."

She didn't need more information. "It was probably him."

"I'd like to help, if I can. I know Gage has him out at the ranch this afternoon."

That was news to her. She must have made a face because Slade grinned.

"Gage is trying to be helpful." She didn't mean to say it like she didn't appreciate his help. She did. She just didn't need this much Gage Cooper in her life.

Why in the world did she always love the bad boys? Her mom had said it was in her genes, that she had to fight it and find a good boy who would stay close to home, love Jesus and work hard.

She hardly thought Gage qualified.

Slade cleared his throat, an obvious attempt to stop her woolgathering, she guessed. She took his menu.

"Gage gets him, Layla. And maybe helping Brandon will help Gage find himself."

She didn't comment on that. "I'll get this order in."

Slade nodded and before he could say anything else, his phone rang. As she walked through the doors to the kitchen, Slade yelled out to cancel his order. He had to leave. Layla tossed the paper in the trash. When she returned to the dining room, Slade was gone, blue lights flashing as he took off.

"It's closing time, girls." Vera walked out of the kitchen, drying her hands on a towel.

Layla's feet couldn't have agreed more. She seriously needed a massage. And better shoes. She hobbled over to the door and turned off the neon Open sign.

"You okay?" Breezy slipped the apron off her waist and tossed it under the counter at the front of the dining room. She reached for Layla's.

"I'm good. Just worn-out."

"It won't take long to clean up our work area," Breezy offered with another big smile. "I already filled the condiments for the morning shift."

"I don't know how you do it."

"I don't work two jobs," Breezy said matter-of-factly.

"You girls head on home. Frank's here, and we'll get things cleaned up." Vera pushed a button on the register. "Layla, you did good tonight."

"Thanks, Vera."

Breezy pushed the door open. The two of them stepped outside. It was colder than cold. Layla shivered and pushed her hands deep into her pocket.

"Where's your truck?" Breezy looked around, eyeing the parking lot, empty except for Vera's Jeep.

"I left it at the feed store. I guess I should have driven it over here, but when I left work it seemed easier to leave it."

"I'd give you a ride, but I'm walking." Breezy lived with Mia, until Mia and Slade got married. "I guess we can walk together."

They walked in easy silence most of the way. The town was quiet, just one lonely truck driving past. The Christmas lights swayed in the breeze. Breezy seemed to have a lot on her mind. Layla enjoyed the peace and quiet. It had been a long day. When they got to the parking lot of the feed store, they stopped.

"I'll wait while you get in your truck." Breezy offered, glancing around the dark area.

"I'm fine. It's Dawson. Besides, you still have another block to go." She pulled her keys out of her purse. "I could give you a ride so you don't have to walk in the dark."

Breezy laughed an easy laugh. "If you had seen some of the places I've slept, you'd know I'm not worried."

Layla said a silent thank-you. At least she'd always had a home. Breezy hadn't been so lucky.

"Breezy, thank you for helping me out tonight. I didn't expect it to wear me out."

"You'd already worked a long day. It had to be exhausting."

"It was. I'm sure it'll get easier."

They parted. Breezy walked down the sidewalk, looked back once and waved. Layla climbed into her truck, happy to sit down, even in the cold cab. She stuck the key in the ignition and cranked.

Nothing happened. She groaned and tried again.

This couldn't be happening. Not tonight. Not in this cold. She'd walked home before when her truck hadn't started, but it had been warm and during the day. She didn't want to walk tonight. And Breezy didn't have a car to give her a ride.

She sat for a minute, waiting. She tried again and nothing happened, not even a click. The gas tank wasn't empty. She knew it wasn't. Her battery was nearly new. She tried once more, with the same horrible results.

She'd have to walk. But she really didn't want to. She stood in the gravel parking lot, looking around the dimly lit area and wishing like crazy she hadn't turned off service to her cell phone. But she couldn't afford it. There were a lot of things she couldn't afford.

She couldn't afford to fix this old truck. She couldn't afford to get sick. She couldn't afford the payments on the loan she'd taken out on the farm. But she'd had to do it. They'd needed a new roof. The farm had been paid off and the bank had felt secure giving her a line of credit. She'd had her job in Grove for six years.

Who would have thought she'd lose it a month after getting the loan?

With no other options, she headed down the road in the direction of the farm. She glanced at her watch, shivering with cold and apprehension. It was eight-thirty. She'd be home by nine. Maybe.

The lights of town faded as she walked. The cold of the pavement seeped into her feet, leaving them numb. The bonus was that they no longer hurt. Her hands burned. Her face ached from the cold and from clenching her jaw.

Ten minutes into the walk, her whole body ached from shivering. She kept trudging on in the dark.

Headlights flashed, coming toward her. She kept walking. The truck slowed as it drew nearer. She sighed as it came to a halt next to her. The door flew open and Gage jumped out.

"What in the world are you doing?"

She looked up at him, teeth chattering. "Walking."

"Layla, why in the world didn't you call?"

"I don't have a cell phone."

"Someone in town would have let you use their phone. Or given you a ride."

"Probably, but I didn't want to bother anyone. Besides, it isn't that far. I've walked it before. Do we have to stand here and talk?"

He opened the passenger door of the truck. "Get in."

She didn't argue. She climbed into the truck, moving the vents so they blew directly at her. The warmth seeped back into her body. Gage got in and headed to her place.

Two minutes later they pulled into her drive. "It wouldn't have taken me long."

Gage didn't answer. He got out and walked around to her side of the truck to pull the door open. "No, just long enough to freeze. Or get hit and left on the side of the road. Or abducted."

"I never realized you were such an optimist." She looked up at him, fighting the sting of tears. The heat had thawed her body and her nose. It had also obviously thawed her emotions. She sniffled and walked past him.

He didn't leave. Of course he didn't. He followed her to the house, marching up the steps of her tiny front porch and pulling the door open.

"Where were you?" he asked as he followed her in.

She kicked off her shoes and limped through the living room. "Working for Vera. Now I need to put on boots and head to the barn."

"Brandon took care of the chores."

She swallowed a lump of emotion and kept walking. She couldn't stand there and look at him, not when she felt raw, and he looked like a man ready to hug a woman. She had to pull herself together. A cup of tea. She needed tea. Ginger tea. It would settle her nerves and her stomach.

Gage didn't take the hint. He followed her into her tiny kitchen, where he seemed too tall and took up too much space.

"Where's Brandon?" The house was too quiet.

"In his room. He has homework."

She didn't know what to say. To fill the void, she reached into the cabinet and pulled out two cups. "Do you want tea?"

"Let me do it." He took the cup from her hand, their fingers brushing in the process. It was a simple gesture, she told herself. She'd touched plenty of hands today. Making change. Taking menus from customers. It didn't mean anything.

Until now, when he looked down at her, his gaze soft and far too understanding.

"I really can take care of myself."

"I know you can." He said it like he meant it. "But sometimes you could let people help."

"Gage, this goes above and beyond. It was a long time ago. It wasn't the end of the world for me. It was a lesson learned. And it didn't work out that great for you, either, did it? Cheryl never really liked you."

He laughed and took the cup, pouring cold water in it and putting it in the microwave. "Sit down. And thank you for reminding me."

"It's the truth. And you've done enough. You fixed my fence. You've helped my brother. The debt is paid. Your conscience should be cleared. Go rebuild that chicken pen for Jack Morris."

To her delight he turned a little pink beneath his tan. "I didn't think fireworks would set the thing on fire."

"You were very bad."

He was rummaging in her cabinet. She watched him as she sat down at the table.

"What are you doing?" she finally asked. The timer on the microwave beeped. He took out the cup and dropped a tea bag into the water.

And then he went back to rummaging. He found an aluminum roasting pan she'd bought to cook a turkey and turned on the hot water. Next he pulled out a gallon pitcher. She didn't know what to say.

What could she say when he set the pan down in front of her and filled it with warm water. He went back to the cabinet and found salt. Really, salt?

She still couldn't comment. He brought her tea. He brought a towel from the drawer and then he pointed to the pan.

"What are you doing?" she asked again.

"You're soaking your feet."

Heat climbed into her cheeks as she stared at him and then at the pan of water. He pointed and she couldn't move. Gage sighed.

"I can't kneel." He pointed to the brace on his leg, "Or I would put your feet in the water for you. As it is, you're going to have to do this. But I promise you'll feel a lot better."

Her eyes filled with tears that she couldn't blink away.

Gage dropped the towel on the table and for a long minute he stared at her as tears rolled down her cheeks. After a heart-stopping moment he leaned. His hand brushed her cheek, and then gently swiped away a tear that trickled down. She wanted to say his name, but couldn't.

She should have told him to stop. But her heart wouldn't let her. Her poor, lonely heart.

When he leaned in close, she held her breath. Her eyes closed while hot tears traced a path down her still-frozen cheeks. His lips touched hers, salty from her tears. Somehow, her hands moved from her lap to his neck. Her fingers twirled in the soft strands of hair at his collar.

His lips continued to move over hers, whisper-soft, then moved to her cheek, and then her ear. She heard him whisper her name as he leaned, still cupping her cheek in his hand.

"Now," he whispered, "put your feet in the water before it gets cold and I have to start all over again."

She nodded and moved her feet. She looked up. Gage had straightened, but he was still standing close. He picked up the cup of tea and placed it in her hands.

"I should go," he said.

She blinked a few times at the announcement.

"Okay."

He brushed a hand through hair that just moments earlier she'd had her hands tangled in. Soft hair. And he smelled good, like soap, spices and lime.

She probably smelled like fried chicken.

Of course he wanted to leave. He was Gage Cooper and she was Layla Silver, the girl who had believed him when he said they were friends. But she had believed her heart more when it said that Gage could be more than a friend.

"I'll give you a ride to work in the morning and then we'll see what we can do with your truck."

"Gage, you don't have to do that."

"I know that I don't."

"Really?" She somehow managed a smile.

"Really." He leaned in, and kissed her cheek. "See you tomorrow."

After he left she sat for a long time, holding a cup of tea that had gone cold, her feet soaking in water that was no longer warm.

Gage woke up early the next morning. He had something to do but he couldn't remember what. His dad had mentioned moving cattle from one section of pasture to another. They were expecting a buyer for a couple of younger bulls they were selling off.

He sat up on the edge of the bed and reached for the brace that he was just about tired of. He'd considered going without it, but he didn't want to go through surgery again.

The alarm clock went off, playing loud country music. He slammed his hand down on the buzzer and fought the urge to go back to sleep. Then it hit him. What he had to do. He had to be at Layla's. That's what he'd been trying to remember.

How could he forget that?

And how could he forget a kiss that shouldn't have

happened? Man, he was losing it. He'd meant to help Layla. Then last night, he'd thought he should take care of her. He guessed it had been a long time since someone had taken care of her.

Layla Silver was about the sweetest woman he'd ever met. If a guy was so inclined, she'd be the kind he wanted to marry. But she deserved better than a guy who was just passing through.

He guessed his mom was right, all the times she'd told him he'd grow up and start to think about other people. She had faith in him. He smiled as he walked down the stairs and headed for the kitchen. It was barely six in the morning, but he could hear her moving around, humming softly. "Amazing Grace." He smiled, because some things never changed, and he was glad.

"Morning, Gage." She poured two cups of coffee and handed him one as he walked into the kitchen. "Sleep good?"

"Yeah, better than I deserve." He took the coffee and grabbed a slice of toast off the plate.

"I can make eggs."

"No, toast is fine. I need to run."

"Where are you going so early?"

Did he tell her the truth or pretend he didn't hear? He smiled, knowing how that would end for him. He couldn't even avoid looking at her.

"I'm taking Layla to work. I found her walking home last night, half-frozen. Her truck wouldn't start."

"She's never been good at asking for help." His mom shook her head. "I think she learned at an early age to keep things to herself."

"I guess she did." He downed his coffee, because

he needed to go and he knew where this conversation was heading.

"Gage, be careful."

Yep, there it went. "I'm careful, Mom."

"Honey, you can charm apples off a tree without trying. Layla is vulnerable. She's been taking care of herself and Brandon for so long, and there you are, helping. She might get the wrong idea."

"I don't think she will. I think Layla has the right idea. She'd prefer to keep me out of her life." But he remembered that kiss last night. It didn't take much to realize he might be the one getting wrong ideas.

He turned to look out the window, because his mom had a way of seeing things. She knew how to read her kids, their expressions, their body language. She sometimes knew them better than they knew themselves.

What would she see if she got a good look in his eyes? He had to get out of the kitchen before she got too close. Or asked questions that made him think more than he wanted to.

Avoiding her wasn't easy, though. He managed to get a thermal cup, fill it with coffee and grab another slice of toast as he headed for the door.

"Later, Mom."

"You be careful." Being the woman she was, she laughed as he hightailed it out of the house.

## Chapter Eight

Layla worked her second shift at the Mad Cow Tuesday evening. It had been a long, long day. Gage had shown up early that morning, helping her feed and making sure Brandon got on the school bus. She'd put an end to him catching a ride with friends. He'd skipped too many days, and the school was threatening action because he had gone over the allotted number of days a student could be absent.

How had she not known that?

As she finished cleaning her workstation at the diner, thoughts were swirling around in her head. What if he'd been better off with foster parents? It was probably too late to be questioning the judge who had given a nineteen-year-old custody of an eight-year-old.

"Hey, you look like you're carrying the weight of the world on your shoulders tonight." Vera walked up behind her, placing a hand on her shoulder as she talked. "Try to get some rest and enjoy your day off tomorrow."

"I'll try."

"You need to take care of yourself, Layla. Vera's

orders. Sleep." Vera patted her shoulder. "And if you need to talk, I'm here."

Layla nodded and finished wiping down the workstation.

Vera frowned. "You do realize, don't you, that you're not giving God the chance to help you through this."

"I'm sorry?" She blinked, trying to focus.

"Layla, honey, I know you pray. I know you believe that God can and will help you through all situations. But I also know that you think Layla Silver is a rock unto herself. And when you think that way, then you aren't trusting the solid rock."

*Ouch.*

Vera gave her a quick hug. "Honey, let God help. And accept the help of the people He brings into your life."

"It should be getting easier, Vera. But it isn't."

Vera stood there for a minute watching her clean. And then she put a hand over Layla's, stopping her. Layla looked up, meeting the kindness in Vera's dark eyes.

"Layla, I knew your folks from the time we were all little kids in Dawson. I knew your dad and his bad habits. I knew the bruises he put on your mama. And I know that she was a private person and taught you to be one. But there's no shame in asking for help. Your mama should have taught you that."

Layla nodded, and looked away. A wave of heartache swept over her. Vera didn't push. She took her hand off Layla's and waited.

"She never wanted people to know."

"But they knew. They just didn't know how to help.

But they would have if she'd asked. And now I'm telling you, people want to help you, too."

"Thanks, Vera."

"Are you thanking me for that good advice?" Vera smiled big. "Or are you thanking me so I'll stop talking?"

She stored lettuce in the cooler and closed the sliding door slowly, trying to find the right answer "I'm thanking you for the good advice."

"That's good, because I just saw Gage drive your truck over from the feed store. He must have gotten it running for you."

She tried but couldn't stifle a groan. "Is he still out there?"

"No, he hopped in with Jackson. I imagine he left the keys in it. Don't let that Gage Cooper get under your skin."

Layla smiled. "I won't."

A short time later she left the café. There was a note on the seat of her truck telling her to pick Brandon up at Cooper Creek. She started her truck and gave it a few minutes to warm up before taking off.

When she pulled up to Cooper Creek Ranch, lights were blazing in the barn. There were several trucks lined up in the driveway. Whoops and hollers greeted her as she stepped out of her truck. She heard the clank of metal gates and the low moo of bulls, making it pretty obvious: they were bucking bulls.

It didn't take much to know that her brother was on the back of a bull. She walked into the stable, past stalls of quarter horses worth more than her house. She headed toward the arena, and when she got to the gate she stopped to watch.

Gage stood on the back of a chute, leaning over her brother. He was pulling the bull rope for Brandon. At least Brandon wore a helmet this time. Travis stood in the arena. He saw her, then shouted something to Gage.

A few others looked her way. She saw a couple of neighbor boys as well as Wyatt Johnson, pastor of the Dawson Community Church. He was probably there for a reason. When Gage got an idea, he sure didn't let go.

Later she would probably thank him for that.

She walked through the gate and around behind the chutes as her brother spun out into the arena on the back of a big, gray bull. She continued watching as she headed for the risers where a small crowd watched the action, clapping and cheering for the riders.

Gage caught up with her as Brandon went off the side of the bull, scrambling to get on his feet and then running like crazy while Travis distracted the one-ton animal and kept it from running her little brother into the ground.

"He's doing great." Gage offered as he walked next to her.

"I'm sure he is." She took a deep breath, released it and looked at the man who had taken care of her last night. He'd run hot water for her to soak her feet. He'd made her a cup of tea. He'd kissed her until she couldn't think straight.

Now it was as if none of it had ever happened. How did he do that?

"Did your truck run okay?"

She nodded. "Yes, thank you. That's what I'd meant to say, but I got sidetracked, watching my little brother on the back of a bull. Not a steer."

Gage flashed that famous Cooper grin. "Yeah, that would kind of leave you speechless."

"I need to get him and go home."

"The two of us took care of feeding. Hey, why don't we trailer that mare of yours out here tomorrow and ride her in the arena?"

"Why?"

He shrugged. "No reason. I know you're working her, and that's hard to do in this weather."

"I don't know, Gage." She glanced back to the arena, to the next kid sitting on a bull. Jackson was pulling the bull rope as the boy tried to get his seat on an animal that seemed pretty intent on getting him off before the gate even opened. "You should go help Jackson."

"Think about my offer." He shot her another grin that made her knees go weak.

"I will." No. She wouldn't think about it. She couldn't.

Gage touched her arm, then leaned in close. "Let yourself have fun."

His breath fanned her cheek and he smelled so good, like leather and the outdoors. Have fun, he said? She couldn't remember the last time she'd really gone out and had fun. She didn't have the time or money for fun. She didn't have the energy.

"Gage, I don't…"

He grinned. "What…? Have fun?"

"I'd love to have fun. I don't have the time." She saw his smile fade. "Look, I'm not trying to make you feel bad. I just want you to understand."

"I do understand. I know that you work hard. I also know that you need a break."

She glanced around, making sure they didn't have

an audience. Everyone else seemed focused on the bulls and the riders. "You have no idea what my life is like. You can take off at the drop of a hat. You can buy a horse, sell a bull, or travel to Colorado for a rodeo. I have to make sure the electric bill gets paid, that there is food for a kid that eats more in a day than I do in a week and outgrows his shoes every month. I have to make a payment or…"

She stopped because she'd said too much. Gage didn't need to know her reality. It wasn't his fault that their lives were worlds apart.

"Make a payment or what?" Gage's hazel eyes locked with hers, looking ten years older. Of course he would zero in on that part of the conversation.

"Nothing. Listen, I have to go. Can you bring Brandon home later? He has school tomorrow, so he can't stay out late."

Gage nodded slowly, but his smile didn't return. "I'll bring him home."

"Thanks."

She started to walk away but he caught up with her. He walked with her out the side door, into the cold night. She looked up at a sky with millions of stars sparkling like diamonds in the velvety darkness.

"Layla, is there something I can do to help?"

She smiled up at him. "You've helped, Gage. You fixed my fences. You've spent time with Brandon. Really, you don't have to keep this up."

"I know."

"Okay, then it's over now. I'm sure there are other people on your list."

She had to say the words because it was the only way she could protect her heart from him, from the soft look in his eyes and the gentleness that changed everything.

"There are definitely other people on my list. But I'm committed here. Not just to you, but to Brandon."

"But what happens to Brandon when you leave?"

"I'll make sure there are people who will spend time with him. If you'll let them. You have to admit, you haven't actually invited people into your life."

"I know." She sighed at the words that mirrored Vera's and looked away, watching as lights came on in the Cooper home. A dog barked in the distance. "I should have asked for help."

"Now you have help."

"Right."

"I'll be over in the morning with the trailer." His smile came back full force as he spoke. She should tell him no. It was easy to let him be in Brandon's life. But in hers?

She stood there looking at him, waiting for the words to form. What was it about him that tied her tongue in knots?

Cage Brandon watched the play of emotions that flickered across Layla's always-expressive face. He should have let it go and not pushed her. She'd given him an out. But the truth was he didn't want an out. Nope, he wanted to be in her life.

He couldn't kiss her again, though. A kiss implied something. It connected two people. And connections were not his thing.

But standing there in the moonlight with her, he thought maybe there was a connection. He wanted to pull her close, bury his nose in her hair, then kiss her until they both forgot how cold they were.

"I have too much to do, Gage."

He smiled at her objection. It sounded familiar. She was still the good girl. He was still the bad boy asking her to skip school. Back then she had informed him, in all seriousness, that she didn't have a 4.0 grade point average by accident. She wasn't going to blow it on a day of random fun.

He laughed, remembering, and she shot him that same serious look that she'd given him years ago. Back when he'd considered that she might be prettier than her friend Cheryl, if only she'd smile more.

"What's so funny?" she asked, looking a little peevish, like a librarian dealing with rowdy students.

"Nothing, just that you've told me that before. And I still don't buy it. You need to have some fun, Layla. You need to laugh and relax."

Tears filled her dark eyes. "I don't have time to relax."

"Tomorrow you're going to make time. I'll be over early to help with chores and then we'll bring that mare over here for a real workout."

"I have laundry and housework."

"Those things can wait. A sixty-degree day in December shouldn't be wasted." He winked, hoping to seal the deal. "We'll hang out, have lunch, be friends and maybe share secrets."

A smile reappeared on Layla's face, and he felt pretty happy that he'd been the one to put it there. Yeah, he could make people smile, but this was different. He hadn't known many people who needed to smile the way she did.

Man, he didn't know many people whose smile he needed as badly as he needed hers.

"Be friends?" She continued to smile. "You can tell me who you want to marry."

"I'm afraid to report that's a pretty short list, so we'll have to move on to my favorite color."

"What is your favorite color?" she surprised him by asking.

"Brown." He tucked a strand of hair behind her ear. "Light brown with streaks of blond."

She was still smiling. And he wanted to keep that smile on her face. In that moment he wanted her smile more than he wanted a ninety-point ride on a bull that had never been covered for eight seconds.

"That smile looks good on you." It was the corniest line he'd ever uttered, and of course she didn't fall for it.

"I'm leaving now." She pulled her keys out of her pocket.

"Oh, come on, I didn't mean it."

She opened the truck door, then shot him a look. "So you don't like my smile?"

"Of course I do, but I didn't mean to sound like an actor in a romantic comedy."

She stood on the running board of her truck. Somehow her hand held his. He didn't know how that had happened. To his surprise, she pulled him close, leaning to kiss his cheek. "Thank you."

She closed the door and started the truck with no problems. The engine didn't sound good, but at least it was working. A new engine, a new transmission, the list for that old truck went on and on.

She waved and drove off. As she went past the

house, the dog ran out of its doghouse and followed along behind her. Gage headed back to the barn.

The guys were putting the bulls back in the pen. Brandon was sitting on the risers, an ice pack on his cheek. Gage walked around the chutes to where Layla's little brother sat, blinking against the sting. He pulled the ice pack off the kid's cheek and flinched.

"Oh, she is going to be mad at you." Gage grinned at Brandon. The kid shot him a dirty look.

"She's going to be more mad at you."

"I was outside. This can't be my problem."

Brandon stood up. The kid was almost as tall as Gage, and standing like he meant to throttle him. "Gage, I think you're great, but don't mess with my sister."

"I'm not going to mess with your sister, Brandon. I'm trying to help her out a little." Gage meant to walk away but he stopped. "You have to admit, things haven't been easy for her."

"I guess not." Brandon walked alongside him as they headed out of the barn. "She worries a lot."

"I know she does." Gage pushed the door open and motioned Brandon out ahead of him. "You could make it easier for her, you know."

"Yeah, I guess."

"You guess?"

At the truck, Brandon shrugged. "I don't know why you care all of a sudden."

He hadn't thought about it but she made it easy to care about her. Maybe because she was so determined to do everything on her own. Maybe because something happened in his gut when he made her smile.

"Well?" Brandon climbed in the truck and shot Gage a look.

"Well, what?" Avoidance was his greatest gift. He knew how to avoid conversations and avoid relationships in equal measure.

"Do you like my sister?"

"I'm not sixteen, Brandon."

"What's that got to do with anything?" The kid didn't look like he meant to give this up anytime soon.

"Brandon, I'm a grown man and I'm not worried about finding a girl to wear my class ring."

"They don't do that anymore."

"Really?"

"Yeah, really. And my sister sure isn't going to wear any ring of yours."

Gage nearly choked. He hadn't been planning on giving her a ring. Any kind of ring. And he sure hoped Granny Myrna didn't have any more heirloom rings stashed away somewhere. Statements like Brandon's made him want to pack his bags and head out sooner than later.

It would have been easy to do, but he'd made promises and he wasn't going anywhere until he knew he'd settled things with Layla.

## Chapter Nine

The sky was dusky gray, and frost covered the ground when Layla walked out to the barn Wednesday morning. She exhaled and her breath turned to steam in the cold air. It was cold for early December, but the weather was supposed to break soon. The forecast said it would be close to sixty, then for the rest of the week it would be back to normal temperatures. That meant cold again.

She didn't mind a brisk morning and frosty grass crunching under her feet. When she walked through the doors of the barn, her mare greeted her with a soft whinny.

"Hey, Pretty Girl, I'm glad to see you, too." Layla brushed aside the thought of selling the mare. She didn't want to think about it. Not yet. She loved the bay with her refined head and the beautiful gait that caused cars to slow down and watch when she pranced through the field.

Layla tossed a flake of hay into the metal rack and headed to the feed room for grain. The dog barked. She walked out, almost expecting Gage. Instead she found her brother, tall and awkward with his dark hair unbrushed and his eyes still half-sleepy.

"You'd best get ready for school."

He pinched the cloth of the dark blue hoodie he wore and shrugged. "I'm ready.

"Oh." She didn't know what else to say.

"I thought I'd help you feed."

"Okay. Well, can you grab a bag of grain and feed the cows."

"Sure." He trudged into the feed room and walked back out with a bag of grain. "What about hay?"

"I put a bale out two days ago. They should be fine for now."

The big round bales would last her small herd quite a while. And since the price of hay had gone up during the drought, that was a good thing.

Brandon hefted the bag of grain to his shoulder and walked out of the barn. She watched him open the gate and head for the feed trough. Her little brother, willing to help. Without being asked. She didn't know how to process the turn of events, but she wasn't going to question it.

A few minutes later Brandon returned. He brushed a hand through his hair. "Got it. I put the bag in the burn barrel."

"Okay."

"Is that all you can say?" Back to moody teen voice.

"No, it isn't. Thank you for helping."

He shrugged again. "Yeah, well, I gotta go. The bus will be here."

"Right, the bus."

He started down the drive, but he stopped. She

waited, and he turned back around. "Hey, I'm sorry that I've been such a pain."

"It's okay."

He shrugged and took off, walking fast because the bus was coming over the hill and would stop at the end of their drive in about two minutes. As great as his help had been, she didn't trust him completely. She stood in the opening of the barn, watching until he got on the bus.

"Pretty Girl, I don't know what to make of that, but I think we have Gage Cooper to thank." It pained her to admit it, even to a horse.

The horse reached, nibbling at the sleeve of her coat. Layla pulled a carrot out of her pocket.

"You always expect a treat, don't you?"

The mare ate the carrot in three bites, nodding her head up and down as she chewed. A truck lumbered up the driveway, the diesel engine distinct. She peeked out the open double door of the barn, knowing it would be Gage.

"Great, he didn't give me time to find an excuse to turn him down."

The mare stared, finishing the last bite of carrot and then dropping her head to nibble at the pieces that had fallen on the ground. The truck door slammed shut, and the horse's head came back up as her ears twitched and she whinnied.

"Don't greet him like you're glad to see him. It'll go to his head."

"Is that what you think of me?" Gage walked through the door of the barn, a cowboy in a heavy canvas jacket and his hat pulled low. He had shaved, and she could see where he'd nicked his chin. The clean scent of his aftershave still clung to his skin.

"I guess you're not terrible," she conceded, and of course he smiled.

He walked up to the stall door, admiring her horse. "Layla, you can't sell this horse."

"I don't know if I have a choice."

"If you need money, I can loan…"

She held up her hand to stop him. "No, you can't. I'm not going to borrow money from you. I'm going to make it through this. I've made it all these years, and I'm not giving up now."

"But this horse is special."

"She's just a horse." Layla said the words, wishing she meant them. If it had been any other horse, maybe. But this horse, she *was* special. It showed in her deep brown eyes, in the way she interacted with people. She wasn't just any old horse. Layla's eyes stung, and she blinked away the moisture before turning to Gage with what she hoped looked like an easy smile.

"Right, just a horse." Gage shook his head. "And elephants fly."

"There was that Dumbo character."

"Yeah, sure." He tossed her a lead rope that she'd left hanging on a hook. "Let's go."

"Go?"

"To the ranch."

"I have to clean house and do laundry. This is my only day off."

"You have to have some fun."

"I can't, Gage. In your world, the clothes will get washed and the house gets cleaned while you're in the barn with the bulls or the horses. In my world, I do those things."

"I can do those things."

"I'm sure you probably can."

"Okay, let's go." He reached for her hand. "I'm going to show you what a Cooper man can do."

"What does that mean?"

He leaned in close, grinning. Layla took a step back.

"It means, Miss Layla Silver, that I'll show you how well I can sweep and mop. My mom is an equal opportunity chore master. It isn't only housework for girls and farmwork for the boys. And I don't always live at home."

"Oh."

"What did you think I meant?"

"Nothing. Gage, I can clean my own house."

"And I'm going to help you." He took a step closer, narrowing the distance between them. Distance she needed in order to think clearly.

"Really?" The word came out as a whisper.

"Really. Because Cooper men are pretty amazing." He slipped a finger under her chin, and she looked up as he leaned to kiss her.

This was becoming a really bad habit, she thought as he stole her breath with that kiss. His lips were warm and gentle. He brushed them across hers, sweet, achingly sweet. Layla closed her eyes and wished she was anyone else, so that she could allow herself to fall in love with Gage Cooper.

But she wasn't anyone else. She was Layla Silver, and she knew that he played games. She knew that he loved the freedom of his life.

She pulled back, shaking her head as she put space between them. "Stop doing that."

He whistled, surprising her, because he looked as stunned as she felt. "Layla, I keep trying to stop. It isn't easy to do."

"It should be."

"If you say so." He continued to look at her, serious, unsmiling. "I promise you, I didn't plan on this."

"On what?"

He shook his head. "Never mind. Let's get that house cleaned up."

Before she could answer, he took off. She followed him across the yard to the back door of the house. He reached it first, holding it open for her. *Always the gentleman,* she thought.

She couldn't quite be sarcastic because she knew he did try very hard to be considerate. His parents had raised him right. Thinking back to high school, she realized that he had offered her friendship. He hadn't pretended to want more. She had wanted it. She had wanted him to love her.

It was an uncomfortable thought that she quickly shed as she walked into her tiny kitchen and faced the sink full of dishes and floors that needed to be mopped.

Why had she allowed him into her life this way? Back then, she'd been young, naive. Now she had no excuses. So what was her reason?

Almost two hours later, Gage dumped a bucket of dirty mop water off Layla's back porch. The border collie, Daisy, ran across the yard, barking as if he had just realized Layla had company. Gage turned back into the house, walking into the kitchen where Layla was putting kitchen towels in a drawer.

She had filled a kettle of water and placed it on the back burner of the gas cooking stove. When he walked in, the whole thing seemed a little too homey. Layla in the kitchen, her brown hair pulled back in a ponytail, a smudge of dirt on her cheek. She had put out a few Christmas decorations, including a nativity on the kitchen table.

He yanked off the yellow rubber gloves she'd given him to wear while he mopped.

Yeah, way too homey. He shuddered and shoved the bucket into the utility closet next to the fridge.

"Do you want tea?" Layla pulled two cups out of the cabinet. "And I have pumpkin muffins."

"Tea is good. I had a big breakfast."

She shrugged and dropped tea bags in the cups before filling them with the hot water from the kettle.

"Thank you for helping." She looked back at him.

"No problem." He reached for one of the cups. "You drink a lot of hot tea."

"It's comforting. My mom used to…" She looked away. "My mom made tea for me. It was her way of making things better. When I needed to talk, she would make tea. When things were… When things got bad, she made tea."

He wondered if any of those talks had been about him. Layla smiled at him, her eyes soft, like a dusky evening sky. "Yes, we discussed you."

"I wasn't going to ask."

"I know." She nodded toward the table. "Have a seat."

"Are you going to…"

She shook her head. "No, I'm not going to tell you what my mom said, or what I said to her. It wouldn't do your ego any good."

"You haven't exactly been easy on my ego."

"I don't think it will hurt you if there's one woman in the world who doesn't fall at your feet."

He grinned as he sat down. Man, she was killing him. His ego was battered, his knee ached. And yet he was still smiling. How in the world did she do that?

"We should go soon."

She looked up from her cup of tea, barely hiding a smile. "Go where?"

He pointed at her. "Ha, good try. To the ranch. As if you didn't know. I didn't clean your house for my health. I did it so you would agree to bring your horse to the ranch."

"Her name is Pretty Girl, and I don't need to take her to your place to work with her."

"We have a nice, cozy indoor arena."

"Yes, I'm aware of that." She bit down on her lip and stared at the cup she still held.

"You're tempted. I can see it in your eyes."

"Yes, I'm tempted."

"Your house is clean. You got your laundry caught up."

"Right, I know. And thank you for that. It was nice, having help."

"So let's go. Get your riding clothes on, and let's head to the ranch. You might have noticed I'm pulling a trailer."

"I noticed that you take a lot for granted."

"It's my special charm. I'm confident."

"Yes, you are." She eyed his left leg. "How will you ride?"

"It isn't that difficult. The brace gives."

"Are you supposed to ride?"

He stood, grimacing as he put weight on his leg. "I'll be fine. Go get ready and I'll load your mare."

Before she could stop him, he headed out the door. She'd either be ready when he came to get her or she'd be sitting at the table waiting to tell him she wouldn't go.

He was leading the mare into the trailer when Layla appeared in jeans, riding boots and a plaid jacket. Her white knit cap was pulled down over her head and her eyes glistened. From the cold or tears?

"Ready to go?" He stepped down from the trailer and closed the back.

"Yes." She looked from him to the horse.

"Layla?"

She nodded. "Ready."

He watched as she walked around the front of the truck and climbed in the passenger side.

Now he was starting to doubt if he was prepared for this, and he didn't know why. It was starting to feel a lot like the way a guy must feel when something was about to tie him down. He'd always imagined he wouldn't want that to happen to him.

Neither of them spoke on the way to Cooper Creek. He reached to turn up the radio. "Do you like Alan Jackson?"

"Of course."

"What about Gibson Cross?"

Cross was a country singer who owned property in Dawson but hadn't been around much in the past few years. "Yes. He helped, you know. With my parents' funerals. He put money in my account."

He hadn't expected this. Why hadn't he really known her before? They'd grown up in the same town. They'd gone to school together. She'd tutored him in chemistry and introduced him to her best friend. And he'd known little about her, other than she kept to herself and sometimes she tried to cover up bruises.

"That was good of him." He cleared his throat. "He's a good man."

"The Coopers helped, too."

He glanced her way and then back at the road. "Yeah, we're good people, too."

Silence hung between them. He didn't know what to say as he parked near the barn. Reese was getting out of Jackson's truck. Great, he needed a big dose of brotherly love the way he needed a stomach virus.

"Why did you groan?" Layla asked as she reached to open her door.

"Brothers."

"You do have some."

"They're always in a guy's business."

She laughed at that. "Which is another reason to take off to parts unknown."

"Something like that."

"You have family, Gage. Be happy about that."

Okay, suddenly he felt like a heel. He tried to smile but couldn't. "You're right."

They were unloading the mare when Jackson walked out of the barn. He whistled when he saw the mare.

"Your horse, Layla?"

She nodded. "Yes, she's mine. She's the only one I have left."

"She's nice." Jackson walked around the horse. He ran his hand over her back, nodding his appreciation.

"Thank you." Layla took the lead rope from Gage.

"We're going to work her a little."

"While you're at it, work that gray for Dad. He needs a good hour under the saddle."

"And the chestnut gelding?" Gage closed the trailer.

"Yeah, if you have time. He always tries to buck when you get him in the arena."

"Good to know." Gage opened the double doors at the end of the barn and Layla led the mare through. He watched as she tied the horse, then he went back to the truck for her bridle and saddle. He'd loaded it, knowing she would want her own tack.

When he walked back in, Reese had joined Jackson. The two were discussing Layla's mare. He was surprised she didn't try to sell the animal to Jackson. But he knew she didn't want to part with the horse. That was evident in the way she brushed the horse, spoke to it, touched it.

Something about that made him itch a little. He'd never had a hard time parting with anything. But then, he hadn't parted with anything he really cared about. Not a loved one, a favorite horse, not even his first truck. He liked his life unencumbered. He craved the open road and new places. He loved riding bulls because it kept him on the road.

It was easy. Load up the truck and go.

He could do it today if he wanted. No one would question him. But his gaze landed on Layla, and everything changed.

He told himself it was because he still had a lot of

fences that needed mending. If God really had given him another chance, he needed to make the most of it.

That's what was keeping him here. Or at least that was the story he was sticking with.

# Chapter Ten

Layla slid off the back of a pretty gray mare that Gage had asked her to ride. She smiled as she reached to pat the horse's face. Super sweet. She loved the mare. She loved riding in the Cooper arena. And she had to admit, it had felt good putting her mare in one of the large stalls in the stable.

"Having fun?" Gage walked up to her, leading the gelding he'd been riding. He was limping more than usual, and she gave a pointed look at his leg. "I'm fine. And you're having a good time, so don't ruin it by lecturing."

"I think we should be done." She glanced at her watch. "It's getting late."

"It's only one o'clock." He pulled the reins of the gelding tight when the animal nudged at him. "Let's go have lunch."

"Lunch?"

"At the house." He inclined his head toward the exit. "Let's get these two brushed and turn them out to pasture."

"What about my mare?"

"She's fine in the stall. She's munching on hay and acting pretty pleased with herself."

Layla walked next to him, leading the mare, who was practically resting her head on Layla's shoulder. "I'm sure she is happy. As long as she isn't too happy here. She does have to go home with me."

"She wouldn't want to stay here. Too many men."

"When are you leaving, Gage?" she blurted out. As soon as the words left her mouth, she wanted to pull them back in.

Gage shifted to look at her. "In a hurry to get rid of me?"

"A little." She smiled as she said it, but maybe she meant it, just a little. She didn't want to get attached to him. Maybe the sooner he left, the better.

"Probably after the first of the year." He tied his gelding and flipped a stirrup over the saddle to undo the cinch. "I can't ride until the doctor releases me. Unless I decide to ignore him."

"What will you do when you get tired of riding bulls?"

He looked at her as he pulled the saddle off the horse's back. "What's this? Twenty Questions?"

"I've known you my whole life, and you've always been Gage Cooper, megaflirt and bull rider."

"Great. They should put that on my gravestone— Gage Cooper. He was a happy man."

She rolled her eyes at him. "I didn't mean it quite like that."

"I hope it'll say more than that. I'm not going to be young and immature forever."

"So what will it say?"

He shrugged. "I guess, Gage Cooper, One Good Guy."

"That's perfect."

"Thank you. I'm glad you approve. But that isn't what you mean, is it? You want to know if I'm going to grow up, get a job and settle down?"

He looked sad, just for a minute, then he wasn't. He smiled and laughed, the way he always did. But she wasn't fooled.

"Gage, you are a good person."

He led the horse to the end of the barn, opened a door and turned the animal loose, sending him off with a light swat on the rump to get him moving before he closed the door. He limped back down the aisle to where she had tied the mare she'd ridden. She looked up from brushing her.

"I'm not the good one, Layla. I'm not Reese, or even Jackson. Travis is a great husband and he'll be a great dad. I'm not the kind of guy who settles down. I always feel like I need to be moving on to the next adventure." He stepped close and brushed a strand of hair behind her ear, sending shivers down her spine. "And you are worth marrying."

Her heart quaked a little at the soft words, the soft look in his eyes. "Gage, don't."

"What do you want, Layla?"

"I want to survive raising my brother." She smiled and shrugged. "I used to want more, but life changed. There aren't many men who want to date a woman raising her younger brother. I love Brandon and I can't put him second."

"You shouldn't. But someday you should put yourself first."

She nodded. His hand was still close to her ear. He stroked her hair and then backed away.

"You asked what I want. I want to win the world title, and then I want to come home and work at Camp Hope."

"Camp Hope?" That surprised her. The camp located outside of Dawson catered to inner-city youth three weeks each summer, three weeks to low-income rural children and two weeks to military families.

"You might not know this about me, but I have a degree. I'm a test away from being a licensed social worker."

"Social worker?"

"Family services. Low pay, long hours, not a lot of glory."

Everything she had ever known about Gage Cooper changed in that moment. He became a person she had never expected.

"I'm impressed," she finally managed to say.

"Don't be. I've been out riding bulls, putting money in the bank. Other people are working the long hours and taking the grief for the job they do."

They turned the mare out to pasture and headed for the house. The day had warmed up as forecasted, close to sixty degrees. Layla slipped out of her jacket as they walked.

"What made you choose social work?"

"Natural choice, I guess." He motioned with his hand at the house, the farm. "I grew up here. I have everything. And my parents filled this house, and our lives, with kids who wouldn't have had anything if it hadn't been for my parents and their ability to love. My folks realized the important fact that love doesn't run out. You can love one kid or a dozen, and love them all. That's pretty impressive."

Where had her fun-loving Gage Cooper gone? She looked at him, saw his face and his smile. But now she knew he had more layers than she'd ever guessed.

His hand reached for hers and she let him hold it. She squeezed back and he chuckled a little. "Don't go all soft on me, Silver."

"Why do you say that?" She lifted her chin a notch to show that she wasn't going soft.

"The look in your eyes, like you just discovered my secret. I'm still Gage. I've never had a committed relationship, other than with my family. I'm still going to leave in a month."

They kept walking.

When they entered the kitchen of his family home a few minutes later, they were greeted by Angie and Myrna Cooper. Gage hugged his grandmother and kissed his mom on the cheek. She wrinkled her nose and stepped away.

"You smell like horses."

"You married a cowboy and you still haven't gotten used to it?" Gage laughed and kissed his mom's cheek a second time. "What's for lunch?"

Layla stood off to the side watching them, wanting. She shook her head to break free from what she wanted. Family. She'd never wanted family more than she did right now. She wanted it for herself and for Brandon. She wanted a house that looked and smelled like Christmas.

There was even a little tree on the counter, a tiny tree with tiny decorations.

"Layla, I bet you're starving." Myrna Cooper motioned her into the room. "Don't let Gage keep you in the barn, honey."

"Oh, I didn't mind. It was wonderful."

Myrna's brows arched, and she looked from Layla to Gage. "Was it really now?"

Gage shot his grandmother a look. Then he grabbed a pitcher out of the fridge.

"Tea?" he asked.

"Please."

As he poured, his mom pulled lunch meat from the fridge, then cheese, mayo and a bowl of grapes. "Layla, do you like smoked turkey?"

"Yes, thank you." Layla eyed the sink. "May I wash my hands?"

"Of course. While you do that, I'll make your sandwich."

Layla turned as Angie pulled slices of bread from the loaf and put them on plates. "I can do that."

Angie looked up from making the sandwiches. "Of course you can, but I don't mind. Relax, Layla. You deserve a day off."

A day off. She tried to remember the last time she'd had such a thing. Then Gage was at her side, sharing the sink. He was responsible for today, for the way she felt relaxed for the first time in so long. He had helped her to forget the harsh realities of her life.

As they sat down to eat, Gage's phone rang. He got up and left the table. Myrna Cooper started a conversation about Christmas plans. Layla listened as she continued eating. They talked about the meal, gift giving, who would be there and who wouldn't.

"Layla, why don't you and Brandon join us this year?" Angie asked, repeating an invitation she'd offered more than once before. "I know you think it would be too much, but with this crowd, I promise two more people won't put us over the limit."

Both ladies were looking at her, waiting. She considered it. But the idea of being surrounded by their family on Christmas Day seemed like too much.

Angie patted her arm. "You know, we're all family in God's eyes. Besides, we would love to have you with us."

"I'll think about it." She was still unsure, but knew Brandon deserved some Christmas memories that included more than the two of them eating turkey and watching old movies.

"That settles it, then." Myrna Cooper clapped her hands together, then she was off on the topic of rings. She showed Layla the engagement ring from her fiancé Winston. As she held her hand up, the light caught the brilliant gem and it sparkled.

"We plan on being married in May, Winston and I. I hope there are more weddings this summer. There's nothing like a good wedding to keep a community alive."

"Myrna." Angie shook her head.

Layla looked from one woman to the other. They were giving each other looks, and Myrna seemed far too pleased with herself. Layla felt a bit apprehensive because everyone knew Myrna loved to involve herself in the lives of her grandchildren. Especially their love lives.

"I love diamonds." Myrna positively glowed as she looked at her ring. "Are you a diamond kind of girl, Layla? Or maybe you favor pearls. Yes, I think that's it."

"Pearls are very pretty."

Gage walked back into the kitchen. "Layla, don't answer her."

"You okay, Gage?" His mother stood, her smile dissolving into a frown.

"I'm fine. Layla, that was Slade. We need to leave."

Her heart thumped hard, and she stared up at him, searching for more information.

"Gage, tell her what's wrong. Can't you see you're scaring her?"

Yes, Layla thought, she was scared. Her legs were weak and she couldn't breathe. Gage closed his eyes just briefly.

"I'm sorry. Layla, Brandon skipped school today. He's fine, but they were in an accident. Ran a truck through a fence. Slade has them out at the Tuckers fixing the fence, and Mr. Tucker said he won't press charges."

"Why did he call you?" Layla's voice shook. She didn't want to be shaky. She had to be strong. This was her life, her brother and her responsibility.

"Layla, you don't have a cell phone." His voice was rational. Reasonable. And too soft. The way it would be if he was talking to someone about to lose it.

"But he's okay?"

"He's fine."

She carried her paper plate to the trash, put her glass in the sink and turned, trying desperately to hold back her tears. Seven-year-old memories rushed to the surface. Angie Cooper put an arm around her shoulder.

"He's okay," Angie whispered, holding her close.

"I know." She fought for a deep breath. "I know." But in that moment, it reminded her too much of that night.

* * *

Gage had missed it, that panic, that fear. He shouldn't have. He should have remembered that not that long ago a trooper had asked Gage's parents to go with him to Tulsa to break the news to Layla.

"I'm sorry." He reached for the hat he'd dropped on the counter. "I should have done that differently."

"It's okay." She sucked in a breath, and he could tell she was pulling herself together. "Let's go. I can drive my truck, if you have other things to do."

"I don't have anything else to do."

"What about my mare?"

"She's fine in the barn."

She nodded, turning to Angie and Myrna Cooper. "Thank you for lunch."

"You're so welcome, Layla. And don't forget about Christmas."

They were walking out the front door when it dawned on Gage. His mom had invited Layla to Christmas at Cooper Creek. He was used to his grandmother meddling in the romantic lives of his siblings, but his mom usually stayed out of it. Or at least gave the appearance of it.

"Gage, you really don't have to drive me."

"I know that, but I want to."

She nodded but continued to stare out the window as they drove. "He's a good kid. I didn't have problems with him until the past year or so."

"He's a teenager, Layla. He needs a man to give him a little guidance."

"I know." Her voice was soft. He reached for her hand and she clasped his fingers tight. "It's my fault. I grew up keeping people out, and then when I needed them, I didn't know how to let them help."

"Old habits are hard to shake."

She smiled at him, finally. He thought about that smile, then decided it was better if he didn't. When they pulled up to the scene of the accident, the old truck driven by Brandon's buddy was sitting in the field. Brandon was busy pounding fence posts back into the ground.

"I want more for him than this. I just hope he wants more."

A dozen thoughts ran through Gage's mind, about growing up, realizing a person wanted more out of life. But he didn't know how to express it so it made sense.

"He'll grow up." That's all he said as he got out of the truck.

Brandon glanced their way as he pounded another fence post. He finished and swiped at his brow. Layla just stood there looking at him. To Gage she looked half mad, half brokenhearted.

"Layla, I know I messed up." Brandon pulled his ball cap a little lower on his dark head. He shrugged in his hoodie and looked to Gage. "I should have known better."

Layla sighed. "You *do* know better."

"Yeah, I do." He looked down at the ground and then at his sister. "I'm sorry."

"I know you are. But there are consequences." She looked from Gage to Slade to Brandon. "I think you'll have to stop riding bulls."

"But..." Gage said at the same time as Brandon.

Layla silenced them both with a look. "For the next month, no bulls. Brandon can do chores for Mr. Tucker, and he can continue to work at Cooper Creek. He can't go anywhere with Jason."

Jason, Brandon's friend, looked a little sheepish. Gage wondered where his folks were.

"Fine." Brandon went back to pounding posts.

"Seems to me you're getting off pretty easy, Brandon." Slade McKennon, soon to be Gage's brother-in-law, had that voice of authority Gage admired. Both of the boys lowered their heads and kept on working.

Brandon said, "Yes, sir."

It took another hour for them to get the fence repaired. Jason got in his truck and headed across the field to a gate. Brandon turned to look at Layla.

"Get in Gage's truck. He'll give us a ride home." She walked up to Mr. Tucker. "He's all yours. Any chores you need done, you let him know. I'll have him get off the bus here, if that's okay with you."

Mr. Tucker nodded and looked at the teenager. "After he's done, I can give him a ride home. Or to Cooper Creek. Mondays and Thursdays I can use some help. Those chicken houses I've got take a lot of my time. My wife has been on me to take her to dinner once in a while. Brandon can help me get work done and that'll keep the missus happy."

"Thank you, Mr. Tucker. If there are any other expenses, just let me know." Layla slowly trudged along the fence line to Gage's truck.

Gage followed them to his truck, knowing full well that Layla couldn't afford to have any other expenses piled on top of the ones she already had.

Brandon had to know that. So why did the kid keep getting himself into trouble?

Gage climbed in his truck. Layla sat in the middle

between him and her brother. That meant the whole ride back to her place, their shoulders touched and her sweet scent teased. He had more troubles than Brandon Silver ever dreamed of.

## Chapter Eleven

Friday night at Vera's started out busy, but then the Mad Cow cleared out. The sky looked iffy, and people were worried about sleet. Layla looked out the window at the light coating of white sleet already covering the sidewalk. A block down from the Mad Cow, headlights flashed on the road. It looked a lot like Gage's truck.

She hadn't seen him for a few days, not since the day after Brandon's accident. Gage seemed to have gotten it when she told him he no longer owed her anything. The day after Brandon's accident, Gage had brought her mare back, unloading a dozen bales of good hay with the horse. And then he'd left, telling her he had to drive livestock to an auction outside of Tulsa.

"Do you want to help me decorate the tree?" Vera asked, walking up behind her.

Layla smiled at Vera's reflection in the window. "Of course."

"Have you put a tree up yet?"

"Not yet. Maybe next weekend."

"It's only a few weeks till Christmas."

"I know." Layla spied the box with Vera's tree. "Let's decorate."

"Layla, why don't you kids spend Christmas with me and my family?"

"We're fine, Vera. The Coopers invited us over."

"Then you should go. Honey, they won't notice two more. The more the merrier on Christmas."

"Thanks, Vera. I'll think about it."

Vera's dark brows arched. "No, you won't."

With a smile and a little chuckle, Layla started to put up the tree. And while she worked, Vera set up her nativity collections. She had several. She bought them in different parts of the country, and she loved them.

Vera loved Christmas. She overdecorated every year with tinsel, garland, glittery decorations and lights. Soon the inside of the Mad Cow would look like Christmas had exploded all over the small café.

But it was more than the beautiful decorations. Vera loved Christmas because she loved Jesus. Every day, every hour, she lived her faith. Over the years Layla and others in the community had been touched by that strong faith.

Vera walked away from the nativity on the counter by the register. She peeked out the window and shook her head. "That sleet is coming down pretty hard. You should probably head on home."

"It would only take a few minutes to decorate the tree."

Vera glanced to the window and then back at the tree. "No, I'll do it in the morning. You take that extra fried chicken for you and Brandon."

"I'm not really hungry and he's probably already eaten."

"Layla, honey, you need to eat. You're pale and you're losing weight."

"I haven't felt so great this week. It'll pass. But I'll take the chicken home for Brandon."

"I'd be happier if you went to a doctor for a checkup."

Layla shook her head. "I can't."

"I know you have no insurance, but it isn't worth risking your health."

"I'll be fine in a day or two."

The sleet was really coming down. Layla shivered at the thought of driving home in the cold and snow. The heater on her truck didn't blow especially warm, and the defroster had a hard time clearing the windshield.

"Go home before the roads get slick." Vera hurried to the back and returned with containers of chicken.

"I can stay and help you close up."

"No, I can get this. And you have farther to go than I do."

Layla decided not to argue. Not only was it point-less, but Vera was right. "Thanks, Vera."

"You're welcome. And promise me that you'll stay home tomorrow if you're still feeling sick."

"I promise, but I know I'll be fine."

"Of course you'll be fine." Vera handed her the container of food. "But in case you aren't…"

"I'll call."

Vera let her out the front door and then locked it behind her. Layla hurried to her truck, sliding a little on the sleet-covered sidewalk. The sleet stung her cheeks as she ran. She cranked the truck's engine a few times and finally it roared to life. Headlights flashed through the cab. A big, blue Ford truck pulled next to her. She rolled down her window as the driver's side window on the other truck lowered.

"I just dropped Brandon off at your place and saw that you weren't home yet." Gage smiled, and something inside her relaxed.

No, she couldn't do this. Couldn't feel this. She fought for something to say, some way to dismiss him. She didn't have time for a broken heart. She didn't have the energy to stop him from storming into her life and taking over.

Gage was still talking. She blinked a few times and refocused as he said something about following her home.

"You don't have to." She could make it the short distance to her house without the truck dying. She told him so.

"I'm sure you can," he answered. "But I'm still going to follow you. I want to make sure you get home safe."

"Really, I do this every day. And you're probably ready to get home."

Gage let out a sigh. "Layla, you're just about the most stubborn woman I've ever met. You do what you want, but you can't stop me from going in the same direction as you."

And for whatever crazy reason, she smiled. And he smiled back.

"Fine, Gage, follow me home."

"Are you going to make me a cup of tea?"

"I thought you were following me, then heading on to your house?"

"Why would I do that when I'm obviously going out of my way to follow you home?"

She didn't answer. She couldn't. Instead she rolled

up her window and eased out of the parking lot with Gage a safe distance behind.

Safe? There was nothing safe about the man. And yet, she smiled all the way home.

When she pulled into her drive, he followed. He parked next to her, getting out before she did. She had to rummage in the seat for her mail, gather up the containers of chicken, grab her purse and open her door. But he had her door open and stood there, tall and broad-shouldered in his heavy coat, his face shadowy in the dark night.

"Let me carry something."

She handed him the containers of chicken.

"Thank you." She remembered her manners.

They walked up the steps together, stomping to shake the sleet off their shoes before entering the house.

"No tree?" Gage asked as they walked through the door.

"Not yet. I haven't really had time."

"I can cut you down one."

She shook her head. "Nope, we're done, Gage. You don't owe me anything. You never owed me."

"What are you talking about?" He took off his hat and raked a hand through his dark brown hair. He tossed the hat on a coffee table, as if it belonged there. As if *he* belonged.

Layla looked at that dark hat, and then back to the man standing in front of her. Once, a long time ago, he'd been a boy. A teenager with acne and a big smile. He'd loved all the girls, flirting and conquering their hearts as if he'd been a conquistador taking new lands for his country.

Now? She didn't really know him now. She didn't

know why he was standing in her living room with that puzzled half smile on his face.

"Making amends, remember?" She walked on to the kitchen. He followed, setting the chicken on the counter. He leaned against the counter, arms folded across his chest.

"Yeah, making amends." He nodded.

"You thought you owed me something. You needed to feel better about yourself. Right?" She ignored the soft smile on his lips. "You never really owed me. I haven't thought about high school and what happened since. Well, not since high school. My life has been too busy to sit around and worry about a silly game you played with…"

"With your heart." He didn't smile.

"Sure, but that was ages ago. It's over. You've been great, helping me with Brandon. He loves you, the Coopers and your ranch."

"And our bulls."

"Yes, your bulls. He thinks he'll make a great bull rider someday."

"He could. He has talent."

"Gage…" He still had the ability to undo her common sense. She definitely needed him out of her life so she could get back to her normal routine.

"When I got hit by that bull in Vegas—" he looked down at the floor "—I could have died. When I think about that, and how I'd been treating people… It made sense to me that I should right some wrongs."

"Gage, you need to deal with this. Deal with your anger toward God."

"Why do you think I'm angry with God?"

"I've seen you walk out of church mad. The night

Reese spoke about his blindness, you left. Not just the church, but Dawson."

Gage scratched the back of his neck and then, without asking, pulled cups out of the cabinet and filled them with water.

"What are you doing?"

"Making tea. Chamomile. My mother says it's very calming."

"We're going to have tea?" As if they had tea every day. She watched the cowboy in his flannel shirt and faded jeans as he limped around her kitchen.

"Where's your brother?"

"Probably in his room."

"Should you check on him?" Gage put the two cups in the microwave.

Yes, she should check on Brandon. She should do a reality check on herself, too.

Gage watched her walk out of the room, then he slumped, resting his elbows on the counter. He wasn't no old house dog, hanging his head because he couldn't find the bone buried in the backyard. He was a grown man. A grown man who was real good at skating in and out of life.

He loved being on the road. He loved getting on the back of a bull and riding until the eight-second buzzer. New places, new people, new challenges. Those were the things he loved.

As soon as they got through Christmas, maybe New Year's Eve, he'd be on the road again, shaking off the dust of this town and people who thought they knew him. Most people didn't. Not really.

But Layla, with a few sentences, had just undone

him. Man, she'd seen right to the heart of him. That scared him.

It scared him almost as much as looking into her eyes and knowing her in a way that a lot of people didn't.

He'd never gotten that close to a woman. He'd dated a lot. Women he met at rodeos. Models representing different products. Daughters of stock owners or sisters of other riders. Those were the women he went out with. They ate dinner, they laughed, maybe they kissed a little. And then he ended it.

He didn't know their favorite colors, their middle names, or their secrets. And he didn't really care to.

They didn't know him, either. They didn't know his anger or his fears. They sure didn't bring up his faith.

She had walked back into the room on silent feet, taking him by surprise. He stood straight and smiled his best charmer smile. And she didn't respond. She stood there in soft sweatpants and a long-sleeved T-shirt, bunny slippers on her feet, giving him a look that said she wasn't falling for it.

He pulled the cups out of the microwave and tossed the sopping tea bags into the trash. He stirred a little sugar into each cup and held one out for her.

"Brandon is asleep. He woke up enough to mumble that you worked him hard today." She squinted at him a little. "Something wrong?"

"Why would you think that?"

"Because you're always smiling, like you've got the whole world in the palm of your hand. But I see the anger, the sadness behind it."

"You've been watching too much *Dr. Phil*." He sat down at her rickety old table and stretched his legs out.

Here he was, sitting in her kitchen, drinking her tea, never really thinking about getting up and leaving. Something was really wrong with that picture. Wasn't there?

"I don't have time for television." She sat down at the table across from him. "I'm talking about you, the guy who showed up in town and decided to right past wrongs, starting with my life. But that isn't going to fix what's wrong with you."

He sipped his tea, speechless.

"Gage?"

He looked at her, really looked at her. Her brown hair hung straight and long, framing her face. Her eyes were bright. And her lips… He really was losing it.

"I'm fine, Layla."

"You're not fine. What happened to Reese was a hard blow, to all of you. Especially for the brother who always looked up to him."

He sat there staring into his empty cup and then he looked at her. Was this his life now, sitting at her table, sharing tea and talking? He should go immediately, get on a bull and get in touch with his cowboy side before she had him planting flowers in her garden.

"I'm dealing with it." What else could he say to a woman digging into his life and his heart? "I'm working through it."

"Good. Because angry doesn't suit you."

He stood up, because he needed to go. He hadn't meant to stay. He'd meant to make sure she got home safely, then head to Cooper Creek. She was right—his time for making amends was over. Somehow she had turned it all around, making it all about him, his life. He hadn't seen that coming.

"I'll see you later." He carried their cups to the sink. "Brandon said you work tomorrow. I'll pick him up in the morning."

"I'll let him know."

She stood, and followed him to the door. They stood there for a minute, his hand on the doorknob, while she leaned against the wall, looking sleepy and a little pale.

He wanted to kiss her good-night, but he held himself back.

"Layla, you're right. I was doing this for myself. But then it became something else." He reached for the coat he'd left on the coatrack. "I'm not even sure what to say except, I'd like for us to be friends."

"We can be friends."

For whatever reason, her softly spoken words made him smile. He needed her friendship in a way he couldn't explain. Maybe because she didn't mind being honest with him. If she could stay in his life, he thought he might be a better person.

But right now, he needed to say something. And he needed to leave.

"Thanks, Layla." He hugged her. It felt right. And she hugged him back.

She stood there in his arms for a moment. He kissed the top of her head. Friendship. Yeah, right. He loosened his hold and she stepped back.

"Good night, Gage."

He nodded and slipped outside, back to the cold and sleet of a December night. The icy air felt good as he hurried to his truck.

He glanced back at the house. Layla was watching, her face pressed against the rectangular window. He wondered what she could be thinking, standing there.

Maybe she was wondering when the weather would switch back to normal.

Or maybe she was thinking about him.

He laughed at the idea. Since when did women think about him when he left?

She was probably standing there wondering what the roads would be like in the morning, thoughts of him not even crossing her mind. On the other hand, he couldn't stop thinking about her. Layla Silver, strong, quiet, never giving up. She'd had it tough, but she kept on going.

All of his life he'd taken for granted everything he had. He hadn't put much effort into his career, because he hadn't really needed to. He'd always had bull riding, the ranch and wherever the road took him. It was the perfect life.

Until now.

The thought stopped him in his tracks. Sitting at the end of Layla's drive, he wondered why all of a sudden his life no longer fit. It felt like a favorite pair of boots that were suddenly too small. Man, he hated that. Breaking in a new pair of boots was never a good time.

Finding out that his life was no longer what he wanted it to be, also not good. He glanced back at Layla's little house. He couldn't see her from where he sat in his truck. Probably better that way. He needed to head home.

He needed to do a lot of thinking, figure out what in the world he was going to do next.

## Chapter Twelve

Layla stood in the kitchen of the Back Street Community Center, shivering a little, wishing someone would turn up the heat.

"Are you cold?" Heather Cooper stepped close, placing a few cans of vegetables in a box next to the one Layla had filled with cereal and snack bars.

"Freezing. I keep thinking if I work faster, I'll warm up. But I've been cold all day." She'd been cold at church, at lunch and even when she'd sneaked in a nap. But it wasn't cold outside. After the sleet on Friday and the frigid temperatures Saturday, Sunday had dawned sunny and almost warm.

"Maybe you should go home?" Heather suggested in a soft voice. "We can bring Brandon home later."

"No, I'm good."

While the women and teens boxed up the food, a group, mostly men, were outside putting the finishing touches on the set for the Living Nativity.

Today was a community service day. They were boxing and delivering food to families in the Dawson community. The Dawson Community Church youth group was wrapping gifts of coloring books, crayons and other small toys. There were also hats knitted by women in the church. No way would she miss out on all this.

She already had to bow out of the Living Nativity. She usually had a small speaking part or sang in the choir. Working two jobs, she just couldn't fit it into her schedule this year.

"Brandon is enjoying himself." Heather inclined her head in the direction of the group of kids wrapping gifts.

"He wasn't thrilled with the idea until he got here and realized he might be the only guy."

He'd wanted to be outside with the men. He was a man, he'd told her, not a kid. But he'd settled into the wrapping gig when no other guys showed up to help— making him the only guy among a group of pretty girls.

She went back to filling the boxes, hoping she could avoid Myrna Cooper, who was packaging cookies. Layla picked up a few of the packages to place them in boxes.

"Layla, how have you been, honey?" Myrna handed her another package of cookies. She had failed her task of evading Myrna.

"I'm good, Mrs. Cooper."

"Call me Granny Myrna." She smiled wide and patted Layla's hand.

*Oh, I couldn't,* were the first words Layla thought. But she knew better than to argue with her. She nodded. Myrna continued to give her a piercing look.

"Are you feeling well, dear?"

"I'm just cold."

Myrna lifted her hand to Layla's cheek. "My goodness, you feel warm. I hope you don't have the flu."

"I don't think I do."

"Maybe Gage should drive you home."

"No, I have my truck. And really, I don't feel sick." Okay, a little nauseated, but nothing she couldn't handle.

"If you're sure." Myrna patted her cheek. "One of these days you have to think about your future, Layla. Brandon is growing up. When is it your turn?"

"My turn?"

"To be young?"

Layla smiled at Myrna. "I think that ship has sailed. I haven't felt young since…"

"Forever?" Myrna supplied the word.

"Maybe." Layla smiled again, wanting Myrna to know that it was okay. She didn't sit around bemoaning her life. She loved her brother, the farm and her community. Someday, maybe, she'd meet someone. But life wasn't all bad. She sometimes thought people assumed that because of everything that had happened, her life must be horrible and desperate. It wasn't.

It hadn't been easy, but it hadn't been horrible. There were good moments in every day. There were bad. Didn't everyone have good days and bad?

"Well, I think your day is coming." Myrna turned to wrap more cookies.

"I'm fine, Myrna."

Myrna smiled at her again. "I know you are, honey. I know. You always have been. I think that's what puzzles people. They don't understand the kind of faith it takes to tackle life the way you've had to do."

"Thank you." Layla hurried away with the cookies.

They were nearly done packing the food boxes. The clock on the wall said it was five o'clock. They would have to start delivering soon.

As if on cue, Layla heard footsteps heading down the stairs. The men returning from their work outside. Angie Cooper and a few other women had put out trays of sandwiches and fruit. There was coffee and tea to drink. The workers started lining up with plates. They would eat, and then the boxes would be loaded and delivered.

Heather walked up behind her and gave her a little push toward the food line. "Get something to eat."

Layla nodded, but food was the last thing she wanted.

Getting in line behind Gage, whether Heather planned it or not, definitely wasn't what she wanted. She held back a little, trying to come up with an excuse to head in the other direction. She'd never seen herself as a coward, but today that's exactly how she felt. Two days ago she had pushed him to talk; now she wanted to avoid all conversation.

Gage turned and saw her. He smiled shyly at her.

"Better get in line, ladies, before it's all gone." He motioned them ahead of him. "Get ahead of me. I'm pretty hungry."

"He'll take it all," Heather confirmed as she moved Layla forward in the line.

She somehow ended up in front of Gage with his hands on her shoulders, keeping her in line in front of him. He leaned in, and she felt his warm breath against her ear. "Nowhere to run."

"I hadn't planned on running." She grabbed a paper

plate and handed one to him, hoping to keep his hands busy.

In front of her, Heather laughed. Layla had never been close to Heather Cooper. They were a few years apart in age. They lived in different worlds, had different friends. Heather didn't even go to church in Dawson. Although someone had told Layla that Heather was moving back to town.

Layla took half a sandwich and a handful of grapes. Gage reached for a bag of chips and dropped one on her plate, one on his own.

"I didn't want those." She looked back at him.

"You have to eat more than a half of a bologna sandwich."

"I'm not hungry."

He took the bag of chips from her plate. "Suit yourself."

And then, somehow, she ended up at a table with Gage and Heather. One on each side of her. Brandon sat across from them. Conversation buzzed. Layla got lost in her own thoughts. As Brandon talked about the kind of truck he wanted when he turned sixteen and playing baseball in the spring, she thought about the electric bill, the loan payment and Christmas.

It wouldn't do her any good to worry. Somehow she'd get through. She always did.

"We should go." Gage stood up, taking his empty plate and hers.

Layla looked up at him, trying to process what he'd said. "I'm sorry?"

"Jeremy paired you with me. We have five boxes to deliver."

She glanced around the room and spotted Gage's

half brother, Jeremy Hightree. He stood next to his wife, Beth, and her brother, Jason Bradshaw. Jason held his little boy in one arm while he talked.

Layla looked away from the group and back to Gage. She always delivered boxes with Beth. She started to say something, but Gage smiled and reached for her hand.

"Come on, Layla. We have a lot of work to do and not a lot of time to get it done."

"But I always go with Beth."

"She isn't going this year. She's exhausted. In the family way, you know."

She knew, but she hadn't expected that to stop Beth. Maybe baby number two changed things for a woman.

"Stop looking so cornered. We'll have a good time handing out these boxes of food and watching little kids smile." Gage grinned at her, and when he did, she melted.

Unfortunately he knew it. His smile grew bigger. His hazel eyes sparkled with mischief, the green flecks in his eyes made more green from the sun shining through one of the small basement windows and dancing across his face.

"Let me get my coat." She headed for the closet under the stairs.

As she slipped into her coat, the men started grabbing boxes and carrying them up the stairs. Suddenly Layla felt weak and her stomach ached. She knew full well she didn't have time to get sick.

She hurried up the stairs, wrapping a scarf around her neck as she went. The boxes were being loaded into various cars and trucks. People were pairing up. She searched for Heather and didn't see her. She thought maybe she could switch partners, that maybe Heather would rescue her.

Gage waved and called to her. He was closing the tailgate on his truck. She took a deep breath and headed his way, smiling. Because she was going to deliver boxes of food to families in need, to children in need.

She loved Christmas traditions. She wasn't going to let a virus ruin this for her. Her gaze connected with Gage's. He smiled an easy smile and she knew it wasn't about the virus. What she felt was a good case of her heart going into defense mode, trying to protect her from what it knew would happen when Gage Cooper tired of spending time with her.

Gage drove down Back Street. He and Layla had been given houses on the west side of Dawson and just outside of town. He pulled the list out of his pocket and handed it to her.

"Where do we start?"

She looked over the addresses. "I say we go to the house farthest from town and work our way back."

"You're the boss."

She laughed at that. "Go left on 1011."

"Got it." He headed west on the main road until he found the farm road she'd indicated.

He pulled into the driveway of a house that had seen better days. Smoke poured from the chimney, and as his truck came to a stop, the front door opened and a little girl peeked out. She was dressed in pajamas but wore rubber boots on her feet. Her blond hair stuck out in all directions, and as she watched them, her thumb went into her mouth.

"She comes to church on the bus." Layla spoke

softly as they sat there in the warmth of his truck. "Her name is AnaLilly."

"She's a cutie."

"Yes, she is. Their mom is single. There are three kids."

"Well, let's see if we can't make their day a little brighter." He got out of his truck, aching a little on the inside as he looked at the small house with the patched-up roof, a rusted-out van sitting in the driveway and a few scraggly chickens pecking at the frozen ground.

Layla joined him at the back of the truck. He glanced her way. She looked pretty, with jeans tucked into brown boots, a pretty brown sweater and a scarf around her neck.

Gage hefted up the box and followed Layla to the front porch. The little girl had gone back inside, and the door was closed. Layla knocked.

Finally the door opened. The mom stepped out, looking way too young to have three kids. Her blond hair was pulled back in a ponytail. She smiled at them, shy and teary-eyed.

"Gabby, we brought you a few things." Layla had taken over, smiling at the young woman barely out of her teens, he guessed.

The three kids pushed around her, trying to see who had come to visit. Gage smiled down at them. A boy and two girls, all under six or seven.

The boy looked to be about five. He had his eyes on Gage's cowboy hat. Gage smiled at the kid as the mom allowed them to enter her house. He carried the box of groceries into the kitchen and put it on the counter. When he turned, the little boy was standing there, smiling up at him.

"Buddy, I think you need a cowboy hat." Gage took off his hat, his favorite, and put it on the boy's head. "There, it's all yours."

"Oh, Mr. Cooper, he can't take that hat." Gabby tried to get the hat back. "Jimmy, give him his hat."

Jimmy ran off.

"Really, I want him to have it. Every boy needs a cowboy hat."

Gabby nodded, her dark eyes overflowing with tears. "Their daddy got himself killed in Afghanistan. We wasn't married yet or nothing. It's been real hard."

"I'm sure it has."

Layla hugged Gabby. "It'll get easier, Gabby. You make sure the kids come to church next week. We're having a big Christmas dinner."

Gabby wiped at her eyes. "Thanks, Layla, I appreciate that. And this food. Thank you. My folks went off to Oklahoma City to see if they can find jobs. I guess if they do, we'll be moving down there. Until then, we're just trying to get by."

Trying to get by. Gage knew a lot of people in her shoes, just trying to get by. He cleared his throat and looked around the little house. "Is there anything else you need, Gabby?"

She laughed a shaky laugh. "A million dollars would be nice, but I haven't seen any prize patrols wandering my neighborhood."

At least she still had a sense of humor. "If you think of anything, let me know. My brothers and I are pretty good at fixing things."

"Thanks, Mr. Cooper, I'll keep that in mind. The roof had been leaking last fall, but I found some shingles and climbed up there. It's not leaking anymore."

"Well, if it should leak again, you let us know."

"We should go." Layla hugged Gabby. The three kids were circling around her, smiling big. The little blond still had her thumb in her mouth. Layla hugged them all and then hurried out the door.

Gage followed her to the truck. They were back on the road before she could speak.

"Childhood shouldn't be so tough." She covered her eyes with her hand and he heard her sniffle. "It should be about sprinklers in the summer, building snowmen in the winter."

"I'm sure Gabby does her best to make sure those kids do a few of those things." Gage kept driving, not knowing what to say, wanting to ask her the next address. He tried to peek, but she had the paper clutched in her hand.

"I know she tries, but they see her tears, they know she worries. She barely had a childhood of her own. She was a mom by the time she was seventeen."

Man. He really couldn't imagine. He was twenty-six and not sure he was ready for marriage. Kids. He'd rarely thought about having kids. But all of a sudden, the thought crossed his mind and stuck.

"Where's the next place?"

"Down the road, turn right. The Morrison house."

"Gotcha. I'll see if Jackson and Travis can help me get her house in shape. Mom might be able to get her some services she hasn't realized she's entitled to. My mom is a genius when it comes to finding resources for people."

"That would be good."

They drove about a mile. "Layla, what about your childhood?"

She smiled at him, looking amused. "It was feast or famine, happiness and chaos. My mom tried to make everything good. My dad couldn't stay sober. And when he drank, he wasn't the nicest person to be around. Sober, he could do anything."

"I'm sorry."

"Compared to what so many people are going through, I had it easy."

They pulled up to the next house. The Morrisons. He knew them. The wife had something wrong with her and couldn't work. Jeff, her husband, tried to hold down a job, but had to take time off a lot in order to take care of his wife. Good people trying hard to make it.

He guessed that people might judge them. But Gage knew how hard they tried. Last year his dad had given Jeff a job at one of their apartment complexes. He worked part-time and was allowed time off when he needed to be at home. No more getting fired, but it wasn't an easy life.

As they walked up the steps to the ranch-style house, the door opened. Jeff's daughter, almost a teenager, Gage guessed, stood in the doorway. She wore an apron and a smudge of flour on her cheek.

"Hey, Mr. Cooper, Layla." Patty Morrison smiled, motioning them inside. "What are you all doing?"

"We're delivering some Christmas boxes, and we just happen to have one for your family." Gage followed the girl to the kitchen. The room was a wreck of dirty dishes, bowls and something boiling on the stove.

Layla turned the stove down. "Are your folks home?"

Patty shook her head. "No, my mom got real sick

last night, and Dad took her to the doctor this morning. They're still in Grove. I'm cooking for me and my brother."

"What are you cooking?" Layla looked in the saucepan.

"Potato soup. I'm boiling the potatoes right now." Patty looked in the pan. "I guess I almost boiled them over. Haden was throwing a fit about something and distracted me."

Layla carried the saucepan to the sink. "Why don't you put away the things in that box that need to go in the fridge, or the freezer. And if you get me the milk, I'll help you finish up here."

Gage looked at his watch. They had several more boxes to deliver yet. But as he watched Layla help Patty Morrison, he knew they weren't going anywhere.

"Where's your brother?" He reached up to take off a hat he no longer had.

He grinned. Sure, he was going to miss that hat. But he was more than glad his hat had a new home.

"He's in the tub. He went outside and got filthy dirty."

The tub. Gage didn't do tubs. He must have looked a little green, because Layla laughed. "Don't worry, we won't make you take care of a four-year-old."

"Good thing."

Haden hopped into the kitchen wearing only a towel and a big grin. "I got a bath."

"I see that." Gage smiled at the boy.

"My mom is sick." Haden climbed on a chair and peeked in the box. "And I love cookies."

"Not until after dinner." His sister grabbed them, placing them on the counter.

"We had potato soup last night."

"I know." Patty frowned at her brother. "I don't know how to make anything else."

"Potato soup is fine." Layla poured milk in the pan. "Do you have cheese? A few slices of cheese makes it really good."

Patty opened the door of the fridge and pulled out a package of sliced cheese. "Plenty of cheese."

Gage watched as Layla stood next to the teenager, telling her something about potato soup. They sprinkled some salt and garlic into the mix and stirred again. Then Layla hugged the girl.

"Patty, you call me if your dad can't get home tonight. I'll come and get you and Haden," Layla offered as they walked to the door a few minutes later.

Gage knew her plate was full. She had Brandon, two jobs, and he knew she had bills she was struggling to pay.

Patty cried a little as they left. She hugged Layla again and promised to call. Gage slipped an arm around Layla's shoulder as they walked back to the truck.

"I think you might be the nicest person I know." He told her as he opened the truck door.

"And it took you this long to notice?" She smiled as she hopped in, and then he saw a grimace of pain.

"Are you okay?"

"Fine." She reached for the door and closed it before he could ask more questions.

He had a lot of questions, but they had more boxes to deliver and it was getting late. Fortunately the next few houses went a little faster than the first two. Two hours after they started, they were heading to Back Street again.

"Do you want to run to Grove and get a real dinner?" he offered as they pulled into the parking lot of the community center.

Layla shook her head. "No, I'm beat."

"Are you feeling all right?"

"Not great. It's probably a bug. And now I've passed it on to everyone we've touched. I should have stayed home but I didn't really feel sick this afternoon."

"You're sure you're okay?"

"Gage, I'm fine."

He knew he wouldn't get more from her, so he let it go. He watched as she got out of his truck and walked to hers. She started it and took off, leaving him to ponder a day that might possibly have changed his life.

Because Layla Silver was surely one of the most amazing people he'd ever met.

And he didn't know what to do about it.

Four hours later, Gage's phone rang. He had dozed off watching TV and was groggy as he answered.

"Gage, this is Brandon. Layla is really sick. She didn't want me to call anyone, but I'm worried about her. I'm going to put her in the truck and drive over to your house."

Gage woke up at that. "Wait a second. Brandon, you can't drive. Give me a minute and I'll be there."

"No, I'm bringing her to you. Your mom can help her. I can't."

Gage could hear the panic in Brandon's voice. Before he could tell him to calm down the call ended.

## Chapter Thirteen

Layla had tried to fight Brandon, but her brother had been impossible. He had wrapped her in a blanket and carried her to the truck that was already running. She didn't complain because it was warm inside and she hurt so badly. Her stomach kept tightening and she just wanted to curl up on her side, the way she'd been when he found her in the bathroom.

She drew her knees up in the seat as the truck sped down the driveway, slid sideways as it hit the road and then barreled toward Cooper Creek.

"Slow down. It isn't worth having an accident. And the bumps are killing me."

"Okay, okay." Brandon slowed down. "Layla, you have to be okay."

"I'm okay." She kept her eyes closed and prayed she wasn't lying.

"You don't look okay." Brandon's voice was quiet, and she wondered if he was crying. He hadn't cried since the day they'd buried their parents.

She opened her eyes and glanced at him, seeing for the first time the man he would become. A sob sneaked up on her, tightening in her throat as she fought the tears. Somehow she'd done it; she had raised him. He wasn't grown, but he was getting there.

"Don't worry," she whispered.

He only nodded, his jaw clenched, his grip on the steering wheel tight.

They drove a few more minutes. "I know I've been... I've been a real pain in the..." He cleared his throat.

"Don't say it. And you are a pain, but you're my pain, and I'm not going anywhere. Could you not hit *every* bump in the road?"

"I'm sorry. And I'm going to do better. I've been praying, and I'll do whatever you want, just don't..." He choked a little. "Don't die."

"I've got food poisoning... I'm not dying. I'll be here to stay on your case and make sure you grow up to be a doctor or something."

"I'm not that smart."

"You are. Stop arguing." She grimaced as another wave of pain hit.

And then they pulled up in front of the Coopers' big house. The lights were on. Brandon had called. He'd woken them all up. Layla groaned, because this wasn't what she did. She handled things. She didn't go running to people....

The door of the truck opened and Gage leaned in. He felt her forehead, touched her cheek. And then Angie Cooper stood next to him, in a heavy jacket, her face pale in the dark night.

"Layla, can you walk to the house?"

Layla shook her head. "I can try."

"No, don't." Angie touched her cheek. "Can you tell me what's going on?"

"My stomach. Vomiting. Maybe food poisoning?" Layla drew her legs up and trembled in the cold air from the open door.

Angie Cooper moved the arm that rested on her stomach. She pushed on Layla's side and Layla had to bite back the cry. Angie whispered that she was sorry.

"Gage is going to take you to Grove. I'll call Jesse. If he isn't on duty, he can wake up and be on duty."

"Grove?" Layla shook her head. "I don't think… I don't have insurance."

"I think you need your appendix checked, honey. That isn't something you can fix with a cup of tea and time. No arguing. Brandon can stay here with us."

"But…" She tried again but Gage's hazel eyes were dark, his mouth firm and unsmiling.

"We'll take your truck. It's already warm. You ready?"

She shook her head. How could she be?

He smiled a little, and she hadn't realized how much she needed to see that smile. She reached out to touch his face, his very sweet face. She hadn't realized how much she needed him.

He climbed in behind the wheel and they took off again. It was a quicker trip to Grove than she would have liked. He kept glancing at her, his brow furrowed, his hair messy from having been woken up.

"I'm okay," she finally managed to whisper.

"Right, of course you are. You're always okay." The words came out gruff and then he sighed.

"You don't have the right to lecture me." She thought about telling him that he didn't really know her. But in the past couple of weeks he had managed to know her better than most people.

"No," he admitted, "I don't. But as stubborn as you are, I do care."

"I'm not stubborn. I'm strong."

He laughed at that. "And still arguing."

Her old truck didn't have the best shocks in the world, and it felt as if it were hitting bumps even when there were none. The few curves they rounded felt as if they were taking them at NASCAR speeds. She held on to the door handle and somehow held on to the contents of her stomach.

"I hate to sound like I'm five, but are we almost there?"

"Almost." He turned at a light and headed down the quiet road to the hospital. Instead of parking, he pulled up to the emergency room entrance.

Before Layla could blink, there were emergency personnel rushing from the hospital. Her body started to shake and her teeth chattered. The door opened and someone reached for her.

Where had Gage gone to? She searched for him, finally seeing him off to the side. He winked. She wanted to reach for his hand but couldn't.

"Layla, I'm Dr. Arnold. Dr. Cooper is on his way in, but we're going to assess your situation and run some tests." The doctor, tall, lean, with thinning hair and glasses, put a hand on her shoulder. "Can you answer some questions for me?"

She nodded, then they were moving through the halls of the E.R. and Gage was gone. She closed her eyes and answered the questions. One question made her pause, nearly made her cry; *Who is your contact person?* Did a fifteen-year-old boy count?

What would happen to Brandon if she didn't make it through this okay? She should have thought of that. Should have decided who should take care of him if something happened to her. He was her responsibility, not the other way around.

She opened her eyes and looked around the room. "I need to go."

"I'm sorry. I can't let you do that." Jesse Cooper leaned close to her, his dark hair and dark eyes strangely familiar and comforting.

"You need to relax, Layla. I know that's hard to do when the world is spinning, but Brandon is okay. And I listed my mom as your contact person, not your brother. Okay?"

Tears filled her eyes. "I'm sorry."

He shook his head and handed her a tissue. "Don't be. You've had a rough night. And unfortunately you're going to have a rough few days. We'll be doing some tests, and then I have a feeling you're in for surgery."

"I can't. I don't have insurance."

"That's something we'll worry about later."

"But I have to worry about it now. I can barely…" She shook her head. "Never mind."

"We'll get it taken care of. You don't have a choice. If your appendix is the problem, it isn't as if you can opt out on having it removed."

"You're right."

He laughed a low laugh. "That's why they made me a doctor. I know about things like this."

Layla managed a smile. But it quickly disappeared. Was she alone? She didn't know if Gage had stayed.

She hoped he had. She wanted to believe that he would be in the waiting room while she went to surgery.

Loneliness really did stink. She closed her eyes, trying to block the wave of emotion that competed in the pain of her abdomen. A nurse apologized, as if she had done something. Layla mumbled that it was okay.

After all, wasn't she always ok? This time would be no exception. She would get through this. She didn't have a choice.

As she drifted on the pain medication they'd given her, she thought about the hospital bills, taking care of Brandon, Christmas and Gage.

She dreamed about his hand on hers.

Gage sat next to the bed, watching as Layla fought something imaginary in her dreams. She kicked and moaned, whispering something he couldn't quite make out. Her surgery had gone well, but Jesse had told him that there was some infection because she'd obviously been sick for longer than a day. Stubborn. He planned on telling her that when she woke up.

Or maybe he wouldn't.

She didn't need lectures from him. She needed support. His mom had told him that when she called to check on Layla's condition. He'd asked his mom if Layla had family he could call. She had to have someone. Aunts? Uncles? People who could be there for her.

No one, his mom had assured him. So he had to stay. She'd said it in a quiet voice, but the meaning had been crystal clear. He was it.

He, Gage Cooper, the last person in the world to be there for anyone, was at Layla's side. Didn't anyone get it? He wasn't good at being there for people. He wasn't the person people confided in or turned to when the chips were down.

He leaned forward in the chair and watched Layla sleep. Her brown hair was pulled back in a ponytail, her face was pale. He guessed he'd gotten better at being there for her. But who would take care of her when he left?

One thing was certain. He'd make sure she had support. It was the least he could do. He'd make sure her house was fixed up, that she had plenty of hay to get through winter. He'd also make sure Travis, Jackson and his dad kept Brandon busy.

He watched her sleep and thought about the two of them being apart. He'd keep riding bulls, wandering the country.

She would keep working two jobs, trying to make ends meet, hoping she could keep her brother out of trouble. Maybe she'd date. Someone would take her to Grove to a nice restaurant. Or maybe to Tulsa.

He rubbed a hand across his eyes. He had better get to sleep because he was definitely losing it. He glanced at the clock on the wall and groaned. It was almost morning.

Soft-soled shoes came down the hall. A minute later, the partially closed door opened. Jesse walked in, not looking much better than Gage felt. His brother smiled at him, and then at Layla.

"She should be out of here by this afternoon."

"That soon?" Gage forced his voice lower so he wouldn't wake her up.

"It's typically outpatient, but we want to keep an eye on her, get some fluids and antibiotics into her system, especially since she doesn't have anyone at home to really take care of her." Jesse gave him a pointed look.

"Yeah, I get it." Gage shot his brother a look that he hoped stopped any speculation as to who would be taking care of Layla.

He would have said more, but he heard more footsteps in the hall, the soft whisper of a nurse and then his grandmother. She walked through the door a minute later, quiet, but observant.

"How is she?" Granny Myrna walked up to the bed, looked the patient over and turned to Jesse. "She's okay?"

"Of course she is," Jesse answered.

When had Layla Silver become the newest adopted Cooper? The Coopers had always tried to help her out. But in the weeks since Thanksgiving, things had changed. Gage guessed it was because he'd charged into her life, thinking he could fix his own mess of a life by focusing on hers.

And the whole family had gotten on board with the plan. Unfortunately they all seemed to have a different idea of things. He'd already talked to his matchmaking grandmother about that pearl-and-diamond ring she'd mentioned to Layla. He knew exactly which ring it was. She'd shown it to him about a year ago.

As beautiful as it was, he didn't plan on putting that ring on anyone's finger anytime soon.

"Get up and let an old lady sit down." His grandmother swatted his arm. He moved out of the chair.

"I needed to stretch anyway."

"You're such a gentleman." She sighed as she sat down. "Go buy your brother breakfast. I'll sit with Layla."

Jesse chuckled a little and headed for the door. "This all seems very familiar, Gage. If I was you, I wouldn't leave her alone with Layla. You'll be engaged by sunset."

Gage shook his head at the warning. He wasn't going to be the next Cooper to fall victim to her matchmaking schemes. "Gran, try to stay out of my business."

"I'm not even sure what you mean by that. But make sure you bring me a doughnut and coffee. Not a filled doughnut. I don't want pudding inside my cake."

"Yes, ma'am. And make sure you don't do anything crazy."

She grinned big. "Oh, Gage, you should trust me."

"Not even for a second." He leaned to kiss her cheek. "But I love you."

She patted his cheek. "I love you. And you need to shave."

"I'll do that later."

He walked out the door, and Jesse was waiting for him in the hall. "You know she's already planning your wedding to Layla Silver."

"I think she might want to scrap her plans. I'm not marrying anyone anytime soon."

"We'll see about that." Jesse pounded him on the back. "You're living in another world if you think our grandmother isn't already having invitations printed up."

They headed down the hall in the direction of the cafeteria. The hospital was still quiet, the halls still mostly empty.

"Gage, it wouldn't be the worst thing in the world," Jesse offered as they got close to the cafeteria's double doors.

"Maybe not, but I'm not ready. I still have a lot I want to do, places I want to go."

"I was heading for South America when Laura showed up in my life."

"I get that, but I'm not you." He sighed. "This is why I don't date in Dawson."

"Why's that?" Jesse pointed toward the buffet line.

"Because if you buy a woman a cup of coffee, this whole town has you married off."

"Yeah, I guess that does happen sometimes. But don't run from what you want just because the people in Dawson see it before you do."

"You're no help at all." Gage ordered an omelet and walked away from his brother.

He even tried to sit at a different table. Jesse laughed and sat down across from him. "Back to your old tricks of leaving when things get a little tough?"

Gage took a bite of omelet and ignored Jesse.

"You didn't used to be a chicken." Jesse grinned, flashing white teeth that Gage thought he shouldn't be so quick to flash.

"I'm not a chicken."

"Really? Because from my side of the table, that's how it looks. Something gets under your skin, makes you a little mad, or gets uncomfortable, you run."

"Stop." Gage kept his gaze leveled on Jesse, almost nine years his senior and probably in a lot better shape physically.

But Gage was pretty sure he could still take him.

Jesse wasn't intimidated. He laughed and leaned forward. "Or you'll do what?"

"I'll drag you outside and make you wish you had a doctor on call."

"I don't think you can."

Jesse pushed his empty plate aside. "I think I can."

The voice of authority boomed near them. "If you boys are through acting like kids, your mom is in Layla's room, and Layla is awake."

Gage looked up at his dad. "We weren't really going to fight."

"I figured that, but I thought I would warn you that your mother doesn't like getting bloodstains out of clothes."

Gage laughed, grabbing his tray as he stood.

Tim Cooper, best dad in the world, put an arm around his shoulder. It made him think about Brandon and what the kid had missed out on. What Layla had missed out on.

"You did good last night." His dad walked next to him.

"I did the right thing."

"Right, but people don't always choose the right thing."

Jesse took their trays to the dishwasher window. He fell in next to them and didn't comment.

Gage would have preferred the previous conversation, the one bordering on a fight, to this one. The one that felt like his dad was about to tell him the facts of life, and those facts had something to do with Layla.

Everyone wanted to give him some advice. Maybe someone could advise him how his life had gotten taken over by a pint-size female and her rebellious brother in just a few short weeks.

# *Chapter Fourteen*

Layla didn't enjoy being told to lie down on her couch and stay there. But that's exactly what Gage had done when he drove her home from the hospital that afternoon. He'd carried her into the house, placed her on the sofa with an afghan and a pillow, then he'd taken off to feed animals. She'd used the time alone to do what needed doing. She placed an ad on the internet with a photograph of her mare. And then she'd cried.

She would have to pay the hospital bill and her loan payment. And she didn't know when she'd be able to work. Jesse had told her not to get in a hurry to go back to work, that her body had been through a lot and she needed time to recuperate.

What Jesse Cooper didn't understand was that she didn't have the luxury of staying at home for a couple of weeks. She had to get back to work. Now.

It wouldn't do any good to worry. She knew that. She knew it as she listed her house for sale, too. She knew it as she wrote down all of her bills coming due, and the amount of money she wouldn't make if she was off work for even one week. But Jesse had said to count on two. He'd prefer more.

The list of numbers on the paper brought a wave of fear. She crumpled it and tossed it on the table next to her.

"Lord, I can't do this alone." She closed her eyes and prayed.

She must have dozed because she woke up to the sound of soft snoring. She glanced over at the leather recliner she'd hauled home from a yard sale last fall. Gage was sprawled out, his feet up on the footstool and her dog sleeping next to him.

"Daisy," she whispered to the black-and-white border collie. "Down."

Daisy's tail thumped on the arm of the chair, and she rested her head on Gage's leg. Layla tried patting the sofa she slept on. The dog whined softly and curled her tail in close to her legs. Obviously she'd made a decision.

"Stop trying to take my dog," Gage grumbled, and opened his eyes.

He looked scruffy, and his green plaid shirt was untucked and wrinkled. Layla watched as he yawned and rubbed a hand over his face. Even scruffy, he was deliciously cute.

"She was my dog first," she said.

He grinned, sitting up a little straighter in her chair.

"Your dog likes me because it's cold out and she realized it's a lot warmer in here."

"Where's Brandon?"

"With my folks. They were putting up more Christmas lights, maybe cleaning out the garage. I don't know. He's fine."

"He has school."

"He came home, packed a bag and he got his books."

"Oh." She didn't know what else to say. Gage couldn't stay here, at her house. Brandon couldn't move in with the Coopers. She couldn't continue to lose herself this way, to him.

"Are you hungry?"

"Not at all."

He lowered the footstool, and Daisy hopped down, shook and walked to the front door. Gage grinned at Layla, as if to say he had been right. She watched as he hobbled to the front door and let the dog out.

"My mom brought over some soup." He eased himself down on the end of the couch. "Jesse said you have to eat something. Chicken soup. I've heard it's good for the soul. I thought I might eat some and see if there's a change in mine."

Layla reached for his big, calloused hand. "Your soul is just fine."

"Is it, Layla?"

"Yes, I think it is. I think you expect a lot from yourself, and you expect a lot from God."

"I think I should go fix us a bowl of soup."

"I think I should get cleaned up and change clothes."

Gage reached for her hand and helped her to her feet. "I'll walk with you."

"I can make it."

"I'm sure you can, but I'm not going to let you." He wrapped an arm around her. "Lean on me."

"Thank you." It felt good to lean on him. Too good.

He left her in the hall. "I'll be back to help you. Do not go anywhere without me."

"You know you have to go home later."

He leaned in close. "I know. Mom is going to spend the night."

Her eyes filled with tears. Gage touched the back of her head, guiding her to his shoulder. She leaned in close and cried. She cried because she'd been lonely for a long time. She cried because people were good and kind to her. She didn't have to be alone.

Gage brushed his hand down the back of her head, stroking her hair. His lips grazed her forehead.

"I'll heat the soup and be back in a minute."

She nodded and walked into her bedroom.

When she came out of the bathroom a few minutes later Gage was waiting, leaning against the wall. He reached to slip an arm around her. She eased into his embrace. A long time ago she had told herself she wouldn't do this. Wouldn't let herself fall for the guy most likely to take off and leave a girl heartbroken.

But today he felt like the guy most likely to always be there. His arm around her was strong, and his shoulder was easy to lean on. At the sofa she turned to sit down but his arm was still around her. He pulled her close and ducked his head to kiss her. She wanted to tell him they couldn't, but her heart didn't agree. She very much wanted to be in his arms, kissed by him.

Loved by him. The thought shook her. His kiss shook her.

He cupped the back of her head and moved the kiss beyond a quiet moment. Layla grasped his arms and held on, needing this.

She didn't want to love him. But maybe she did. She knew the heartache in loving someone like Gage. She'd watched her mom, trying to hold on to a man who couldn't be held. She remembered her own heartache when Gage had used her to get to Cheryl.

She looked up, meeting the tenderness in hazel eyes that would be her undoing. Gage wasn't her father. She didn't think he was still the thoughtless boy she'd known in school. Time changed people.

"Stop thinking," he whispered close to her ear as he nuzzled her cheek.

"I have to, Gage. I don't get to not think."

"You think too much." He trailed kisses from her cheek, back to her mouth.

She had to be responsible. She had Brandon. She knew how the wrong choices could tear a person's life apart.

She leaned in to his shoulder and then slowly drew back, pulling out of his arms. "I have to think."

"I know." He brushed strands of hair, tucking them behind her ear.

She sat hard on the sofa and reached for the afghan that she'd left on the back of the couch. She needed to think, but she couldn't.

Gage smiled down at her. "I'm going to get you that bowl of soup."

"Thank you." Maybe if he left the room she could put two thoughts together and make sense of what seemed to be happening.

Car headlights flashed through the window. Layla looked at Gage and he shrugged. "I'd say that's my mom or Granny Myrna. Either way, we're busted."

"Busted? For what?"

He winked at her. "For that kiss."

"They didn't see."

"No, but they have mom radar. I bet they know. Don't worry, though—I don't kiss and tell."

"You're horrible."

He tipped his hat. "Now you're catching on. I'm nobody's hero, Layla."

"I didn't think you were."

He laughed as he walked into the kitchen. And she smiled, because as much as he twisted her inside out and made her question everything, he also made smiling easier than it had been in a long time.

His mother found him in the kitchen. She filled a cup with water and placed it in the microwave, then turned to look at him. He squirmed a little. It was the same look she'd used on him and his brothers when they were kids.

"I didn't do anything." He found a spoon and placed it in the soup that he'd fixed for Layla.

"I didn't say you did. My word, you have a guilty conscience. I was actually thinking how proud I am of you. How glad I am that Layla finally decided to let someone help her out and that the person was you."

"Are you staying here tonight?"

"Yes. Brandon is here. He's getting a few things he forgot, but he'll go back to the house with you. He's pretty happy over there, but he's worried about Layla."

"I'm sure he is. They only have each other."

"It was quite a scare for him. We talked a long time after you left to take her to the hospital. He has a lot on his mind for a young man."

"I think they both do, and they're trying to protect each other by not discussing it." Gage picked up the bowl of soup. "I told her she has to eat something."

"Oh, I see."

He didn't need his mom reading too much into this. He was bringing a woman a bowl of soup. Soup. Not flowers, a ring or a lifetime commitment.

He shook his head at her, which only made her smile more. He walked out of the kitchen with the bowl of steaming hot soup.

"Here's your soup." He forced an easy smile as he walked into the living room.

Layla was sitting up on the couch. She smiled at him, then at his mother. But the smile was strained, probably a lot like his. He knew Layla was probably wondering how she could get rid of the people invading her home, her life.

"Eat your soup and don't argue. You're not going to convince us you don't need us here."

"I didn't say anything." She wrinkled her nose at him and took the soup. And then she smiled a real smile. "Thank you."

"You're welcome. I'm going to head back to the house but Mom is staying with you."

"Thank you, Gage. Thank you for everything."

She looked sweet and soft, curled up in an afghan, the bowl of soup in her hands. He wanted to kiss her again but he couldn't. He wouldn't.

He cleared his throat. "You're welcome. I'll see you tomorrow."

Brandon walked into the room, and Gage couldn't have been happier to see him. The kid was a great distraction.

"I'm ready to go." Brandon glanced at his sister and then at the door.

"Tell your sister goodbye." Gage reached for his jacket and gave Brandon a shove in the right direction.

Brandon looked at the ground and then at Layla. And then he hurried forward, gave her a quick hug and out the door he went.

Layla smiled a weepy smile that sent Gage out the door as quickly as her brother. He met up with Brandon out by his truck. The kid looked red in the face, like he might make a run for it.

"She's going to be okay, you know," Gage offered as he pulled his keys out of the truck.

"She shouldn't have to worry all the time." Brandon got into the truck. They were heading down the road before he continued. "It's because of me. I've messed up. Last year I broke my arm and she had to take out a loan. And the roof needed fixing and she didn't have the money for that, either. Now she won't be able to work. I need to get a job, Gage."

"You need to calm down and remember that you're only fifteen and still in school."

"I've checked into it. I could quit and get some special permission to work. I could still go to night classes or something."

"You're not going to quit school. End of story."

"You're not my boss. You're just the guy who feels bad because you broke her heart years ago." Brandon glared at him in the dimly lit truck. "If you hurt her again, this time I'll hurt you."

"I'm not going to hurt her."

"Are you going to marry her?" Brandon's dark eyes were fixed on him, and Gage worried that the kid would decide to suddenly defend his sister's honor.

"I'm not planning on marrying anyone."

"Don't hurt her...that's all I'm saying."

"I'm just trying to help her out."

They were silent for a few minutes before Brandon spoke again. "She'll probably lose her jobs."

"We'll make sure she doesn't." Gage sighed as he turned down the road that headed to town instead of to Cooper Creek Ranch.

Brandon grinned.

He drove toward the Mad Cow. It was almost closing time but he thought he would talk with Vera before she replaced Layla. And he knew she'd have to replace her. Vera couldn't go even a couple of days without a waitress.

The parking lot was empty except for Vera's Jeep. Gage left the truck running and set the emergency brake.

"Stay here," he warned Brandon.

"You going to talk to Vera about Layla's job?"

"I reckon I am."

Brandon grinned again. The kid was getting as bad as Gage's mom and Granny Myrna. When Gage walked through the door of the little café, the cowbell over the door clanged, and Vera looked up from the cash register.

"Didn't you see the Closed sign?" Vera smiled, making it okay to be there at closing time. She glanced at her register tape and then raised her gaze to his again.

"You know me, Vera, no sense of time and no respect for rules." He pushed his hat back and grinned at her, not really knowing what he would say without starting a few new rumors.

"You're going to have to come up with something

better than that." She pulled off her reading glasses and let them hang from the chain on her neck. "So?"

"I just wondered…" He looked around at the empty dining room. He could hear someone in the kitchen rattling dishes and singing to the radio. He cleared his throat and thought about that pile of bills he'd seen while he'd been watching Layla sleep.

"You was wondering?"

He cleared his throat. "About Layla's job."

Vera pinned him with a look. "I'm going to have to hire someone, Gage. I'd do it myself if I had more hands and a lot more energy, but I don't."

"She's worried about it."

"I'm sure she is. This is going to be hard on her in a lot of ways. I'm just not sure what I can do. The job I gave her was temporary while my other girl is out having her baby. Now I've got Layla out."

"I'll do the job for her while she's gone. We can set up an account for the tips I earn and give it to her."

The words were out before he could stop himself. What in the world would people say? So much for keeping Dawson out of his business. Vera gave him a look, eyes narrowed and lips pursed but twitching like she might start laughing.

"What?" He crossed his arms over his chest.

"Oh, nothing. I just always wondered what you would look like when it happened." Then she started laughing, and he blushed from his ears to his neck.

"I'm helping out a person in need."

Vera's brows arched. "Of course you are, honey. I'm just saying, this is about the sweetest thing you've ever done. I'm not surprised, just real impressed."

Gage shifted from foot to foot and adjusted his hat. "Well, I should go."

"Don't you want to know your hours?" She laughed a little more. "What about the feed store? Are they going to replace her?"

He'd forgotten about the feed store. "Guess I'll talk to them tomorrow."

"You're going to work her job over there *and* here? Gage, that could start some serious rumors."

"I know that, Vera. But people will just have to talk, won't they?"

"I guess they will." Vera came out from behind the counter. She stood on tiptoe and kissed his cheek. "She deserves someone like you."

"I'm not her someone, Vera. I'm just her friend."

"That's exactly what I meant. Now, you wait right here. I'm going to box you up a coconut cream pie for being so sweet. And I'll expect you here tomorrow afternoon at four."

"I'll be here." And for the first time since the conversation started, he managed to take a deep breath.

People were going to talk. There was no getting away from that. He shook his head and wondered what they would say that he wasn't already thinking.

## Chapter Fifteen

Layla moved from the kitchen to the living room, cringing as she sat down. Her abdomen was still tender but she actually felt pretty good. And she was tired of sitting. Three days of being on the couch was enough. But Jesse had insisted she not do any chores outside, and definitely no waiting tables at the Mad Cow.

She closed her eyes and thought about all of the bills piling up and the money not coming in. She opened her eyes when someone rapped on the front door and then opened it. Angie Cooper had left just an hour ago, after fixing lunch and doing some housework for Layla. She'd had errands to run and promised to be back later.

The person walking through the door wasn't Angie, it was Gage. And he had a Christmas tree. He smiled as he dragged it in through the door, a big evergreen, the smell of cedar strong, filling up the house before he even had it completely inside.

"I brought you a tree."

"You certainly did." She wondered where they would put that big tree and how it would fit in her tiny living room. It looked to be about nine feet tall.

"It might be a little big."

"You think?" She laughed a little as he pulled the tree into her tiny living room and tried to stand it up. "We might have to move the furniture out."

"We might. But who needs furniture? A tree, on the other hand, is pretty important."

"You're right…a tree is definitely important."

The tree brushed the ceiling. He'd already shoved it into a tree stand. It looked as if he'd tried to trim it. One side seemed fuller than the other, the way trees cut from the field often are. It smelled awfully good, though.

"Do you like it?" He grinned, steadying the tree and looking from it to her.

"I think it's perfect. I do have an artificial tree we could have used."

"No way." He scooted it around the room. "Where do we put it?"

"Middle of the room? But that might cause problems."

"Hall?"

"More problems." She looked around the room. "The rocking chair can go in the kitchen for now."

"You're sure?"

"Positive."

He dragged the rocking chair out of the room and when he came back he moved the tree where her chair had been. It took him a few minutes of turning and positioning, but he finally had it so that the fullest side faced out. She enjoyed watching him work. He'd pulled off his coat and he wore a heavy, button-up shirt and jeans. His boots were a little muddy. His hat was cocked to the side thanks to the tree brushing his face as he angled it to make it stand straight.

"Perfect." Layla clapped her hands and smiled at him. She forgot everything but Gage standing in her living room with the perfect tree.

"Decorations?" he asked her.

Layla responded, "Attic."

"Great." He grinned. "Nothing better than climbing a ladder into an attic.

"It can wait for Brandon to come home."

"Nope, I can do it." He looked around. "How do I get up there?"

"There's a door in the ceiling of the utility room."

He headed out. She watched him go, and then looked at the tree he'd cut down for her. Any other woman would have been doomed by such an act of sweetness. But she knew his charm. She knew how easy it was to fall for that smile and the sweet things he did.

And yet, she felt her heart stuttering and stammering as it tried to convince itself that Gage Cooper had to be off-limits. For so many reasons.

A few minutes later she heard him banging and bumping around her attic. She waited, cringing at the vibration of her entire house. And then he returned carrying a rubber container full of decorations.

He set it down and swiped at a cobweb that clung to his hat. "For someone so organized, that attic is crazy."

She laughed at the description. "Yeah, I guess it probably is."

He arched his brows at her and pulled the lid off the container. He grimaced. "Is this it?"

"You were expecting more?"

"I don't know." He pulled out a box of lights. "Lights first. Do you feel up to helping?"

She was already on her feet. "Of course."

He walked to the back of the tree and started at the top. He strung the lights at the top of the tree, and as he reached to hand them to her, their hands brushed. And then on the next pass, brushed again. He moved around the side of the tree the final time, and smiled down at her.

"Almost done." He spoke softly, finishing the lights as she watched.

Layla needed to do something. She reached into the tub and pulled out a box of angel decorations. "These first. I always make sure these go on first."

"Are these special?" He took the box from her hands.

"They were my mom's favorites." She shrugged, trying to make him think that it didn't really matter. But it did. She and her mom had always decorated the tree together.

"Layla, I'm so sorry."

She looked up, blinking quickly to clear her vision. "Gage, don't. Please. Not right now. I wanted you to know they were her favorite. They're special to me. But I don't want to cry."

He tucked a strand of hair behind her ear. For a moment she thought he would kiss her, but he didn't. He ran his fingers through her hair and then he brushed a hand across her cheek.

As she turned to hang ornaments, her legs weak and her fingers trembling, he reached into the container and pulled out a box of homemade decorations. She smiled, remembering the year she'd made them with Brandon.

Gage looked at the baked dough decorations. "Also special?"

"The year after they died, Brandon and I made those together."

"Good memories, Layla."

"Exactly. That's why I don't want to cry. Each year I decorate the tree, I remember the special moments. It's more than just decorating a tree—it's the memories, the laughter." She smiled up at him. "It's corny, I know."

He shook his head. "Not at all."

They worked in silence, hanging each ornament while Layla thought about the past, about her parents, about the advice her mom had given her, sometimes at night while her mom nursed a new bruise and Layla's dad slept off another drinking binge. Advice meant to help Layla have a better life, but advice that had caused her to put her heart away, safely locked up where no one could ever hurt her the way her dad had hurt her mom.

Those memories weren't the ones she wanted. What they needed was Christmas music. She reached for the television remote and turned to a station with seasonal music. Gage started to sing along to "Silent Night." She sang with him.

Emotions tangled inside her, drawing her closer to the cowboy at her side.

"I think you should sit down." Gage wrapped an arm around her waist and led her back to the sofa. "I'll finish. You boss me around."

"That's a good idea." She sank into the soft couch and pulled the afghan around her shoulders. "Gage, you've been wonderful. I don't know how to thank you."

"I have a suggestion." He smiled as he continued to

decorate the tree. "One of these days you'll agree to have dinner with me."

"Gage."

"I mean it, Layla. I want to take you out. Maybe to Tulsa. I know a really good steak house."

"I don't know."

He hung the last decoration, finding a spot that looked a little bare. "I do know. I know that we've become friends and I'd like to take you out."

"My life is really complicated."

"I know that."

"No, you don't. You've been gone a lot. You don't know how complicated it is to be working two jobs and raising a fifteen-year-old brother."

"You're right, I don't."

"I haven't been on a date in a long time. It isn't fair, to go out to dinner with some nice guy when I have all of this going on."

"Well, there you go. If you go to dinner with me, you're not going with a nice guy." He winked and then he dug around in the tub. "No star or angel for the top of the tree?"

She shook her head, trying hard to keep up with him, trying to understand where this conversation would take them and what she should say next.

"This is going to have to be a cowboy tree." He pulled off his hat and placed it on the top. "Perfect."

She had to agree. The tree was perfect. He was perfect, even with his perpetual five o'clock shadow and hair messy from the hat. He wanted to take her to dinner.

"Gage, I can't go out with you. A few years ago I

tried to date, but it was too complicated. I work a lot. I have a little brother to raise. It's a package deal."

"I know that." He sat down next to her on the couch. He looked at the tree and smiled. "We did a good job. Now it feels a little more like Christmas in here."

"Yes, it does. The hat is a nice touch but you might want that later."

He shrugged, reaching for her hand. "I might. But I have others at home."

He lifted her hand and brushed a kiss across her fingers.

"Gage." She shook her head. "I can't."

"I know. When it comes to stability, I'm not the poster child."

"It isn't that." Not completely. The late-night talks with her mother came back to her, the warnings, the careful advice.

"I have Brandon, and he's pretty much all I can cope with right now."

"I know."

She touched his hand, tracing her fingers over his. "You have helped him so much."

"I'm not sure how." He chuckled, soft and husky. "It's not like I'm the best role model."

"You're a good person."

"Now I know you're making things up." He lifted her hand again, holding it against his cheek. "If you keep telling me that, I'm going to start believing it."

"Good."

He released her hand and looked at his watch. "I have to go. You'll be okay until my mom gets here?"

"Yes, I'll be fine."

He stood, looking down at her with a careful look. "Think about dinner."

She nodded. "I will."

He left. She watched as he pulled on his coat and reached for a hat that wasn't there. He brushed a hand through his hair and smiled back at her. Then he was gone and she was alone. She sat on the sofa looking at the tree, at his hat where a star should have been.

She thought about how it would feel to go out to dinner with man like Gage. She thought about how much Brandon needed him, and how it would break both their hearts when Gage left again.

Gage walked in the back door of Vera's instead of the front door. He didn't want people to know he was waiting tables until he actually walked out on the floor. Before coming to the Mad Cow he'd stopped at the feed store to talk to them about working for Layla, and they'd agreed. They needed the help, and Layla needed the money. It was a win-win for all of them.

Layla would be surprised. And probably a little bit mad.

"Hey, there's my new waitress." Vera stepped out from behind the grill and gave him a careful look. "You'll do, but you aren't as pretty as Layla." Vera laughed at her own joke.

"Where do I start?" Gage asked.

"I'll get you an apron and an order pad. You've eaten here enough to know how it works. You give 'em menus, get their drink orders and then go back to see if they're ready to order. My specials are listed on the board. Salads are in the cooler at the waitress station."

"I've got it." He followed her into the dining area.

People turned to stare. A few of them called out his name. He waved and kept following Vera.

She made a big production of handing him an apron and an order pad. "You're ready for this?"

"Don't look so doubtful." He grinned as he tied the apron around his waist and dropped the order pad in one of the pockets.

"I'm still surprised that you offered. This is a big deal, Gage. People are going to talk."

"I know." He looked around the dining room at the early crowd that had showed up to make sure they got an order of Vera's fried chicken.

"The Pullmans just got here." Vera nodded to a table with parents and two kids. "Go ahead and take their order."

"Will do, boss."

Ted Pullman watched Gage with a glint of humor in his eyes that Gage didn't really appreciate. "Gage, you're a waitress now? I knew cattle prices were down, but didn't think they were that bad."

"I'm helping Layla Silver out. She can't work for a while."

Mira Pullman smiled at that. "That's real sweet of you, Gage."

"Thanks, Mira. All of my tips go to Layla."

"You could just give her the check from the finals," Ted offered as he picked up the menu.

Gage had thought about it, but he knew she wasn't going to take his money. He wrote down their order and headed back to the kitchen. When he walked back to the dining room a few minutes later, the big table in the middle of the room had been filled. His older brother Lucky and his family, Jackson and his family sat down. Great.

"Hey, little brother, we heard you were waiting tables." Lucky leaned back in his chair and grinned. "How's that working out for you?"

"Well, I thought it wouldn't be too bad until I saw the Cooper clan."

Jackson touched his coffee cup. "Could I get coffee? And maybe you should be nicer. We're real good tippers."

Lucky laughed at that. "I'll give you a tip. Marry the girl. It'll be a lot easier than waiting tables."

"Thanks, I'll remember that." Gage walked off.

"Coffee," Jackson called out, and then his wife, Madeline, spoke softly, warning him to go easy. Gage glanced back over his shoulder and made eye contact with Madeline, who was one of the nicest people Gage knew.

At least he had one ally.

But he didn't have time to think about it. The Mad Cow got busy. He had seen it like this before, with every table filled. He'd just never realized how hard a job waitressing was until he was the guy facing all of those customers. Vera helped him out when she could.

Toward the end of the evening, he was doing everything he could to keep up with his tables. Vera laughed as he rushed out of the waitress station with a few salads. He turned to look at her and she pointed.

"Salads are better with more than lettuce."

"Of course they are." He looked down at the bowls of lettuce.

"You're doing great, Gage. My goodness, people are leaving tips in the jar at the register, plus what they're giving you. And Breezy suggested we have a benefit. She said she'd be willing to sing. But we should get a better waiter."

"Nice, Vera."

Vera held her hands up in surrender. "Breezy said it, not me."

The front door opened, setting off the cowbell that had never bothered Gage until he had to hear it over and over again. A gust of cold air came in with the newcomers. Gage turned, smiling at a couple that lived down the road from Cooper Creek, and then at Brandon.

How'd Brandon get to town? The kid looked madder than spit. Or maybe just upset.

"She put that horse of hers online," Brandon nearly shouted, catching several curious looks.

"Calm down." Gage grabbed the kid by the arm and pulled him toward the waitress station, knowing people were listening.

"She put her horse up for sale," Brandon said again.

"I didn't know." Gage grabbed his phone out of his pocket. "Give me the website link."

Brandon did, and Gage punched it into his phone while Vera shouted to him that he had an order up.

"Take that order to Jackson and his family." Brandon just stared at him. "Yeah, you."

Brandon grumbled something about not being no waitress, and Gage ignored him. The kid could help out, too.

While Brandon took the order, Gage glanced over the website until he found the mare. Great. Now what would he do? She couldn't sell that horse. He glanced out at the crowded restaurant. Someone had to buy it. She'd guess if it was him. But she wouldn't suspect Jason Bradshaw, and he'd just walked through the doors of the café.

Gage walked through the crowded dining room and sat down next to Jason, who happened to be sitting with his wife, Alyson.

"I don't think the waiter is supposed to sit with the diners." Jason laughed, as he turned a cup right side up for Breezy to fill with coffee. She gave Gage a dirty look, filled the cup and left.

"Hey," he called after her, "you get what you pay for."

"What's up?" Jason poured a couple of packets of sugar into his coffee.

"I need you to buy a horse. Maybe pay for it and say you can't pick it up for a week or so."

"I don't want to buy a horse."

"I'll pay for it." Gage put his phone on the table in front of Jason. "It's Layla's mare. She must be panicking about money and she put it on this website."

Alyson sighed a little. "Poor Layla, she loves that mare. She has so much hope for it."

"I know. That's why we're not going to let her get rid of it." Gage felt like he was the only one getting it. "I'll write you a check, Jas, but you have to send her a message and tell her you'll put the money in this pay account, and send someone to pick the horse up."

"Why don't you just tell her you'll give her the money and she doesn't have to sell the horse?" Jason said it like it made sense.

"She isn't going to take my money."

"Yeah, she probably wouldn't."

"Not after you broke her heart," Alyson mumbled as she reached for her water glass.

"Thanks, Alyson, for that knife to the heart."

"She's one of my dearest friends. If you break her heart this time, I'll do worse than that to you." She glared at him, and he knew she meant it.

"I'm not going to break her heart. Why is it if a guy does something nice for a woman, everyone assumes they're dating?"

"Well, when someone spends this much time with a woman, it looks like a relationship."

Gage tapped his phone screen. "Do you have that website?"

Jason picked up his own phone and typed it in. "I'll buy the horse, Gage. And you bring me the check tomorrow. But you'd better listen to my wife."

"Yes, sir."

Vera came out of the kitchen, looking like she was on the warpath. He jumped up.

"Are you working for me or not?" She glanced from Gage to the crowded dining room.

"I'm working. I had to take care of an emergency."

"There's a fifteen-year-old kid carrying orders to customers," Vera informed him. "And he's doing a better job than you."

Jason laughed.

"Yeah, well, I'm injured." Gage pointed to his braced knee. "I'm supposed to rest a lot."

"You've been resting all your life. Now get to work." Vera handed him the coffeepot. "Fill up some cups and remember why you're doing this."

How could he forget? As he filled up coffee cups, he tried to guess Layla's reaction when she found out he'd bought her horse. She'd be mad. Really mad. Or she'd love him forever.

He didn't know how to feel about that. People wanted to order, and others were waiting for drinks to be refilled. When he'd come home for the holidays, he hadn't expected his life to get tangled up with Layla Silver's. But now that it was, how did he get it untangled?

And did he want to?

## Chapter Sixteen

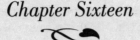

On Friday the new owner picked up Pretty Girl. Layla stood on her front porch and cried as the mare drove away. A week from Christmas, at least she had a nice check that would keep her from defaulting on the bank loan. She wiped at the tears streaming down her cheeks. She had to stop crying because crying wouldn't make it any better.

Telling herself that never seemed to work. Sometimes a girl just needed a good cry. Especially when her horse was being trailered down the drive, whinnying as she got farther and farther from home.

Layla had to go inside, away from the heartbreaking sound. Daisy sat next to her, whining and nuzzling Layla's hand with her cold nose. She brushed her hand through the soft fur at the collie's neck.

Beth would come by any minute. She had called earlier. Now that Layla was feeling better, Beth wanted to take her to the community center. They were putting finishing touches on the Living Nativity that would take place the following weekend, right before Christmas. After watching the rehearsal, they would head to the Mad Cow for dinner.

Layla slipped off her barn boots and put on suede boots that had a warm lining. She grabbed her jacket off the hook next to the door just as Beth's truck pulled up the drive. It was only the two of them tonight. Jeremy was caring for their son. Layla needed a night like this. She needed a break from the house, from people taking care of her. Not that it hadn't been wonderful. She had a freezer full of casseroles from neighbors and church members. She wouldn't need to cook for weeks.

Beth honked. Layla grabbed her purse and went out the door, not running as she would have done. Her side was still tender, and she found that naps had become her friend.

She climbed into the truck and smiled at Beth.

"You look great." Beth shifted into Reverse.

"Thank you."

Beth's eyes narrowed. "What's wrong? Did Gage…"

Layla laughed a little and wiped at more tears. "I sold my mare."

"Oh, Layla, I'm so sorry."

"It's okay. I mean, it's not, but it will be. I had to do it. And she's going to a good home."

"I'm sure she is." Beth looked away, and Layla wondered at her friend's sudden loss of words. But Beth wasn't a person to push.

"It hurt to let her go, but tomorrow will be a better day. And I'm hoping next week Jesse will allow me to go back to work."

"Don't rush it, Layla." Beth slowed to make the turn that would take them to Back Street. "Give yourself time to heal."

"I'm trying. It's hard to sit at home when I know that the bills are piling up."

"I know you're worried," Beth said as she pulled into the crowded parking lot of the community center.

Beth parked, and the two of them walked over to the nativity scene. The actors were walking through their parts. The animals milled restlessly in a pen. Layla watched as Mary and Joseph took their place in the stable.

The eternal story of the birth of a savior. Layla shivered in the cool afternoon, watching as an angel appeared to the shepherds in the field. She thought about what this story meant to her life. It meant faith. It meant believing in something more than herself, her own abilities.

If she'd only been trusting in herself all of these years, she would have given up. But God hadn't let her down. She had people in her life who were there for her, when she allowed them to be. She should allow it more often. This past week had taught her just how easy it was. It had taught her to be thankful for their help.

The Coopers had been at her side the entire time. Because of them, Brandon seemed to be doing better. Of course he would still have bumps along the way, but she thought they might make it through his teenage years. And because it meant so much to Brandon, she had accepted Angie Cooper's offer to spend Christmas with the Cooper family.

Gage. She hadn't seen much of him since the day he brought over the Christmas tree. Maybe he'd finally realized that he didn't owe her. Didn't have to make amends for something that had happened years ago.

It seemed silly, but she realized she missed him.

"Are you okay, standing this long?" Beth had walked away to talk to someone, but she returned, giving Layla a cautious look.

"I'm fine for now." She smiled at her friend. "As many times as I've seen this program, it still moves me. Makes me think about that night and how much God loves us."

Beth nodded, watching with Layla. The choir sang "O Little Town of Bethlehem" and Mary and Joseph greeted the shepherds who had come to see the baby Jesus. Beth looped her arm through Layla's.

"It's going to be okay."

Layla smiled. "I know it is."

"Do you want to go to Vera's for coffee and a piece of pie?"

"Sure." Layla answered as she was pulled toward Beth's truck. "Why not."

When they pulled up to the Mad Cow, Layla had a funny feeling something was going on. The parking lot was full, and almost everyone she knew was there. She got out, feeling uneasy, maybe a little sick.

"I think I'd rather go home."

Beth laughed and guided her toward the diner. "Not on your life."

As they walked through the door of the Mad Cow, Layla's feet refused to move forward. The restaurant was packed. Breezy stood in the corner with a guitar and a mic—and Gage. He was wearing an apron and taking orders.

"What's going on?" Layla looked around, managing somehow to smile and greet people who called out to her.

Vera walked through the crowd, her hair in its neat

bun, her smile familiar and welcoming. "Layla Silver, your friends and family put this night together to help you."

"I don't know what to say." Layla allowed herself to be led to a table where Angie Cooper patted an empty chair.

"Say thank you to that crazy Gage Cooper. I think he has a surprise for you."

"Why is he wearing an apron?" Layla sat down next to Angie.

"Honey, he's been working both your jobs for you while you've been sick." Vera hugged her from behind and placed a noisy kiss on her cheek.

"Working my jobs?" Layla repeated. She locked eyes with Gage. He winked, and she didn't have a clue how to act or feel.

"He wanted to make sure you had money coming in." Angie Cooper patted Layla's hand. "I think if bull riding doesn't work out, he'd make a fine waiter."

"He didn't have to do this."

"No," Angie said, "he didn't. He did it because he cares."

Layla wanted to argue, to tell Angie that Gage did it because he felt guilty. He felt like he owed her. But she couldn't. All of these people were here to support her, to help her. No matter what his motivations were, Gage had put this together. *She* owed *him.*

She closed her eyes and said a silent "thank you." Once again, God hadn't let her down. The people in Dawson hadn't let her down.

For the next two hours she sat at the center table, thankful but a little embarrassed by all the attention. People would come and go, stopping to talk with her for a few minutes, to hug her, to tell her that she was strong and they all admired her.

Toward the end of the evening, Angie rubbed her back a little. "Why don't you let Gage take you home? You look exhausted. This was probably too much for one day."

"No, I'm fine. And Beth can take me."

"Beth left thirty minutes ago, honey. I think she even said goodbye to you." She looked around the room. She was right. Beth was gone.

Layla hadn't even noticed.

Angie waved at Gage to grab his attention. He ambled over and pulled up a chair to sit close behind the two of them.

"I don't know how you do it, Layla. This is hard work."

She smiled at that. "It isn't easy."

"Why don't you give Layla a ride home?" Angie patted his arm. "I'll help Vera clean up."

Layla wondered if he felt cornered, as if they were being pushed together. He had to know people were getting the wrong idea. But he didn't look cornered. He shrugged and then grinned at her.

"I'm game if she is. Let me get rid of this apron and let Vera know the plan."

Ten minutes later they were in his truck. He'd insisted on warming it up before they left. Layla sat on the passenger side, wondering how it would feel to have her heart broken a second time by Gage Cooper.

"Were you surprised?" Gage glanced at the woman sitting as far from him in the cab of the truck as she could get.

"Very. Thank you for doing that. And for working for me." Her voice broke a little. "I didn't know."

"Because if I'd told you, you would have told me no, and mentioned that I didn't need to make up for what I did ten years ago. This wasn't about that, Layla. This was about me doing something for you because we're friends."

They were more than friends, but if she hadn't figured that out yet, he didn't know how to explain it to her.

"You're probably right," she finally admitted.

"Thank you for that. I do like to be right every now and then."

She laughed a little, and the sound was a relief. He wanted to reach for her hand but didn't. It didn't take a genius to see that she still thought he was only in her life to make amends for the past. Eventually he'd convince her otherwise.

"I'm leaving in January." That probably wasn't the best way to let her know he was feeling more than friendship for her. He was thinking about the future, and she played a big role in those plans.

But it wasn't quite time for that yet.

"Back to bull riding?" She didn't look at him.

"Yep. But before I go, we're going to that steak house in Tulsa."

"Are we?"

"Yes. We are."

She turned to look at him then. He saw the dark circles under her eyes, her pale face and the strain of a long day. He reached over and laced his fingers through hers.

"Do I have a say in this?"

"Are you going to turn me down?"

She unlocked her fingers from his. "I'm not sure."

He pulled up to her house. Brandon had gone home with Gage's dad about an hour before the event at the Mad Cow ended. They had a horse about to foal, and Tim hadn't wanted to leave her alone too long. These days, Brandon stuck to Gage's dad like glue.

Layla gave him a long look. "I'm not sure if I can do it, Gage."

"You'll be better by then."

"No, I can't do this. I can't go to dinner with you." She looked so sad he wanted to hold her and never let her go. He wanted to find a way to make her smile every day.

Somehow he doubted Layla was in the mood for caveman tactics.

"Why?"

"Because you'll break my heart." She opened the truck door. "I have a fifteen-year-old brother to raise. I'm not young and carefree. I can't do casual dating. You're gone more than you're home. This is it for me. This is my life. I raise Brandon. I work. I try to keep this old farm from falling apart. You go where you want, when you want. You date who you want and then you move on. And for a lot of women you meet, I'm sure that's fine."

"So going to dinner is out." She didn't get it. Maybe he should have told her that he had more in mind than a casual dinner with her.

He didn't get a chance. She was out of his truck in a flash, and hurrying toward the house. Stubborn female. He watched her go, deciding it was for the best. She needed to cool off, and he needed a better game plan.

Man, he'd never needed a game plan before. How did a guy go about courting a woman as stubborn as Layla Silver? He headed for his granny's, because if anyone knew about courting, it would be Myrna Cooper.

He drove back to Dawson, glancing at the clock on the dashboard, and wondered if his grandmother would be awake. When he pulled into her driveway, the lights were still on.

He walked up to the front porch and knocked lightly. A moment later, she peeked through the curtains, turned the porch light on and opened the door.

"What in the world are you doing on my front porch at ten o'clock at night?"

He shrugged and stepped in, pulling off his boots before he walked into the living room. "Wanted to visit."

"I'd say I was glad for the company, but you look like something the cat hacked up, and you smell like fried chicken."

"Thanks, Gran. Can I sit down?"

"Take my chair and put your leg up while you're at it. You're going to end up having surgery again because you won't listen to a thing anyone tells you."

"Another compliment, thank you for that." Gage sighed, doing as she said, not because he wanted to, but because he knew she still had a flyswatter and she wasn't afraid to use it.

"Well, I can think of a few more compliments if that's why you're here. Like maybe you ought to shave once in a while."

"My self-esteem is tanking here." He grinned up at her, and he'd never felt less like smiling. His grandmother eyed him, like she knew what he was going to say.

"You are in a bad way. So tell me what happened."

He sat there on the sofa, wondering how exactly he should broach the subject of Layla with Gran. He decided to jump in, feetfirst.

"I told Layla I'd like to take her to a nice restaurant in Tulsa. She told me politely, no, thanks. Then told me I basically am just a good ol' boy, and she's got to think about raising Brandon and working to keep her place from falling apart."

"The truth is so hurtful." His grandmother fanned herself with a magazine, giving him a sly look. "She hasn't dated in years, Gage. Do you think you can bat those pretty eyes at her and she'll suddenly come running?"

"I'm not looking for her to come running. I'm looking to marry her." He choked a little because he hadn't expected to say those words out loud. To anyone. Now that they were out there, they kind of made perfect sense.

His grandmother couldn't stop laughing. "Oh, now, isn't that wonderful. But she thinks you want to date a little, then run back to bull riding and who knows what."

"Could you stop making me sound like a womanizer?"

"Are you one?"

"No, I'm not. You know me better than that. I'm not Jackson."

"Well, that ended well for him, didn't it?"

"Yeah, I guess it did."

They sat in thoughtful silence for a moment, letting

his words sink in. He still couldn't believe he'd said them out loud.

"I have the perfect ring. Pearls and diamonds, so very much like Layla. She's a gem, so quiet and beautiful, truly one of a kind."

"Yeah, she is."

"Don't monkey around, honey. She isn't the kind of girl you play around with. She's got a lot on her shoulders. You're going to have to make it clear from the beginning that you're in love with her and you want to marry her."

"After three weeks, I should just declare my intentions? That's kind of rushing things, isn't it?"

"I guess it is. You do what you want, but that's my advice."

Gage left his grandmother's with a diamond-and-pearl ring in his pocket. If a man was going to learn about all things related to love, she was the one to learn from.

## Chapter Seventeen

Layla didn't have to drag Brandon to church Christmas morning. He was actually up before her, having fed the cattle, broken the ice in the pond and taken a shower. She hugged him tight before handing him a plate of bacon and eggs.

They had opened their gifts the night before. He was wearing the new jeans and button-up shirt she'd bought him.

"Sis, thanks for the clothes." He looked pretty happy.

"You're welcome." She sat down across from him with a small plate of scrambled eggs. "Thank you for the perfume."

He grinned at that. He'd used the money he'd earned working for the Coopers. "Mrs. Cooper helped me pick it out."

The scent was perfect—subtle, not too sweet or too overwhelming. She had thought he must have had help. She also knew the bottle of perfume cost far more than he could ever afford. But she loved the fragrance, loved her brother for giving it to her.

Christmas changed everything. Layla thought that

as they drove to church. She'd worried over the holiday, over money and gifts. As they pulled into the parking lot of the church she realized people had changed the focus of the day. The focus should still be a baby born in the manger.

The church wasn't crowded, not on Christmas morning. Many of the regulars were out of town. The Coopers were in their usual pew, along with the Bradshaws, the Johnsons and several other local families. Layla noticed the church had been decorated with poinsettias and twinkling lights.

Myrna Cooper waved her over, patting the seat next to her. Brandon and Layla slid in and sat down as the choir stood. She loved this, singing the songs that told the Christmas story, of faith and promises kept.

Layla closed her eyes as she sang, wishing the peace of this moment would last forever. She wondered why it didn't. God had said He gave peace, not as the world gave it. She remembered the verse: *Let not your heart be troubled, neither let it be afraid.*

Layla stood with the congregation to sing "Joy to the World." As she sang, Gage looked at her, making eye contact. She noticed the tears in his eyes, and her heart faltered. She had found peace during this Christmas service. Maybe Gage had found a way through his anger.

She smiled at him, hoping he would know that she understood. He had come home in more ways than one.

As the service ended, people stood. Hugs were exchanged, and friends wished one another a merry Christmas. Layla turned to look for Gage. He had gone. The door at the back of the church opened as people filed out, and she saw his truck pulling out of the parking lot.

"Ready to go?" Angie Cooper appeared at her side.

"Oh, yes, of course." Layla smiled, as if nothing had happened. She wouldn't be the person who heard a message and then quickly forgot what she'd learned. Peace, not as the world gives it. Peace coming down from the Father above, she reminded herself.

She turned to find Brandon. He was at the front of the church, and he looked strangely proud of himself. His smile seemed a little too big and his eyes a little too bright.

"What did you do?" she asked as they walked out the door and down the steps together.

"I didn't do anything." He looked young and sheepish. Then he looked over at Jade Cooper, with her pretty blond hair and her big smile. Great, the last thing she needed was her brother going girl crazy.

"She's a year older than you, you know," Layla warned as they drove away.

"What?" He sounded pretty surprised and a little puzzled.

"Jade Cooper. She's a sweet girl, and I really do like her, but I'll like her better when you're twenty-two and out of college."

He turned a little red. "Jade is just a friend."

"That's cool. Brandon. We haven't really talked about dating."

Brandon groaned. "Could we *not* talk about girls and dating right now? It's Christmas."

Layla laughed. "You're right. It's Christmas."

They followed the line of Cooper cars and trucks up the long drive to the big brick, Georgian-style home.

Lights were wrapped around the columns on the porch, and a big wreath hung on the front door. Layla knew it would be beautiful later, when the lights twinkled in the dark evening.

They parked next to Jackson. Gage's truck was nowhere to be seen. She tried to pretend she didn't mind that he had disappeared. He was a grown man. He could do what he wanted.

Layla walked up to the front porch. The Coopers were filing inside, laughing and talking. Layla felt her guest status keenly as she and Brandon entered the big house, taking off their shoes and lining them up alongside the others. Myrna Cooper had stationed herself at the entrance to the living room. She hugged everyone as they walked through. She hugged Layla tight and kissed her cheek.

"I'm so glad you're here. You are a pearl." Myrna held her cane in one hand and slipped her other arm around Layla. "You're a pearl, my darling girl. You're beautiful and beyond compare."

"I'm not sure about that, Myrna."

"Oh, Layla, I'm never wrong about such things."

The two of them walked arm in arm to the kitchen, where the Cooper women were gathered, putting the finishing touches on lunch.

"I should help," Layla said, but Myrna didn't agree. She kept her arm around Layla.

"You're still recovering. And look at the crowd of women in there." Myrna led her to a stool at the counter. "Sit down."

Angie pulled a beautiful beef tenderloin from the oven, then turned to her. "We have it under control.

I'm going to bake the rolls and then we'll have dinner. I think it will be about thirty minutes."

"Where is that grandson of mine?" Myrna asked, glancing at the clock.

Angie gave her what Layla would classify as a warning look.

"Do you all mind if I interrupt?" Gage's voice behind her surprised Layla. She turned, nearly falling off the stool.

Angie looked back, her smile big. "Well, there you are."

"Yes, here I am." He walked up right behind Layla. "I need to talk to you outside."

"I'm helping."

"No, she isn't." Myrna gave her a little push. "Go."

Angie echoed the sentiment. "Go. You have thirty minutes before dinner's ready."

"That's long enough. I hope." Gage reached for her hand and waited.

Layla slid off the stool. Gage didn't let go of her. He also didn't explain. They walked to the front of the house where she'd left her shoes and coat. All the while, her heart was doing a strange dance.

Gage helped Layla into her coat, his fingers trembling. He hoped she didn't notice. Trembling fingers couldn't be a sign of strength. She reached for the front door, but he stopped her.

"Not so fast."

Her eyes large, so expressive, searched his. "Why?"

"I need to blindfold you."

"I won't be able to see."

He laughed at the obvious. "No kidding?" He pulled a bandanna out of his pocket. "Hold still."

He wrapped the cloth around her face and tied it tight in the back. And then he took advantage of the moment, leaned in and kissed her. At first she hesitated, then she kissed him back, holding tight.

"Merry Christmas, Layla," he whispered close to her ear, smiling when she shivered a little.

"Merry Christmas to you, too."

He placed her hand on his arm. "Be careful on the steps. I'll help you."

"I trust you."

"Good. Okay, step." He allowed her to go slow. "Next step. And two more."

He led her down the sidewalk. The sun was warm and the breeze had calmed down. Snow would have been nice, but a guy couldn't have everything.

"Where are we going?"

"If I told you, it wouldn't be a surprise."

"I don't like surprises."

"I kind of figured you for a person who didn't like surprises. But I promise, you'll like this one."

They stopped walking. She stood still, her hand still on his. "Gage?"

"Hold on." He stepped away from her.

"Gage?"

"Give me a second." He untied the mare, adjusted the big bow around her neck and led her close to Layla. He slipped the lead rope into her hand, then stepped behind her to untie the bandanna.

When it dropped, she gave a gasp that turned to a sob. And then she hugged the mare's neck. He stood behind her as she ran her hands across the horse's face, then hugged her again.

She looked up at Gage, tears streaking down her face. "How?"

"I bought her. I arranged for one of Jason's guys to pick her up, and I kept her there so you wouldn't know."

"But why?"

"Because you wouldn't let me give you the money, and I knew you wouldn't let me buy her and hand her right back to you." He brushed hair away from her face, then gently touched her cheek. "You're stubborn that way."

"It isn't stubbornness. It's strength."

"Yes, of course it is." He kissed her again, soft and easy, as the horse pushed between them. He pushed back. "Go away, Pretty Girl."

"I don't know what to say."

"Say yes," he whispered, waiting, holding his breath, wanting to hear that one word more than he'd ever wanted anything in his whole life.

Layla stopped breathing.

She held her mare in one hand, Gage's arm with the other. He remained close, his head touching hers, his breath soft on her neck.

"Yes to what?" she managed to get out.

Gage pulled back, his face serious, his eyes full of emotion. She loved his eyes. She loved his smile. She loved that when he held her, she felt safe.

"I guess we could start with you saying yes to dinner in Tulsa." He grinned as he said it. "You keep telling me no. But I think we have a misunderstanding."

"Do we?" She tried to keep up with what he was saying.

"We do. I think I failed to communicate my intentions to you, Miss Silver."

"Your intentions? How very Victorian of you."

"Not Victorian. Romantic." He leaned to kiss her again, and she held tight to his shoulders, the lead rope of the mare slipping from her grasp.

"What are your intentions?" she whispered as he held her close.

He smiled down at her. "My intentions are to show you that a cowboy can learn to stay home if the right woman is there to keep him close."

"Is that a fact?"

"Yes, it's a fact. Another fact is that when I asked you to dinner, I didn't mean I would take you out just once before I left town. I meant I wanted to take you out. And keep taking you out."

"Oh, like a steady girlfriend?" she teased.

"Stop talking, woman." He sighed and let go of her. He yanked the brace off his knee and tossed it aside. Before she could stop him, he dropped to one knee and reached in his pocket.

"Gage?"

"Layla, I love you. I'm going to court you, romance you, buy you flowers every day if I have to. And then I'm going to marry you."

"But…but…" She was so full of love for him, she was speechless. Her heart ached from the tenderness in his voice and his eyes. She reached for his hands and pulled him to his feet. "Stand up."

"I'm going to make it to a few rides this winter, then

I'm going to stay home and build a life with you." He stood and pulled her close again.

"What about Brandon?"

"We're going to raise him together. And my family will help. Layla, it's time for you to open your heart and let people help."

"You can't propose to someone you haven't dated."

"I've been trying to date you, and you kept turning me down."

"I'm sorry." She smiled up at him. "I haven't made this easy for you."

"No, you haven't. And you haven't said yes, either." He pulled back. "Come to think of it, you haven't said you love me."

"I do love you. I've always loved you. Since I was fifteen and writing your name in my notebook, I've loved you."

He reached for her hand. "My grandmother says you're a pearl."

She laughed at that. "She told me that just an hour ago."

"She said not to tell you that you're shiny, because a girl doesn't want to hear that she's shiny."

"What does a girl want to hear?"

Gage Cooper loved her. He loved her, and he'd just put one of his grandmother's rings on her finger. He'd bought her horse and given it back to her. He wasn't going to leave.

"That she's the only one in the world for a cowboy. That she's beautiful beyond compare." He kissed her lightly and whispered, "And that if this cowboy can't marry her, he's not sure what he'll do."

Layla touched his cheek. "I love you, Gage Cooper.

I do want to go to dinner with you. And I do want you in my life forever."

"I'm going to love you forever, Layla Silver."

Layla wanted to tell him that he had changed everything for her. She hadn't expected it that day he stopped to help her on the side of the road, but she was so glad he'd stopped.

Before she could speak, there was a burst of applause and cheers. Layla and Gage turned toward the house, where the Coopers were crowded on the front porch. Brandon stood with them, clapping and smiling big.

"Let's go have Christmas dinner." Gage held her close to his side.

"What about my mare?"

Gage groaned. "I didn't really plan the logistics of a horse with a big bow around her neck."

Before they could figure out a plan, Jackson was there. "I'll take her. The two of you oughtta show that ring to the family."

The family. Layla looked at the group of people gathered on the porch, including her brother. Family. She reached for Gage's hand as they walked up the steps into the arms and hearts of the Coopers.

# *Epilogue*

Layla stood in the yard where her house had once stood. Gage had insisted on moving the little house, not tearing it down. It had a new foundation at the other end of the property. In its place stood a beautiful ranch house with log siding. Gage walked down the front steps, beaming at her. She walked to meet him.

His hand immediately went to her belly. "How's my little girl?"

"Boy," Layla insisted. Further argument ended when he kissed her.

"Girl," he whispered. "My grandmother insists it's a girl, and that we have to name her Pearl."

Their baby was due at Christmas, two years after Gage's very wonderful proposal. Her mare, Pretty Girl, whinnied from the barn. Andie Johnson, Ryder's wife, had turned her into a champion barrel horse.

"If she's a girl, we name her Pearl." Layla hugged her husband. "I want to go inside my new home now. You've kept it a surprise long enough."

"You'll love it."

"I know I will."

"Brandon will love it," Gage said, and they both laughed.

"If Brandon ever sees fit to leave Cooper Creek, that is. He loves staying with your parents."

They walked up the steps of the big, log home. The front porch ran the length of the house. They had designed it together, then Gage had taken over, wanting it to be a surprise and insisting it would be better for their marriage if he did the work and she stayed out of it. She hadn't quite agreed, but she'd let him think he was in charge. His sister Heather, who had decided to move back to Dawson, had taken charge of the decorating, and she'd run everything by Layla first.

The inside of the house was every bit as beautiful as Layla had anticipated. The walls were painted warm colors. The kitchen had everything Layla had ever dreamed of, from the hickory cabinets to the granite countertops, to the stone flooring.

"It's beautiful."

Gage hugged her close. "Mrs. Cooper, you're beautiful. I love you."

"I love you, too." She stood on tiptoe, kissing his chin, and then she grimaced. "Your daughter is going to be a soccer player."

She moved Gage's hand across her belly so that he could feel what she felt. He leaned down to talk to their daughter.

"I'm going to protect you and your mommy forever, little girl. And you'll grow up thinking you're a princess."

"You can't spoil her," Layla warned.

"Wait and see, Mrs. Cooper. Wait and see."

She couldn't wait.

* * * * *

Dear Reader,

I hope this book finds you all well and that you are preparing for Christmas with joyful hearts, and with a knowledge of Jesus that makes this holiday season special.

This story is one that has been in the making since the very first Cooper Creek book. Gage has been a favorite character. We've all watched him struggle. We've worried over him and wondered when he would find peace. Finally, in this story and at this special time of year, Gage comes home to Dawson and he makes peace with himself, with God and with his past.

Merry Christmas to you all!

*Brenda Minton*

# SEASON OF HOPE

Virginia Carmichael

For my sister, Susan,
who loves without boundaries.

But Jesus said to them, "It is I. Do not be afraid."
—*John* 6:20

# Chapter One

Late, as usual. Evie swung the door of the Downtown Denver Mission open and dashed inside. The lobby was toasty, even though a bitterly cold November evening wind blew off the Rockies and right down Broadway without pausing to add a few degrees. She strode across the polished floor, her gaze taking in the large wooden cross that hung from the upper level.

She loved that old cross. It was so simple, so strong. It had brought her back to a life of forgiveness and hope. Her steps slowed and she took a deep breath. There wasn't anything to be gained by running, except a few more seconds.

Now that she wasn't flying through the lobby, she noticed a large poster announcing the Christmas tree–lighting ceremony. She smiled, knowing how excited the city's kids would be. One of the biggest parties of the year, it brought the whole Mission family together, as the tree was delivered on an old-fashioned sled pulled through downtown by horses. Often as not, it snowed through the party, but that was part of living in Denver.

The sound of her own footsteps rang in the cavern-ous lobby. Must take a ton of money to keep this place warm. She couldn't imagine trying to balance the com-fort of the residents and the reality of the electricity bill. But that was why she was here. An empty spot on the finance committee, her brother, Jack's, annoying ability to get his way and an extra dash of guilt meant Evie was the Mission's newest volunteer.

She glanced at the large, decorative mirror mounted to the nearest wall and tucked her dark hair behind her ears. Snow melting along the collar of her coat, blue eyes, generous mouth and the flush of a woman who'd been running late all day. She'd heard she was pretty, even beautiful, but sometimes when Evie looked in the mirror, all she saw was her twin brother, Jack. Same quirky smile, same off-center dimples, same arched brows that made them look just a bit mischievous.

Except for that little bit of sadness in her eyes that was all her own, a shadowy reminder of too many years running after the wrong things, too many nights awake staring at the ceiling. She smoothed her slightly wrin-kled office clothes and forced her mouth into a smile she hoped would pass as genuine.

Evie paused at the long, low front desk. She'd been volunteering for years at the Mission, mostly during the holidays or when they were short-staffed. Now, for the first time, she had a position. The responsibil-ity felt heavy on her shoulders. "Hi, Lana. Do I smell cookies?"

"Gingerbread. It's a rule that we can't have finance meetings without cookies. Take one." The secretary lifted up the plate, a smile creasing her face.

"Oh, great rule." Evie snagged a soft, round cookie

and took a bite. She'd pay for the cookie later. Power walking an extra mile or two at the gym might cover it. But she wouldn't think about that right now.

Lana tipped her head toward the offices. "It's hard enough to make tough money decisions. A little bit of gingerbread goes a long way toward keeping everybody happy." Purple-tipped hair, cut military short, gave the impression that the secretary was a little nutty. Add in the wheelchair and Lana was the poster child for unconventional. But Evie had never been anything but impressed by Lana's warmth and professionalism.

"Thanks for this," she said, turning toward the office area.

"Welcome. We've got all your papers filed, but remember to turn in the background check waiver."

Evie popped the last bit of deliciousness into her mouth and nodded. She wondered briefly if she would have any chance of stealing Lana away from the mission. Better pay, fewer hours, more vacation. Working at a big newspaper wouldn't be so different from what Lana was doing now, with coordinating all the paperwork and the staff.

Her whole body turned taut with anger as she caught herself. Old habits die hard. Plotting to steal away the Mission secretary might be a momentary bit of shallowness for some, but for her, with all the ugly past she carried, it burned like a searchlight on her weakness. Over and over she had made the very worst choices with only her selfishness as a guide.

And even now, years after she'd walked away from a miserable situation made by her own bitter jealousy, she caught herself slipping. Self-loathing and frailty, it all felt so familiar. She dragged in a breath, willing

the chill to pass. All she could do was continue to ask
for grace and hold on to hope. A girl with a past like
hers didn't have much choice.

"Evie!" She knew even before she turned it was
Jack, his cheery tone echoing around the lobby. He was
half a foot taller and a hundred times more fun. Just
the sight of him, with his energetic bounce, made her
forced smile morph into something absolutely genuine.

"Wait up. I got stuck in traffic. Oh, and here's Gavin.
Looks like everybody's late tonight." Jack motioned toward the entry and tugged off his ski jacket as he spoke.

A man with sandy blond hair stepped through the
glass double doors. He didn't look up, gaze focused a
few feet in front, mouth set in a line. More than preoccupied, he seemed to be carrying the worries of the
whole city.

Evie cocked her head, watching him. So, this was
the Gavin Sawyer who liked to snowboard with Jack
up on Wolf Mountain. From what her brother had said,
she'd gotten the impression Gavin was sort of an awkward science type, obsessed with viruses and germs.
The man striding toward them was the furthest thing
from a pale, nerdy lab rat that she could have imagined.
Broad shoulders, strong jaw, he was classically handsome but for the little bit of a hunch to his shoulders,
like he'd spent his life feeling too tall for the room. His
suit fit well, the shirt pressed and tie straight.

This was not a guy who would be happy behind a
desk all day, or in a cube farm. She gave him another
head-to-toe survey, trying to pinpoint what it was that
gave her that gut feeling. Athleticism, maybe. He was
only a few feet away and still hadn't noticed them. He
seemed to be in his own world. He looked down at his

watch and she grinned. There was something bright on the face, like a cartoon, and the strap was cherry-red.

"Wow. Earth to Evie." Jack's comment was followed by a loud snort of laughter.

She turned, face already heating. "Sorry, what did you say?"

"Let me introduce you." He stepped directly in Gavin's path.

"Wait, Jack. I don't—" She gave up and let him go. Trailing behind her twin, she attempted to look collected and cool. Jack was the outgoing, popular one. Give her a frantic newsroom an hour before the paper went to press anytime, but small talk just wasn't her strong point.

Jack clapped a hand on Gavin's shoulder in greeting. "Hey, you made it. This is my sister, Evie. She's the editor of *The Chronicle* and our new board member."

He turned, face polite, perfect mouth lifted in a smile. But Evie saw a flash of something in his expression that made her catch her breath. A narrowing of the eyes, a thinning of his lips. It was dislike, clear and simple.

"Hi. Glad you've joined us." Gavin's deep voice caught her by surprise. His tone was perfectly pleasant, if a bit distant. Nothing there suggested the feelings she'd sensed just seconds ago.

"Thank you." She flashed a bright smile and focused on slipping out of her blue wool coat. She struggled to compose her thoughts, letting her hair hide her face for a moment. Had Jack told him an unflattering story? Was Gavin one of those naturally distrusting types? She could understand that, just a little. But the expression he'd had was more disdain. Her stomach dropped a few inches as she wondered just what he'd heard. Or seen.

"Gavin is our resident disease specialist so if you have any odd rashes, be sure to let him know," Jack teased as he walked to Lana's desk and took two cookies.

There was an awkward pause. She crossed her arms and looked at Jack, who was grinning at her. She wanted to smack him.

Gavin let out a deep chuckle and shook his head. Disease specialist didn't sound like a particularly fun job and certainly didn't fit with her first impression, but the guy took Jack's teasing in stride. Better than Evie, who barely resisted giving her brother the look of death.

"Thanks for the cookies, Lana," Jack called as he headed toward the Mission's locked office area.

"Consider it a bribe. Don't forget the Christmas tree is being delivered this weekend. I want you all to be there to help us keep the kids under control." The secretary grinned and pushed the button on the desk that unlocked the doors and Gavin waved Evie ahead.

He held the door and as she passed, the smell of fresh air and soap wafted her way. As if acting on instinct, Evie glanced at his hand to see if he wore a ring and then grimaced at her own blatant curiosity. Gavin was handsome, smart and smelled wonderful. He also seemed to have taken an instant dislike to her. She was here to help the Mission's finance board, not find a date.

As she started down the hallway, Evie caught the toe of her glossy black pump on a wrinkle in the old brown carpet, pitching forward. Strong hands quickly gripped her elbow, rescuing her from the headfirst trajectory.

"Careful. The Mission definitely needs new carpeting." His low voice in her ear held more than a hint of laughter.

Of course he would have to be a witness to that acrobatic turn. Jack was halfway down the hallway, oblivious. Evie blew out a breath, calming her pounding pulse. Nothing like a near miss with the floor to get your heart rate up. "Right. It's practically unsafe to walk around in here." She met his eyes, wishing it didn't matter how ungraceful she seemed.

Fine lines marked the corners of his brown eyes. His hands felt warm and sure against her arm, lending her a support she hadn't known she needed. Evie wanted to lean close, to soak in the strength, to let someone else make all the big decisions, just for a moment.

Instead, she drew her elbow back from his gentle grip. "We'd better get in there before they start without us."

Gavin nodded, the ghost of a smile still playing around his mouth.

Turning back toward the conference rooms, she steeled herself against the feelings that swirled in her heart. Besides the fact she was here to focus on the Mission, she wasn't the type of girl who spent much time on her social life. There were a lot of reasons, really. Potential candidates were meager, even in a city as large as Denver. Running a paper wasn't a nine-to-five job, either.

But mostly, if she was truly honest, it was the knowledge that in every relationship there would be the moment where she would have to be honest. Honest about her past and the person she had once been. That was enough to give her second thoughts about any man, even one as handsome as Gavin Sawyer.

Gavin moved on autopilot down the hallway, Evie just steps ahead. So, the new member of the finance board runs the local paper. Okay. Nothing he couldn't work around. He took a calming breath. They were here to help the Mission build a healthy financial cushion, not pry into each other's ugly secrets.

Jack had mentioned her and something about *The Chronicle,* but he hadn't realized she was the editor. And so beautiful. Her smile was infectious, with a quiet confidence that made him want to follow her anywhere. But with his sister on her way to Denver, that would be a recipe for certain disaster.

Besides, right now he had a lot more to worry about.

The old fear gripped him and he felt his heart grow cold. He'd promised to do everything he could to save lives, promised on the memory of his best friend. No child should ever die of a preventable disease. No family should ever have to suffer that kind of anguish. He fought back the remnants of old grief and focused on the moment ahead. Finance meeting, then back to work. Nothing else really mattered.

Evie stepped back in a hurry as Grant Monohan rushed out of the meeting room, cell phone in hand. The usually unflappable director looked a bit worse for wear.

"There you two are. Go ahead and get settled. I'm just going to call Calista and check on her." His voice was warm, if just a little anxious.

"Is she in labor?" Gavin asked. Grant's wife was due soon, maybe tomorrow.

"Three days overdue. She told me if she doesn't have this baby by Monday, she's going to stage a sit-in at the hospital until they induce her." He didn't crack a smile. Gavin didn't know Calista very well, but he'd definitely gotten the impression the woman liked her schedule nice and tidy. Babies just didn't work on schedules.

"Uh-oh. My cousin went overdue and we all tried to stay out of her way until that baby arrived," Evie said, her tone light.

"A few more days and I might wish I had that option." This time Grant laughed outright, his joy shadowing his words. "But for now a lot of foot rubbing seems to be keeping her happy." He held the door open and motioned them in.

The drab conference room was nearly empty. Evie chose a seat next to Jack, who promptly slung an arm over the back of her chair.

Seconds later, the door opened and another board member walked through. Her curly brown hair was pulled back from her narrow face, high arched brows framing bright eyes. She smiled, reaching out a hand. "You must be Evelyn. I'm Nancy Winkoff. I think we've met once before."

"I think we sat together at the fund-raising dinner for the Denver Children's Symphony last year," Evie agreed.

Nancy passed out papers. "I'm so glad you've joined the five of us. Well, four, now that Tom moved to Los Angeles with his company. And I guess we're three at the moment, without Grant." She looked up, meeting

Gavin's eyes. "I didn't expect to see you. I know you're fighting a real battle over there at the CDC."

Gavin nodded, his face tight. "Pray that we can stem the rate of new cases. I've never seen numbers like this before."

He could feel Evie's gaze on him and turned to face her. She looked mystified. Could the editor of the biggest paper in town really not know what was happening in her own city?

"We will," Nancy said, her brow creased in worry. "So, welcome to the new member. There's no mystery why we're having a hard time filling spots. It's a thankless job. Nobody enjoys pinching pennies in a place where every program is a good one." She put a few papers in front of Evie. "Some catch-up homework. We've already gone over these, but here are the ideas for next month's fund-raising, a few grants we apply for every year and a list of new corporate donors who have committed to sponsoring the Mission."

"I'll look them over tonight and make sure I'm up to speed." Evie was all business and Gavin had to smile at the contrast between Jack and his sister. A more laid-back guy would be hard to find, yet his twin was speed and efficiency.

After a half hour of acquiring signatures and making sure the papers were in order, Nancy laid her pen on the table. "Looks like this meeting has reached its natural conclusion. Next week, same time, same place. And I'm praying that Grant will be showing us some pictures of that new baby." She stood up, gathering a thick gray sweater from the back of her chair.

Gavin hoped he would be there to see the pictures, because the way things were going, the CDC would be running night and day. His stomach clenched at the thought of what might be happening by then. More children in critical care, a city in the midst of an epidemic, the Mission Christmas parties canceled. He gathered up his papers and followed Jack's conversation with half an ear.

"Here, you guys, have another cookie." Lana was pushing the cookie platter along the top of the desk as they emerged. The Mission residents were filing out of the cafeteria at the other end of the lobby, and the smell of something delicious reminded Gavin he hadn't eaten dinner.

"Oh, Lana, you're tempting me." Evie flashed a brilliant smile and did as she was told.

"How did the meeting go? I saw Grant go by a few minutes ago."

"I think he said he needed to check on Calista, didn't he, Gavin?" Evie asked.

He nodded, keeping his gaze on Lana. Thinking back to that moment reminded him of Evie's near accident in the hallway and how warm she felt to his hands. A friend's sister was the very worst candidate for romance, even if he had the time, which he didn't. Throw in her profession and she should come with a warning sign.

"He's hovering over the poor woman." Lana's lips twitched. "At least Evie's here to help out. I bet she's got some great plans."

Gavin cleared his throat. "Right. Feel free to bring any ideas to the table. Nancy would be the one to ask about specific projects, but the board is fairly informal."

"Well, I figured, since Jack is part of it." She gave

her twin an ultra-innocent look. He responded in true Jack fashion by flicking his pen cap at her.

"Gavin, what sort of watch is that?" Evie asked.

He glanced down at his wrist, brows lifting in surprise. "My sister had it made for me." He moved toward her, extending his arm. "She's got a great sense of humor. See, every number is replaced by a different microbe. Instead of the number one it has *Yersinia pestis* or the black plague, two is ebola…" His voice trailed off. Every microbe actually looked like a number, wasn't labeled, was brightly drawn. "Just geek humor, I guess."

Evie stared, transfixed. "Okay, your sister should get an award for that."

"She should. For a singer, she sure knows her science. I don't deserve her at all."

Reaching out to touch his wrist, she turned his hand to see the watch better. Her fingers were warm, almost hot to the touch. She leaned closer, dark hair falling forward. She smelled wonderful, like Christmas.

"Gavin's out to rid the world of disease. If he had his way, no one would ever get sick." Jack leaned against the desk, his mouth lifted in a grin.

She brushed back her dark hair and met Gavin's gaze with those bright blue eyes. "That's wonderful. Like a modern-day superhero."

He felt a tug in his chest, right under his ribs. He'd always found his drive in the memory of Patrick, his best friend. He worked and studied and fought hardest when he thought of children suffering like Patrick had, of families grieving the loss of a child. But right now, more than he ever had before, he wished he had the power to wipe out the viruses that cut children down in the prime of their young lives. All because of one sweet smile.

He shrugged off the compliment with a good-natured laugh, but inside Gavin was waging a full-on war. He couldn't afford to be distracted right now. Especially if the distraction came in the form of a beautiful woman who just happened to run her own paper. He had a walking, talking family secret on the way to Denver and right now, a journalist was the very last sort of woman he needed.

The shrill sound of a cell phone stopped the conversation and Gavin searched his pockets until he grabbed hold of his work phone. Flipping it open, he already knew who would be on the other end.

"Gavin? It's Frank Ray. I think we're going to have to go to a twenty-four-hour schedule. The labs are swamped with all the samples the hospitals are sending." His coworker's voice sounded rough with exhaustion.

"You're probably right. I'm still downtown. Give me five minutes and I'll be over." Gavin snapped the phone closed and faced his friends.

"Trouble?" Lana's expression said it all. Concern, fear, worry. Evie's brows were drawn together, and she opened her mouth to speak but seemed to think better of it.

"You could say that." He straightened his shoulders and tried to look confident. Part of his job was to keep the public informed, but not panicked. "Thanks for the cookies."

He made as quick an exit as possible, buttoning his coat with one hand and searching for his keys with the other. The main hospitals would be full to the brim with cases, and their labs weren't equipped to handle all the pertussis samples.

As the frigid night air hit him, Gavin felt the warmth of the Mission being stripped away. He pushed aside all the feelings that had swelled in him when Evie was near, the regrets of being too busy for a romantic life, the wishful thinking that did no one any good.

He hunched farther into his coat, walking into the biting wind. He couldn't let his focus slip, not for a day. He had made a promise to Patrick and lives depended on him.

## Chapter Two

"Over here!" Evie waved at Jack above the crowd of kids, but she wasn't sure he heard her over the noise. The Downtown Mission's children were gathered in groups on the sidewalk, eagerly awaiting the delivery of the annual Christmas tree. Grant wandered the sidewalk, crouching down every few feet to chat with some small child or another. The Mission workers passed cups of hot chocolate and took turns peering down the road for any sign of the tree.

Evie huddled inside her wool coat and tried to stamp some feeling back into her feet as her twin made his way over. The paper had been put to bed for the day, so there was nothing left but to jump back into the fray. It could be a 24/7 job, if she let it. She'd been down that road before, back in Aspen. A fast crowd of photographers, chasing a faster crowd of celebrities, made for a perfect storm of selfishness. She could feel her perspective slipping, just like old times. Her brain needed a little time away from the drama, and this was the perfect way to get a grip on her priorities.

Snowflakes drifted gently down over the crowd

of excited kids, and Evie whispered a silent prayer of thanks. Christmas was her favorite season, all about hope, new beginnings and fresh starts. She was living proof of second chances.

"I heard the wagon got stuck on Lincoln Street." Jack tugged his ski hat down over his ears and gave Evie a hug.

"Traffic at this hour?" She frowned up at the sky. Drivers in Denver were used to the weather.

"Something about a frayed rope. I didn't catch the whole story." Jack broke off as a cheer went up through the group.

Around the corner came a pickup truck pulling an old-fashioned wooden wagon. The large spoke wheels were caked with clumps of snow. On the cart was strapped an enormous, bushy fir tree. The truck stopped and Gavin jumped from the passenger's side. His coat was unbuttoned and he wore no hat, but he had a length of rope over one shoulder. He waved to the kids and flashed a thumbs-up, which resulted in another round of cheers.

Evie sucked in a breath at the sight of his smile. Last week he'd seemed so preoccupied. Of course, she didn't expect a finance meeting to be a barrel of laughs, but this was a different side completely.

"I'll see if he needs help with the tree." Jack loped off toward the wagon, joining Grant and a few other Mission workers in the job of wrangling the tree into the lobby.

"Will you help me hand out the cookies?" Evie turned to see a young woman holding a tray of brightly colored treats. Her name tag was sporting a blob of snow, but it was still legible.

"Sure, Simone. My pleasure." She took the tray and started toward the swirling group of preschoolers.

From the corner of the group, Lana sang out the first lines of "Jingle Bells" in a sweet, clear voice. Evie joined in, moving through the crowd of waist-high kids, distributing cookies into mittened hands. The snow fell faster, large clumps landing on brightly colored hats. She couldn't help grinning, although it was hard to sing and smile at the same time. To think she could have missed this moment by spending another evening at the office.

Her tray was almost empty when the song changed to "Deck The Halls." She felt a small hand slip into hers and looked down into the face of a little girl.

"I love Christmas," the girl said. Her lisp was so pronounced, her large eyes such a deep brown, that Evie almost laughed. So much sweetness in one little person shouldn't be allowed.

"I do, too." They both stood watching Gavin and Jack help carry the tree into the lobby. The children sang with gusto, if not perfectly in tune, and Evie blinked back tears.

Five years ago she was the very worst kind of person, without a real friend in the world. She'd turned her back on everyone who loved her. Chasing money and fame was all that mattered. Evie sucked in a shaky breath.

*Thank You, Lord, for second chances. I won't let You down again.*

Gavin stood back to admire the tree. The Mission kids had decorated every inch as far as they could reach, then handed ornaments to Jack as he stood on a ladder. He really should be at the lab, but Frank had told him to take the evening off. Something about not being any use if he worked himself into the ground.

"You guys picked a great tree." Evie stood by his side, shy smile on her face. She smelled lightly of something flowery, maybe roses.

"Gerry picked it out. I just tied it down." He pretended to think it through. "But I should definitely get points for standing in the middle of Lincoln St. replacing the broken rope. I never want to stand in traffic again."

She snorted. "Let's hope that's your once-in-a-lifetime moment."

A short Hispanic woman bustled out of the double doors that led from the kitchen. Her black hair was pulled back into a bun, black eyes snapping with energy. "Gavin, is Grant in the office?"

Evie answered for him. "Marisol, I think he went to call Calista. She wasn't feeling up to the party so she stayed home. He'll be right back. Would you like a cookie? We have a few left."

Lana held out the cookie plate with a smile.

"Uh-oh. Lana is making Grant cookies now. He won't want any of my enchiladas. I made them especial." Her words were a rebuke but she was smiling.

"Lana, why you not married? You cook like this and the men gather round." Marisol gestured at Jack and Gavin, who froze like a pair of deer caught in headlights.

Covering her mouth with her hand, Evie looked like she was working to get her expression under control.

Lana snorted. "I'm not averse to marrying a younger

man, but I'm pushing fifty. I don't think good cookies will make up for a wheelchair and grandma status."

Marisol paused, black eyes gone wide, cookie in midair. "*Abuelita* already? When did it happen?"

"No, no. Eric's only thirteen." Lana brushed a hand across her forehead, as if the thought pained her. "My son's a great kid, but let's give him a few more years. Like ten or so."

"Ah, well, I am sure you will have many babies to cuddle." She said this like a benediction, her dark brown hand lifted toward Lana.

"Thank you, Marisol. I can't imagine how wonderful it will be. But you're closer to that than I am." Lana's face crinkled in a smile, and both women sighed happily.

"You're waiting for a new grandbaby?" Gavin wished he had a cheat sheet for the Mission staff and their families.

"Calista is having her baby soon. Very soon." The older woman put a hand on her heart and closed her eyes. "*Dios le bendiga.* We must pray for her."

Gavin glanced at Evie and grinned. He'd seen Calista, and the woman was as white as they came. And Grant, with his tall frame and blue eyes, was probably not related to Marisol, either. He was getting the full picture of this place and it was all about family, but not the kind he'd known.

The seriousness of what he'd seen this morning in the neonatal critical care unit intruded on his thoughts. He reached for his keys. "It was a wonderful party, but I'd better go."

"Anything we can do, Gavin? Is the office running

twenty-four hours?" Lana turned, concern lining her face.

"We are. Just keep trying to get the word out. We're racing to stay ahead of the outbreak, but..." His voice trailed off and he could feel Evie watching him. It was the stuff of nightmares, his very worst fear, that his city would be hit with a disease he couldn't control. That more families would suffer like Patrick's had.

Lana reached up and squeezed his hand, sympathy written large on her features. "We're praying."

"Thank you." Gratitude swelled in him. "And I'll see you on Tuesday."

"What's on Tuesday?" Jack mumbled through a mouthful of cookie.

"Gavin's helping set up a soccer league for the kids."

"Overachiever. Now I suppose I have to volunteer for that, too." He pretended to huff, but Gavin knew he lived for sports, any sports.

"Actually, I need another coach. So, yes, you do." He was already heading for the door. "Be there at six." He let his gaze wander to Evie, just for a moment. When their eyes met, he felt a tug deep inside that had nothing to do with the finance board or coaching and everything to do with the fact she was a beautiful woman who had a smile that took his breath away.

A second later, Grant pushed through the far door, his phone clutched to his ear. The director's tie was crooked and he was running one hand through his dark hair. "Yes, yes! I'll be right there!"

The four of them froze in shock, watching the normally calm man snap closed the phone and take two steps forward. And then two more. He looked like he was sleepwalking, except for the wide-eyed expression.

"Grant, honey." Lana's calm voice cut across the lobby. "Are you okay?"

He looked up, a huge smile on his face. "It's time! She's already at the hospital!"

Gavin and Jack exchanged looks. Uh-oh. Looked like the dad-to-be was having a mental breakdown before he even got to the labor room.

"Why don't we have someone take you over?" Gavin walked back across the lobby, holding out one hand to Grant like a lion tamer approaching a wild beast.

"He's right. Let me get someone to cover the desk and we can take my car." Lana rolled out from behind the desk and was heading toward the office doors. She punched in the code and hit the blue button that opened it automatically. "I'll grab our coats." And she was gone before he could answer.

"How long has she been in labor?" Gavin wasn't an expert, but Calista was probably going to take a while.

"Twenty minutes. She just checked in. She didn't want to interrupt our party if it was nothing." Grant shook his head, dark hair falling over his forehead. "She sounded so calm. I wonder if they already gave her drugs. She said she didn't want any."

"Hmm. Sometimes they can be helpful." Gavin led Grant toward the desk, one hand on his shoulder.

"Especially for the dads," Jack murmured and Evie tried not to giggle.

Gavin glanced up, eyes creased with mirth. Their gazes locked and he watched her lips curve up at the corners.

Lana wheeled herself back through the door, her coat draped around her shoulders, purse on her lap. "Eric just left. Michelle and the child care folks helped the parents take the kids back to the family area. I've called a few more people." She looked at Gavin and he nodded.

"Don't worry. I'll man the desk. Good thing you showed me the switchboard in case of emergencies."

"Emergency? There's no problem. I can drive," Grant said.

Three of them spoke at once. "No, Lana should drive."

Grant looked from one to the next, then grinned. "Okay, Lana can drive. Let's go!"

And then they were gone, with only a cold gust of icy wind as a farewell.

Gavin walked behind the desk and slipped off his jacket. A new life, a precious gift to the mission family. "I was afraid we were going to have to take his keys."

"Too excited to drive," Evie agreed.

"Well, I'd better get. I've got a ski date early tomorrow morning." Jack was already heading toward the door.

"Same girl as before? The bank teller?" Evie sounded hopeful.

"Who? Oh, right. No, she didn't like to go out and do anything. Sort of a homebody." Jack shrugged, as if that said it all. And it sort of did. Jack was all about the going and doing.

Evie looked at Gavin. "Won't you need someone else here?"

He didn't look up from the switchboard but poked a few buttons and frowned. "I'm sure someone will be here in a few minutes. They have staffers everywhere."

Out of the corner of his eye, he saw her look toward the office doors, then the deserted lobby. Okay, so maybe there weren't staffers everywhere. But they would come, and he wasn't really certain about hanging out with Evie.

"I'll just wait until someone else arrives."

Emotions flashed through him. Concern, relief, dread. The Christmas tree sparkled in the corner, the air smelled like cookies, and the excitement of a new life hung over them like a blessing. It was the perfect opportunity to get to know her better—something he was determined to avoid.

## *Chapter Three*

Gavin could feel the heat at the back of his neck as he stared at the switchboard. It seemed to have at least a hundred more buttons than the day Lana walked him through the system. But this was what the Mission needed right now, so he was going to sit behind the desk and answer the phone. At least until someone else got there, and he prayed that would be soon.

"You really don't have to stay." He tried to keep his tone even, but the focus of the gorgeous brunette with the bright blue eyes was almost as unnerving as the switchboard panel. The way she laughed with Marisol, held a little girl's hand and sang carols with Lana told him this wasn't the gossip-hungry editor he'd imagined. She radiated energy, as if she was plugged directly into a current. He shouldn't have been surprised, since she was Jack's twin, but he hadn't expected her to be so…vibrant. Quiet, yes. Jack had mentioned that part. But not this live wire of a personality.

"Not a problem. It's not going to interfere with my social life to stay here a little longer." She smiled then and he was glad he was sitting down. Perfect, matching dimples. And that was a definite reference to the lack of a boyfriend. He sat up a little straighter, needing to remember who she was and what she did. A journalist was not his type. The very opposite of his type, really.

There was a small pause, and then she seemed to make a decision. "So, did you and Jack meet here at the Mission?"

"No, up on the mountain. I pulled him out of a drift when he went off-trail last spring." Gavin shook his head at the memory. Crazy guy could have died that way, upside down in ten feet of snow.

"He never told me that."

"Probably didn't want to worry you."

She laughed and the sound made him smile without his permission. "No, he loves to worry me. More likely he was embarrassed at having pulled a less-than-stellar move."

"You don't ski?" Maybe she did and he just hadn't noticed her under a ski hat, ski suit and goggles. No. He was pretty sure he would have noticed her even under all that. She sure looked like she spent time at the gym. Then he realized he was giving her an extended once-over and dropped his gaze.

"Not my thing. In fact, exercise and I have an awkward relationship. On-again, off-again, depending on the number of cookies I need to burn." She shrugged one shoulder.

It was as if his mouth had declared independence from his brain. He needed to stop asking questions and pray a call came in. "Well, if you ever feel the need for more commitment, we could go snowboarding for the day. I'll even let Jack come along." Was he flirting with her? What was wrong with him? Gavin wished he was alone so he could give himself a punch in the arm.

She didn't say anything for a moment, just smiled at him as if he'd said something cute. "Does your family live around here?"

Reality check. "Yes. My grandmother lives here, and my sister and her little boy are moving here next week."

She leaned forward, interest shining from those bright blue eyes. "Younger or older sister?"

"Allison is four years younger." *And you don't want to know the rest of the story on my prodigal sister, so don't ask.* Then again, as a newspaper editor, she just might. They were all about dishing the dirt.

"My cousin has a little boy. We can arrange a playdate at the park if she wants. Moving is hard on kids."

Moving was extra hard on a kid who didn't really have any place to call home. But he was ready to change all that, if Allison would let him. Sean would love to make some friends. He nodded. "That would be great."

There was a beat or two and then he said, "Hey, I'm sure someone will be here soon. I feel bad about you wasting your time."

Her eyes narrowed, and she glanced around the deserted lobby. "True, it's pretty slow right now."

The far door that led to the offices opened with a bang and Jose strode through. His hair was cut short, red polo and khakis neatly pressed. Except for the massive multi-colored tattoos covering each arm from wrist to biceps, he looked like your middle-management employee. His name tag bounced as he advanced on them, expression intense.

"Did I hear that right? Calista's in labor?" His Mayan features were lit up with excitement.

"Sure is. Grant left a few minutes ago."

"And you let him drive?" Jose raised both hands in a "what's up" gesture.

"No, Lana took him over."

Jose relaxed against the desk, a smile creasing his face for the first time. "Good thing. When my wife had her baby last year, I almost wrecked the car and we only had to drive three blocks."

"He didn't look like he was fit to do much besides walk. Maybe not even that," Gavin said, remembering Grant in the lobby, too excited to put one foot in front of the other.

"I'm Jose." He seemed to notice Evie for the first time and put out a hand. Gavin watched her shake it and introduce herself. Her expression was friendly, her tone even, but Gavin had seen alarm pass over her face when Jose appeared. He was definitely scary-looking, but there wasn't a man in this Mission who was more committed to peace.

"You must be tapped into the community if you're heading *The Chronicle*. Best hometown paper we've ever had."

Evie smiled that megawatt smile, both dimples making an appearance. Gavin could see the pride in her eyes.

Jose tapped a finger on the desk, thinking. "You and Gavin should work up something about the whooping cough epidemic. Last year we had a few cases, but this year they've already had seventeen. The babies get sick the worst. No fatalities yet, but there will be if people don't get on board with the vaccinations."

Gavin looked to her, suspecting she was already giving the idea a pass. Sure, the outbreak had his office going crazy, but that would be low priority at the paper.

"I was thinking the same thing when Jack told me you worked with the CDC, but I didn't want to pressure you." Evie was nodding at Gavin, as if this made perfect sense. "You need to get the word out, and we can help."

He forced his face into something that he hoped passed for encouraging. She was right. But he wouldn't be the one to walk into the lion's den. Journalists were all the same. Drama for profit. There were real people suffering and they showcased it for greed. Gavin dropped his gaze to the desk, struggling to compose his thoughts. But babies would die without the information out there, so it didn't matter what he felt about papers.

The large glass front doors opened and two women in red Mission jackets came into the lobby, probably Lana's replacement.

He stood up and angled himself out of the desk chair. Thankfully nobody had called.

A young woman with a name tag and a long dark braid came toward the desk. "Jose, what's going on? Lana said there was some sort of emergency?" She scowled, features twisted in surprise.

"Grant got a phone call, Lissa." He waggled his eyebrows. The expression on the young woman's face went from confusion and annoyance to all-out glee.

"No way!"

"Yes, way. But keep it on the down-low for now. She just got checked in." Jose put his finger to his lips.

He couldn't help laughing. He locked eyes with Evie and she was grinning from ear to ear. The joy was

contagious. A *baby* was going to be born. The whole
Mission was waiting for this baby. That was the way
it should be, for every kid. Family and friends and
well-wishers waiting to give a big welcome. He felt his
smile fade a little. That's not the way it was for Allison and Sean, for sure. There was no one to welcome
him, to hold Allison's hand. He hated that it had happened that way.

"Call me tomorrow about the article. We can get
started on it right away." Evie pulled her keys from her
purse and gave a wave. A second later she was wading
through the little kids, toward the middle of the lobby.
Her dark hair was loose around her shoulders, and her
steps were quick.

Gavin watched her for a moment, noting the glass
doors and the darkness outside. Her keychain had been
a tiny bottle of pepper spray. It was downtown Denver, not New York City. The sidewalk shone with fresh
snow. People passed the Mission at a steady rate. There
was no real reason to need an escort to the parking lot.
And Grandma Lili would thump him if she found out
any grandson of hers let a woman walk alone at night.

Gavin took a breath. "Hey, wait up a minute," he
called.

Evie turned, surprise on her face.

"Let me walk you to your car." He slipped on his
coat.

"You think I'm afraid of the dark?" She laughed up
at him. The black of her coat hood contrasted with the
pink in her cheeks, and her eyes sparked with interest.
He dragged his gaze away.

"I'm sure you're not." He pulled on the long metal

handle of the front door and held it open for her. "Better safe than sorry."

He grimaced inwardly. That was his personal motto, would probably be written on his tombstone. *Here lies Gavin, better safe than sorry.* Just as soon as he walked Evie to her car, he'd go back to being safe, because was she the type of woman that promised a whole lot of sorry. Smart, sweet, funny…and tied to a newspaper. Couldn't get much further from safe than that. He had a lot on his plate without adding trouble to it. Now, if he could just remember that when he looked in those gorgeous blue eyes.

Evie walked out the doors of the Mission, and the cold cut through her wool coat like a knife. She shivered and hugged her arms to her chest. Being homeless was horrible, but being homeless in Denver in the winter was downright deadly.

She cut a glance at Gavin. His broad shoulders were hunched in his parka, his face set in a grim expression. She sighed inwardly. He obviously hadn't offered to walk her to her car so they could chat. Evie appreciated the gesture, especially in this neighborhood. But she wouldn't have minded if he wanted to get to know her even a little bit better.

"How long have you been on the finance board?" When in doubt, talk shop. Evie wasn't any good at small talk, anyway.

"About five years. It's been rough the past two, but things seem to be turning around." He put out a hand and cupped her elbow as a group of ragged teens pushed past. Their raucous laughter echoed down the street.

"Do many public health disease specialists have experience in business?" She said it with a smile. So it was an awkward way to ask the question, but she was curious.

"Certainly not as much as running a paper would give me."

She nodded. "Well, most of the profits from papers come from advertising, so I have to watch the business angle. We vet everything through our lawyers. We don't want to tick off any deep pockets." Evie said it matter-of-factly. Maybe he thought she sat at her desk and smoked cigars, yelling for the copy boys. "I think the pertussis article is important enough that we'll make space, even if it means cutting out some fluff. *The Chronicle* is about informing and serving the community."

Gavin stopped and turned to her, eyes intense on her face. He didn't seem to notice the frigid December wind. "You're saying the community comes first? That if you got a big story, a real shocker, you'd make sure it wouldn't ruin anyone's life before you ran it? If it was against your moral standards, it wouldn't run, no matter how many copies it might sell?"

Evie could have sworn her heart dropped four inches and settled at an angle. Did he know what she'd been so many years ago? She opened her mouth to defend herself, to say how she'd only been trying to pay the bills, to get through journalism school. They'd said it would be easy. Just take some pictures. Follow the famous people and maybe expose a few liars in the process. But she didn't say anything. There was no excuse for what she'd done.

"*The Daily* is the paper that runs the gossip. When

I bought *The Chronicle* back from the bank, it was bankrupt and worthless. I wanted it to be something better, a paper that people could trust. And when I die, I don't want to have to explain to God why I printed what I did." Any more than she already would be. She felt her eyes burn and angrily blinked back tears. She couldn't make up for ruining lives, exposing sins, but she was going to keep going anyway. The only other option would be to give up. And Evie wasn't a quitter.

The chill breeze ruffled his dark blond hair, the orange glow from the streetlight casting his features into half shadow. Finally he nodded. "I see a lot of suffering on a daily basis. We need to reach the people that are falling through the cracks."

Evie looked up at him, taking a deep breath. "I agree." She hadn't had to defend herself for a long time, and she felt off-kilter. Or maybe it was that steady gaze that let nothing past him.

"I can write up something tomorrow morning and bring it to you by noon. The booster shots are our best hope, especially for pregnant women, but nobody knows about it. When do you think we can run it?"

Evie did a quick mental calculation and came up with a time frame that included skipping lunch and staying hours after most of the crew had gone home. "It could run the day after tomorrow, but let's put it in the Sunday edition. It's the biggest. Everybody gets the Sunday paper."

He nodded, a flicker of hope passing over his face. "Thank you. This means a lot to me."

"What got you interested in diseases?"

Emotions flitted behind his eyes faster than she

could capture them. Confusion, surprise. "My best friend died in the fourth grade from chicken pox."

Shock made her silent for a moment. "I didn't know it could be deadly. I thought everybody got chicken pox. Parents even try to expose their kids, to get it over with."

His face was tight with pain. "You're right." He paused, gaze locked on hers. "I had it. Patrick's mom brought him over to my house so he'd catch it and be done before Christmas break was over."

Evie felt her mouth drop open. Gavin had given his best friend a disease that killed him…at Christmas? "I'm so sorry."

"Me, too. I'm still sorry." His voice had a hard edge to it. "And that's why I work at the CDC."

Evie wanted to reach out and hold him, to tell him it wasn't his fault. But there wasn't anything she could say that would make that kind of grief disappear.

He seemed to want to say something more but thought better of it. He nodded toward the parking lot. "I think it's going to snow again. We'd better get you home."

She walked toward her light blue Volkswagen Beetle and unlocked the door. He made a noise behind her that sounded suspiciously like a snort.

"What? You don't like my car?" She was used to people poking fun at the powder-blue classic. She searched around on the floorboards for the ice scraper. There was a light film on the windshield, and she didn't want to wait for it to defrost. Which would be about three hours with her outdated heating system.

"It's great. I just figured you drove something nicer."

She stood up, scraper in hand, and shot him a look. "Nicer?"

"Maybe I mean safer."

"True, no airbags."

"You can get those installed." His lips quirked up in a smile, he held out one hand and she passed him the small plastic wedge.

"And what do you drive, Mr. CDC?"

"A Saab. I highly recommend them." He made short work of the ice on the windows and brushed off the extra snow, handing back the scraper.

"Well, Edna and I are committed to each other. It's till-engine-failure-do-us-part."

He was grinning now, hands deep in his pockets, staring down at her. "Your car is named Edna."

"That's what she says." Evie angled into the seat, dropped the scraper back on the floor and buckled up. "Thank you for the escort. And the window service."

He didn't answer, just raised a hand as she shut the door. As she pulled out of the lot, he was still standing there, looking amused.

The heater was going full blast and it was still twenty degrees in the Beetle, but Evie didn't feel the cold. She turned toward *The Chronicle* offices, struggling to get her head back in the game. They had a big story shaping up and she needed to be ready to make decisions. But her mind kept returning to the man she had just left. He took a terrible tragedy and turned it into a life mission to help others. Handsome, yes. Educated, yes. Smart and purpose-driven, yes and yes. But all of those things added up to a man who wouldn't want a woman with her sort of past. It was the kind of past that never went away, no matter how many community service articles she ran.

## Chapter Four

"Did you get the message about the O'Brian's car dealership ad? He says it's faded and the type is hard to read." Jolie plopped into the chair across from Evie's enormous, battered oak desk and huffed out a breath. "Obviously somebody told him that. He was fine with the full color copy I showed him last week."

Evie massaged her right temple and tried to smile. It was turning into the worst Friday on record. The newsroom was in chaos because the lawyers had nixed a major feature they'd planned. All they cared about was whether the paper would get sued. She would fire them, except that's what she'd hired them to do, so she was stuck with following their advice.

"I'll call him. Maybe he got ahold of a bad copy. Maybe it was passed around too much. What I saw looked great."

She hated bad news, but Evie couldn't shoot the messenger. Especially since Jolie was the best computer graphic designer she'd ever hired. No one else wanted to take a chance on a nineteen-year-old college dropout with hot pink highlights, but something about

Jolie reminded Evie of herself at that age. Not the nibbled nails or the crazy punk-inspired clothes, for sure. It was more her obvious desire to prove to the world that she was more than just a girl. And the bucketfuls of attitude might be a little familiar, too.

"It was great, don't you doubt it." She shrugged and crossed one slim leg over the other, wiggling a foot until her polka-dot ballet flat hung by her toes. "Hey, why doesn't your dad want to place an ad? I was looking at a Colorado Supplements brochure and the graphics were totally old-school. We could do a whole lot better than whoever he hired for that flyer."

Evie dropped her gaze to her desktop and pretended to scroll through a few pages. Her father would never hire her. He thought she was just goofing around, playing at running a paper while Jack was the one who did the real work. But anybody who really knew the guy understood that Jack had about as much of an aptitude for business as the proverbial fish on a bicycle. "Yeah, I should ask him about that."

"Of course, maybe it's better to keep business and family separate?" Jolie pursed her lips and tapped a black polished nail against her chin.

She couldn't suppress a snort of laughter. "Excellent advice. But since my dad has been grooming Jack to take over the family business since he was five, that boat has already sailed."

"Speaking of that luscious brother of yours…" Jolie leaned forward, eyebrows raised.

"No, not on your life." Evie shook a finger at her.

"But why not? He's so handsome, and those eyes!"

"Because. He has a hard enough time getting to work as it is with snowboarding season in full swing.

Throw in a girlfriend and he'd be MIA most of the time."

"Well, I work as hard as I play, so maybe I'd inspire him." Jolie flashed a grin as she popped out of her chair and left the office.

Evie waited for the door to close before she dropped her head in her hands. Her paper needed the revenue desperately. They were walking a fine line between solvency and bankruptcy, again. *Lord, I'm trying to do the right thing here. I'm not asking for wealth beyond measure. Just enough to pay the bills.*

When she'd first bought the paper, she'd fought hard to get them on solid ground. But things had slowed and *The Daily* was getting a good cut of their advertising customers. It was human nature that people would rather read gossip than human interest stories or exposés on slave labor. But she'd been there, done that. No going back. Even if they published community hero stories all the way into foreclosure.

"Thanks for distributing these, Lana." Gavin handed over an armful of posters on pertussis prevention.

"Anything we can do to help, you know that." The secretary laid the posters on the desk and cocked her head. "You look exhausted."

"No, I'm fine. Just running a little low on sleep." The low end of empty.

"Take care of yourself. We wouldn't want you to miss Christmas." She gave him a look that meant business and he nodded obediently. He would rest when there was time. If he didn't keep working, the Mission would have to cancel all public gatherings anyway. It wasn't something he wanted to say out loud.

Gavin's phone buzzed in his pocket and he stepped away from the desk with a wave of apology. Lana smiled, making a shooing motion with her hand.

He snapped the phone open. "Allison, everything okay?" He hated the note of anxiety in his voice. She was a grown woman, with a son she'd taken care of all by herself, but he would always be her big brother. They weren't related by blood, but he'd given up the *step* word a long time ago. She was his sister, end stop.

"Everything's fine, Gav." He could hear her smile and felt the muscles in his neck relax. "Just wanted to let you know we're headed into Denver tonight. We made good time through Kansas. Nothing there to see but corn."

Gavin leaned against the lobby wall and grinned. "Can't wait to see you. Are you heading straight for my place?" Office workers wandered in and out of the double doors, staring at their smartphones or chatting with colleagues.

"No other place to go, is there?" Her tone was light, but the words held a lot of sadness.

Gavin knew what she meant. She'd been on her own for so long. Moving back to Denver was a big step, and hopefully it was one in the right direction. As long as Sean's father didn't make trouble, they would probably do just fine.

"I think it will be a whole new start for you both."

"You're right." She paused, as if choosing her words. "Because I'm tired of hiding."

Gavin straightened up. "What does that mean?"

"I'm just…ready to be honest about who I am and what happened."

He felt his eyes widen.

"But let's talk about it when I get there."

Gavin took a breath, calming his thoughts. Allison didn't need to explain everything, especially while driving. "Right. Be careful. See you real soon, sisty ugler."

"Watch it. There's still time for me to turn this rig around." There was the brief sound of her laughing and she disconnected. Gavin snapped the phone closed. He'd wanted her to move here for years, right after he'd found out about Sean. But she'd been determined to make her own way. Maybe she was stubborn. Maybe it was shame. Whatever it was, he was glad she'd finally given in. His sister needed family around her, and his godson needed his uncle.

His brows drew down as he thought of her words. She was ready to be honest. How honest? To everyone? To the media? The idea of another bout of newspaper scandal made him ill. He never wanted her to go through something like that again.

But now wasn't the time to worry about it. He strode out into the bright winter sunlight and headed for his car. God willing, they would get the whooping cough cases under control and he could really focus on welcoming her to Denver.

Of course, getting the epidemic under control involved a certain collaboration with a certain newspaper editor. Evie Thorne's beautiful face passed through his mind. If he could just ignore those flashes of humor, that quick wit, those bright blue eyes, then he wouldn't mind so much that he had to deal with a journalist. He had an unsettling feeling that his calm, predictable life was veering into completely unknown territory.

\* \* \*

Yanking the cord that released the long window shades, Evie pressed the palms of her hands to her eyes and gritted her teeth. Her office had a heart-stopping view of Wolf Mountain, but the bright winter sunlight was making her head throb. Sometimes she wanted to be someone else, anyone else. Getting a call from another advertiser who'd rather pay *The Daily* than *The Chronicle* had her feeling like she should just pack her bags and head out of town.

A soft knock on her door brought her head up with a start. Gavin Sawyer stood in her office doorway, a concerned expression on his face, brows drawn together. His suit was nicely pressed, as if he was just starting his day, instead of heading into the afternoon. He had a badge clipped to his shirt pocket. Warm brown eyes and softly wavy hair made him seem casual despite the business wear. It was as if he always walked into *The Chronicle* on a Friday morning. Her mind stuttered to a stop.

"Are you all right?" His low voice brought her back to reality. Delusions weren't usually concerned with your welfare.

She nodded, struggling to smile confidently.

"I'm sorry I didn't call ahead, but I have the main issues we need in the article, along with the most recent statistics from this week." He took a few steps into her office, set the folder on her desk and looked out the large glass window to his right. "Nice view. Sure beats looking at posters on diphtheria."

"Probably anything would be better than that. Does your lab have windows? Or are you a basement dweller?"

His lips tilted up a bit, as if she'd said something charming. "I don't usually work in the lab. I have degrees in microbiology and epidemiology, but I get to spend my days in the fresh air. Mostly."

"Until something awful comes along, like whooping cough."

"Right." He sighed. "It would be nice if we spent all our time trying to get kids to drink water and not soda, but it doesn't always work that way."

"Do you have an idea which languages need to be on the inserts?" She gestured to the chair across the desk.

"There's a federal handout in there with brief guidelines in fifteen languages." He settled into it, stretching out his long legs. He looked tired, a small frown between his brows. "Did you hear Calista and Grant had a little boy?"

"Sure did. I got a call from Jack, who heard it from Lana, who heard it from Jose, who got a visit from a deliriously happy Marisol." News traveled fast in the Mission community. Plus, it seemed the entire group had been holding their breath until that baby was born.

"I peeked in at the hospital. Grant seemed to be back to normal. Proud as can be and mentally sound. We had a good laugh about him not being able to walk across the lobby that night."

He looked around, still taking in the small office. Evie was painfully aware of the teetering piles of papers and the jumbled books haphazardly tossed onto shelves. She felt the heat rush to her cheeks. His office was probably neat as a pin.

"They say a messy desk is a sign of a tidy mind."

"Do they?" Evie glanced around, wondering if the perpetual mess had anything to do with her mental state, or if it had everything to do with her organizational skill. "One of my employees says I use the EAS filing system. Every Available Surface."

He grinned, tiny lines appearing around his eyes. "I would never survive in this office. How do you find anything?"

"Strangely, it doesn't seem to be a problem."

"So, if I moved something, right now, you could probably tell?"

Evie bit her lip, staring at the piles of papers and Post-its scattered like colorful snowflakes. "Depends on what it is."

He stood up, leaned over her desk and wiggled his fingers. "Let's try it."

She fought to keep from laughing. They were going to play a game with her messy desk? Something about that grin made her want to play along. "Fine, I'll close my eyes. Try to be very quiet." She was almost surprised at her own flirting, but then that smile made her forget a lot of things.

She scrunched her eyes closed and put a hand over them for good measure. As if someone had thrown a switch, all her other senses went on high alert. She could hear the rustle of his shirt against his suit jacket, his slow breathing. The scent of his aftershave was deep and woodsy. She could hear, no *feel* him, moving very close to her. There was a tiny sound and then he said, "Done."

She peeked between her fingers and frowned. Maybe she didn't know where everything was. Maybe not even half of it. And then she saw the change and triumph surged through her. "You moved my pen."

The look of shock on his face made her laugh out

loud. His eyes had gone wide. "Well, I guess that proves it. Messy doesn't mean disorganized. But how did you know?"

"I'm left-handed. I keep my pens on this side." She waved with her left hand.

"I hadn't noticed that." He cocked his head, appraising her.

"Why would you?" Evie felt her face flush under his gaze.

Gavin ran a hand down his tie and cleared his throat. "So, how much space can you spare for tomorrow's article?"

Evie struggled to switch gears.

"Half of the front and two full pages in the first section."

"You usually have that much room on short notice?"

"Only when the lawyers tell us to shut down our biggest story of the year." Even saying the words made her feel slightly sick. She could see the newsroom over his right shoulder, through the half-open door, and it looked like someone had hit the panic button. Her head throbbed a little, as if for extra emphasis. She sighed and rubbed her eyes. So much work, down the drain.

"Lawyers." The word wasn't a question, more like he was repeating her.

She nodded. "We keep them on retainer so we can pass stories by them. Otherwise we might be left open to lawsuits. It's the kiss of death for a paper."

"So, what exactly got shelved?" He was working on keeping his body relaxed, but he heard the tension in his own voice. Of course they'd need lawyers. Walking the fine line between getting sued and delivering the daily gossip must be a lightning rod for litigation.

"I don't know how much you hear about the dark places in this city," she paused, gathering her thoughts, "but there is a slave labor ring. It keeps moving. We can never quite catch them. We know some of the businesses involved. But the people we're getting the information from are too unreliable. The lawyers said it was a no-go."

There was a beat of silence, then another. His throat felt tight. "I do hear things, now and then. I have friends who work in the free clinics. They see girls coming in for treatment, always accompanied by men, never left alone."

Evie raised her face, stricken. "There are those, too. Girls brought here with the promise of jobs and then enslaved. No one thinks it can happen in this city, but it does."

"What about the police?"

"We can't get word to the police fast enough. By the time they arrive, the groups have decamped."

Her words hung in the air between them. So many people needed help, desperately, and sometimes he didn't even know where to start.

"Thank you." His voice was softer than he intended.

"For what? Failing?" Bitterness was written on every feature.

"For caring."

She gave a small shrug and sat up a bit straighter. "Did you bring the current stats on the reported cases?"

He handed over the file.

She was busy studying the graphs and numbers. "This is bad."

"I know. My grandmother's been praying like crazy. She's got the whole Women's Guild at St. James on the case."

"I didn't know you went to St. James. I mean, I've never seen you there." Then she paused. He knew what she was thinking. Just because someone's grandmother went to church, didn't mean they did. Usually grandmas held down the fort and everyone else went about their lives, sleeping late on Sunday and counting on the trickle-down effect of the prayers.

"Usually the early service."

"Oh, I went to that one last summer when we were leaving on a trip. It was me and Jack and about forty old ladies."

Too accurate to be funny, but he couldn't help chuckling anyway. "Right. Just me and the old ladies. My grandmother has trained them all to treat me like their own. We have a great time at coffee after."

Evie let out a throaty laugh that made him want to scrap his plans for the day and do something better, more fun, just the two of them. But that wasn't really an option, in a lot of ways, no matter how that laugh tugged at him. Work was ramping up to round-the-clock shifts and Allison... Just the thought of his sister made him sit up straighter. All he could think of was how good Evie smelled and how that husky laugh made him want to take a day off work. He gave himself an internal shake. People reacted to stress in different ways, and he must be grasping at anything that wasn't related to pertussis or fragile sisters. This was a working relationship and it needed to stay that way.

## Chapter Five

His heart thudding in his chest, Gavin took the stairs down from *The Chronicle*'s upper floors at a quick clip. Everything would be fine. They would get the word out about the epidemic, Allison and Sean would settle in nicely and the Mission would get some big donations before the holidays. He let out a deep breath and paused in the stairwell.

It was a good thing Jolie had knocked. He had been about to make a fool out of himself, having an entire internal debate over whether to ask Evie out. So she had a heart. It didn't mean he had to get any closer. Keep it simple and everything will be fine. Gavin took the last flight of stairs slowly, the sound of his dress shoes echoing in the empty stairwell. Timing was everything, and now was exactly the wrong time. He pushed the long metal handle and exited into the lobby. If he was honest with himself, *never* would be an even better time.

Twenty minutes later, with a tray of hot coffees in hand, Gavin punched in the code to the top floors of the Center for Disease Control. The building was humming with activity and not in a pleasant way. Gavin didn't know if this epidemic was going to be something they could control. Babies got the first diphtheria, tetanus and pertussis vaccine at two months, and most of these babies were newborns. The older ones had one of the vaccines, but not the whole series. It wasn't enough to keep them from developing the disease if they caught it from an older sibling or a parent. The most fragile infants were falling victim.

At the first door, Gavin peered in and saw Tom's desk was empty. Piles of papers were strewn around. It reminded him of Evie's desk, which made him think of the way she'd covered her eyes during their impromptu "spot the difference" game. His lips tugged up.

"How many more cases?" Tom asked from just behind him. His voice was quiet, subdued. He reached around and took a cup of coffee from the tray, raising an eyebrow.

"Three more confirmed, total of eleven babies in the NICU, and there are two isolated in the emergency area."

"Well, if we're trading bad news, Senator McHale is in your office." Tom took a sip and nodded down the hallway.

Gavin felt like ice had dropped into the pit of his stomach. His first thought was of Allison, and the next was of Sean. The door to Gavin's office was almost closed, revealing nothing, but they both stood watching it anyway.

"He didn't say why he was here. I also didn't ask. I didn't figure he'd want to share his business with a lowly administrator." Tom was more than that. He could run the whole local organization in a pinch. There were few things he didn't know, and that Gavin was connected to McHale in a very ugly way was one of them.

"He's been waiting about an hour." Tom tossed the last bit over his shoulder as he wandered back to his desk, but the look they exchanged said it all. The senator never waited. Ever.

McHale had visited the CDC before. It was part of his election year rounds. Gavin had been struck by his utter arrogance. There were people who loved power. It happened in every profession. Unfortunately, McHale was determined to keep his power at any cost. Anything that made him look bad was blacklisted, no matter the reason. And an uncontrolled pertussis epidemic could certainly be considered a negative.

Allison was another. She'd ruined his presidential aspirations once. Revealing that he'd fathered a child out of wedlock and refused to acknowledge him might be the final nail in his political coffin.

Gavin steeled himself before opening the door, resisting the urge to knock. It was his office, after all. McHale was sitting behind Gavin's desk, looking right at home. His dark hair was perfectly combed, manicured hands casually flicking through a stack of papers. Gavin wasn't overly territorial, but if he hadn't already had a bone to pick with the man, he certainly would have at the sight of McHale reading his personal notes.

"Finally back." The man didn't even have the good grace to pretend he hadn't just been rifling through Gavin's desk. He took one last peek and then tossed the stack down. Expensive suit perfectly pressed, silk tie straight as an arrow, a light tan that was more California than Colorado. He'd aged well since the last time they'd been in the same room. Or hadn't aged at all, really. Politicians and celebrities seemed to hang at thirty for a few decades before they got wrinkles like the rest of humanity.

Gavin itched to straighten the papers, but he was so angry he forced himself to remain perfectly still. If he started moving toward the desk, he might just keep going until he grabbed McHale by the tie.

"How can I help you today?" He was proud of his easy tone and wished he could force a smile to go with it, but that was too much to ask of any man.

"I need copies of every outreach program, every vaccine push and every community education session you've put together. This outbreak is unfortunate, but it's spreading unchecked." He leaned forward, black eyes narrowed. "That's your job, in case you didn't know. And when you don't do your job, it makes me look like I'm not doing my job."

Gavin had known what was coming, had prepared for it, and it still made his blood pressure skyrocket. McHale wouldn't know one end of a graph from another; the papers wouldn't do him a bit of good. He was blowing hot air. And Gavin was in no mood to be bullied.

He bought a few seconds to calm himself by slipping off his coat and hanging it on the rack behind the door. His face felt hot, his collar too tight. He lowered himself into the guest chair. "I can do that. And we're starting a new series in *The Chronicle* tomorrow."

"Better be a good series. But is *The Chronicle* the biggest paper? What about *The Daily?*" McHale leaned over the desk, long fingers laced together in a contemplative pose. "Anyway, whichever one you put it in, you've got to be working day and night. Make sure everyone knows that this office is doing something, not just testing samples and visiting the hospitals. I don't care if you have to go door to door. These numbers are way too high, and if it spreads from Denver to other places, they'll come looking to see who let it happen."

Of course they would. And there wouldn't be any support from McHale, clearly. If Gavin hadn't already been working on *not* hating the guy, he would be now.

"Well, if I'm out going door to door, they won't be able to find me. Maybe the lab crew can give them a statement."

The placid expression vanished from McHale's face. "This isn't a joke," he barked, eyes angry slits.

"I'm not laughing." Gavin stood up and stepped closer to his desk. "You may be concerned about how this makes us look, but I'm trying to save lives. I won't play media consultant when there's an epidemic."

The senator may have been pushing fifty but he was still fit. He stood up so quickly it looked like he'd bolt over the desk. "Those papers are here to make us look good, when we need them. You think this is all about keeping babies healthy? It's not. You're funded by the government, which is run by politicians. If people think you're inefficient, they complain to me. I get enough complaints and we'll cut every program you have down to nothing."

The words thumped and rumbled around in his head like shoes in a dryer. "I'll give you the files and a copy of the story that's running in *The Chronicle*." He didn't offer more.

He stood silently, debating. Gavin waited, watching emotions flash over McHale's features. Anger, frustration, cold calm.

"Fine. And if I hear anything negative about this office, anything at all, I'll be back. Use some of your time to cover your backsides. Even if it takes manpower away from reaching the at-risk people in this city."

Gavin's muscles tensed from the base of his skull all the way down his spine. "You're telling me to take people off the regular task force and put them on media outreach, just so we can look good?"

Walking around the desk and standing inches away, his pale blue eyes cold and calculating, McHale said, "If looking good keeps your office open, then I would think you would be on board."

They stood nose to nose, Gavin refusing to blink. He clenched his fists and willed himself to speak calmly. For Allison's sake—for Sean's sake—he kept his cool.

"Looking good should be keeping the pertussis from taking over the city. I don't care if the public thinks I sit here and watch football all day. I'm going to do my job to get the preventative measures in place and try to stay ahead of the storm. The rest will have to wait."

"Know what your problem is, Gavin? You think if you work hard, the public will see it. But honestly, the average American isn't that perceptive. They have to be told when someone is doing their job. And part of your job now is to make sure they know how hard this office is working. You need me to make it official and put it in your job description? I'm sure I can get the director to do that."

With those finals words, he turned on his heel. As

his hand reached the door knob, he paused. Gavin felt the hair on the back of his neck stand up.

"I know your sister's back in town. She should have stayed in Florida."

Blood was rushing in his ears. "She needed to be near family. Her son—your son—is growing up fast." He was surprised at how calm he sounded.

McHale's eyes glittered with anger. "Don't ever say that again. She ruined my chances for a party nomination. She won't destroy my career."

In two steps, without his brain giving directions, Gavin crossed the room. He was twenty years younger and six inches taller, and rage was fueling his every movement. He wanted to wrap McHale's tie around his fist and pull him in close. Through sheer force of will, his hands stayed where they needed to be: by his sides. "She didn't ruin your chances, you did. And Sean is a child, an innocent victim. You need to reevaluate your priorities."

For several seconds they breathed the same air, locked in furious silence. Then McHale turned on his heel and walked out.

Breathing heavily, Gavin tried to get control of his anger. Wasn't it enough for Allison to be estranged from the father of her child? Did he have to be a power-obsessed politician concerned only with his own image?

Falling into a chair, Gavin stared unseeing at the stack of papers on his desk. His chest ached at the thought of Allison in the same city as McHale and not even getting a phone call. What a waste of a man. She'd wised up as soon as she'd found out she was having Sean. But her little boy deserved better than that.

Between a rock and a hard place, that was his life. McHale above him, pertussis creeping up from behind, and all the time there was his nephew, a little guy who never asked for any of this drama. Time to call Evie, see if she could put in some lines about the disease prevention center working overtime. Hot anger swept through him. He hated to even think of trying to spin the facts. This wasn't how he wanted to spend his time.

Was it possible to run an article that made McHale happy and still got the information out to the public? It would be an article that was three quarters sunshine and one quarter lifesaving, ugly facts. Journalists spun a web of words that changed opinion, sometimes regardless of the reality. It made him sick to even consider their expertise to sway public opinion. But McHale was going to be watching the pertussis outbreak very closely for any negative comments from the community.

Gavin took a steadying breath. Evie seemed like she walked her faith. Only time would tell if that was true. Meanwhile, he needed to focus on Allison and Sean and getting the epidemic under control. *Help me remember, Lord, the only opinion that matters is Yours.*

Evie felt the slam of a very small body against the back of her knees and tried not to pitch forward. She grabbed the bike rack to her left and let out a yelp.

"Sorry, Evie! Jaden, give your auntie some warning." Stacey was trotting up the sidewalk, obviously left behind when Jaden saw Evie and made a break for it. Her rounded tummy was her only handicap, but that had been enough to give him a head start.

"It's okay. I was just surprised." Evie twisted around

and rubbed the top of Jaden's knitted hat. His arms were wrapped firmly around her waist, and he was grinning up at her, one front tooth missing.

"Do you see it, Aunt Evie? Do you?" He opened his mouth wider and wider, pointing with one mittened hand.

"Buddy, your mouth is open so wide I can see your lunch. But if you're talking about that gap in your teeth, I would bet that somebody lost a tooth."

"It was me! I'm the one!" He let go long enough to jump up and down. Huge brown eyes were even wider with excitement.

Evie shot a glance at Stacey, grinning. Her cousin was three years younger than Evie and about ten years further down the road to domestic bliss. Every now and then Evie caught the slightest sir of jealousy in her heart. Okay, maybe more than a slight stir. More like a full-blown green-eyed monster attack. The pretty blonde had lucked out first try and was married to her high school sweetheart. Another baby was on the way, who would probably have Stacey's blond hair and Andy's big brown eyes, just like Jaden did. *Blessed.* That was the word Evie would use for her cousin's life.

"Let's head over to the park before it gets any colder. I heard the temperature is going to drop this afternoon." Stacey handed Evie a deli cup of what smelled like vanilla chai.

"Wow, how did I miss this?" Evie took a sip, almost scalding her tongue.

"You missed it when Jaden tackled you." Stacey fell into step beside her as they walked toward the city center park. Lots of moms and dads and kids around on a freezing Saturday, but Denver worked that way. If you couldn't handle the cold, you'd better stay inside or, better yet, move to Texas. The city didn't stop for a few inches of snow, or even a few feet. It was just normal to look up and see snow on the mountains. And the streets and the cars.

Jaden raced ahead and went straight for the slide. Kids swarmed the area, adults clustered every few feet, trying to keep warm with coffee and oversize parkas.

"There's a free bench. Somebody already scraped the snow off." Stacey settled on one end and hunched over her coffee.

"Before I forget, there's someone who's just moving here and she has a little boy Jaden's age. Would you want to have a playdate with them? To help them settle in to their new city and everything."

"There's no harm in that. We're always up for a park date. How do you know her?"

"I don't, actually. It's the sister of someone on the finance board at the Mission. They just mentioned it and I thought of you." Evie wrapped her hands around her cup and stared out at the playground, thinking of Gavin. She wondered if his sister would have his warm brown eyes, or his quiet sense of humor.

"Just a someone?"

"What?" Evie was caught off guard.

Stacey shot her a calculating look. "You normally use names. And a gender. Unless you've vowed to keep his identity a secret."

She could feel her face getting warm. There wasn't anything between them so there was no reason to be embarrassed. Or whatever it was she was feeling. "That wasn't on purpose. Gavin Sawyer, male, no secret identity that I know of yet."

Stacey grinned at her and said nothing.

"We're also working on an article about pertussis. He's a disease prevention specialist, works in community outreach." There, that was Gavin in a nutshell. Except for that slow smile he had, the one that made a girl forget she hated flirting. And maybe it would be fair to mention the way his hair curled just a bit over his collar. And how he stood a good head taller than she was, and was very fit, but he never made her feel weak.

"Is he cute?"

Evie rolled her eyes, pretending to dismiss the question.

"Do I have to ask you again?" Stacey was smirking into her cup.

"Okay, a little cute." She shot her cousin a glance. "A lot cute. He's one of those guys that gets a first *and* a second look. But then when you talk to him, you forget about how gorgeous he is because there's so much going on in his head." She huffed out a breath. "Happy?"

"Cute and smart. Gotcha. So you're going to use me to get to him through his sister? Not that I mind, I'm just trying to figure out my role here."

"No! Of course not." Evie glared out at the park, watching kids running every which way.

"Sure you don't want me to put in a good word for you?" Stacey's voice was shaking with laughter.

Evie said nothing, wishing she hadn't tried to explain. She wasn't even sure what Gavin was, except he was interesting in a way not many other men were. She met a lot of people in her job at the paper. Some good, some bad, most of them just like her. But he was different. Of course, that didn't mean he'd want a woman like her, with an ugly little past tagging along behind her everywhere she went.

Stacey grabbed her hand. "I'm just teasing you, cuz. You don't need my help at all. You can reel this guy in all by yourself. It's my way of saying how thrilled I am you've found someone."

Evie shook her head. "I haven't found anybody. It's not like that." She would have said "at all," but that wouldn't have been completely true. She wished there was a little bit of reality to Stacey's overactive imagination.

"Okay, we'll just wait and see." But Evie could tell Stacey was already planning bridal gowns in her head.

"How's the new guy?" The baby was due in three weeks and Stacey looked tired.

"Active. Keeps me up all night with his gymnastics." She grinned over her cup, blond hair falling around her face. "I don't mind so much. It's been tons easier than when we had Jaden."

Evie thought hard, going back five years to when Stacey and Andy were expecting the first time. She shook her head. "Sorry, you must not have whined enough. I don't remember anything but being excited."

A group of little girls raced by, screeching. Stacey watched them with a smile that slowly slipped from her face. "I probably didn't share what was going on, but we were in a really tough spot."

Evie turned her whole body, staring at her cousin. "You and Andy were having trouble?"

"No, not like that." She took a sip and stared out at the playground. "He'd just started that new job when we found out we were having Jaden. And then the apartment building was foreclosed on so we had to move. We lost our deposit and last month's rent, then had to come up with first, last and deposit all over again. And then I was on bed rest for a month and had to quit my job at the library. And then Andy got rear-ended by that old guy who was trying to keep his dog's tail out of his face while speeding through an intersection."

Evie nodded. She remembered all of those things. But she hadn't put them together quite the same way. They'd been so thankful that Andy hadn't been seriously hurt. The car wasn't such a big deal. They had seemed like they were doing okay. Everyone was safe and healthy.

"When Jaden was born, I didn't even have a crib." Stacey's voice wavered on the last word and Evie felt her heart contract.

"I didn't know it was that tough. I'm so sorry." She was whispering, shame choking the words.

Stacey wiped her eyes with one hand. "Don't be sorry. It was our fault for not asking for help. Everyone thought we were doing okay, two college-educated people starting a family. I was too ashamed to say we couldn't pay the electric bill."

Evie sat back against the bench, watching Jaden zoom down the slide, arms in the air, glee on his face. Shock stole her voice. She'd never even suspected.

"My mom held the baby shower, and I got a lot of cute outfits for him. But we returned most of the items for cash."

"I wish I'd known. I wish you could have told me."

"Me, too. Looking back, it seems so silly. Just tell someone you need help. But I couldn't. I went to the Goodwill to look for a crib and some clothes, but I only had about fifteen dollars and the crib was twenty. It wasn't even that important. We had a little basket we lined with blankets. It was just that we were living on the edge, financially, and this tiny baby depended on us." Stacey pressed her lips together but tears slid down her face. "Sorry. I'm feeling hormonal."

"I think you're having flashbacks because the baby is so near." Evie had a sudden thought and squeezed Stacey's hand. "Are you okay now? Do you have what you need?"

She laughed, shaking her head. "Oh, boy, we've got more than enough now. It's like night and day." Her expression settled into something a little more grim. "But I can't forget the way it was. I wonder how many people are in the same position. I know the shelters have cribs, but we weren't homeless. Andy had a job, we had an apartment, but we were barely scraping by. Even the cheapest stuff from the bargain stores was more than we could pay."

Evie was silent, thinking back to Jaden's birth. Stacey had seemed tired, stressed out, but her clothes were all right. Andy wore a suit to work in the insurance agency. They looked like any other young, middle-class couple.

Jaden ran up, hood bouncing behind him, knit cap slipping over one eye. "Mommy! My snowsuit makes the slide work even better!"

"Sounds fun, Jay, just be careful." She waved as he raced away again. "We don't need any medical bills." She glanced at Evie. "We're okay, really. Just medical bills would stink."

Evie grinned. "I hear you. And broken bones are never fun when you're five." She took another sip of her cooling chai tea. *Lord, how had I missed this?* They had been in need, right in front of her, and she hadn't seen it. She felt like her eyes had been opened at the same time her heart was being crushed. She'd been blind. But not anymore.

"Stacey, could you give me a list of things that young parents need? The kind of things that you had a hard time getting ahold of when Jaden was born?"

Her cousin gave her a quizzical look and nodded. "Sure can. But why?"

"I have this idea. I'll tell you when I get it clear in my head."

Evie felt excitement rush through her. A plan was forming in the back of her mind, and she knew it was a good one. Nothing could make up for the hurt she'd caused another young woman so many years ago, but at least she could help people in need right now.

# *Chapter Six*

"Thanks for meeting me down here. I'm sure you have better things to do on a Saturday." Gavin kicked a soccer ball back to a small boy with jet-black hair and hoped he didn't look too sweaty.

"Not a problem. Is this the new soccer league?" Evie folded her red coat over her arm and watched twenty-five young kids chase balls around the shiny gym floor. The noise was deafening, but she didn't seem to mind. In fact, she seemed to be enjoying the chaos.

"Right. Just a junior league for the youngest players. Once they're in middle school they can join the city leagues. But these kids get left out of the community run teams because they live here." Gavin intercepted another errant ball and rolled it back. He halfheartedly smoothed his hair. That wavy-hair gene was a curse. He should probably just shave his head.

"So, you played soccer in college? Or on a city team?"

"I played some. Not much. My theory is that if we offer to serve wherever there's a need, God will honor that."

She squinted back up at him, thinking. "God will honor it by helping you out, or by sending in other people to do the job, right?"

"Right. Either of those. Probably sounds iffy. And I'm not saying we can be lazy because we have good intentions and we know God will pick up the slack. I mean…" It was hard to explain, especially as Evie watched him, a small frown line between her brows. It was hard to think at all when he looked into her eyes.

"I think I understand." She looked out at the horde of kids kicking and chasing soccer balls. "It's funny you say that, about God picking up the slack." She paused, as if unsure whether to go on. "I had a great idea today but then thought it might be too big for me. For anybody, really."

"It's probably not." He felt his lips tug up, remembering all the times he'd spent hours thinking of all the ways he wasn't right for the job, and then he'd stepped up anyway. Because it wasn't about him.

"As long as God is behind me?"

"Right."

She nodded, clearly making some kind of decision. "Thanks for that. You probably just saved me a few days of giving myself a headache."

"That's what friends are for."

He watched emotions flicker behind her bright blue eyes. They were friends, weren't they? He wouldn't have said so before, but it seemed right, somehow.

"So, my friend, why are we in this gym?" Her tone was light, teasing. Back to work was the message.

"I know I could have called, but this is a little complicated." Gavin dodged a flying ball and wished they were somewhere quieter. It was hard enough without the soccer-style war zone. "It's important that this article mentions how hard my office is working to contain the spread of pertussis." There, it was out.

Her dark eyebrows rose. "All right." The words were drawn out a little, as if she was thinking something completely different.

"I received a visit from Senator McHale, and he was very concerned about the image of our organization during the outbreak."

"Image is always linked to funding." It was a statement, not a question. "I'll make sure it's clear how hard you guys are working."

Gavin felt the tension ease in the back of his neck. She wasn't going to sacrifice the article in favor of running a feel-good fluff piece. Every time he thought she'd act like a gossip-hound or a politician, letting the newspaper dictate her morals, she surprised him with something completely different.

He blurted, without thinking, "You're perfect." He felt his eyes go wide. "I mean, that's perfect. Your plan for the article. It's perfect."

Her eyebrows had zoomed back up, but there was the tiniest twitch to her mouth. They stood there for a moment, a pause stretching to fill the empty space. All the noise of the kids yelling and the balls bouncing off the walls seemed to fade away. He wished for half a second that they were somewhere quieter, and not so they could talk about the paper. What were the rules about dating fellow board members? He didn't know if there were any. Maybe he didn't even care.

She cleared her throat. "I saw my cousin today. She said she'd love to have that playdate."

Right, his sister, who had spent the past five years

hiding from gossip magazines, had arrived. He needed to keep his head on straight. Work and family first. That was all. "Great. They arrived last night. And I better get back to the kids. First practice, we're all just finding our feet."

"Sure, let me know when your sister is all settled in. I'll email you the article by noon tomorrow. Shouldn't take much to tweak it."

He looked over her head toward the double doors. Jose was just coming through, registration forms in his arms. "Okay, sounds good." And he turned away with a polite smile, telling himself it was better to nip it in the bud now. Whatever *it* was.

Just flirting, nothing real. There were thousands of single women in this city. The doors clanged shut behind her and he stood there for a moment, wondering what she'd been thinking during that long pause. Did she see him as a sweaty geek who spent his free time hanging around little kids? Or a lab rat who didn't know his way around women? That "you're perfect" line would haunt him for a while.

The sound of a throat being cleared made him snap to attention. "Jose, sorry. You've got more forms?"

Jose handed over a pile of purple sheets and some pens, his face creased with a rare grin. His dark mahogany skin made his smile Cheshire cat–like.

Gavin felt his neck getting hot and he shuffled the forms. "We're working on a column for the paper."

Jose made a noncommittal sound and the grin stayed fixed.

"It's important we get everything right for the community's sake." He didn't know why he was still talking.

"That's the way it always happens at the Mission, you know."

Gavin frowned, trying to connect the dots.

"Did I tell you I met my wife here? She was working with food distribution, helping sort nonperishables into aid boxes. Took me about three minutes to know she was the one. Took her about six months longer, thanks to..." His voice trailed off and he motioned to his tattoos. "But she came around."

A soccer ball sailed past and Jose went on, "When Calista walked in the door, Grant got a look on his face." He paused, laughing. "Like he'd been hit with a frying pan." He made a swinging motion with one hand, like he was beaning someone with an invisible skillet. "And every time he walked in the room, she turned red."

"Oh, wait a minute. You're trying to say that Evie—" Gavin shook his head.

"That's exactly what I'm saying."

"That's not happening. We're..." He wanted to say opposites. But they weren't. There was the paper, and his sister, and some family drama, and the fact he didn't have the time to spare for dating. But if they were on a desert island, they would find plenty to talk about.

"Coach, are we learning any fancy kicks today?" A skinny kid ran up, all knobby knees and sharp elbows. His hair was shaved short, dark eyes bright with happiness.

"Just one, and I'll show it to you right now," Gavin said, thankful for the reprieve from the uncomfortable conversation.

Jose turned on his heel and gave him one last rendition of the frying pan move and a big grin.

Walking to the sidelines, Gavin tried to shake off the conversation. Life was complicated, and his work didn't leave room for anything important, like a girlfriend. That was all he needed to know. It didn't matter how much she made him think about getting a real life outside of chasing diseases across the state. Besides, if he was parceling out extra time, Allison and Sean came first.

"Have you seen him yet?" Lana rolled up to Evie as she came through the Mission front doors. Her purple-tipped crew cut was freshly dyed and her eyes were wide with excitement.

"Who?" Evie glanced around, wondering if the whole world could tell she'd spent half the afternoon thinking about Gavin. It had been three days, but she couldn't seem to shake the vision of him jogging through the gym, muscles straining at his T-shirt, hair a bit damp at the nape of his neck. He had looked like a giant next to all the little kids. A benevolent, soft-eyed giant with a killer smile.

She smoothed her hair self-consciously. Maybe the soft pink cashmere sweater and tailored black wool skirt was too much. Maybe she should have stayed in her office clothes.

"The baby! Calista just brought him in. He's so tiny." Lana waved her toward the office doors.

Evie followed Lana through the long hallway. "Didn't they just leave the hospital? She should be home resting."

"Oh, you don't know Calista. You can't keep that girl down. She's got him wrapped in some sort of sling. Snug as a bug." Lana pushed open the meeting room door. Calista and Grant were busy passing the baby around the room, huge smiles of pride on both their faces.

"Evie's turn," Jack called out and stepped toward her with an impossibly small bundle.

She glanced down and felt her breath leave her in one big whoosh. He was perfect. Amazing. Miraculous. She couldn't tear her eyes from his sleeping face, peacefully unaware he was being admired by total strangers.

"I have to sit down," she breathed. Gavin was there, pushing a chair up to her, and she settled on the edge. Dark, fine hair covered the baby's head, and she admired his miniature button nose, pursed mouth. He was out cold, dreaming whatever it was babies dreamed of when they'd known only warmth and love. "He smells like the sweetest thing on earth."

"Those are Lana's cookies. Iced oatmeal." Jack took one from the plate on the table for emphasis.

"What's his name?"

"Gabriel," Calista said, glancing at Grant. A look passed between them, part joy, part sadness. "After Marisol's son."

She remembered the short Hispanic woman, huge hug, smelled like vanilla. Evie wanted to ask about Gabriel but sensed a tragedy. Marisol should be the one to tell the story, if she wished.

"Look how long his fingers are." Gavin stretched out a hand and pointed, not touching the baby's skin. Gabriel had his hands crossed over his chest, fingers on full display.

Hyperaware of Gavin's presence, a radiating warmth near her shoulder, Evie was overwhelmed by emotions.

He smelled clean, a little woodsy, like he'd been up on the mountain today. She glanced at him, feeling her eyes well up with unexpected tears. "He's so beautiful." Is this what it was like to welcome a child into the world? She couldn't even begin to imagine the love they must feel for him and for each other.

Gavin nodded, his eyes soft and dark. His expression spoke of tender wonderment.

"He's so Zen." Jack shot a glance at Calista. "Don't know where he gets that."

"Hey, I can be Zen." Calista tossed her blond hair and frowned. Evie wasn't too sure, but from what she'd seen, Calista was more Pilates than Zen.

"From distant relatives, probably." Grant laid a large hand on his son's head, running his fingertips through the fine, dark hair. There was such peace in his eyes that Evie felt her heart contract. This baby had brought excitement and joy. Effortlessly.

"Welcome to the world, little guy." Evie brushed her lips over Gabriel's soft hair, inhaling his sweet scent.

She glanced up and caught Gavin's gaze. Something in his posture changed. She sensed him stiffen. She straightened up, wondering if he worried about germs. Maybe like editors hated typos, he worried over microbes. She shouldn't have kissed the baby. But she didn't see revulsion there. His eyes held an emotion she was very familiar with: struggle, conflict.

Evie dropped her gaze, heart pounding. There was a story in Gavin, she was sure of it. The journalist in her could smell it a mile away. Her woman's intuition was setting off alarms that were making it hard to hear the conversation in the room.

"We'd better let you all get to work. Babies won't

pay the bills, you know." Grant reached out for Gabriel, and Evie reluctantly passed the warm bundle back to his father.

"Must be their only failing because he's pretty perfect, in my eyes." Lana gave him one last gentle touch and wheeled out the door.

"I agree. I don't know how you get anything done. I'd just sit around and stare at him all day." Evie was convinced she could still smell the baby on her sweater.

"I budget time just for gawking." Calista said it so seriously, Evie wasn't sure whether to laugh or not.

"All right, let's get this meeting going. We've got some decisions to make on the grant money that came in last month," Nancy said.

Evie settled in her chair and got down to business. Working on a shoestring budget was something she was used to.

But the awareness of the man sitting next to her, and the emotions that had passed between them moments before, were making it difficult to concentrate. She wasn't a girl who thrived on drama. Those years were done and gone. She'd once thought that living for the moment was for the brave and the free. She'd learned the hard way it was just another trap. She wasn't interested in unearthing old secrets, of exposing wounds best left to heal.

But her heart was aching to know Gavin's story, to bless the hurt he carried inside. The loss of his best friend wouldn't have caused that sort of reaction. Did he have a child given up for adoption? Had he once been married and he and his wife had lost a baby? She lived her life in God's grace, but there were memories that still gave her pain. If Gavin trusted her, if he ever let her into his heart, she would share the hope that kept her going—that a past like hers could be used for something great. Hope that she had a divine purpose, a calling, that wasn't lost when she'd worked as a paparazzo.

Her elbow brushed his whenever she moved. She was left-handed and sitting on his right, a recipe for awkwardness. Gavin shifted on his chair, willing himself to focus. Spreadsheets were passed around, funds allocated, and still he couldn't hardly concentrate. It felt like someone was running a hand down his arm whenever the sleeve of her pink sweater touched his jacket. She looked so soft and she smelled delicious.

He let out a long breath. He hadn't had dinner. He'd missed his run that morning. The pertussis epidemic was weighing on his mind. He wasn't sleeping like he should. McHale was breathing down his neck and asking him to do something he felt was unethical. Nothing more than that. Nothing a vacation wouldn't straighten out.

Okay, truthfully, maybe he was feeling like it was time to settle down and start a family. Maybe it was seeing Grant and Calista wrapped up in their new baby. He'd dated a few girls who had turned into great friends. But he'd never felt this pull, this inability to get his body to follow his brain. And his brain was telling him that this woman next to him was going to complicate his relatively straightforward life in all sorts of ways.

*Allison and Sean are complications, and you wouldn't let them go for the world.* The little voice in his head reminded him that sometimes love was that way. It walked in and rearranged the furniture in your heart, changing everything around, making you feel like a stranger in your own place. And when it was all done, you realized you were happier.

Evie had held that baby like the precious gift he was. He'd been caught up in the moment; his chest had contracted at the sight of the tears in her eyes. Then he'd remembered Allison. His sister who had made terrible choices, who had given birth to a child no one wanted, who had hidden from the world until her shame was too heavy to bear all alone.

Allison, the sister who always walked on the wild side, believed she would be a big star someday. When she met a man and fell in love, she hadn't cared that the man was married and had children. It was always about her feelings, her dreams. But he was in the public eye, so it was only a matter of time before the gossip hounds found them out.

Sean, who should have been welcomed into the world because he was innocent, was hidden away like a stain on the family honor. Gavin hadn't even known Sean existed for a year. The thought of those missed moments, and of Allison's broken heart, made him sick inside.

"Gavin?" Evie was watching him, a question in her eyes.

"Sorry, I was thinking." *About you and love and complications.* He tried to catch up to the topic they'd been debating. He couldn't let his feelings dictate his actions. That was for weaker men, men like McHale. Commitment and focus was his rule, because the world didn't need more messy drama.

\* \* \*

"It's Friday. Go have some fun. You never take a day off." Jack slouched in the chair across from Evie's desk, feet propped on the corner of a cabinet. He sounded bored, which was his usual reaction to frustration. He'd spent the morning schmoozing new clients.

"If I did, I wouldn't spend it snowboarding." Evie shuffled papers and tried to ignore her brother's annoying presence. He'd had only one meeting today and the rest of the day was free. That's what happened when you were a figurehead and not a real manager. He knew it. She knew it. They didn't really talk about it.

"Do you even know how to take the day off? Or would you end up back here, sorting through stories and fighting with the lawyers?"

Evie rubbed her temples and tried to beat back the angry words that swirled in her head. Jack was acting like she didn't want to have a life. She did. It just didn't include acting like a teenager. She wanted to do something real.

There was a light knock on the door and Amy Morket popped into view. Evie was fairly sure what was going to come out of Amy's mouth in the next few seconds.

It was a surprise she'd gone most of the morning without bumping into the overeager reporter. Working dynamics were complicated, especially where women were concerned. A woman who took charge was labeled differently than a man who had initiative. But Amy grated on her nerves. She was always nosing into stories that were assigned to more senior reporters. Where Jolie was bright and tough, Amy was sly and determined.

"Ms. Thorne, I've heard there was a lot of trouble with the sweatshop story. I think I could help out, if you'd let me in on it. I could go undercover."

Evie wanted to drop her head to the desk. Amy had dark hair but ivory skin that paired perfectly with her bright blue eyes. She was going to infiltrate a slave labor ring that shuttled groups of South American aliens from warehouse to warehouse? It would have been laughable if it wasn't such a terrible idea.

"We're working on it. We've got source issues. When it's back on the front burner, I'll let you know."

"I have lots of contacts. I hear rumors." Amy leveled a gaze at Evie and narrowed her eyes. One manicured hand on her slim hip, shoes that cost more than the normal weekly take at *The Chronicle,* and Amy was probably the last person to hear rumors about slave labor. But Evie wondered what she could have been hearing. She cut her eyes to Jack, who shrugged.

"What kind of rumors?"

Amy's eyes widened. "Does this mean I'm on the story?"

"No, it means if you have something helpful, we could see if it will *save* the story."

Amy looked like she was deliberating. "I'll write up what I know and send you an email."

"Okay, that's fine." Evie gave her a smile and waited for the door to close. Then she waited another few beats. "What do you think she knows?" she asked Jack softly.

"When all the big sales are scheduled. She has nice shoes. And legs."

Evie rolled her eyes. That story was on hold, and it

made her angry that they couldn't run something that would save people from modern-day slavery.

"She sort of reminds me of you."

"Excuse me?" Evie tried to put all her umbrage into two words.

"I don't know what it is. Her drive, maybe." Jack was staring at the door, frowning.

She wanted to protest but felt the uncomfortable brush of the ugly truth. Amy was driven, just like she had been. No matter the cost, she was going to be successful.

Shaking off the thought, Evie rubbed her eyes. "I just want to do something real. I'm tired of stumping for advertising dollars."

"Real? Everything you print is real." Her brother paused, choosing his words carefully. "I think you're overcompensating. You made bad choices, repented, changed your life and bought *The Chronicle*. But that doesn't mean you can't have fun once in a while. Plus, nobody even reads papers anymore. If you really want to do some good, you need to get an online presence."

"You call it overcompensation and I call it doing something worthwhile. And we're working on the online subscription system." They'd told her it would be up by the end of the month. She hoped they could hold out that long. If the paper lost many more subscribers, she wouldn't have to argue whether running so many community service articles was overcompensating or not because there wouldn't be any articles at all.

She rubbed her temples. The hum of the enormous machines running thirty feet of newsprint a minute echoed through the floor below. Of course she could do good in the world without a paper, but this was what she did best. God knew her strengths and weaknesses, and this paper was a weapon she could wield against poverty and injustice. As long as she could keep it running.

"Good. You can't afford to ignore the internet." He sat forward, eyes somber. "Seriously, Evie. I don't want to see you beat yourself up about a few mistakes made a really long time ago. I think if you weren't still holding on to guilt, you'd be away from this desk a lot more."

"I know that I can't fix what I've done with a few columns." How ridiculous to think she could. "But I'm not working from a place of unresolved guilt. I just don't want to waste any more time."

"Do you ever think you'll miss something important by working all the time?" His voice was quiet. The afternoon light from the large window put half his face into shadow, sharpening his features. "I just don't want you to miss your chance at happiness."

She felt her eyebrows rise. "Do I only get one? Why the sudden philosophical bent?"

"I've been thinking about things."

Uh-oh. So, it wasn't just her that had a revelation while holding Gabriel. "Things?"

"Specifically, my present employment."

Jack, groomed from birth to take over the family business and shuttled off to business school, rethinking his job? "Colorado Supplements would survive without you."

"Of course they would. I don't really do anything. But Dad might never forgive me."

The sound of the busy newsroom faded away as Evie

waited in the moment. She'd never believed it would come. "You have to be true to your purpose in life."

He looked up, eyes bright. "Exactly. I've let myself live a life that was designed for someone else. That's like a slap in the face to God, don't you think?"

She nodded, her breath tight in her chest. She knew exactly what that type of life felt like.

"I want to be who I was meant to be."

"And who is that?"

He sat back with a sigh. "I have no idea. But you know, I'll figure it out."

Evie nodded, eyes moist. "I'm proud of you. Have I said that recently?"

He grinned over at her, his usual teasing tone back in evidence. "Not recently. But that's gonna change."

She tried to wipe the tear from her cheek without being too obvious. Was there anything more powerful than watching a person embrace their calling? Jack wasn't sure what his was, yet, but he was willing to be led wherever God wanted him to go.

"Now that I've made you cry, I should say something to make you mad. It will be just like old times." He put a finger to his chin and pretended to be deep in thought. "How's Gavin? Seen him lately?"

Evie rolled her eyes and pretended to straighten papers. Why did the phone ring all day long until this conversation? And where were all her reporters?

"He's got a thing for you."

Evie snorted. "He's got a thing for the paper. We're working on a series about the pertussis outbreak."

"And you don't feel anything for him?"

Evie felt her mouth drop open. Jack wasn't one to ask about feelings. "I'm not sure what to say. There are feelings and then there is something that has an actual chance at surviving the reality we live in."

"Have you ever been in love?" Jack's voice held no hint of sarcasm or teasing. In fact, he was deadly serious.

She'd know if she had been, right? "I don't think so."

"A few years ago you said there wasn't a man in Denver you'd really consider."

Evie knew what he was saying; she'd felt it herself. Gavin was different. But she was afraid to hope, afraid to say anything in case it all crumbled to dust.

"I think there's one that deserves a second look."

"I'm not sure what I feel. Maybe it's something important and I'm going to miss my one chance. Or just maybe it's that he's a disease specialist and he's infected us with something horrible and we're all going to die."

Her brother dropped his feet to the floor with a bang. "You're the most unromantic person I've ever known."

"I don't really have the time to be romantic." She tried to keep the frustration out of her voice but couldn't quite manage it.

"Maybe you should make some time."

She glared at him, weighing her words. The door cracked open and Jolie stuck her head inside. "Sorry to interrupt. You've got someone coming from the Downtown Association in ten minutes."

"Thanks for the reminder." Evie gave her a smile and tried to ignore Jolie's obvious appreciation for Jack's backside as he stood up, stretching his arms over his head.

"Later, little sis." He leaned over the desk, dropped

a kiss on her head and went to open the office door. "And where love is concerned, you better trust me."

He passed through the door and Jolie reappeared. "Safe to come in?"

"Why wouldn't it be?" Evie sat up straight and pretended like she wasn't absolutely rattled. Jack was going to quit their family business. He'd given her a speech on getting a life. He said she needed to give Gavin more than a passing glance. As if she could help it.

"Usually I hear you two laughing up a storm in here. Today was…quiet." Jolie dropped into the chair across the desk, a folder on her lap, fluffy neon pink skirt in sharp contrast with her black-and-white-striped T-shirt, lime-green tights and black Converse shoes.

"Well, we were just disagreeing on a course of action. And he doesn't like it when I disagree." She said the words lightly, as if it didn't matter what her twin thought.

"It's about that vaccine guy, Gavin, isn't it? Is Jack getting overprotective? Wants to run him over with his car?"

Evie let out a startled laugh. "Why would you ever think that?"

"I finally outsmarted Miss Observant, didn't I?"

"It's not what you think. It sort of concerns him, but not the way you're implying." Oh, boy, Evie was digging a hole.

"Uh-huh. A gorgeous man shows up here, there are all sorts of sparks flying around, and then Jack's unhappy? It doesn't take a genius to figure that one out."

"It's too complicated to explain. And I don't know where you get the sparks part because you saw him for about four seconds when he came through the news-room."

"Which was three seconds more than I needed. I may be a lot younger than you, Ms. Thorne, but I can definitely tell when a man is interested." She sighed. "Which is a horrible burden to bear when you realize your crush isn't into you. Jack didn't even stop to chat on his way out."

Evie offered up a short prayer of thanks for that one. She thought Jolie was wonderful, but Jack really didn't need a nineteen-year-old girlfriend.

"Anyway, here's the next set of ad mockups for the Sunday inserts." She stood up, handing the folder to Evie.

"Jolie, you always do such a great job. I don't know where this office would be without you."

"A lot slower and a lot less interesting." She grinned on her way out the door.

## *Chapter Seven*

Gavin paced back and forth near the bench. It was a park playdate on a normal Saturday afternoon, nothing to be nervous about. He couldn't help glancing at the parking area every few seconds. Evie said her cousin was blonde and had a little boy Sean's age. They were fifteen minutes late. Allison didn't seem to mind, but he desperately wanted them to see Denver as a friendly, welcoming city. Being stood up for their first playdate didn't fit that picture.

Of course, a lot of people ran late. Or maybe the cousin forgot. It wasn't personal, these things happened.

But if felt personal. He shouldn't even be here with the office running twenty-four hours. He should be checking on the lab, meeting up with the hospital emergency-room doctors, something other than hanging out in a park on a Saturday.

The article had run in last week's Sunday edition, and the office had been flooded with calls for pertussis boosters on Monday. And Tuesday. And every day after. That was a small measure of success.

He hadn't heard anything from McHale's office on whether the article was sufficiently slanted to positively reflect on the office. He didn't want to call and find out. He battled back a surge of anger at the thought of the office conversation. He hadn't said anything to Allison. She didn't need the anxiety. At least Evie's columnist had made it seem effortlessly connected, a human interest story on the epidemic and the hardworking CDC officials.

He stared out at the playground teeming with kids. Spin was second nature to reporters. They seemed to handle the truth like it was something to craft, to mold into whatever image they wanted to portray. He couldn't imagine living like that, day in and day out. Evie was different and sometimes he got the faintest flash of sadness in her eyes. That didn't jibe with his idea of journalists. Arrogant and pushy, maybe. Ready to sell their souls for a buck, definitely. A heart for social justice and an active concern for vulnerable people of the city, not at all.

Sean yelled and waved from the top of the slide and Gavin raised an arm, grinning. Evie was young to be a full-fledged editor, and an owner. Even a small paper in bankruptcy must have cost an enormous amount. Maybe she'd taken an early inheritance. He shrugged inside his coat, irritated with himself for wondering. It wasn't any of his business, really. He railed against gossips, but sometimes his own curiosity brought him just as low.

There was a touch at his elbow and he sucked in a breath of surprise. Evie had come up from behind him, cheeks pink from the cold, breath coming fast. For a moment, his mind went completely blank. He forgot about the playdate, about being welcoming. He wanted to put his hands to her face and drag her perfect lips to his. He stepped back, instead of the direction he wanted to go.

"I'm so sorry, they can't come. Stacey had her baby!" She was smiling widely, and she put her hand on his arm.

"Wonderful! Everyone healthy?"

"Perfect. He was early, but he's just fine. I saw them a few hours ago. I was going to bring Jaden to play, but he was absorbed in watching the baby. Do you think your nephew will be too disappointed?"

"He'll be fine. We can reschedule." He wanted to tuck the wisp of dark hair into her hood, but didn't. He also wanted to introduce her to Allison. His head was telling him to keep them apart, but his heart said Evie wasn't a danger. She was solid, faithful. He took a breath. "Do you want to meet them?"

"Sure." Evie smiled, both dimples showing. "Oh, before I forget, Jack says 'hi' and something about…"

"About?" he prompted.

"There were cords on the cheese wedge, I think it was."

His expression cleared. "Oh, okay."

"And that means something to you?"

"Sure. Snowboarder lingo. But I can't tell you what it means or I'd have to teach you the secret handshake, too."

"Fine. I didn't want to be part of your little club anyway."

His smile deepened and he held her gaze for longer than could be considered necessary. The world had shrunk until they were the only two in it.

"So, are you going to point them out or should I try to guess?"

"I suppose you could try." Gavin crossed his arms over his chest. He tilted his head at what seemed like hordes of small kids each running in different directions. "In fact, I'd like to see it."

"Challenge accepted." She narrowed her eyes and scanned the playground.

Gavin watched her from the corner of his eye. It felt so right to stand here with her on a Saturday, surrounded by families. In fact, it felt right to have her by his side wherever they were. *Lord, if this isn't what You want, tell me, because I want to go with my heart.*

She gave him a mock salute with one blue mittened hand and scanned the playground. That smile always gave her courage; she wasn't sure why. Courage to flirt, to tease. Totally unlike her. It would be scary if it didn't feel so right. The top of his coat was unzipped and she could see his tie was crooked, which gave her a jolt of pleasure at the familiar sight. Evie gave him a quick once-over and told herself not to gawk. Dark blond hair peeked out from under a dark knit hat, just a hint of stubble, brown eyes intent on her.

She couldn't help noticing the shadows under his eyes. She knew his office was under a lot of pressure. Maybe he was headed back to work after this. There weren't many guys wearing ties on Saturday morning between the swings and the rock climbing wall.

Surveying the play area, she tuned out the rhythmic shriek of the swings, stopping at a pair of young boys near the slide. They were rolling snowballs up the slippery chute and trying to catch them on the way down. One little boy was wearing a coat that looked a little too new, as if he'd just moved from a warmer place, like Florida. But the next moment his mother called his name and he ran toward her, across the play area and away.

Evie felt Gavin shift next to her, following her gaze. She sensed his amusement and tried not to laugh. This was silly, but she couldn't help playing along. She was determined to win. Struggling to block out the sight of him, the sound of his slow breaths, the faint scent of soap, Evie focused.

She was going at this all wrong. She should be look-ing for Sean's mother. Evie's lips twisted in triumph at her new plan, but she kept silent. Within seconds she spotted Sean. His mother was near but not hovering. Tall, slender, with a red scarf wrapped haphazardly around her throat, the strikingly pretty brunette leaned against a metal pole. A few feet away, three little boys worked on moving a large snowball through the toys. Allison didn't scan the park for friends, wasn't texting on her phone. Sean's mother was watching him intently but from a short distance.

Evie could guess from Allison's line of sight which boy was hers, and when he turned she could see the resemblance to his mother. Straight blond hair peek-ing out from under a brightly striped knit hat, but his eyes were blue, features a little sharper.

"And what's the reward if I prove myself?" She slid a glance at him and felt her cheeks warm as he raised his eyebrows and made a sound that was part surprise, part laugh. She should be ashamed of her flirty tone. But it was hard to feel guilty.

"You won't be able to pick him out of the crowd, I'm sure. If you fail, I have a proposal."

Evie turned, mittens on hips, and shot him a look.

Gavin turned to face her, one side of his mouth quirked up as if he was trying not to laugh. He rubbed a hand over his jaw and pretended to contemplate the situation. "I was thinking that when we're not working together professionally... Dinners are always so awkward. Sitting at a table, trying not to spill food on your nice clothes. I think we could find something more fun to do. If you wanted."

Chewing her lip, she glanced at him, then back to Sean. Her cheeks were feeling downright toasty. She thought she knew where he was headed. Then again, maybe they weren't on the same page after all. "You mean, like a park date?"

This time he laughed out loud, a deep sound that made her unable to tear her gaze away from him in spite of herself. "I don't know how I've given you the wrong impression, but I don't need free babysitting."

She'd gotten a lot of impressions. And one of them was that he didn't like her at all, but it seemed like that was changing.

"And if there's a man who thinks you'd make a better babysitter than a dinner date, he's certainly not standing right here." Voice low and words measured, he meant what he said. His warm brown eyes were locked with hers, speaking volumes.

That small space inside, the one that held all the old grudges and hurts, eased just a bit. So many times she'd felt invisible, growing up as Jack's twin, the daughter of a business owner who didn't think girls were good enough. It had become second nature to assume people were interested in her paper, her brother, her family. But not Gavin. He made her feel as if she were captivating.

"How about we head up to Echo Mountain for the day? Maybe on Saturday, we could go skiing, or boarding, whatever you'd like. There's a great restaurant at the ski lodge."

A drive, mountain scenery, gorgeous slopes, excellent restaurants, cozy chats by the enormous lodge fireplace as they sipped hot cocoa. Evie couldn't help grinning.

"Sounds great, but there's one problem."

"You don't accept rides from strangers?"

Evie gave him a shot to the arm. It was the unconscious, playful move of a girl crushing on a boy. Part of her wanted to groan. The other part thrilled at his answering expression of mock pain.

"I don't ski that well. I would only slow you down."

"We don't have to ski. There are nature trails, too. We could snowshoe. If all else fails, we can just wallow around in the snow like little kids do." He flapped his arms for emphasis.

"I suppose I could manage that." She stood, smiling up at him, lost in the idea of a day in the mountains with Gavin on a Saturday when she'd have a little more time off from the paper. But he'd said she couldn't pick this kid out of the crowd, and she was stubborn. It would be easy to point out the wrong kid, but she didn't play dumb for anybody. It just wasn't in her. "But you can't win a day with me. You have to ask nicely." She pointed. "Sean is the little boy in the yellow ski jacket, by the jungle gym. Allison is the woman leaning against the pole a few feet away."

If she wasn't a little irritated at herself for having to be right, she would have laughed at his expression. "I just looked for the mom who wasn't all wrapped up in her own circle of friends, or stuck to her smartphone. She's new here so she's sticking close to him."

"That will teach me to set myself up for disappointment."

"She doesn't look anything like you." Evie swept a glance over his wavy blond hair, strong jaw and broad shoulders. Allison was dark and slight, with a pointed chin and delicate features. She looked familiar, somehow.

"We're not related except by marriage. Her father, my mother. She's technically my stepsister, but I don't bother with the step part."

She smiled a little, thinking of the way the world was always drawing lines in the sand and raising invisible fences. Gavin preferred to step over them, arms wide open.

A few fat flakes of snow drifted lazily down between them. Did she really want to give up a date, just to be right? Before she thought it through, Evie slid a glance at him. "But Shakespeare said, 'the quality of mercy is not strain'd, it droppeth as the gentle rain from heaven.'" She held out a hand and a wet, clump of snowflakes dotted her mitten. "Or snow, as the case may be."

Gavin faced her, hands in his coat pockets, head tilted down. His voice was soft. "He also said, 'it blesseth him that gives and him that takes,' an attribute to God Himself."

"Right. So, we both win. I think we should go to Echo Mountain and have some fun." The flakes were falling thick and fast. Evie lifted her face to the sky, unable to keep the warmth from spreading from near her heart, settling somewhere in her belly and translating into a goofy smile.

He reached out and turned her mitten, examining the snowflakes in her palm. Their eyes met and Evie felt the warmth in her chest transform into something full of possibility, tenuously hanging in the air between them. The thrill that went through her was chased by a healthy dose of fear. Getting close to Gavin meant telling the truth, all of it, including how she'd bought the paper.

"Uncle Gavin!"

They both turned as Sean ran toward them. His small face was alight with happiness, huge smile revealing widely spaced front teeth. "It's snowing, it's snowing!"

"Yup, it tends to do that here, buddy." Gavin leaned down and rubbed his hand over Sean's knit cap. "This is your welcome to Denver."

"You must be Evie." Allison was just steps behind her son, dark hair pulled to one side and tucked into the collar of her coat. She held out her hand, but her smile contained a bit of wariness. Again there was that flash of memory, something struggling up to the surface of Evie's consciousness.

"It's nice to meet you and Sean. I hope you'll enjoy your time here."

"I do, too. We're making a whole new start in Denver. We've been hiding for too long." She took a deep breath and smiled.

Evie wondered if Allison was being literal. Hiding from what? Gavin's expression was cautious.

Allison went on, "I don't know if we'll be able to get Gavin to lay off the eighty-hour workweek for a while." She cocked her head. "We've never been able to before. But maybe things are different now you're in the picture."

Heat rising to her face, her gaze slid to the man beside her. His expression was inscrutable, but he didn't look at all irritated by the implication that Evie was going to cut into his workaholic ways.

"Which reminds me, I've got to get back." Gavin dodged a snowball that Sean lobbed at his kneecap.

"You're not staying?"

"I really wish I could. But there were five more reported cases just today. They're talking about restricting travel in and out of Denver International. That would mean disaster at any time, but right now, near the holidays, it would be a bigger crisis than we've seen in a while."

Evie paused, wondering what to say, to ask. She could feel her pulse pounding in her throat. "City-wide quarantine?"

"Not quite. For this they'd make sure people stayed home, skipped the holiday parties. It would put a huge damper on the Christmas festivities at the Mission. The kids would be crushed if the parties were cancelled."

Rubbing a hand over the back of his neck, he went on, "Antibiotics can help, but not after the first three weeks because the damage is already done. People just aren't bringing the kids in soon enough. They just give them cough medicine, and then their lungs are already filled with fluid, their kidneys are starting to fail. The way this is going, it's only a matter of time before there's a fatality."

The snow seemed to pause in the air, time slowing down as Evie processed his words. Her hand went to her throat of its own accord. A fatality, just like his best friend. She couldn't imagine how hard it was for him.

Gavin's face was pained, tone subdued. "Almost certainly it will be an infant. All the cases have been, so far."

Feeling her throat closing in fear, she struggled to get the words out. "I knew whooping cough was hard on kids. But I thought you just got vaccinated and everything was okay. I didn't imagine it spread so fast, or could kill. Is Stacey's baby safe in Memorial?"

"They're keeping the pertussis cases under strict quarantine." His expression turned stony and he was silent. Then he said, "Unless you recognize the signs, you can still be infected and pass it to an infant. It's the education that's missing. People aren't heeding the signs. Soon it will be too big to stop and we'll be working under a city-wide alert that includes shutting down all public spaces. Schools would close, the Mission would be shut for the holidays. People who need services will go without until it's under control."

People weren't heeding the signs because no one read the paper anymore, just like Jack said. Their column hadn't made much difference. She should get out of the paper business and get an internet news domain. She felt sick with powerlessness. "Oh, Gavin, we're almost ready with the internet site for *The Chronicle*. The IT crew told us a week, maybe two." She reached out and touched his arm, feeling her heart constrict. "We've got to pray hard this doesn't claim any lives."

"We've had a lot of calls. I don't mean to sound as

if there's no hope." He drew in a breath, as if her touch was giving him strength.

"Uncle Gavin! Catch me!"

Sean was waving from the top of the slide, a bundle of hat and scarf and coat. His uncle lifted a hand and jogged toward the bottom of the slide, boots squeaking on the fresh dusting of snow. Evie watched silently as Gavin crouched down and held out his arms, neatly intercepting the boy-shaped projectile as he whizzed down the icy plastic. Sean let out a whoop as he got an extra swing out of the bargain.

Evie tried to marshal her thoughts. This man, strong and sturdy, a shelter for his loved ones, was fighting to keep people from dying the way his childhood friend had. She wanted to help, wanted to do something meaningful. It felt like something from the Old Testament, the smiting of the firstborn. *Lord, help us!*

"Poor kids. I'm so glad Sean is old enough to have all his vaccinations." Allison sounded like she was almost talking to herself. She turned to her and smiled. "And I'm really glad we came. Sean needs someone like Gavin. I promise we won't take up all of his time."

Evie blinked, hurrying to catch up with the conversation. "I think you've misunderstood something. See, we barely know each other. We're just—" She'd started to say "friends," but that didn't seem right at all.

"Just? Even halfway across the playground I could see the happy vibes." She gave Evie an appraising look. "He was right, you know."

She was afraid to ask, but she couldn't help it. Gavin was soldier straight at the bottom of the slide, waiting for Sean to make his way the last few steps to the top. Could he hear them? She didn't think so. "About?"

"Your eyes. They're gorgeous. Such a deep blue, like sapphires." Allison paused, her lips tugging up. "Of course, he didn't say it like that. He just mentioned it in passing. But I noticed. He usually chats about *E. coli* and single-celled organisms."

Gavin had talked about her eyes?

She stuck her mittens in her pockets and pretended like her heart wasn't hammering in her chest. There was something real, something wonderful happening here. And it was a terrible time for it. All this talk about getting him to cut back on work. He had a purpose and a calling. Who was she to interfere with that?

Allison tucked her long dark hair behind both ears and tugged her hood up over her head to block out the snow as it fell more steadily. "Gavin is always so driven. Patrick's death really affected him. He's totally consumed with eradicating every known disease from the city. Like one man could do that!"

Every word seemed to reinforce her fear. Of course Gavin was just one man, but wasn't that what they'd talked about in the gym? Doing so much more with God's help? Stepping in to fill a need? She'd been giddy with infatuation, and now she felt like her heart was being battered. Let other people take the weekend off. His job was to save lives, hers was to keep the community educated and safe. They could work together. Anything more than that was asking for trouble.

Sean let out a squeal of delight as he flew down the slide, snow dotting his hat. Evie watched Gavin grab his nephew in another swinging hug.

Turning back to them, snow clinging to his dark blond hair, his face was lit with laughter. Her breath caught in her throat. There weren't enough hours in the day for all of them. She watched the smile slip from his face and his brow furrow. Evie raised a hand.

"Mom, I'm cold." Sean had gone from having fun to freezing cold in seconds.

Evie crouched down to his level. "There's a great little coffee shop across the street that my brother and I go to all the time. If your mom says it's okay, we can grab some hot chocolate and warm up."

"Can we, Mom? Please?"

"Well, I don't see why not." Allison looked over at her brother. "Come on. You can't work all the time. Join us."

Gavin sighed, stuffing his hands in his coat pockets. "I wish I could. Next time."

Evie nodded at him, hoping she betrayed nothing that was swirling in her mind. He had a serious job, the city had a serious problem and lives were at stake. It didn't matter how many people pushed them together, or how he made her want to reconsider her own workaholic ways. There wasn't time for them, and there might not ever be.

Gavin trudged toward his car, toes of his boots white with clumps of fresh skiing material. He should have waited before asking her out. He really needed to get the pertussis crisis out of the way before he even thought of bringing Evie into the situation. But somehow their conversation had hung a left turn somewhere around those dimples and plowed on through to its conclusion: the promise of a full day together. Up on Wolf Mountain, enjoying the fresh air and the great pines, maybe some time by the main lodge fireplace getting to know each other better? They couldn't go wrong with that plan.

He snorted. Wallowing in the snow. She probably thought he was nuts, but he didn't want their first date to be the same old routine of dinner at some overpriced restaurant.

His lips started to lift of their own accord. The way she'd picked out Sean and Allison was uncanny. He thought he was detail oriented, but she made him look like a big-picture guy. Maybe if it wasn't in front of a microscope, he didn't pay as much attention, but she sure had his attention and she was as far from the lab as she could get. His half smile widened to a full grin as he remembered the way she'd smacked his arm. Natalie Jenkins had done that in ninth grade when she'd had a crush on him. Everything he said got him a whack on the arm. It was such a classic girl move.

He pressed the remote unlock and tugged open the car door, glancing behind him one last time. She was laughing at something Sean had said, leaning over to hear him better, holding out one mitten as if she was afraid of his snowball-throwing powers. Beauty was one thing, but Evie was stunning inside and out. Her faith seemed so effortless, seamless. Her work flowed directly from her desire to fulfill her God-given purpose. He needed to pray as hard as he worked; she'd reminded him of that.

Gavin slammed the door closed and took a deep breath. It just seemed a losing battle, some days. He was Sisyphus, pushing that boulder up a hill every day and then having to watch it roll back down again. Quitting wasn't an option, but he wasn't even close to being the man God needed him to be.

The way Evie talked, there wasn't a doubt in her mind she could do what she had to do, as if she couldn't fail. She made him want to be braver than he was, to live a little more.

Backing slowly out of the parking space and turning into the street, Gavin could see tiny reflections in the rearview mirror. Sean was trotting toward the corner, waving Evie on. His sister followed with her shoulders hunched in her dark coat, hair flying free. *Be with Allison, Lord. Help her know Your love.* It was going to be a hard transition for them. The old worry over his little sister—the funny, talented one—resurfaced in his gut. She had an awesome talent and wouldn't have trouble making a living singing in Denver's live clubs, but life was more than surviving. It was about finding a place to call home.

Following the club crowd in Aspen had led her down a dark road full of disappointment and heartache. He knew being this close to the area where it had all gone wrong would be tough for her. She'd decided all by herself to come back, be closer to Grandma Lili. He didn't want to discourage her, but seeing McHale made him afraid for her all over again.

But he needed to commit her to God and focus on his job. The memory of the tiny babies he'd seen sedated and struggling made dread course through him. They were getting closer to a breakthrough, he could feel it. But it may not come fast enough.

He slowed at a yellow light and clenched his jaw in frustration. The base of his neck was starting to ache.

Gavin stepped on the gas as soon as the light turned and sped through the intersection. He felt wound tight with anxiety. It wasn't just the pertussis. He loved Allison, but she brought drama to his formerly boring life. He tried to be fair and treat her like an adult. Warning Allison not to share her past would be acting like the bossy big brother, although he was tempted. He had only told her that Evie worked at a paper and hoped that would be enough. His sister was so trusting, always believing the best about everyone. That had gotten her a broken heart and complications that no young mother should have to deal with, let alone carry around for the rest of her life. She wanted to make a fresh start, live her life in the open, but he didn't know how that would happen. She had to think of Sean.

Sure, he was young, not even in kindergarten yet, but some day he'd be in grade school. Kids were cruel. Just having separated parents could make you a target. It was more common to be the child of a single mother, but if it was a weak spot, a tender point, the kids would seek it out. Sean would be bullied for the fact he was conceived in scandal and born in secret. It was a few years ago, but nothing ever went away on the internet. A few keystrokes and those photos would come up for the world to see. His sister, dressed like the twenty-year-old club singer she was, stumbling out of the senator's hotel room, laughing, holding her shoes. The senator behind her, wrapped in a hotel bathrobe, dark hair rumpled. That was the end of his presidential aspirations, even though he denied it all. And that was the end of Allison's reckless years. Within a matter of months, she had moved to Florida and taken a job as a secretary for a large electronics factory, a baby on the way.

Gavin sighed. He wanted to make everything better, but there wasn't any way to fix the past. All they could do was work with what they had, and that was a beautiful little family. He wanted to protect them, cushion them from every sarcastic comment and every sneer.

He rubbed the back of his neck. *What is done in the dark will be brought to the light,* as the verse says. Eventually Allison would have to deal with the fallout from her affair. But it wouldn't be right now, if he could help it. At least he and McHale agreed on one thing.

## Chapter Eight

"How did you two meet?" Allison took a sip of her latte and eyed Evie over the rim of her mug.

Here she thought Gavin wanted her cousin to befriend his lonely sister. The girl across from her didn't seem lonely at all. She looked like she was making sure her big brother wasn't going to be eaten alive. Evie couldn't help but admire that. It's what family was for.

"Well, we have friends in common. We're both on the budget committee at the Downtown Denver Mission."

Allison glanced over at Sean, who had gulped down his hot chocolate and was busy stacking wooden blocks the coffee shop kept in a bin for kids. The rustic shop had a family-friendly atmosphere that wasn't just for looks. She tucked her hair behind both ears, a gesture Evie was learning to recognize.

There was something about Allison that tugged at her. She squinted, thinking. It couldn't be her, could it? No. Maybe. Younger, thinner, blonder. She couldn't help the tears that started in her eyes. It was a wound that had never healed. She had wondered, prayed, cried and grieved for that girl.

Evie cleared her throat, forcing the thoughts away. Some days she thought she saw that unnamed girl everywhere. Evie had ruined her life, and there was no way to forget it.

"Do you miss Florida?"

"I miss the sunshine, the Cuban food, the way every street seemed to have music coming from a little shop. But it was time for us to be nearer our family. My grandma lives here, too. She's an amazing woman, not to mention she makes the best blueberry scones ever. Have you met her?"

Evie shook her head.

"And of course, Sean is at that age where he needs a father figure."

Feeling awkward, Evie said nothing, but the question hovered in the air between them.

"I'm assuming that Gavin told you the whole, ugly story." Allison said the words matter-of-factly.

"No, he told me you were moving here. That was all."

Allison watched Sean carefully set a small block on a tall tower. "He should have told you. If you're going to be close to him, you'll have to know everything. No surprises, no skeletons in the closet."

Evie felt her face heat with Allison's words and she took a sip of her mocha, scalding her tongue. She had more than a few of her own skeletons rattling around, disturbing her peace of mind. *Close to him.* Was that what she was becoming? In a way, she hardly knew him. In another, it felt like they'd known each other for years.

"You don't need to tell me anything you don't want to."

"But I do want to." Allison leaned forward, eyes bright. "I'm really starting to understand that what I was afraid of doesn't matter. I have Gavin and my grandma and Sean. Even though our parents are holed up in Arizona, pretending Sean doesn't exist, I think they'll come around. I've come back to my faith. I feel like my life is ready for a change."

She liked Allison before, but she empathized with her now. She knew the feeling of wanting to change and change big. Grace made it possible. "Your story is for you to tell. Probably why Gavin didn't say anything."

Allison's brown eyes turned sad. "He thinks I should keep hiding, and I understand his reasoning. But I want Sean to respect me, and I can't live my life honestly when I'm lying all the time."

Evie dropped her gaze, watching the swirls on the surface of her drink. Did she lie about her past? She hoped not. She just didn't ever mention it. It never came up. Usually.

"I got into a wild crowd when I started working the clubs in Aspen, right out of high school. By the time I was twenty, I thought I knew everything. I had an affair with a married man. Sean is the product of that affair." She spoke the words quietly but clearly.

Her stomach dropped about six inches. She'd worked the Aspen crowds right out of college, hoping to catch somebody famous doing drugs or kissing the wrong girl. Those pictures sold for a lot, if the person in the picture was just starting their downward spiral. After a while, nobody cared. But a picture of the innocent ones, on the first step down, paid well.

"Does his father ever try to make contact?"

"He sent a few messages. Mostly to keep out of sight and keep my mouth shut."

Evie wanted to ask his name but couldn't bring herself to do it. A sickening suspicion was settling over her. She struggled to speak. "I'll pray he has a change of heart."

Enough money and some men thought they could rule the world. Add in a reputation to protect and things got ugly. She glanced over at the little boy, wishing the world didn't have fathers who denied their sons, wishing she hadn't seen those dramas acted out over and over again. Sean let out a laugh as the blocks came tumbling down with a crash.

"Sweetie, not so loud." Allison laid a gentle hand on her son's shoulder. She raised her eyes to Evie's, her jaw set. "I want to do better for him. I made some poor choices and we have to live with the consequences. When I asked God for forgiveness, I knew it was going to be a really hard road. But Sean's my joy." She gazed back at him for a moment, her lips tugging up. "I don't even think I knew what love was before I had him."

Eyes filling with tears, Evie swallowed hard. Allison had taken that second chance and run with it. How was it that people could wander aimlessly through life, making bad decisions and poor choices, and yet… in a tug, in a seemingly insignificant moment, it all changed? *Love* changed everything.

She blinked a few times, trying to find her voice. "I thank God every day for my own second chances." She wasn't like Allison, she knew that now. She couldn't tell her the whole story. But she could let her know she understood. "I think you're doing a great job, and I know Gavin's glad you're here."

The words seemed to boost Allison's spirit. She straightened her shoulders. "I was wrong to keep anything from him. I should have trusted him more. But when he advised me to give up my baby, I didn't have the strength to argue. I was so weary and discouraged, disappointed in myself. I shut him out instead."

Advised her to give up the baby? She couldn't help the surprise that must have shown on her face.

"He wanted the best for us. But I wanted to keep Sean, and instead of telling Gavin, I just dropped off the radar." Allison's eyes were dark and sad. "He didn't know what had happened to us. Our parents had cut me off, so I convinced myself that he didn't care, either. But he did, and he spent every spare moment trying to track me down. He thought I was dead."

Evie was silent, working phrases in her head. *We all have regrets. Sometimes we make terrible choices.* They sounded weak and inadequate.

"Of all the things I wish I could take back, that's one of them. He missed out on his nephew's first year because I was afraid to be honest. I knew with God's help I could raise my baby, no matter how hard it was going to be. But I was so scared to tell my family. It was just easier to go it alone." Allison circled her mug with both hands, her face tight.

"I understand." It wasn't much. She really did get how hard it was to show your true self when you've spun a web of lies so thick, so strong, that it seems nothing can cut through.

Allison looked up, almost laughing. "Do you? Really?"

Evie swallowed, her throat feeling dry. Was she playing truth or dare? They'd known each other only a few minutes.

She forced a smile. "Maybe not."

"I hope not. For your sake." Allison shot her a glance, turning her attention to Sean, who was placing the very last block on a teetering tower. "Sweetie, let's keep it under control, okay? That's a little too tall."

Evie took a hasty sip of her mocha and pretended to admire Sean's engineering skills. "It's been nice to chat with you, but I told my brother I'd meet him in a few minutes. We should do this again. Or maybe a movie. It could be girls' night out."

"Sure." She smiled warmly as Evie gathered up her coat and mittens.

"I usually never get out unless Jack forces me." Evie slipped on her coat. "In fact, you should meet him. You're a singer, right? He's got a friend who's looking for some new talent for weekend gigs in their club."

"Now that's an offer I can't refuse. I know Gavin wishes I'd find a real job. Maybe he's worried I'll fall into a bad crowd again, but I'm a different person than I was then. And singing makes me happy."

Evie paused, processing the words. "Actually, that was one of the first things he said about you, that you were a singer."

Her brows rose and she seemed pleasantly surprised.

"Bye, Evie!" Sean ran up and threw his arms around her waist. "And thanks for the snow!"

This surprised a laugh out of her. "What can I say? It was just for you." Apparently, she was now in charge of the weather. She hoped he liked snow. A lot.

The handle of the door was chilly to the touch. Evie

knew it was going to be a deadly cold night. The snow swirled around her as she stepped onto the sidewalk. It felt like ice was melting in the pit of her stomach as she wondered how many new babies would show up at the hospitals and walk-in clinics tonight.

The street was pleasantly deserted, just a few people walking quickly, heads down through the falling snow. She wished that this was all there was to her city. Coffee shops and parks and mayors holding sledding parties for the kids. But it wasn't. There were so many people in need, and some of them were too scared to ask for help.

As she drove back to her apartment, Evie went over and over Allison's words.

Her throat tightened and she fought to focus on the slick road filled with downtown traffic. Allison said that she was tired of hiding, and Evie knew just what she meant. There just weren't enough ways to make up for what she'd done. But that was where the similarity ended. If Gavin's sister was the girl she'd photographed with Senator McHale, then Evie had come out miles ahead. She sold those pictures for enough money to buy a whole paper. And what did Allison get? Disowned by her family, shunned publically.

The old VW heater finally kicked to life and Evie tugged off her scarf. She felt as if her limbs had been filled with lead. Fear had sucked the energy from her, localizing it near her frantically beating heart. *Lord, I will do what You want me to do.* Even if it meant ruining her good-girl reputation, even if it meant destroying this new thing that was growing between her and Gavin Sawyer.

# Chapter Nine

"You look tired. You're not sleeping."

These weren't questions, and Gavin knew better than to argue with his grandma. She handed him a plate piled high with spaghetti covered in homemade sauce and juicy, fragrant meatballs. Allison had wanted to put Sean to bed early and was already gone to the little apartment they had found on the other side of town. She'd taken with her a container filled with enough spaghetti to feed them for a week. The dining room, cozy and calming, had always been the perfect antidote to whatever was giving him stress. But not tonight. He was a bundle of nerves and couldn't seem to concentrate.

"The kids are going to make me run laps if you don't stop feeding me like this." So it wasn't very funny, but he didn't want to get into the exact reason he tossed and turned all night.

Fixing her brown eyes on him, she cocked her head like a bright little bird. He tried to ignore her, focusing with grim determination on his spaghetti. Finally, he sighed and put down his fork.

"I already know what you're going to say."

She smiled brightly, her lined face creasing into tens more wrinkles. Some women paid top dollar for face cream, but Grandma Lili said she was proud of every one of her laugh lines and every one of her wiry gray hairs. Fifty-five years of marriage to a cigar-smoking cab driver who worked around the clock could have given her reason to complain. But she wasn't that sort.

"Then I'll just keep my mouth shut when you're all done telling me about those dark circles. Women don't find that look very attractive on such a young man, let me remind you."

Evie's face popped into his mind, but he brushed it away. It didn't matter what women liked right now. It mattered that the city was under a pertussis epidemic, his prodigal sister had returned and the woman he found incredibly alluring was his best friend's sister. That was enough to give anybody sleep deprivation.

"You know the whooping cough has hit the city hard this year."

"Of course. I've never been prouder of you." She reached over the table and patted his hand.

For some reason those few words made his shoulders sag. He took a deep breath, but she spoke first.

"You can't be held responsible for a whole city, dear."

"But I can. It's my job to make sure people are aware of the booster shots, that pregnant women are aware of the need to get vaccinated again and that we keep on top of any cases. Something went wrong. And now there are very sick babies suffering." He lifted his face to hers, mouth tight. "It is my job, and I failed." It was an old feeling, from all the way back when Patrick died.

Grandma Lili let out a laugh that was part chuckle and part snort. "Sweetie, I think you're part superhero, don't get me wrong. To come out the way you did, so serious and calm, when all the rest of the family is a group of hot heads... Well, it's impressive. But you can't run the world."

Gavin stared in disbelief. "I'm not trying to run the world."

"Then you're trying to take responsibility for it. Do the best you can. Commit the rest to God."

Gavin pushed a meatball around his plate. "It's more than the epidemic."

Grandma Lili said nothing. She waited, bright eyes fixed on Gavin's face.

"I'm glad Allison is finally here, with Sean. But she's changed. Just in the last few weeks she seems intent on being as transparent as possible."

She leaned back in her chair, tapping the long slim fingers of one hand against the tablecloth. Gavin wasn't sure if this was the moment she'd promised not to say anything, or if she was just thinking.

"She says she won't cover up her past, or the identity of Sean's father. I don't think it's a good time to start being brutally honest."

"It's her choice."

"You don't think it will hurt Sean?"

She sighed and put her hand on his. "Gavin, Sean is a bright little boy. Let her judge how to approach this topic."

His gaze slid to the framed black-and-white photos on the wall. His grandpa in a cabby station surrounded by men in suspenders and hats, Grandpa shaking hands with the mayor, Grandpa accepting an award of service, his grandparents in their wedding outfits and smiling into the sun.

"I wish he was here to tell us what to do." He wanted to be strong, competent. But he missed the man who had held their family together. His parents were distant at the best of times. Now that they lived a few states away, enjoying retirement, he hardly ever heard from them.

Grandma Lili regarded him, her hand under her chin. "Gavin, he never told anybody what to do. He would say his piece then you had to make your own decisions. You've always been so driven, ready to take on the world. I love that. But sometimes I wish you would remember that other people want to take care of you, too. Allison didn't move here just because she needed us. She knows we need to be near her and Sean, too."

He wondered what Evie would think of Allison's "history." A typical journalist would jump at the chance of revealing such a big secret. Juicy gossip like that would sure sell a lot of papers. But she wasn't that type. He had the feeling she wouldn't be publishing that kind of story in *The Chronicle*. It might be the golden cow for a gossip rag, but she'd made it clear that those kinds of stories were repugnant to her.

"But it's more than that, isn't it?" Grandma Lili's voice was soft, but her hand was softer as she laid it on her grandson's arm.

He met her eyes and sighed. "There's this girl. I mean, woman." Heat flooded his face. "It's nothing important, I just—"

The rest of his sentence was lost as she started to laugh, one hand over her mouth, eyes crinkled in mirth. "No, go on. Sorry."

But he could tell she wasn't sorry, in fact was enjoying every moment of his embarrassment. "I thought you promised to listen."

"No, that was when you were talking work trouble. But woman trouble, all bets are off. Sweetie, if I've seen that look once, I've seen it a hundred times."

Gavin frowned. He didn't want to know what look she meant. He sucked in a breath. "When I'm with her, everything seems possible. I feel like we can tackle all the problems of the world and win. My mouth starts running without my brain being engaged. Suddenly, I'm inviting her to a ski date when I should be holed up on the fifth floor with the lab guys."

He studied his plate. "When she's not around, I wonder what she's up to. I worry about her advertisers, her workload. My phone rings and I hope she's calling me, even though there's no reason for her to call me. It snows and I hope she's driving safely." He rubbed his forehead. "I hate her car. It's completely unsafe. It doesn't even have airbags."

Grandma Lili was silent, listening.

"I can't help thinking that if the epidemic gets worse, and my office is blamed, she won't want to be anywhere near the fallout."

"She wouldn't be the girl for you if she walked away because of that."

"And then there's Allison."

His grandmother's gaze was steel, her lips a thin line. "Gavin, her past is her own. She's made peace with God. So it's not anybody else's business. If this girl is scared away by someone else's mistakes, then she's all wrong for you."

Grandma Lili didn't understand, but he couldn't figure out how to explain. He was worried about what Evie might think, rather than about people who were desperately ill, and it made him crazy.

"It's not a big deal. We've never even been on a date." He smiled ruefully.

"Can you invite her to church tomorrow? I want to see this girl who makes my big, strong grandson lose sleep."

"I don't know if that's such a good idea."

"She doesn't go to church?" Her expression took on a hint of caution.

"No, no, she does. I think she even goes to St. James, at a later service. But you and all your friends might be a bit much."

"You're not painting a very attractive picture. She can't handle trouble with your job. She can't handle Allison or any family problems and can't go to church with a group of harmless old ladies?" She ticked them off one by one, daring him to disagree.

"I know what you're doing."

Her eyes opened wide, innocence written large over her face. "If she's really worth your time, it won't be a problem. Call her. It's not so late."

Gavin paused, wondering. They had just seen each other that morning. Would it be too much? He reached for his phone, heart speeding up against his will. "If this goes badly, I'm blaming you."

"I'm okay with that." Grandma Lili winked and then took the bowl of salad to the kitchen so he could dial in peace.

Evie was parked in front of her apartment building, watching the snow drift down through the orange glow of the street lights. The glass-fronted condos were brightly lit, figures moving behind thin curtains. She didn't know if she quite considered this her home, but no place else had felt right, either. Maybe she was doomed to exist in a sort of limbo, happy at work and filled with emptiness at home. Jack said she was over-compensating by working all the time but whenever she stopped to enjoy herself, the memories came flooding back. Evie laid her head on the steering wheel, closing her eyes. Allison might have been the girl she'd photo-graphed; it was hard to say. She could go search Google for some images and try to tell for sure.

Or she could ask her. The thought made her heart sink in her chest.

Her cell phone trilled and she jumped. *Gavin.* Evie stared at the display, fingers trembling, struggling to get it open. "Hello?" Her voice cracked on the last syllable.

There was a pause, and a terribly familiar voice sounded in her ear. "Are you all right?"

Was she? There wasn't any good answer to that.

"Evie? It's Gavin. You sound upset."

She cleared her throat. "No, sorry. I'm just sur-prised." She tried to force her face into a smile, know-ing it could be heard in her voice.

There was another pause. "This is probably a bad time. But I was at my grandmother's and she was won-dering if you'd like to come with us to the early ser-vice tomorrow."

Evie shook her head to clear it. She'd been wrapped up in memories of hiding in bushes and bribing lowlifes for information. She struggled back to the world where kind, handsome disease specialists called about church with their grandmothers. "I'd love that. There's no way to pry Jack out of bed at that hour, but I'll be there."

"Would you like me to pick you up?"

For just a moment, Evie clutched the phone tighter. She wanted him to come here, right now, and tell her everything was going to be okay. She wanted to explain how she used to be someone very different but had grabbed on to the promise of grace. She wanted him to say that everyone made mistakes and she was only human.

"Evie?" She loved the way his voice sounded in her ear, so close.

"I'll meet you there. And Gavin?"

"Yes?"

She didn't know how to say any of what was rocketing around inside her head. "Thanks for inviting me."

"Better wait until after you get grilled by the Granny Group." But she could hear the smile in his voice before he disconnected.

Evie was still clutching the phone when it rang against her ear. She fumbled to answer it, wondering what Gavin had forgotten to say. Maybe he'd already changed his mind.

"Did you get home okay?" Jack's tone was a bit accusatory. She always gave him a quick text when she hit the door.

"Sorry." She gave the shorthand version of Gavin's invitation.

"Church date? I didn't think that was legal. Nobody pays attention to the sermon."

"His grandmother suggested it."

"And so it begins."

Her stomach dropped. "Disaster?"

"Nope. I was thinking that he must be serious if he's talking about you to his grandmother."

"Maybe they were just talking about—"

"Pertussis articles? The Mission budget? And then she said he should ask you to church because that's the logical next step."

"Well, when you say it like that, it sounds weird." So, that made two family members who knew about her. A warmth spread in her chest. She wanted to be someone important in his life, not just as an editor. "It's just church. It's not like they're going to march us to the altar."

"Your choice. But like I said, so it begins. Sleep well. Call me tomorrow after your church date."

"Stop calling it that."

She snapped the phone closed on his laughter and Evie rested her forehead on her palms and prayed, long and hard. *Please help me know Your will for us.* Because nothing else should really matter, especially not the feelings that had taken root in her heart and were threatening to push out any other concerns.

Evie took a deep, calming breath. She had plans, projects and a mission of her own. She didn't want to lose sight of it. But when she was around Gavin her world seemed to shrink until it just included the two of them. How could she be sure that she wasn't falling into that old trap, of thinking she knew best, no matter what God was telling her?

Adjusting his tie reflexively, Gavin hovered near the large double doors. Why did he ever think this was a good idea? Oh, right. It was Grandma Lili who thought it would be nice to sit through a service with

Evie. Knowing how he could hardly get through a conversation with all his brain intact, he just couldn't see how he was going to focus on what Rev. Bright had to say today, especially if she sat beside him. Memories of the budget meeting flooded back. Every brush of her elbow made him lose his train of thought. Maybe he could get her to sit on Grandma's other side.

No, then she'd be grilled mercilessly. Better he should sit between them. He yanked at his tie again, feeling less like going to church than he had in his life.

"Am I late?" Somehow she'd snuck up on him, and her cheery voice made him whirl around.

"Not at all. Just getting some air." He glanced down at her, trying not to stare. A long, black skirt, dressy leather boots, gray wool coat, familiar blue mittens, dark hair sleek and shiny. She was so beautiful. No, that wasn't it. She was vibrant. Her eyes were clear and bright, cheeks flushed. She looked so *alive*.

Evie checked her watch. "We should go in before there's no place to sit." Then she grinned. "Never mind. We're at the early bird service. No fighting for pew space. That will be perk number one."

His heart lifted. *Perk number one,* as if there were more. This wouldn't be hard at all. Just two people going to church, not a big deal. "Let's head on in before my grandmother sends out a search party." He opened the door and followed her in, breathing in the familiar smell of the sanctuary space. It was a peaceful place, filled with good memories, and the gleaming pews beckoned to him. There wasn't room for confusion and anxiety here, and suddenly, being with Evie seemed to fit right in.

He touched her elbow and whispered, "She's up in

the front, wearing light blue. Says she has trouble hearing. I think she just likes to sit behind that big family with all the little kids. Usually gets passed a baby by the middle of the service."

Evie nodded and headed up the aisle.

He guessed he shouldn't have worried about the seating because Evie had no problem entering the pew, introducing herself to his grandmother in a soft voice and reaching for a hymnal. A strange feeling of contentment spread through him as soon as the bells stopped ringing and the choir started the first hymn. He peeked over at Grandma Lili, who was singing gustily.

Not hard, nothing to it. He shouldn't have worried. Grandma caught him looking and gave an enormous wink.

Of course, he should probably reserve judgment until after the service. That's when the real test of Grandma's restraint would be. Would she ask Evie a million questions or would she give the poor girl a break? And although Evie seemed shy at first, he suspected she was just observing before speaking, taking the temperature of the room before diving into the conversation.

He peeked at the two of them sharing a hymnal. Grandma Lili's gray head was bent near to Evie's dark one, their voices blending sweetly. Looks could be deceiving, especially with his grandmother. Would they get along, or would he be calling in the National Guard?

He couldn't even guess; it was a toss-up.

"Have another doughnut, dear." Grandma Lili pushed a maple frosting coated twist toward Evie and smiled, brown eyes crinkling. The church hall was echoing with chatter and sounds of coffee mugs being filled.

"I can't. One doughnut a day, that's my rule." Evie said it with a straight face and was rewarded with a chuckle. The little old lady was a lot more relaxed than she'd been expecting. But then again, the real conversation had just started.

Gavin looked from one to the other, a bemused expression on his face. He hadn't said much, but she had loved having him beside her during the service. Jack always tended to fidget about halfway through and Evie struggled to ignore his tapping foot or murmured comments. Gavin's presence was strong and steady, as comfortable as if he lived there. There was a peace about him that was contagious.

"Just like Allison, always on a diet. You're not plump. Just have a half."

Evie shook her head. "That's a slippery slope. A few months from now the fire crew would be cutting me out of my house. My twin brother, Jack, he can eat anything, but that's probably the male gene acting up. The universe is grossly unfair."

"In my day, men liked a little meat on their women. But nowadays, all I see are collarbones and knobby knees. I just can't see the attraction. What is there to hold on to?"

Gavin coughed, startled. "Grandma, please. We just got out of church."

"And your point is? You think church people don't fall in love? Who made all these fine folks here? Men and women just like you two." She waved a hand in Gavin's direction. His face was turning pink around the cheekbones and Evie was struggling not to laugh.

"There's no reason to skirt around the issue. It's as old as time itself. Now, your grandfather always told me he wished we'd met a few years earlier. By the time we got married, he was already working fourteen-hour days and—"

"Grandma, please." Gavin had one hand to his forehead, as if to shield his eyes from the light. Evie could see his face turning pinker by the moment.

"I see your point, Mrs. Sawyer." She hurried to join the conversation, wondering if Gavin was going to give his grandmother an earful later. Or maybe she talked like this all the time. Evie's parents hardly seemed to exist on the same planet as their own children, let alone hand out tips on marital happiness.

"Do you? Gavin tells me you run your own paper. Aren't you a little young for that?"

"I bought it from the bank when it was bankrupt."

Grandma Lili tilted her head. "I love a good sale. Smart girl. But why don't you just hire someone else to be the editor? Hal Golden owns *The Daily* and he hardly steps foot in the place, from what I hear. He just collects the profits and lets someone else do the dirty work."

Evie glanced down at her plate, dabs of maple frosting the only remnants of her breakfast. The dirty work, that's exactly what went on over at *The Daily*. She hadn't been any better, but she was different now. "I prefer to be in charge of the content, too. If I didn't own the paper, I might have to print a story I didn't think was good for the community. If I hired someone else to be the editor, we'd have to have a rock-solid friendship and a lot of trust. I haven't found that yet." She paused. "And I enjoy what I do."

"That must take an awful lot of time." Grandma Lili narrowed her eyes, hands still wrapped around her mug, blue veins visible through her fragile skin.

Evie nodded. "My office gets busy, but I have a great crew. Most of them came with the paper." She paused, glancing at Gavin, who looked like he was in pain. "I've seen what happens when work is everything and the family comes last. It's not the way I want to live."

"So, you're not one of those women who think they can have it all? That you can run a big business and raise kids and have a happy marriage and a perfect house without dropping a single ball?"

Evie blinked, surprised. Of all the conversations she thought they'd have, this wasn't one of them. It ranked right below "How to make your husband happy."

"Nobody can have it all. Everyone has to make priorities. But I also think that with all the technology, the old roles of work and home are more fluid. I have two employees who work flexible hours from home."

His grandma nodded, approving. "Nice of you to let the moms stay with their kids more."

"Actually, one is a man who runs a pottery business and needs the daytime hours for teaching classes, but it works for moms, too. I just believe that you can't have two separate items in the number one spot. I'd prefer my employees to feel fulfilled, happy. Which means family usually gets the top spot, work comes next." Evie wasn't trying to be difficult, but a serious question got complicated answers

"Anything else, Grandma?" He dropped his head toward hers and pretended to whisper. "She promised she wouldn't interrogate you."

She patted her gray hair with one hand and lifted

her chin. "I'm not interrogating, as you call it. I've got to find some good spouses for you and Allison. But you wouldn't believe the things I've heard from my friends. Angela DiLindo, down there on the end, with the blue scarf? Her daughter got divorced for the third time. Want to know why?"

Evie glanced at Gavin and felt her lips tug up at the sight of his expression.

"The man didn't want to live in a place where it snowed for months at a time." She looked from one to another, brow arched. "I mean, honestly. They didn't talk about the snow? He hated winter so much and she never knew?"

Gavin made a noise in his throat. "Is it possible to marry somebody and not know what season they like the best?"

She chuckled, but her eyes were sad. "Oh, dearie, I think it's very possible. There are so many other things competing for attention. Looks, money, status. Then after a few years you get a good look at the person and realize you didn't know them at all."

Grandma Lili lifted her mug and took a long sip. "But that's my lecture for the day. I'm headed over to Mrs. Werlin's table there. She's always got the news of the week. Better than your paper, Evie. You should hire her to dish the dirt." She patted his hand and grinned. "You two go have some fun. Get to know each other. And it was lovely to meet you, Evie."

"Thank you. I'm glad I came. But won't you be needing a ride?"

"I drove myself. I'm only eighty-two." And with that parting shot, she stood and waved them goodbye on her way toward a table packed with chattering old ladies. A few old men had staked out their own table and were busy arguing over something that needed a lot of hand gestures.

There was a short silence and Evie snuck Gavin a glance. He probably was waiting for the right moment to set her straight. Poor man, practically married off without saying a word. And every time Lili had mentioned Allison, Evie's conscience had twinged in response.

"Do you want to take a walk? There's a beautiful trail behind the church that comes out near the old sledding hill. Probably lots of boarders out there today. We can count the nose grabs."

"The what?"

"The ones who catch air and grab the end of the board." He was already standing, clearing their coffee mugs.

"Sure, let's go walk off these doughnuts." Evie stood, grabbing her coat. He obviously wanted to wait until they were alone to put in his objections. She'd make it easy on him, try to start the conversation first. But something deep inside warmed at the memory of Grandma Lili and her advice. She was missing that kind of solid strength, yearned for it. If only there was a way to share her. Some people had all the luck.

## Chapter Ten

Gavin felt the snow crunch under his boots in a satisfying way. Evie walked beside him, eyes focused on the footpath that wound through tall pine trees toward Ruby Hill. He shot a glance in her direction. Her hood was down, but her face was unreadable, her mouth set in a soft smile. He sighed. She was probably thinking what a crazy conversation that had been, but Grandma Lili was wiser than all the people he knew put together. Add that to her unshakable faith and he wouldn't trade her for anyone.

"Listen, I know that was awkward, but she didn't mean any harm."

Evie said nothing, just smiled in his direction. The sound of their boots echoed in the cold air. He could hear the faraway sounds of children testing the brand-new snow on the hill.

"You're probably thinking she's a nutty old lady."

She stopped and stood blinking up at him. The mid-morning sun peeked through the clouds, and her eyes glowed bright blue. "Is that what you think? That I see your grandmother as nutty?"

Gavin frowned, trying to recapture his train of thought. If only she wasn't so pretty, wasn't standing so close. "She had a great marriage, even though they were very different people, and can't see why the divorce rate is so high." He spread his hands, looking out across the snowy trail toward the trees. "She's not a cranky old person wanting to make everyone miserable. She's—"

"Protective." Evie laughed, a sound so light and warm that it felt like waves against his heart. She reached out a mitten and touched his arm. "Gavin, I think she's wonderful. Truly."

He said nothing, wondering how he could feel the heat of her hand through her glove and his coat, then realizing it was his own reaction to her touch.

"I'm not sure what your parents are like, but mine aren't very protective." She dropped her hand and he immediately wished she hadn't. "They give lots of advice, but not about happy marriages, or learning to balance life and work, or even how to attract a man." Her lips curled a bit at the last sentence, as if she really didn't want that kind of help. "It's all about making good impressions on people in power, how to become wealthy, how to acquire things."

He nodded, knowing exactly what she meant. "Perhaps our parents are similar that way."

"So please don't apologize for your beautiful grandmother. I'm jealous of you and Allison. Maybe she'll adopt me if I ask her very nicely." Her dimples were like deep indents in each cheek. He wanted to respond, but all he could think was how Evie seemed to fit into every part of his life. From her passion for social justice, to the Mission meetings, to her dedication to making her employees happy, to sitting in church today with his grandmother. He felt like she got it. She understood. She was real.

Almost against his will, he took a step forward. He watched those sky-blue eyes widen, dark lashes framing them perfectly. If there was anything he could say, he would try to form words, but all he could think of was how much he wanted to brush a kiss over her soft mouth. His gaze dropped to her lips. He waited, wondering if she would put up a hand, warn him off. But she stood motionless.

He didn't remember taking the last step, but somehow they were very close, his arm gently wrapped around her waist. She smelled wonderful, like apples and cinnamon. Her head tilted up, thick dark hair falling back from her face, and she met his eyes. He saw yearning, hope, wild happiness, and at the last moment before he leaned toward her, there was something else, as if she had suddenly remembered where they were. She still didn't move back but returned his kiss without a second's hesitation.

She fit in his arms like she'd been born to be there, felt righter than any other woman ever had. How many times had he said he would wait until things were calmer, less hectic, less chaotic, before getting any closer to her? But like everything else with Evie, his plans meant nothing. The only thing that mattered, that existed in the universe, was her soft mouth and the splay of her fingers against his chest.

After a few moments he forced himself to break away, wishing they could stand there forever but knowing real life was just around the corner. Or the trail bend, as it were. He felt crazy, kissing her behind the church on a snowy day, like teenagers hiding from their chaperone.

"Um, that was not planned. I don't want you to think I lured you out here with an ulterior motive."

"Well, now I'm disappointed. I was hoping this was your plan all along. If I'm just a spur-of-the-moment smooch, then maybe I'll take it back." Her voice was husky.

He felt his brows rise. "Yes, please, do take it back. I don't deserve it one bit."

Evie's eyes were bright with laughter and she stood on tiptoes, gaze slipping to his mouth. His heart hammered in his chest as she drew near, reminding him of so many moments he'd wished they'd been this close. Then at the last moment, she drew back, eyes shadowed.

"Gavin." She spoke his name so softly he wondered if he'd imagined it. "I should tell you something about my past. I meant to tell you before now."

"Wait." He paused, searching for words. "Despite Grandma Lili behind me, I've still made some spectacularly bad choices. We all make mistakes. And we all ask forgiveness. Christ always makes a way for us to change, keep working toward something better. If you want, later, we can sit down and write each other a list. But…" he waved his hand around the pine-shaded trail, the bright white of the snow drifts, the distant sound of kids sledding "…just for today, let's enjoy this."

She smiled, as if coming to a decision. Evie looked up at the trees, her whole posture relaxing. She was almost happy now, as if a burden had slipped from her shoulders.

There was no sound except a slight breeze in the

treetops and the distant noise of kids playing. Evie's hand touched his arm. "What is past is prologue." And she smiled up at him, as if that made all the sense in the world.

Gavin raised his eyebrows.

"It's from *The Tempest*. Not a great scene, sort of depressing. But what I meant is that everything in our past prepares us for our future." She took a breath and let out it out slowly.

Gavin searched her face, trying to decide what else she was trying to say. Or not say.

"When someone shares a failing from his past, it doesn't make me think any less of him. I figure they're moving forward and that's what is most important."

Those were the words he had waited to hear. He had lost sleep, wrestled with his own conscience and argued with God. Evie could be trusted with Allison's secret, when Allison was ready to share it.

"I agree. Because we're all a work in progress, as long as we don't give up." His toes were getting numb from standing still in the cold. He took her mittened hand and turned back toward the sledding hill. "Let's keep walking before we freeze to death."

She strode along beside him, matching his steps, her fingers tight in his. "Back there, when we were…"

He shot her a glance, lips curving up. "We were what? I'm not sure I remember exactly. You should describe it. Or better yet, show me." He loved the pink of her cheeks, the frown that battled with her shy smile.

"Not a chance. Too many impressionable children around. Plus, I'd never remember what I was going to say the third time around." She paused as they came out on the trail head and Ruby Hill stretched in front of them, dotted with sledders and snowboarders. An orange plastic barrier delineated the ski area from the off-limits woods. Bright snowsuits and ski jackets flashed by, and it seemed hundreds of children yelled for someone to pull them back up the long, sloping hill.

He turned to look at her, but she was staring intently at the activity. He wasn't sure if she was choosing her words or was distracted. The next moment, she turned to him, a bright smile creasing her face.

"Never mind. You're right. Let's just enjoy the day." She slipped her arm through his and he felt a warmth expand in his chest, as if the sun were shining just for him.

There would be time for all those conversations, the kind that dug deep and exposed painful pasts. But for right now, he hugged her to his side and said a silent prayer of thanks. Whatever Evie had to say couldn't be anything close to what his family had been through in the past five years.

## Chapter Eleven

"Look who's Little Miss Sunshine." Jack slouched in the chair across from Evie's, one foot propped on the rung of the chair next to him. The Mission conference room was chilly and smelled of stale coffee. The finance meeting was going to be the shortest on record if Nancy didn't show up. Gavin was busy and Grant was stuck in another meeting.

Evie felt her cheeks warm. Gavin's kiss had been replaying in her mind all day. It was enough to make her want to swing her arms out wide and belt something from *The Sound of Music*. "And why not? It's a wonderful Thursday, Christmas is almost here, no advertisers have left us for *The Daily,* and the lawyers haven't shot down a single story."

"There's always tomorrow." Jack's usual contented attitude had taken a leave of absence.

"Why are you in such a foul mood? Did they close the ski season early?" Evie softened her words with a smile. She'd be in a terrible mood, too, if she was employed in name only.

"Dunno. Just thinking." He picked at an invisible

thread on his suit jacket. "I was always the fearless one and you were the responsible one. Now I feel like I'm stuck in an endless loop of meetings and you're branching out."

"Branching out? Like joining this finance board? That's hardly exciting."

"You seem so happy, so ready to take on the world." He cocked an eyebrow. "Maybe it's Gavin."

She wanted to hush him but knew Gavin wouldn't be coming tonight. The lab was completely overrun with work. Evie rolled her eyes, aiming for scorn but ending up somewhere near startled. Jack had said the name of the man who had taken up permanent residence in her daydreams after Sunday.

"Since you met him, you seem different. Less fearful." As she opened her mouth to argue, he raised a hand. "I'm not saying you used to creep around like a scared bunny. But you seemed to think that God was waiting to smite you down if you messed up."

"I thought being afraid of doing the wrong thing was what happened when you grew up." Did Jack think she wasn't as committed to making the right choice just because she was growing closer to Gavin? Cold fear rose in her chest and she struggled to hear his words.

"You know that verse about perfect love casting out all fear?"

"But I'm not in love with Gavin." At least, she didn't think so. Definitely in like. A lot of like.

His lips tugged up. "Not Gavin. God."

Evie blinked and then sat back in her chair, eyes on the ceiling. Jack was the deep thinker, the dreamer, the free spirit. She was the bottom-line girl, the one who made sure all the papers were signed and wor-

ried whether the insurance was current. Twins, but
sometimes as different as night and day. Right now
she felt like following this conversation was like trying to swallow an elephant.

"Somehow, I'm not sure exactly, they're connected."
Jack nodded to himself, as if he made perfect sense.

She thought of their little games, their teasing. But
Gavin's lightheartedness never felt like it came at the
expense of what really mattered. He was strong and
steady, sheltering, protecting. "When I saw him on
Sunday, he said some things about grace that made a
lot of sense to me."

She glanced up, hating to admit she was wrong.
"Maybe you were a little bit right on the overcompensation. Maybe I'm trying too hard to earn forgiveness
instead of just accepting my second chance. Christ
gives it as a gift, and I've been treating it like it was
bartered for my perfect behavior ever since the moment
I..." She wasn't sure what the end of the sentence was.

"Hit bottom?"

"Yup. Maybe there was some fear that God was
going to get revenge, that I'd better not do anything
wrong or it would be on the front page." She shrugged,
feeling the old fear slide around in her chest.

"He doesn't work that way, thankfully." Jack's lips
quirked up just a smidge.

Evie twiddled her pen, thinking. God wasn't one to
hold a grudge. Forgive and forget actually happened
when you said you were sorry for making a mess out
of your life. That was perfect love. And her job was to
grab that grace with both hands and move forward. She
was changed, different, but there was so much more to
do. Not out of fear, but out of *hope*.

"I lost you for a second, there."

Evie shook her head. "Just remembering something I have to do. Will you be free tomorrow? I need some help moving furniture into my apartment."

"Sure. But you'll owe me."

"No problem. You want me to cook you dinner?"

"No. I can't be there to help the soccer team this week. I told Gavin you'd fill in as assistant coach. You've been cleared through all the background checks, so you can hang out with the kids at the Mission. Jose said he'd rather not. Something about winter colds and germs and preferring to chew broken glass."

"I don't know anything about soccer." Evie hated the tone of panic in her voice.

"It's not a date. You kick the soccer ball to the kids. Just don't dress up. It's hot in there, gets real sweaty." Jack got to his feet, smoothing his tie. Evie couldn't help noticing how he'd inherited all the good genes. He was tall and lean and could eat like a horse. Perfect smile, athletic grace and an extrovert to a fault. She'd hate him if he wasn't such a good guy.

"I'm going to go see if Nancy left a message at the desk." He was already pulling the door shut behind him, grin flashing one more time through the crack.

She groaned. Just perfect. Sweaty, dress-down time in a gym with grade-schoolers…and Gavin. That's a nice way to erase the memory of that kiss. At least he wouldn't be tempted to try for a repeat.

Evie struggled to focus on the papers in front of her. Every few seconds her mind drifted back to that trail behind the church. She had melted into the kiss without thinking it through. All her plans for setting things straight between them had drifted into the mist when his gaze had rested on her mouth. She'd known, in that moment, what it felt like for her heart to make decisions for her head.

Gavin was something completely unexpected, and for once she wasn't scared out of her wits about facing the unknown. She was determined: no more slips of the heart until she managed to set everything straight between them. And that included letting him in on her ugly past.

"You're early for soccer practice."

Gavin turned away from the large plate-glass window, searching for the friendly voice. He adjusted his gaze downward. Some part of him was always a bit surprised to see Lana was in a wheelchair. She projected fierce capability. The purple-tipped crew cut didn't exactly scream "softy," either.

"There are worse places to waste a little time."

"True, but you don't really seem the time-wasting type."

Gavin wanted to laugh. Lana was sharp, observant. Jack had left a message that Evie would be subbing for him today. It wouldn't be anything close to romantic, but maybe their next date would be Echo Mountain. Playing in the snow. Hot chocolate. Maybe a little more of what happened on the trail.

"I need some tea. Would you like me to make you some?" Lana turned back toward the desk.

"No, thanks. I never pegged you for a tea drinker."

"I can't seem to get warm today. I think Grant must be fiddling with the temperature. I know he wants to cut costs, but I feel like an icicle."

"Hi, Lana. Hey, Gavin." Calista stepped through

the front doors, her pea coat unbuttoned over a still-rounded belly, a dusting of snow on her blond hair. She was holding a plate of what smelled like fresh cookies. Her green eyes were tired, but her smile was pure light.

"Hi, Calista." Lana reversed herself and accepted a quick hug. "And cookies. You're my favorite boss's wife, you know that?"

"Silly. I better be the only boss's wife around here."

"Let me peek at the little guy." Lana craned her neck and Calista carefully unwrapped the bulge around her middle.

Gavin felt his eyebrows rise. "I forgot you've got that baby smuggler. Bet it's great to keep both hands free."

"Swaddler, not smuggler. But I sort of like the way you say it." Calista flashed him a smile. She seemed so joyful, it made him happy just to see her. "True that it keeps my arms from getting tired, but mostly I like having him close to my heart. Nine months of him tucked right under it, now he feels so far away when he's in the next room."

Gavin thought of the little babies he'd seen in the NICU that morning. The swaddler was actually a good idea. It kept people from getting too close, from touching the baby's face.

"He's so tiny," Lana said, voice soft with awe.

"Getting bigger by the day. He's gained two pounds now. Officially bigger than a bread box." They all stood admiring the baby for a moment.

"Speaking of the boss, is my handsome husband slaving away in the back?"

Lana frowned. "I think he might be walking around near the classrooms. But go ahead on back and I'll send someone over to tell him you're here."

"Let Marisol know we're back here. She'll want her baby fix for the day. And tell Grant if he makes it down here right away, maybe there'll be a cookie left for him." She headed toward the office door and punched in a code. "Maybe." She threw the word over her shoulder with one last smile.

"Oh, boy. The tea has to wait. I better get someone to tell Grant she's here." Lana started toward the long wooden desk.

"Does he mind her visiting?" Gavin knew she was the VitaWow CEO and had heard rumors of her ability to broker deals no one else could. But they always seemed so happy to just be around each other.

Lana laughed up at him, pausing with her hands on the wheels. "Oh, not at all. But I think he's over in the preschool area and they're finger painting today. She gets a little crazy with the kids. Lets them run right over her. Or maybe joins in the fun, I'm not sure. Anyway—" she started back around the desk "—we try to keep Calista occupied in other areas. May the Lord help them when that baby gets up and running."

Gavin turned back toward the window, wondering how Evie would handle kids. When they'd been with Sean at the park, she'd seemed to really like him. Tonight they'd be dealing with forty grade-school kids and a whole lot of soccer balls. He frowned at the snowy street outside. Grandma Lili was afraid no one really got to know each other anymore, just jumped into marriage like it hardly mattered. But he knew Evie. She was so straightforward, clear, upfront. They both weren't the type of person to throw away a marriage over something silly like snow.

He blinked at his own reflection. Did he really just

put marriage and Evie in the same sentence? Gavin rubbed a hand over his face. Was it her, or was he getting to the age where he'd rather have a family than spend Saturdays snowboarding? He let that sink in for a second and realized it was her, Evie. Saturdays should be spent up in the bright sunlight and clear pine-scented air, freeriding down the mountain on fresh snow. The picture seemed to be expanding to include Evie, when it had been just him before. Even better if there was a family in there somewhere, too.

It was a relief he hadn't reached middle age overnight and was just looking for any available woman. It wasn't so reassuring to realize this one particular woman had him thinking years into the future.

Evie's light blue VW bug pulled up at the corner and crossed the street to the Mission parking lot. Gavin felt a smile spread over his face for no particular reason. He felt goofy with anticipation. And realized he'd look pretty odd standing at the window, waiting for her to come in. He turned and headed toward the gym, shucking his coat as he went.

"Don't forget the key to the athletic equipment room," Lana called after him, waving a key in one hand.

Gavin reversed his trajectory and snagged the key. "Thanks. Just going to get the balls and jerseys out."

The gym still smelled like lunch, and if he wasn't mistaken, there was chili cooking for dinner. Marisol could cook anything, but her specialty was the comfort foods of winter. His stomach gave a rumble and he thought of the breakfast burrito he'd had hours ago. It was going to be hard to concentrate with all those delicious smells coming from the kitchen.

The day had been packed with hospital visits and lab visits, and the rest of the evening would be more of the same. But he'd made a commitment to these kids and he would try to keep his promises as long as he could. At the rate this epidemic was going, he was going to have to start sleeping at the office to save time on the commute.

As Evie opened the cafeteria door and walked inside, his heart reminded him that missing lunch and needing dinner were going to be the very least of his distractions this afternoon.

Hair up in a ponytail and exercise gear, check. Lip gloss and running shoes, check. Ready to face Gavin, not even a little.

Evie blew out a breath and pasted a bright smile to her face. She hoped she looked cheery, kid-friendly and physically fit. She could probably pull them all off except the first one.

He was dressed in the usual T-shirt that fit snugly around his biceps, shorts, running shoes. She tried not to give him the once-over but could hardly help herself. He'd been at the front of the line when God handed out good looks.

"How's your day been?" He asked the question over his shoulder, putting the key into a small door near the kitchen entrance.

"Oh, you know." Her smile was in place even though her heart was disagreeing.

He turned, key in hand, door hanging open. His brows came down. "That doesn't sound good."

She waved a hand. "It's not a big deal. I'm ready to help." She tried to look enthusiastic.

Now his eyebrows had gone up several inches. He leaned a shoulder against the wall, perfectly at ease. "That bad, huh?"

Evie held her bright smile for a few seconds more and then let it fall away. "Well, yes, actually. Our story on the slave labor ring keeps getting shut down because our sources can't be verified beyond what the attorneys need to keep the paper out of trouble. Meanwhile we know there are people trapped in this city, working for nothing and probably much worse. Then a major advertiser threatened to pull out and head for *The Daily* because we don't print enough reality TV stories and the style section is only four pages. Everybody is reading the news on the internet. Nobody wants to pay for a paper anymore."

Her shoulders slumped. And the worst moment, just hours before, appeared when she'd grabbed her courage with both hands and searched online for Senator McHale so she could peer at those old grainy photos of a blonde club singer leaving the presidential candidate's hotel room. Photos she had taken, of a girl who looked a lot like Allison. She'd been a totally different person then, someone she would hate now, if she met her old self. And maybe he would, too, when he knew. Especially now that she was sure she was at fault for what happened to his sister, it would be impossible for her to just leave the past in the past.

He said nothing but held out his arms and their eyes met. Evie wanted to walk into them but didn't know if she dared. Another second passed and she moved without thinking, drawn by an unrelenting need to be held. Maybe it was wrong to let him comfort her when she might have shattered his family. Evie couldn't think, couldn't process all the different emotions that threatened to pull her down into chaos.

All she knew was how it felt wrapped in his arms. Bliss. She laid her head against his chest and took a deep breath. She could hear his heart beating steadily, his breathing slow and even. He smelled wonderful, freshly showered and shaved. She felt the pressure of his cheek against her head and could have stayed there forever. She wanted to catalogue and file away everything about him; his smell, his laugh, his warmth. Her heart was all wrapped up in that smile. Those warm brown eyes seemed to see her better than anyone else.

The sound of a throat clearing brought her back to reality. Jose was standing there, fighting a huge smile.

Evie backed out of Gavin's arms, feeling her face flame hot. It was silly. Just a hug. Maybe it was the cafeteria and the smell of chili wafting from the kitchen, but she felt like a high-school kid caught by the principal.

"Sorry to interrupt. Marisol wants to know if you two can help her set the tables out when practice is over. She's short in the kitchen today."

"Sure, I can help."

"Me, too." Gavin turned to the equipment room and started to haul netted bags of soccer balls out to the floor. She wondered if he was as embarrassed as she was.

Jose gave her a smile and wandered toward the kitchen. "I'll let Marisol know."

"I didn't ask how your day was." Evie grabbed some colored cones and brought them to the side line, trying to act businesslike.

"Do I get a hug if it was really bad?" Gavin's voice came muffled from the closet.

She inhaled deeply at the thought. "Sure. Maybe two." She wanted to roll her eyes at herself. It was so easy to flirt with him, it was hard to resist.

He emerged with another bag of soccer balls and whistles on cords. "There were three more confirmed cases of pertussis. The politicians have decided we're not working hard enough on the public opinion front."

"A two-page spread in the Sunday edition isn't enough?" For a moment she was thankful she was her own boss. She never had to deal with impossible expectations from a supervisor.

"Apparently not. And even worse, I didn't get any lunch."

"No lunch?" A voice behind them held tones of disbelief. Marisol was coming from the kitchen, wiping her hands on her apron. Her dark eyes were narrowed in alarm. "You can't play with no lunch. You go get some chili before the kids come. Hurry!" She placed her hands on her hips and waited.

Evie wanted to laugh but thought it was better to get out of the way. Gavin nodded, heading for the kitchen. "Thanks, Marisol."

"Tell Mandie to serve you both," Marisol called out on her way to the office area.

Gavin slowed down until they were walking side by side. He leaned over and whispered, "Whew. I thought you were going to resist for a moment."

"Not on your life. I'm hungry and she's scary, in a good way. Never mess with the cook."

Mandie met them at the serving line and handed

them both trays with a bowl of steaming chili. Corn-bread and carrot sticks were on a plate to the side.

"Do we really have time for this?" Evie checked her watch. Fifteen minutes before the kids showed up.

"Plenty of time. Just watch me." Gavin waved her to a small table behind the serving area and they sat, awkwardly placing trays at an angle.

Evie took a bite of the chili and almost rolled her eyes in delight. "Oh, man," she murmured. "This is delicious."

"Mmm-hmm," Gavin agreed.

After a few minutes of silence, he shot her a glance. "Remember when I said dinner dates were always ter-rible because you spend all your energy trying not to spill anything on yourself and make a bad impression? I think this breaks that rule."

"Is this a dinner date?"

"Well, we're eating dinner. And we're…"

Dating. That was the word he was going to use, Evie was sure of it. She felt her face grow warm. Their gazes held.

"Coach Sawyer?" Someone small was calling in the gym. "Coach? Are you back here?" A dark-haired boy came around the corner. His T-shirt hung on his shoulders like a tent, and his shoes were more than a few months past their replacement date.

"Hey, Harrison. Let me take my tray back to the kitchen and you can help me get everything set up." Gavin shot Evie a wink and stood up. She was sur-prised to see his bowl was clean.

Evie hurried to finish her cornbread and took a gulp of milk. She really needed to focus. As soon as he was out of view, or out of range, whatever it was, she felt like she could think more clearly. Was she pretending to be something she wasn't? You can't go back and change the past; sometimes you can't fix what's been broken. Before anything else happened, she needed to talk about the way she'd made enough money to buy her paper.

How could he possibly get past the fact that her whole life was funded by the fact she'd sold pictures of his sister? That her dreams had come true when she'd destroyed his family? There were other people at fault, but she couldn't ignore that she was one of them. Her stomach twisted and she tried to breathe deeply. Gavin loved Allison and Sean more than anyone in the world. Evie couldn't imagine how he would react if he knew what she'd done to them.

No more church dates, no more impromptu dinners and certainly no more kisses in the woods until she told him the truth. *Lord, give me courage to be honest.*

## Chapter Twelve

Gavin rushed down the long hospital hallway, yanking on the quarantine gown as he went. It was nearly deserted at this time of night. Or morning, technically.

It seemed like the day would never end. The call had come in to the office when he was just heading home, too exhausted to keep working, hoping to catch a few hours of sleep before starting all over again. He'd been up for almost twenty-four hours straight. That bowl of Marisol's chili seemed forever ago. But what he felt was nothing to what he knew was happening to the people in the room ahead.

His heart was pounding out of his chest and he could feel sweat beading his forehead. *I commend this patient to the Great Physician, guide our hands.* He grabbed the patient file from the holder by the door and flipped through it. He snapped on the mask, then the shoe covers and finally the gloves. He pushed open the door to the tiny examining room with his shoulder, calling out a low greeting as he entered.

Calista sat in the far corner, Gabriel cradled against her chest. Her eyes were huge and pleading. There were monitors hooked to Gabriel's chest, and a small clip was taped to his foot, measuring his oxygen levels. The number of machines running in the room made a constant cacophony of beeps.

"Hey, there." He moved closer, slowing his breathing, struggling to seem calm. She was panicked enough without seeing his fear.

"His pediatrician just left. Did he call you?" Her voice was low and unsteady. She looked like a woman doing her best to stay on the far side of total panic. And failing.

Gavin nodded.

"He was fine yesterday at his three-week checkup, and then he felt hot during the night. At about nine this morning, he was running a fever. I thought it was because I was keeping him close to me, so I unwrapped him. He wasn't coughing, but he seemed like he was breathing too fast. That's when he started shaking." Calista's eyes filled with tears and she sucked in a breath. "Grant said we had to come in right away. He's downstairs filling out paperwork."

A fever and fussiness were the first signs in infants. The cough came later. If they caught it early enough, the worst could be averted.

"I'm tough. I've given a lot of bad news in my life and taken some, too. I need to know what's happening. But—" she paused, swallowing hard "—tell me gently. Please."

"I'll tell you everything I know. And we'll talk it through." He knew her fear. Not as a parent, but as a man who had watched this disease ravage infants in this very hospital.

Gabriel gave a whimper and Calista readjusted him against her chest. He was sleeping but restless.

"Pertussis destroys the lung tissue, as you probably know. If we can catch it quickly enough, we can lessen the damage with antibiotic prophylaxis. If Gabriel hasn't begun coughing, then there's a very good chance that he'll make a full and complete recovery. They've got his sample in the lab right now. We're going to go ahead and start on the antibiotics for Gabriel and for you and Grant because there's a real chance that it's pertussis."

Her face seemed to crumple under the weight of her fear and grief.

He reached out and touched her arm. "Calista, you did the right thing to bring him in immediately. If he was a year old, and there wasn't this epidemic, it would probably be just a cold. But we've had hundreds more cases in just a few months, more than we had all last year. We can't take a chance that it's not, as young as he is."

Calista nodded, pressing her lips together. "Will you pray with me? I'm so scared." Her voice broke on the last word.

"Of course. And I'll stay with you until Grant gets here." Gavin held out his hand and she gripped it, hard. They bowed their heads and asked God's mercy on the brand-new life, now struggling against an invisible enemy.

"Thanks for inviting us out. We've been going stir-crazy in that little apartment." Allison gave Evie a brief hug. Sean and Jaden took off for the slide at a run, or as fast as they could manage in six inches of snow. The park was relatively quiet for a Wednesday morning. A few moms huddled on benches, chatting.

"Jaden was sad to miss the playdate last time. I think the excitement of a new baby has worn off." Evie stuffed her hands in her pockets and tried to look at ease. Her heart was pounding already and she hadn't even started.

A few long nights of tossing, turning and a lot of praying had led to this moment. Before she talked to Gavin, Evie needed to ask for forgiveness from the woman she'd hurt. She felt like a soldier headed to war, sick with fear.

Allison didn't seem to notice her nervousness. "Sean wants a little brother. But I told him we might get a dog instead."

Evie smiled, thinking of how most kids want a dog and get a baby sibling instead.

"Gavin said you were a big help at the soccer practice."

"He did?" Evie couldn't stop the tone of surprise. She hadn't felt very useful. "I spent most of the time trying not to get hit in the head with a ball. Some of those kids can really kick."

Allison waved her toward a bench. "I know I'll regret it, but I'd rather sit down. They should have auto-warming benches in Denver, don't you think?"

She snorted. "I can get up a petition in the paper. Enough people write in about it and the mayor just might pay for a few of them."

They watched the two little boys in silence for a moment as they chased each other around the edge of the play area. Sean's tousled hair reminded her of how Gavin always rumpled it as he passed. Evie felt her chest constrict. She wished this was just a play-date. She wanted more than anything to be spending quality time with Gavin's family, rather than getting up the courage to open old wounds.

"Your brother called me about a job singing at a club downtown." Allison's eyes were bright with happiness, her face flushed.

"I'm glad. He's good at that sort of thing." Jack knew everybody, it seemed.

"What sort of thing?"

"Bringing people together. Arranging groups. He knows who will fit best in what place. Too bad he spends all his time in meetings."

"He sounds like he's ready to change careers."

Evie thought on that for a moment. "He is, but I'm not sure what the whole plan is right now. He's always been so up-front, and now there's a little mystery going on."

Allison shot her a glance, lips quirked up. "You sound irritated."

"Do I?" She chewed her lip. "Probably. I'm used to knowing everything about him. It's weird to be shut out."

"Do you tell him everything?"

"Mostly." Evie locked eyes with Allison and they both burst out laughing. "Well, women are different. He can't ever really know everything, right?"

Allison shook her head, still smiling. "And probably wouldn't want to. Gavin never asks me questions. He's worried he'll invade my privacy." She paused. "As if that's never happened before."

*Now.* Evie sucked in a breath and whispered a silent prayer. "You mean the pictures of you and the senator."

Allison didn't look at her. For a moment Evie wondered if she'd even heard.

"I shouldn't be surprised. A little bit of digging was probably all it took to find out the details."

The playground was filling up with kids and adults, but the sounds seemed to fade away. Evie gripped the edge of the bench.

"I took those pictures." It came out in a rush, not even remotely like the way she'd practiced all morning. "I took them and sold them to the tabloids."

Allison turned slowly, her eyes wide, face slack with shock. She blinked and then pushed off from the bench. She got a few steps away and stopped. Evie could see her take a few deep breaths, arms wrapped around her chest, body tensed.

The two little boys were pushing a snowball through the arch under the slide. Jaden's face was red with cold, but he was laughing. Sean was serious, pointing out directions with his striped mittens.

Allison walked slowly back to the bench and perched on the edge. "Wow."

Evie nodded, eyes filling with tears. "I'm so sorry." She choked out the words. Night after night she had lain awake and prayed for the young woman. First had been stories of the girl in hiding, then being in rehab and finally, missing. Now Evie knew that Allison was alive. And a mother.

She straightened her back. "Does Gavin know?"

"No. Not yet." It came out in a whisper. Facing the young woman she had betrayed should be harder, but Evie didn't know how her heart was going to survive telling Gavin. She hated that her own emotions came before another's, again.

"When will you tell him?"

"Soon." She hoped Allison wasn't going to offer to help explain. There were some things you didn't want a witness to, like the breaking of your heart.

Allison blew out a breath. "Well, all we need to decide now, is whether this is for me or for you."

"Excuse me?"

She turned, brown eyes showing the smallest bit of a smile. "Did God arrange this meeting so you could apologize? Or is it my chance to say thank you?"

Evie frowned. How could Allison be grateful for being mocked, hounded and forced into hiding?

"Because—" Allison laid her hand on Evie's "—I'm so very thankful." Her eyes glinted with tears. "I thought I was untouchable. I didn't care he was married. He had money and nice cars and could get into any restaurant. People fell all over him. I didn't feel an ounce of shame."

"Until everyone knew."

"A lot of my friends knew. And I didn't care what my parents thought. They hated my singing career anyway. It was when Gavin found out." She closed her eyes for a moment, face stiff with pain. "He was so disappointed."

Evie squeezed Allison's hand. She wished she could go back in time, to the years when she didn't care what anybody thought, and take a different path. How much time had she wasted chasing the big bucks a scandalous picture would bring? And then she'd thought she'd finally got it, the really big one. The one that would pay off her journalism school bills. Maybe even buy her a cheap paper of her own.

She was right; Allison's pictures fetched a huge price. And cost Evie more than she could have ever imagined.

Gavin ran a hand over his face and wished he'd had the extra five minutes to change into fresh clothes. He'd spent most of the day stripping quarantine scrubs off and on, comforting parents, juggling messages between the labs and the office. His eyes felt gritty, he needed to shave and there was a jelly doughnut stain on his tie. All in all, not a pretty picture.

But he had assured Grant that the Mission would run smoothly. The poor man was out of his mind with worry over Gabriel. Calista needed him there with her. The whole city was being hit hard, but to see it brought home in the brand-new family was almost more than he could take.

The sidewalk had been freshly shoveled, and Gavin trudged toward the Mission, eyes on his boots. Groups of young men loitered around the entrance, hassling each other in loud voices. The sky seemed to hang low and heavy.

He looked up to see Evie, paused at the Mission door, one hand outstretched to the handle. She flashed him a smile and he felt his lips lift completely independently of his own doing. She'd left a message for him that morning, but he hadn't been able to catch her. Her dark hair was loose around her shoulders, bulky red ski jacket not able to completely erase her curves. She was a very welcome sight on a very bad day.

"Hey." He leaned in and gave her a quick kiss on the cheek. He wanted to move the kiss over about two inches to the right and linger there awhile but resisted.

"Hey, yourself." Her voice seemed tense, subdued. "You're early."

"No, just on time for once. I heard about Gabriel." Her gaze raked his face, as if seeking answers there.

Gavin opened the door and motioned her inside. The lobby was bustling with people. The closer it came to Christmas, the more people showed up for dinner. It was the long winter months, the last of the seasonal jobs closing and soaring costs of utilities. In warmer climates you could just put on a jacket if your apartment was cold. In Denver, you'd have to scrape the ice off the inside of your kitchen window if you didn't turn on the heat.

"They've started antibiotics. The lab test takes about twenty-four hours. He's running a temperature and is fussy, but no coughing, which means it could be just a cold but more likely early stages of pertussis. Calista's going to be in isolation with him, but Grant will come and go, as long as he suits up every time he visits."

Evie stood there, her arms wrapped around her middle. Her lips were pressed tightly together and she was blinking back tears.

Gavin pulled her to him without thinking, not caring there were people milling around the lobby. He pressed a kiss to the top of her hair. "He'll be okay. Everyone is praying. Calista brought him in right away."

"I thought the articles would help stop the epidemic." Her voice was muffled against his chest. "Nobody reads the paper anymore."

He leaned back a bit. "But Grant did. He told Calista to come in right away, in the middle of the night. Your paper probably saved this baby's life."

He took a breath, wondering how much to say.

"There are a lot of reasons for it, but I've never been fond of journalists." Her eyes went wide. He hurried on. "When Patrick died, his mother mentioned to a reporter that she'd brought him to my house to catch the chicken pox. The guy showed up at my door. He tried to get a quote from a nine-year-old on how it felt to have killed his best friend."

Her hand was at her mouth, horror etched on her features. "That's awful."

He let out a laugh that sounded bitter, even to his own ears. "I agree. So, the fact that you're using the space in your paper to try to save lives, rather than ruin them, means a lot to me."

She dropped her gaze and he heard her drag in a shaky breath.

He rubbed her shoulders, hoping to bring a little cheer back to her face. "But today you don't seem like the fearless editor I know. More advertising trouble?"

She sighed, bright blue eyes troubled. "Another big client bailed in search of a paper that actually gets read, even if it's only for the celebrity gossip."

"I'm sorry."

Evie's lips tugged up. "You're supposed to tell me to man up, to carry on, to keep working to the end."

"Okay, that, too." He couldn't help grinning. She felt so good in his arms; he never wanted to let her move another inch away. But the lobby was like the downtown Denver transit station, and Lana was giving them a sly grin from over by the desk.

"We should get to the meeting." She moved away, leaving one hand tucked into his elbow. "I ordered a pizza to be delivered to the meeting, by the way. I figured you hadn't had dinner yet."

He ginned at her. "You're a genius. Grant's worried the Mission will fall apart without him. I let him know that as long as Marisol is here, we'll all be okay."

"I just saw her in the kitchen. She was in a state but told me God would never ignore a mother's tears."

"He better not ignore Marisol, that's for sure."

She laughed, a sweet sound that warmed him. "I wish I had someone on my side like her. She's a big, bad spiritual bodyguard in the form of a little Mexican woman."

"Grandma Lili is mine. I've never tried to wander off the path because I know she'd just pray me back on. It would be a waste of time." Of course, Allison tried. Grandma Lili had never given up on bringing her granddaughter back into the fold.

They wound their way past the groups gathered near the lobby couches. Gavin knew he had sounded confident, reassuring, but that was his job. He was supposed to help people feel safe. Even when things were going from bad to worse, when he was trying his best to protect the city from a killer disease and failing. The pit of his stomach felt like lead, but he kept the smile fixed to his face. Fake it until you make it was never his motto, but giving in to panic wouldn't help anyone. The world seemed to be falling to pieces around them, but as long as Evie didn't give up, then he felt he could keep going, too.

"So, if the pertussis cases continue to rise, we'll cancel the Christmas dinner and worship services? What about the caroling?" Evie couldn't imagine what it was like to be a kid, homeless, and have Christmas canceled.

"Discouraging large gatherings helps contain the spread." Gavin's face was tight but his voice was level.

"That's rough." Jack shook his head, voicing everyone's sentiments. He picked up the last piece of pizza but didn't take a bite. The idea of skipping Christmas was unthinkable.

"Let's end the meeting with another prayer." Nancy folded her hands and spoke softly into the conference room. The finance board had managed to get through several large projects that needed approval by Christmas, but baby Gabriel was in everyone's thoughts.

When the prayer had finished, Evie looked up in time to see Gavin's expression turn from contemplative to downright steely. She knew what he was thinking but had no idea how he coped with the feelings.

Evie had been attracted to his quiet wit, his careful speech, that gorgeous smile, but now she knew the man who would lay down his life for his family, who stayed awake worrying about there being enough vaccines for all the babies, who felt a responsibility to an entire city. She'd never considered a biochemist a particularly manly profession, but this science geek was warrior material.

Her heart thudded in her chest as their gazes locked. She wanted to go back in time and change everything. It was too much to ask to erase her own past, but why couldn't she have known about Allison first? Why did she have to get to know Gavin, care for him, and break her own heart?

And she was going to break it the moment she told him the truth, maybe even minutes away.

"Evie?"

She sat up straight, startled.

Jack was leaning forward. "No meeting next week. It's the Thursday before Christmas."

"Got it." Her face felt hot, and she focused on shuffling papers into her folder. The world was bigger than Evie and much bigger than whatever love-life issues she had. She'd love to hang around and mope, but there was work to be done. And a major conversation to be had with the handsome man across from her. She just hoped that her heart didn't get in the way of her mouth when the time came to be honest about her past.

The finance team filed out of the conference room, uncharacteristically quiet.

Nancy waved and was gone, along with a few others. But Jack paused by Lana's desk, a hopeful expression on his face.

"I thought it was against Mission rules to have meetings without cookies."

"Oh!" Lana shook her head, tired eyes going wide. She lifted a plate to the top ledge of the desk. "Have at it."

"Now this is what I'm talking about!" Jack peeled back the cellophane and inhaled deeply. Evie could see small spritzer cookies with red hots, gingerbread men, brightly colored stars and brownies with fudge topping.

"When I get stressed, I start baking." Lana didn't smile. "Gavin, I don't want to pry, but is there anything you can tell me about Gabriel?"

Gavin nodded, one hand resting lightly on Evie's back. She felt her mind go blank as feelings surged through her. She struggled not to turn around and lean into him, tried not to think of how everything would change. For this moment, she would be grateful for small blessings. A touch, a whisper.

"Grant said he would be in tomorrow morning and that I should let you all know that Gabriel is holding his own." Gavin repeated the medical update, his low voice subdued.

"Let them know we're all praying." Lana's eyes were filled with tears.

"All of us," Jack said, nodding. "Poor little guy. But Gavin's on the scene, and if I had to choose anybody to be there when my kid got sick, it would be him."

Gavin smiled but looked pale and sad. Evie wondered how he could work around sick kids and not be overwhelmed with memories.

"Now, I've got to run." Jack selected a gingerbread man for the road and gave Evie a playful nudge. "I've got a first date and I can't be late. Bad manners. Right, little sister?"

Evie rolled her eyes. "Another? First dates are awful. And I was born first."

"First dates with me are the bomb. And you're older but littler." He called the last part from the middle of the lobby and was out the door seconds later.

"I'd better get back to the office. We're running twenty-four hours." Gavin rubbed his hand over his face. Evie could hear the stubble on his chin rasping. She wondered when he ate, when he slept. She shot Lana a glance and knew she was thinking the same thing.

"Take care of yourself, Gavin. We don't want to be visiting you in the hospital, either."

He nodded. "I will. Evie, are you leaving? I can walk you out."

"Sure." Now was the moment to tell him. It was terrible timing, the very worst. He was exhausted and overwhelmed. But if she didn't do it now, she never would. She could hardly swallow, fear suddenly gripping her by the throat. They walked through the lobby, footsteps echoing on the polished floor. Everything seemed sharp and vivid, her senses heightened with crushing anxiety. The Christmas tree sparkled in the corner, ornaments dangling crazily from where small hands had hung them. She felt as if someone was standing on her chest, and she fought to stay calm. It was just her heart, not life and death. But somehow it felt like she was walking straight toward the end of the world.

He took her hand on the way to the parking lot and she gripped it tightly. Like a prisoner on the way to the gallows, guilty as charged. He was quiet, shooting her a glance. She kept her eyes on the sidewalk, ignoring the bright windows twinkling with Christmas decorations. Not more than a foot away, but she felt the distance yawn between them, impossible to breach. As soon as they'd arrived at the edge of the lot, she turned to face him, letting go of his hand. It felt like she'd lost her only lifeline.

His eyes were filled with questions. Evie wished desperately that she could reach out and brush back the bit of curl that escaped from his hat. What she wouldn't give to touch his cheek, kiss him one last time. She took a deep breath, wishing someone would swoop in and fix the mess she'd made. But it was only her and Gavin, standing on a snowy downtown street corner in the freezing cold.

"What is it?" His voice was low, wary.

She met his gaze and knew she couldn't, not now. Maybe not ever. She'd rather walk away from him than tell him the whole truth. She couldn't bear seeing what was growing between them turn to hate, to witness the disappointment in his eyes.

She looked up to see a familiar pair walking—no, running—down the sidewalk toward the Mission. Grant turned, searching for what had caught her attention.

"Allison!" She thought the young woman wasn't going to stop. Her face was pale and her hand was gripping Sean's as if her life depended on it.

"I'm so glad you're here. Something horrible happened." Her words dissolved into a hoarse sob.

Evie moved toward her, but Gavin was there first, shielding her, eyes sweeping the street for what was threatening his sister and her little boy.

Evie's breath caught in her throat. This man would do anything to protect his family, and it showed in his every action. She could never tell him the truth unless she was ready to face the consequences. This strong, faithful man would see her not as a friend, but as the enemy. And Evie knew she would never be strong enough to bear it.

# Chapter Thirteen

Evie slipped an arm around Allison's shoulders, her heart pounding. "What happened?"

The young woman's face was tight with fear. "I was reading the news on my laptop, just scrolling through and saw this." She held up her phone to show them an internet site filled with photos. A little boy playing in the snow, laughing. Close-ups of his face. One of Allison, looking college age, happier. Evie's mind stuttered to a stop.

"Oh, Allison. I'm so sorry." Her voice came out soft, breathless.

"Are you?" Allison's gaze was locked on her face, searching for the truth.

"What does that mean? Of course she is." Gavin stared down at the lurid headline on the screen, anger written in every line of his face. "Left to wander the country without support? An unemployed single mother dependent on her relatives for help? They make it sound like she's a bad mother."

"You can't think I had anything to do with this." Evie should have been angry, furious. But she could hardly speak past the enormous lump of fear in her throat.

"I don't know what to think." Allison clutched Sean closer to her side, never letting her gaze slip from Evie's face.

Gavin looked up at her, a question growing in his eyes. She had meant to tell him, was planning to tell him.

"Oh, Allison, I would never..." Her voice trailed off. She didn't do this terrible thing. But she had, once before. How did one admit guilt and innocence at the same time? Evie swallowed, wishing there was something she could say but everything that occurred to her seemed trite.

Gavin finally spoke, shock dawning in his tone. "Did you write this?"

"No!" Seeing the betrayal in his eyes was the catalyst she needed. "I didn't take those pictures, or write that story, or know who did. I would never do that to you." She looked from the sad young mom to her son, still standing with his face buried in her sleeve. Her gaze traveled to Gavin, this man she'd come to care so deeply for, without even realizing it was happening. "Any of you," she whispered.

As if taking the words deep inside, Allison inhaled, shutting her eyes. "Okay. I'm sorry I accused you." She wiped her eyes. "I don't know what to do now. We can't go back to my place. I rented my apartment in my own name. It must be how they tracked us down." Her face crumpled as she looked behind her at the bleak cement building. "Maybe this is the safest place for us, a homeless mission."

"Stay with me. I've got plenty of room. We can plan

what to do next." Gavin put a hand on Allison's shoulder, his deep voice thick with emotion.

Evie knew he would give anything to keep Allison safe. But what she really needed was a little time to disappear. "Maybe it's better if you stayed with me. Just for a while, until the trail goes cold." She grimaced at her own words. She sounded like a bad spy novel. "I mean, until you decide how to address this. No one knows we're friends. I've got more than enough room, and I'm gone during the day."

Gavin sucked in a slow breath, nodded. He saw she was right.

Allison looked between them, a watery smile covering her pale face. "Nice, now I have two superheroes for the price of one."

Lips tugging up, Gavin turned and shot Evie a smile that took her breath away. Like they were on the same team, partners, protectors. She desperately wished it could be true.

"Are you sure? I mean, Sean is a good kid, but he's still a kid." Allison wavered, dark brown eyes rimmed red from crying.

"I know what kids are like. And I'm no clean freak, so I won't be bothered if he makes a mess or is loud."

"Sounds like it's settled. We'll head right over. We need to get Sean out of the cold anyway." Gavin moved toward the car.

Evie held up her hand. "But first we should probably figure out how we're getting Allison's stuff over to my place."

"Her stuff?" Gavin blinked.

"I'm sure she'd be a lot more comfortable with her own clothes, toothbrush, that sort of thing." Evie struggled to keep from smiling. Just like a man. He could probably hang out on someone's couch for a week without a problem, and Sean would love to have a sleepover, but women liked their creature comforts.

"I'll go, I've got a key." Gavin was already heading for his car.

"Here, you better write a list. If you're anything like Jack, you'll bring some ski boots and a parka and call it good." Allison let out wavering laugh as Evie scrambled in her purse for a pen and some paper.

After a few seconds of hasty scribbling, Allison handed it over. "Be careful," she called after him, and Gavin paused, turning back to give her a tight hug,

"You, too." He included Evie, touching her lightly on the shoulder as he left.

"Let's get you two someplace warm. Hey, Sean, ready to visit my place?" Evie hoped her voice was cheery and not betraying the desperate anxiety she felt.

He nodded, his little face pale and pinched.

"You follow me. We'll go home and make some hot chocolate, okay?" A brief smile lit his face. Allison flashed her a look of gratitude as they turned back to their car.

As Evie slipped into her little VW, she felt her heart dropping into her shoes. Maybe there had been no chance for real love; maybe she and Gavin were doomed from the start. But something deep in her heart fought against the verdict, especially when she let her mind wander back to that kiss. She'd meant to tell him, and now it was too late. It would look as if she'd been forced to expose her past rather than freely offering it up.

Evie cranked up the heater, rubbing her mittens

together. The whole situation was such a mess. She waited for headlights in her rearview mirror and tried to calm her breathing.

If only she'd had the nerve to look him in the eye and speak the words she'd been dreading. Her stomach roiled, imagining the anger, disappointment and pain in his eyes. She hadn't been just a gossip hound, like the journalists he hated. She'd been the person who had exposed his sister to the whole world in the first place. Now that boat had sailed, and the time for confessional talks was gone. There were bigger problems at hand, and one of those was protecting the girl she'd hurt so badly all those years ago.

Evie wandered aimlessly from the cozy little kitchen to the wide-open living room and back. She was glad she'd decorated a bit, twinkle lights at the windows of her little home, a wreath with ribbons. Allison was trying to read Sean to sleep, but from the sound of it, he wasn't buying the idea of "camping out" in Evie's apartment.

First he said he needed a tent, which they rigged up with chairs and extra blankets. Then he decided he needed a lamp, and Evie's book light was attached to the top inside. Now he seemed to be insisting on a husky to keep him warm in the "snow." It didn't seem to matter that it was a reasonable seventy degrees in the apartment. She wondered how Allison was going to manage a husky out of the meager offerings in the room. But as far as she'd seen, the young mom was about the most patient and creative person she'd met. If only she wasn't fighting a losing battle with the press.

The truth would come out, and it didn't look like it was exactly going to set them free.

Her phone rang and she answered it instinctively. Jack's voice was rough, static-y.

"Are you okay? I just got your message."

For some reason, Evie felt suddenly exhausted. "Did you see the link I sent you?"

"How is she?" He didn't bother to acknowledge the ugly article, just the little family it targeted.

"Pretty shaken. I'll fill you in tomorrow. Allison and Sean are staying here for a while."

"Do you need anything?" His voice was wavering in and out of clarity, but the tone was all Jack.

"You have a husky I can borrow?"

"Fresh out." He waited to see if she was going to add more, but she was too tired to talk. "I want to know what I can do. You call me when you're ready. I'll be a good little boy and go to the office bright and early. I'll shuffle some papers and wait for your phone call."

Evie snorted. Honest to a fault.

She hung up just as a knock at the door nearly startled her out of her wits. Evie put a hand to her chest, feeling her heart pounding through her shirt. She stepped softly toward the door and looked through the peephole. The face that appeared didn't help to calm the thudding pulse in her ears.

Evie swung open the door and motioned Gavin inside. He set down two duffle bags, seeming taller than she remembered. His dark gaze swept the small living room and then returned to her face, expression unreadable. His jaw was shadowed with stubble and his tie hung loosely. The smell of fresh soap was so familiar it made her throat ache.

"Sorry I took so long. Grant left a message. The lab has more cases." He stopped and ran a hand through his blond hair, a gesture she hadn't ever seen from him before. He looked overwhelmed, undone. "I'm sorry, that didn't make much sense."

Somehow his anxiety helped the lump in her throat reduce to a manageable size. It didn't disappear altogether. "How is baby Gabriel?" Her face felt tight with fear. *Lord, please heal him!*

"Better." His lips moved up, though his eyes were still shadowed. "But Lana is sick now. They think she must have caught it from one of the kids and passed it to the Gabriel on one of the days Calista brought him in to visit."

Evie put a hand to her mouth and felt her eyes go wide. Lana would be heartbroken to have caused baby Gabriel's infection. "Poor Lana."

His gaze locked on her face and he seemed to be choosing his words. "I know just how she feels." An old pain flashed in his eyes. "It makes me so angry that I couldn't protect him."

"But…" Evie frowned, lost for words. "You can't protect the entire population, Gavin."

He didn't seem to hear her. "The articles helped. But Lana didn't think those symptoms applied to her." Gavin closed his eyes, his voice dropped low. "To be honest, she told me she was feeling off. She said she couldn't get warm. I heard her cough."

Evie reached out, her heart aching for the pain she saw on his face. "But you couldn't have known."

His gaze bored into hers. "No, Evie, I should have known. I should have guessed. I should have warned them." His voice broke on the last word.

Phrases swirled in her head. *Everything is clearer in hindsight. You're not perfect. It was God's will.* But the words seemed inadequate.

He dragged in a breath. "Anyway, thanks for letting them stay." He paused. "I was worried what you would think about Allison, about how I wasn't there to help support her when she needed it."

"Oh, Gavin." She shook her head, the irony of it all twisting her heart. She couldn't speak. What could she say? He was the most honorable man she had ever met, and he had worried what *she* would think of *him*. She felt sick.

"When we left the Mission tonight, you were trying to tell me something."

For a moment, Evie couldn't seem to draw in air. "Not a big deal. It's not the right time."

"Is it related to whatever you wanted to say on the trail?" His voice was pitched low, words measured.

Now? She felt herself standing on a precipice, wavering, heart in her throat. No, it couldn't be now. "Yes, but I want to get Allison and Sean settled." She smiled a little, hoping he would move on, let it go.

He took a step toward her, and she craned her neck up to see his face. Brown eyes burning with intensity, his hands felt hot where he cupped her face. "I want us to be honest with each other. Don't be afraid to talk to me, Evie. Not ever."

Her eyes prickled and she sucked in a wavering breath. To the rest of the world she was a fighter, a woman who made her own way. But deep inside fear swirled and twisted. She could never be completely free of her past, and it was too much to hope Gavin could accept her as she was then.

He stood only inches away from her, a buffer of heat between them. She desperately wanted to move forward, to kiss him until they both forgot about the present and the past, what they'd done and failed to do.

Sweeping a thumb over her mouth, he locked his gaze on her lips. Evie knew she should break his gentle hold, back away, but her body wouldn't obey her mind. She was lost, and she hated her own weakness. Every touch, every kiss, would seem a betrayal when he knew the truth. And she still could not do the right thing.

Sean's high voice carried into the living room. The little boy was overtired and obviously near tears. It was enough to break into the moment. Evie blinked and gently lowered Gavin's hands, squeezing them before letting them drop.

Allison's footsteps sounded down the hallway.

"I think he's finally ready to lie down quietly. Sleep may be too much to ask for, but I'll settle for quiet." She walked in, already talking, both hands tucking her hair behind her ears. "Gavin!" She launched herself into his arms and he hugged her tightly.

This is what family was for, to be the rock in a storm.

"I guess moving here wasn't such a great plan after all," Allison said. She tried to make it sound as if she thought the whole thing funny, but the quiver in her voice was telltale.

"I'm glad you're here. You and Sean." Gavin's face was almost fierce. "Don't think I regret you coming to Denver."

She nodded, looking small and forlorn, and shrugged one shoulder. "Well, I'm glad that I didn't enroll Sean in kindergarten this year. It won't be so hard for him this way."

"What way?"

"Moving again."

"Allison, you know you can't let this go on forever. You've got to face it. Head-on."

For a moment, Evie thought the young woman was going to shout at him, but then she took a deep breath. "You're the one who's been telling me to keep quiet."

"I was wrong." His words were simple, but they socked Evie in the heart. It took a big man to admit he was wrong without batting an eye.

"Well, I can't think about it right now. My son is sleeping in a strange room, pretending he's on a camping trip, because we were outed by an internet gossip site."

She turned to Evie. "I'm so grateful to you. Don't think I'm not grateful."

"I understand. Really." Evie glanced around at her tiny living room. She wished it were more comfortable, more like a real home. She wished there weren't boxes stacked to the ceiling in one corner of the guest room.

"Since you probably shouldn't drive your car in case you're followed, let me take you. Or I can call someone else. But I don't want you and Sean riding around with Evie." Gavin's face was somber.

"And why would that be?" Allison turned, hands on hips, eyes narrowed.

"No airbags." Gavin looked from one to the other. "What? It's not safe. I bet there aren't even any shoulder belts in the backseat."

Evie caught Allison's eye and started to giggle. The poor woman was being exposed to the nation for the second time in her life, and Gavin was worried about her VW bug.

"You are such a bossy brother, but I love you anyway." Allison rolled her eyes.

"Will you guys sit down while I make some tea? Or hot chocolate?"

"No, thank you," Allison said, reaching for the bags. "You should get to bed. I've kept you up too late already."

"I should go check in at work." Gavin headed for the door, giving Evie one more glance.

"But it's almost ten!" Evie froze, shocked.

"Just for a few minutes." And he was gone.

"He thinks he has to save the world." Allison rummaged in a duffel bag. "But he can't."

Opening her mouth to argue, to point out how capable and smart and hardworking Gavin was, Evie paused. Gavin may be a superhero type, but it took an entire fleet of scientists and hospital workers to contain the spread of the disease. He was acting like he was shouldering the responsibility alone.

"And when things don't go well, he thinks it's his fault. Every failure, every sick kid, every bad decision made by other people and he takes it personally, as if he's let it happen through his own negligence." Her eyes had a distant look and the pupils seemed dilated with the pain of remembering.

Evie nodded. She loved that about him, his protective nature, but she'd never thought of the flip side. The guilt, the burden of trying to change a world that didn't want to be changed.

"My own bad choices have hurt him more than he'll say, and it kills me." She paused, brushing back her hair. "Some days I want to tell him that keeping Sean a secret had nothing to do with him, but he thinks my lack of trust in him is his fault."

Allison laughed, a sad little sound that made Evie's throat tighten. "Whatever you do, don't lie to him."

"I'm not…" Her voice trailed away. She wasn't lying. But she was hiding. "I can't tell him right now."

Resting her hand on Evie's arm, she said, "The way he looks at you tells me you better not wait."

She felt her face go hot. "What way?"

"The way his gaze follows you around the room, the way he stands near you and the way he gets this look on his face like he's been stun-gunned." Allison started to laugh. "I've never seen him like this. He's a goner."

She turned, hiding her face while she straightened the couch cushions. "That's silly. He's probably watching me for signs of pertussis." She hoped her voice didn't betray the way her heart was pounding. She desperately wanted to believe Gavin was falling in love with her and just as desperately hoped it wasn't true.

"Very funny."

"Make yourself at home. I'm going to set the coffee-maker for tomorrow." Evie hoped Allison understood she didn't have to ask for anything.

In response, the young mom hugged her hard. "Thank you."

Evie nodded and wandered to the kitchen, realizing for the first time how long ago she'd eaten. She stood at the sink and stared at the small alcove window near the ceiling. Lights from the building caught the drifting snowflakes on the downward spiral. She'd always felt comforted by the snow. Now the thought of Christmas made her swallow hard.

Without realizing, she had placed Gavin squarely in the middle of her visions of the coming holiday. Maybe there wouldn't be any handsome blond man by her side as they listened to the Mission kids sing carols. Maybe she wouldn't be attending the midnight service and sitting next to Grandma Lili, with Gavin a steady, peaceful presence on that special day.

Evie felt a pain in her chest that was so sharp she leaned against the sink, sucking in deep breaths. It shouldn't be a surprise. It was only right that she suffer for her past. Just like Allison was, so she would be. She struggled to stand up straight and blinked back hot tears. Enough of feeling sorry for herself. It never did any good.

There wasn't any other way around it. Gavin deserved to know the truth, and she deserved whatever came from the revelation. And something told her that this fiercely protective man was going to have a very hard time forgiving Evie for what she'd done to his family.

## Chapter Fourteen

"Sean, put that down!" Those were the words that greeted Gavin as he walked into Evie's apartment that evening. Allison was pointing one finger at her tow-headed son, who was swinging something that looked suspiciously like Evie's laptop cord.

"Is the day over yet?" She tucked her dark hair behind her ears and let out a huge sigh.

He gave her a quick hug and ruffled Sean's hair. "I hear you." He'd snagged a few hours of sleep near dawn, but napping in his desk chair wasn't the best way to feel rested. He felt as if he were fighting through a fog.

Couch cushions were lopsided, throw pillows stacked in a pile in the center of the room and the table was covered with paper and crayons. "Looks like you guys are having fun."

"Oh, boy. Not the word I'd use." She rolled her eyes, plopping into a chair. "Evie's not back yet. Thankfully Grandma Lili's in the kitchen cooking something wonderful or I'd have to give up. Like, right now."

"Our Grandma Lili?"

She snorted. "The one and only."

Gavin hoped Evie was telling the truth about loving his grandmother because it appeared his entire family had moved in. "I'll go see if she needs any help."

"Smells great," he said, as he poked his head into the kitchen. Grandma Lili stood up, hands covered in flour, gray hair slightly mussed. The cabinet was open and she seemed flustered.

"Oh, good. You can help. I've had my heart set on biscuits all day, and I can't find the baking sheets." She nodded at the bowl of biscuit dough, raising her hands as proof.

"I can look, but I've never been here except for a few minutes last night." He crouched down and started opening cabinets.

"Really? I got the impression…"

He peered over his shoulder. "Yes?"

"Well, we all know how fast the world moves today. I assumed you'd at least been to dinner here."

Gavin took a moment to reach in and grab the slim metal cookie sheet. "Nope."

"And that's not for wanting." Grandma Lili cocked an eyebrow at him.

Was he that obvious? "My usual charms are proving less than adequate." He didn't bother to mention how she had stepped back from him last night. It was a clear message if there ever was one. Something had changed since that kiss on the trail, and he didn't know what.

"Well, nice to see you again, Mrs. Sawyer." Evie had appeared in the doorway, face pink from the cold. Gavin straightened up with a snap. She must have come in just seconds behind him. With all the noise Sean was making, nobody could hear a thing.

She froze, sweeping a gaze over him. Gavin wished his suit were a little less rumpled, but he hadn't had time to go home and change. He was a few hours past a five-o'clock shadow and definitely the worse for wear.

She recovered quickly and raised a hand. "Hi, Gavin." Peering in the oven, Evie made a sound of utter happiness. "Roast chicken? I could get used to this."

"Nonsense. I bet you can cook pretty well, yourself." Grandma Lili pointed at the row of cookbooks displayed on a shelf in the tidy little kitchen.

"Did you read the titles?"

His grandma leaned closer, squinting. "*365 Desserts. Chocolate Decadence. A Cookie for Every Occasion.* Well, somebody has a sweet tooth."

"Little known fact." She unbuttoned her coat. "Let me hang up my coat and I can help."

Grandma Lili waited a few moments after Evie had left the kitchen and then whispered into the silence. "I think your charms are in perfect working order. You stopped that girl in her tracks."

He shook his head. "Not in a good way. She must think it's a Sawyer family invasion."

Allison popped her head in. "Evie's reading to Sean so I can take a break and come help."

Resisting the urge to shoot Grandma Lili a look that told her how he'd been right all along, Gavin moved to the other counter to chop lettuce. "Come on in, newest kitchen slave."

"The least I can do is make sure you don't burn anything."

"As if." He loved being with these two, fighting for space in the little kitchen. But there had been the tiniest hope that Evie wanted to be here, too. He shrugged it off and focused on his chopping.

"Have you seen any nice little buildings for rent? Evie's got that whole back room filled with supplies but nowhere to store the stuff."

He looked at Allison, struggling to make sense of her question. "What supplies?"

"Oh, I thought you knew." Glancing between him and Grandma Lili, Allison wiped her hands on a towel. "She's got this idea of opening a small drop point for baby supplies."

"A boutique?"

"Nothing like that. She said she had an idea but thought it was too crazy until Gavin told her something about doing the right thing. That you always waited for someone else to stand up and volunteer and finally you figured you should just do it and God will fill in the blanks?"

"I think I remember that." In the gym at the Mission.

"Well, I guess a friend told her about how they had been in a financial bind right before they had their baby. They weren't homeless or destitute, but they were in a bad place. Even the thrift store was too expensive."

"Working poor," said Grandma Lili over her shoulder. She shook a pile of green beans into a colander and rinsed them in the sink.

"They looked okay but weren't staying afloat and really struggled to buy the essentials. Evie got this idea that somehow she could rent a little place that would have cribs and things available. She'd buy them from online thrift sites, yard sales or on sale. Make sure everything was up to code and supply them for free. The need will always outweigh the supply, but something is better than nothing."

Grandma Lili was perfectly still, a handful of green beans hovering near the pot. "What kind of person opens a shop like that?" She nodded her head. "I love this girl."

Allison's voice dropped a bit, and she focused on a spot on the counter. "I know what it's like to be in that position. I think it's a great idea."

There was a tightness in his chest, hope and pain mixed together. Evie didn't have anything to do with her friend's situation, but it touched her enough to make a plan, to try and change the way the world works.

Gavin carefully set the plates on the counter and looked for silverware, conscious of being in Evie's kitchen, touching items she touched every day. What kind of person *was* she? He could hear her soft voice in the living room, reading to Sean. She was someone who stepped into the gap, whether or not she was to blame for the lack.

Allison took a breath and went on. "She'd have to keep track somehow of who got what to keep the system from being abused. Of course, there will always be some people who try to take more than they need, but she doesn't want to focus on that. She wants it to be a place people can bring their like-new baby gear to donate and a place where families in need can find no-cost supplies."

"I'm sure my ladies' prayer group at St. James would be able to help out. Collecting supplies, running bake sales." Grandma Lili looked like she was ready to start that hour, that minute.

"Well, she doesn't even have a place yet. It should

be in a central area, close to the Mission so it's accessible. But not too expensive and not too much like a shop front. The way she described it was a place that was comfortable, private, but big enough to store what they needed." She put a finger to her chin. "Oh, and some sort of loading area near the alley."

"That's a long list," Gavin said. He wiped the cutting board, brushing small crumbs into his palm. She'd put a lot of thought into this store. He hadn't heard anything about it, but Allison had the full story. He noted his own petty feelings of being left out and felt his lips go up in a half smile. Evie didn't owe him anything, least of all an accounting of all her current projects. But he desperately wanted to be that person, the one who heard all her hopes and plans.

A knock sounded at the door and the two of them froze, like a domestic tableau in an old painting.

"I'll get it." Gavin tried to sound calm, assured. What would he do if it was a reporter? What would Allison do?

He peered through the peephole. "Just Jack," he called over his shoulder and swung open the door.

"Just Jack. What does that mean?" He walked in, dark hair covered with a dusting of snowflakes, arms full, something large dangling from one hand.

"It means you need to call first," Evie said from the other end of the living room.

"Hi, Jack." Allison waved shyly, walking in from the kitchen. "Sean, get down from there!" His nephew took a flying leap from the side of the couch, letting out a full-throated shriek as he went. The kid had a good pair of lungs.

"Sorry." The young mom's face was bright pink, her lips set in a line.

"I picked up some essentials." Jack held up his arms and Gavin got a better look at the jumble of items. A small trampoline, a miniature basketball hoop, several boxes.

"What's all this?" Evie pointed at the pile of what was obviously meant for Sean.

"Dear sister of mine, I was a boy once. And boys have energy to burn." He grinned. "I still do. But anyway, I thought you guys would like some activity toys."

Sean was standing near, eyes wide. "Is this for me?"

"Sure, but your mom will probably set some rules before you get to start. Maybe you could try this out while I pump up the balls." He laid the trampoline on the floor and Sean bounced onto it, small body a blur of motion. A wild scream of laughter told them how much he was going to enjoy it.

Jack looked embarrassed. "He may not be quieter, but he might be happier."

Gavin glanced at Allison and was surprised to see tears in her eyes. "Thank you. That means a lot."

"No problem. Glad I can help. Sure wish we could get him up on the mountain for some sledding, but this will have to do." He set down two boxes and pulled out a large yellow exercise ball.

"Will you stay for dinner?" Allison asked, already headed to the kitchen for another plate, her words following her.

Evie snorted. "Jack's never turned down a meal. Ever. We're having roasted chicken with homemade biscuits and fresh green beans."

"I don't want to butt in."

"Butt into what? It's dinner."

"I haven't met the grandmother," he said softly, as if it were a secret.

"And? She's perfectly nice." Evie shrugged and took the giant yellow ball from Jack.

"She doesn't bite," Gavin assured him.

"Okay. I guess I'll stay." He still looked a little nervous but took off his coat.

Gandma Lili called out from the kitchen. "Help me with these biscuits, Gavin. Evie can roll and you can cut."

Evie caught his eye and seemed to be trying not to laugh. His bossy grandmother was taking over her kitchen. He hoped she didn't mind. To him it felt like what a family should be: busy, warm, a little bit loud.

They trooped into the small kitchen and took up their biscuit-making jobs. Gavin knew now wasn't the time or the place, but he couldn't help the rush of warmth when those bright blue eyes flitted from his, shyness written on her face. And those dimples. Her face was like a movie he never wanted to stop watching. He catalogued every detail. She had felt so soft in his arms, so warm.

Gavin shook himself. Get a grip. What kind of lovesick puppy ogles a pretty girl just feet from his own grandmother? He glanced up guiltily and caught Grandma's eye. She winked broadly. He was so obvious he should be wearing a sign. Whipped—Do Not Attempt To Rehabilitate.

"Gavin, take this chicken to the table. Make sure you set it right on the hot pads. We don't want to scar the lovely wood. That would be a poor way to repay Evie for her hospitality."

"Yes, ma'am." He slid on the oven mitts and carried the rosemary-encrusted bird toward the living room, delicious smells rising straight into his nose. He knew what Grandma Lili was doing. A little interfering might not seem like a bad thing, but something was keeping Evie from opening up to him, and there was nothing Grandma Lili could say that would change that.

Evie stood awkwardly in her own kitchen and wished she'd been gifted with a lighter personality, one that chirped over décor or the best recipes or hairstyles. But she hadn't been, and so she waited for Grandma Lili to roll the biscuit dough, saying nothing.

The seconds stretched into minutes, and Evie peeked at the old woman's face. It was serene, thoughtful. The only noise in the kitchen was the steady rhythmic sound and motion of the age-old exercise of rolling out dough.

Grandma Lili passed a biscuit cutter to Evie, meeting her gaze and smiling. There was no need to be anxious. Just two women, making biscuits, preparing dinner. She watched Grandma Lili's capable hands twisting and turning the slab. The raucous sounds of two men and a young boy playing in the living room were like sweet background music. Evie let loose a long breath she didn't know she'd been holding deep inside and felt her shoulders relax.

"I believe in you." Grandma Lili's words were soft, almost as if she were speaking to herself.

Evie looked up, eyes widening. For a moment, she'd thought the older woman had said she *believed* her, and she'd felt her past rise up in her throat.

Her quick hands pinched out the shapes and laid

them on the sheet. "You remind me of Gavin, you know. He took Patrick's death and made it a personal mission. He works so hard, as if the world will come crashing down if he doesn't take responsibility for it."

Evie felt her face flush hot. She carefully pressed her cutter into the dough, making sure the entire circle was separated from the rest. Just the way she felt. Isolated, alone.

"But you're both more than your job." She looked up, pale blue eyes shining with sincerity. "I believe in you as a woman with purpose. You know what happens when you follow your God-given purpose?"

Evie shook her head. Did she even know her purpose? All she'd done lately was try to clean up the mess she'd made years ago, and the only outcome was it coming back to smack her in the face.

"You can not fail." She enunciated the words clearly, one hand cradling a raw biscuit. She put her other hand, dusty with flour, over Evie's. "I believe in you and you can't fail. So do what you have to do and stop being scared about it."

Her eyes burned at the corners, and Evie felt her throat close up on whatever words she could have said, if she could have thought of any. All the years her father had overlooked her, all the times she'd chased after success that had never come, all the hours she'd spent hating herself for making such huge mistakes, they all rose up in her like a dark tide.

She dropped her gaze and took a shuddery breath. "But you don't know me."

"I do, Evie, I do." She squeezed her hand and laid the biscuit on the sheet. "You're just like Gavin. He's a big, strong man who is smarter than anyone I've ever met. So handsome but doesn't know it. Girls just fall all over him."

Evie pushed her cutter into the dough a little forcefully. She knew all about how girls felt around Gavin.

"But he's scared, too. Scared of letting people down, of making mistakes, of not being the man he's supposed to be."

"He doesn't seem like it. He seems so capable. In control. Perfect," Evie said. The last word came out softly, like an afterthought.

She snorted. "Nobody's perfect."

"I know, but compared to the rest of us." She shrugged, lifting a biscuit to the tray.

"Compared to the rest of us, he's still not perfect. And he's not trying to be." Grandma Lili sighed. "No comparisons allowed. We are who we are, pasts and all."

Evie had a momentary burst of panic, wondering if Allison had shared the entire story with Grandma Lili. And it would only be a matter of time before Gavin heard the full story from someone other than herself.

"Let's get these in the oven. Ten minutes and we'll be ready to eat. Why don't you put the plates out, dear?"

She nodded, forcing a smile to her face. She didn't deserve this woman's faith in her. She was too afraid to take that step, to tell Gavin the truth.

"Just a few minutes until dinner's ready, I think." Gavin hoped the idea of the impending dinnertime would give them all a chance to settle down. He chuckled as Jack slung Sean over one shoulder. The little boy's giggles were muffled by the fabric of Jack's plaid flannel shirt. Jack lowered Sean to the floor and Gavin held out his arms to the little boy. "How's my guy?"

Sean wrapped his arms around Gavin's waist and buried his face in his stomach. "Good." The word sounded a bit tired, or sad.

He tipped up his godson's face, one finger under his chin. "Having fun camping out?"

He shrugged, small shoulders moving in unison. "Sure. When are we going home?"

"We'll have to talk to your mom about that." Gavin felt his stomach clench. This couldn't go on forever. But it wasn't the right time to discuss it, either. One thing at a time. And that rosemary chicken definitely came first.

A few minutes later they were all seated at the table, the smell of the roast chicken wafting around their little group. Grandma Lili at the head, Allison and Jack on one side, Gavin and Evie on the other side, Sean at the end. They all linked hands and bowed their heads. "Lord, we thank You for these gifts we are about to receive, from Your bounty, through Jesus Christ. Bless our family and friends, keep us safe from harm and within the arms of Your love. Bless all those struggling with illness, especially the babies who've caught the whooping cough."

"Amen." The word, spoken in unison, made Gavin hope for a moment this would happen often, in better times, without fear.

"How are the numbers today?" Grandma Lili was peering at Gavin, small frown lines etched between her eyebrows.

"Better. Evie, I meant to tell you, another mom told

us she'd read the signs of pertussis in the article and that was why she brought her baby in right away."

Her fork paused in midair, lips lifting up in a bright smile. "Really?"

"Really." He knew what she was feeling, saw the glint of tears in her eyes. Their articles had helped in a very concrete way. Maybe even saved lives.

"I'm so proud of you two. You make a great team." Grandma Lili patted Gavin's hand and beamed at Evie. He felt heat spread over his face, wishing she wouldn't be quite so obvious, but Evie seemed to take it as a straightforward compliment.

"Did you read any of those fun magazines I brought over?" Grandma Lili switched her focus to her granddaughter.

Allison took a bite of fresh green beans and shrugged. "Um, I paged through a few of them. I don't have a lot of time to sit. Sean wanted to play Lego pirates most of the day."

"Did you at least take the quiz I told you about?" Grandma looked to Evie and said, "It's such a silly quiz. You get it all filled out, it tells you what animal in nature you'd be. I was a badger. Which I liked. I think they're hardworking and smarter than most people."

"I think I'd be a monkey," Jack offered.

"At this point, I would probably be anything that eats its own young," Allison commented into her plate.

Evie snorted with laughter. She didn't have to be a mother to understand how long the days must seem for Allison.

"Now, dear, have you been thinking about what you're going to do? There was another article today. Senator McHale is denying everything. What's your

plan?" Grandma Lili passed the biscuits to her granddaughter and asked the question like she was stating
tomorrow's weather. Sean shoveled mashed potatoes
into his mouth and didn't seem to hear a word.

"Grandma, I don't know. I'm not sure." She took
a biscuit and handed the plate to Jack, her face heavy
with worry.

"Well, you can't stay here, hiding in this apartment
forever."

"She's welcome to stay as long as she needs to," Evie
said quickly. Gavin flashed her a small smile. He could
tell she was eager to reassure them, to never let them
feel like burdens. He felt gratitude swell in his chest.

"Of course she is. You're a sweet girl. But are they
never going to go outside again?" Grandma Lili's blue
eyes were wide, questioning.

"Maybe we can discuss this later." Gavin's voice
was quiet but firm. "She's had a hard day."

"We've all had a hard day, dear. Except maybe
Sean." She winked at her grandson, who was busy
covering his biscuit with raspberry jam. He grinned
back at her, black hair sticking up right in the front.

Allison stared down at her plate, appetite seemingly
gone. Gavin felt her anxiety palpably and wished he
could make this entire ugly situation disappear.

He cleared his throat. "I know you don't want me
to boss you around, and I'm not trying to tell you what
to do…"

"But." Allison said the word with a note of bitterness.

"But you were right when you said it was time to
stop hiding. You need to face it head-on. It's only a
story because it's a secret. That's how these things

work. It will be big and ugly and loud for a while, then everyone will lose interest."

Out of the corner of his eye, he saw Evie's shoulders hunch. He caught her gaze, and she offered a wan smile.

"He's going to be furious." Allison's voice was low.

They all knew who Allison meant. She watched her little boy happily working his way through his biscuit. "People will hate me, and I can handle that. But if they hate him…"

"People are half-blind with their own prejudices. And they will hate the person you used to be. But we loved you, wherever you were, always." Grandma Lili reached over and laid a hand on hers.

Evie met his gaze. The expressions that flickered on her face made his heart feel as if it was being clamped in a vise. A mix of hope and terror warred in her eyes. She was carrying a terrible burden—he knew it as surely as he knew his own name.

In the next moment, she'd replaced that raw look of fear with a wobbly smile. He sucked in a breath, hoping he'd imagined it all, but knowing in his heart that he had not.

"He's going to deny it all, the way he did in the beginning." Allison wiped her eyes. Her words brought Gavin back to the drama unfolding at the table.

Gavin's protective side wanted to have a man-to-man talk with Sean's absentee father. But this was her fight. All he could do was stand behind her.

"Okay." She wiped a tear from her cheek and managed a wobbly smile. "We'll have to make this good because I don't want to be making statements every morning."

"That's my girl," Gavin said. He knew she was tough, strong, but she just kept growing.

Jack passed Allison a tissue, and Grandma Lili forced another biscuit on Evie. Gavin snatched a tall glass of water out of harm's way as Sean reached for the jam again.

All was well, for this perfect moment in time.

But he knew, in a matter of days, they would be weathering a storm that had been building for years. What the damage would be, and the lasting effects, only time could tell. He prayed that God would give them all the strength to hold fast to honor and truth, no matter how painful it would be. As he met Evie's eyes, he saw the same worry in her gaze. But it was just a note. The rest was resolution, determination and an iron will.

## Chapter Fifteen

"Coach! Watch this kick!" Gavin barely had time to dodge the soccer ball as it sailed over his head.

"Nice one, Alec." He gave a short clap for the sweaty-haired kid and hoped he got more of a heads-up next time. The Mission soccer team was really shaping up into some dedicated players.

"Good news," Grant called out to him as he crossed the gym at a jog, face creased with happiness. "Gabriel's doing so well, the doctor said he'll probably come home as soon as his course of antibiotics is finished."

Relief flooded through him, and he felt a smile stretch over his face. "I'm so glad."

Grant reached out, laying a hand on his shoulder. "I can't thank you enough. Without those articles you and Evie ran in the paper, Calista wouldn't have brought him in right away."

"I'm so glad that she did. And the numbers are falling by the day. I think you're good to go on the Christmas pageant and the caroling."

"You saved the Mission's Christmas, my friend." Grant's eyes shined with emotion.

"Not me. I wish I could wipe pertussis from the face of the earth, but…" He felt his shoulders slump. Same old story. Never quite good enough.

"Hey." Grant gave him a steady look. "I give you points for trying, but there's no reason to carry the responsibility of the world."

He shrugged. "Just the way I'm wired, I guess." Well, since Patrick died, anyway.

"Don't lose sight of the good you're doing." The director looked concerned but left it at that. "Did you invite Evie to the pageant?"

Gavin nodded. He wondered how many people knew how he felt about Evie. Probably anyone with eyes. "Sure did. We'll be there, Christmas Eve."

It probably would have sounded odd to some people: an evening of kids reenacting the birth of the Savior, then a candlelight church service. But it felt right for them. Everything about Evie felt right. If only she felt the same way. The way she kept him at arm's length told him she didn't.

Gavin's cell phone rang and Grant nodded, motioning he'd help direct the soccer team for a moment.

"It's Grandma Lili. I'm just worried that Sean is cooped up in that apartment all day. It can't be healthy for either of them. Don't get me wrong. I know he'll survive just fine. But Allison may not. She needs to have some time to herself, even if it's just a few hours." Her worried voice traveled over the line, delivering a load of grandmotherly guilt in just a few sentences.

Gavin frowned. "I know, but I'm not sure what we can do about it until she sets the day for releasing the statement. And she's waiting to hear something back from McHale."

"She could be waiting a long, long time. Meanwhile, is there any way you can sneak her out for a movie?"

"It would be easier to take Sean out than Allison. He's not as recognizable. Maybe we could take him up on the mountain for the day?"

"Good idea. You and Evie can take Sean up sledding before Allison goes fruity."

Gavin smiled at the term. "I'll call over there and ask if we can take him tomorrow morning."

He disconnected and jogged back to the kids, thoughts on a beautiful young woman and the promise of a snow day up on the mountain.

"This is the first Saturday I've had off in years." Gavin clapped his hands in readiness. "Sleeping in might have done me more good than ten pots of coffee. I'm ready to sled!"

Sean responded with a whoop and launched himself at his uncle. "Can we snowboard, too? I want to try everything!"

His mother folded her arms over her chest and looked nervously at the pile of gear. "This seems like a lot of stuff for sledding. Are you sure it's safe?"

Evie slipped into the room and stood quietly near the couch. A pair of black leggings and a T-shirt and a pair of bright red woolen socks. It made no sense, but out of her everyday office clothes, she was stunning.

"Jack says helmets are required for kids his age on the larger hills, and the other gear is just in case he decides to try out the boards." She pulled her dark hair swiftly into a ponytail.

"See what we got, buddy?" Gavin held up the Spider-Man ski mask and prayed that Sean would take to it. They would still go if he didn't wear it. But it would be somewhere else, away from people. He had his ski cap and sunglasses in his car, so he'd be less recognizable, too.

The little boy gaped at the bright red-and-blue cotton mask. "Wow," he breathed. "Can I wear it right now?"

"Um, I suppose you can." Gavin grinned at Allison and was relieved to see a dawning sense of hopefulness in her eyes. She needed time by herself, and Sean needed time to be a little boy. Outside.

"Mommy, what do you think?" He jumped around the room, bouncing from spot to spot, arms in the air.

"Just like Spider-Man. Everyone's going to want your autograph." Allison bent down and gave him a quick hug. "Give me a kiss, superhero boy. And be careful."

"I will, Mommy. Don't be lonely." He was already heading to the door, Spidey mask on just a bit crooked.

"Wait, Sean, I'm not quite ready." Evie rushed back to the bedroom and Gavin could hear her rummaging in drawers. She emerged, a striped sweater and ski pants in one hand and a pair of boots in the other. "And just let me find my… There." She pulled a weatherproof bag from the closet and stuffed in the pants. Slipping on the bright sweater, she quickly laced up her boots.

She jumped up. "Now I'm ready!" Her eyes were bright with excitement, and Gavin wondered who was going to be happier to be on the mountain: her or Sean. She had seemed so preoccupied the past week or so, but she'd said there were problems with the paper. It must be hard to watch something you love struggle.

"Have fun and don't leave your phone sitting around." He waved to his sister, who stuck her tongue out at him in a sisterly way. "We'll call you as soon as we get up there."

Evie opened the door and they headed for Gavin's car, each of them carrying armloads of items. Sean bounced in front of them, hardly touching the ground. "I can't wait! I can't wait! I can't wait!"

The sun was bright, and there wasn't a bit of wind—perfect. Nothing like a cold wind to make you want to stay home. Sean needed an outing, and it was going to be better than anything he could imagine. Gavin pushed the thought of Allison's dilemma far from his mind. There was just today. Winter sun, perfect blue sky, a beautiful girl, a crazy little kid and a whole lotta snow. He caught Evie's bright gaze and grinned. It couldn't go wrong.

Evie's calf muscles were burning as she trudged up the long sledding hill. The ski lifts whirred in the distance, and the new dusting of snow sparkled on every surface.

"I think we're going to need some serious food to make up for all these calories burned," Gavin said from her other side, the sled rope in his hand. Sean had wanted to get a ride back up the hill, as well as a ride down, but his uncle nipped that idea in the bud.

"Spoken like a man. I don't usually go looking to make them up." This was their tenth time up the hill and her parka was beginning to feel a little warm. A whole ski suit would have been overkill. She'd avoided the Michelin Man look out of pride, not wanting to look puffy and awkward, but now she was glad she'd worn light ski pants.

"Are you sure you're having fun?" he asked, shooting her a glance. He'd seemed careful, cautious around her. He was probably worried that she was getting tired of Allison and Sean at her apartment. Nothing could be further from the truth. If she was tired of anything, it was worrying about how he would react when she told him the truth about her past. It would be too awkward while Allison was living with her. She had to wait until after the press conference, which Allison said might be in the next week. Evie wanted it to be over, but at the same time, she wanted more days like these in the future. Days of coming home to laughing voices, trips to the mountain with Gavin and Sean and seeing this man almost every day. Her heart constricted just thinking of how fast it would all be over.

Sean piped up, cheery little boy voice echoing in the cold air, "Yes, Uncle Gavin!"

Evie smiled at him. "Me, too."

"This will be good practice for when we have kids, anyway." Gavin shot her a glance. "I mean, kids you have and kids I have. Separately."

Evie stopped, one hand on her hip. "Separately? What exactly are you saying?"

His face was turning pink. "I mean, we could have them together, if you wanted."

"If I wanted. That's not a very romantic offer," she said, her eyes narrowing.

"Come on, guys!" Sean was tugging her hand, and Evie couldn't hold her face straight any longer. She burst out laughing as she trotted after Sean.

"I underestimated your inherent meanness." Gavin

was alongside them, easily keeping pace while dragging the large wooden sled.

"Sorry. It was too good to resist. First we were having kids and then we weren't and then we were having some if I wanted."

As she repeated the words back to him, his lips quirked up. "Sounds like I have a decision-making disorder, but my mind is amazingly clear."

They were almost at the top. Evie was thinking she probably wasn't going to be able to roll out of bed tomorrow morning. She was going to be crippled from all this exercise.

Most of the sledders were on their way back down; only Sean, Evie and Gavin remained at the very peak, like mountaineers attaining the summit. She paused, turning to him. His gaze was intense; it spoke volumes into the relative silence at the top of the hill.

Evie felt her breath catch in her throat. He was so near, she could feel the heat radiating off him. He reached out a hand and brushed a strand of hair from her cheek, his fingers warm against her skin. She wanted to lean forward and inhale his familiar smell. His lips turned up at the corners as if he knew just what she was thinking. Evie felt her face go hot. She must be so obviously smitten, but part of her just didn't care. She wanted him to know how much he meant to her, this fiercely protective man who wanted to save the world. And in the next moment, she remembered that she still had a very big conversation to have with this man. Her heart squeezed in her chest.

She quickly turned to Sean, holding out his mittens. "Hey, let's get these back on you before the next go-round."

"Hey, Gavin!" The shout caught Evie's attention. Jack was loping toward them up the slope, huge smile on his face.

"I was hoping to catch you guys up here today. I found someone to take my beginning snowboarder up the mountain so I could hang out." Huge neon ski goggles were pushed up on Jack's knit hat, and his green pants matched his jacket. The modern paint splatter pattern made him look like a giant ink blot.

"Great. We're just thinking of trying out a snowboard on the bunny hill." Gavin hoisted the sled over his shoulder and pointed to a small lump down near the lodge.

"Jack, I think we should take a bathroom break before we start with the snowboarding lessons." Evie waggled her eyebrows at her brother, hoping he got her drift. Kids Sean's age would get too excited to take time for the essentials. And that would sure put a damper on their outing.

"Evie's right. Let's sled down, hit the bathrooms, grab some hot chocolate and do the bunny hill next." Gavin mouthed a "thank you" as he steered Sean toward the sled.

It only took seconds for Sean to reach the bottom of the hill. "Oh, Uncle Gavin, why? We were just having so much fun and now we have to stop." Sean's shoulders slumped as he trudged after his uncle.

"A quick break, kiddo, then we're back on the slopes."

"But I don't want hot chocolate. I want to snowboard." Even behind the Spider-Man mask and under the helmet, Evie could tell Sean was disappointed.

"No hot chocolate? I thought you lived on it." She

tried to jostle him out of his mood, but his blue eyes just blinked at her. "My hands are freezing and my toes are numb. Don't you want to warm up a bit?"

"I feel fine. I'm not cold at all." He stomped up the flagstone steps to the lodge deck. Evie sure hoped he was telling the truth. She didn't want to bring him back to Allison with frostbite. The bathroom trip was non-negotiable, though.

Gavin reached for the giant lodge doors, swinging one side open and standing aside to let them through.

She glanced up at Gavin as he held the door and smiled. She didn't care where she was, in the bright sunlight on a gorgeous mountaintop or on a frozen park bench, she just loved being with him. Being near him was becoming something essential, like sunlight or food. A thrill went through her that was chased by a healthy dose of fear. Being near Gavin might not always be a possibility.

After she convinced Sean to head into the bathroom, he refused to sit down at the table Gavin had chosen in the corner, away from the crowds. "Jack said he'd take me outside. Please, Uncle Gavin?"

"You guys can sit in here and warm up. You'll be able to see us." Jack pointed toward the bright, glittery slope in front of the lodge. Small, helmeted children were being coaxed up and down the gentle swells by cautious adults.

"We'll be right here if you need us." Gavin looked hesitant but didn't seem to find a reason to object.

"Don't forget your mittens!" Evie jumped up to put on the little pair of gloves and made sure Sean's coat was zipped to the top. His hood was up, the Spider-

Man ski mask hiding everything but his blue eyes and his mouth, which was split in a huge grin.

She watched Jack and Sean head back out the door, snowboards in hand. He was so good with kids, a natural father. Who knew where he got it from. Their own father had never spent much time with them.

"So, you're not going to get tired of us, are you? We're over at your place all the time. I'm expecting Grandma Lili to bring her bridge group on Tuesdays if you don't lay down the law."

She felt laughter rise in her throat. "I'd love Grandma Lili to move in. She cooks like a dream."

"And the rest of us? I'm sorry if I've been invading your space. Up here at Echo Mountain today and then brunch tomorrow and Christmas right after that. You're probably ready to apply for the witness protection program."

"I think it would take more than a few home-cooked dinners and a great ski day to make me avoid you." Evie felt her cheeks warm again. She couldn't resist flirting with him, even if their time together was running out.

He leaned back in his chair and tapped a finger on his chin. "You could always add Sunday church and see if that makes me even more tired of you. Just for kicks."

She grinned. "Oh, but you go to the early service with all the old ladies. Jack would never forgive me if I left him alone at the ten o'clock on a permanent basis."

"So, what will we do? Are we cursed to attend different services for the rest of our lives?"

*The rest of our lives.* Her heart thudded in her chest, but she pretended to consider the problem. "You'll never be able to convince Lili to come later?"

"Not a chance. Only for special occasions. Christmas. Easter. Weddings." He said this last word with a wink and chuckled as her face flamed.

"Well, then we're doomed. Might as well face it."

"I never figured you for a pessimist."

She watched Gavin surreptitiously from under her lashes. He was completely at ease, coat tossed across the bench, gray sweater showing off all the time he spent in the gym, blond hair mussed from his hat. She loved the way his heavy brows made him look a bit serious all the time, even when he was happy. He turned to the window, keeping an eye on Sean. One corner of his mouth tugged up as Sean flailed into the snow and Jack leaped to pull him upright.

He glanced up and caught her watching him. She dropped her eyes to her mug, stirring the dregs with a spoon.

"What were you thinking just now?"

Evie tossed back her hair and tried to look as if she weren't inwardly writhing in embarrassment. What could she say? *I was remarking over your every feature, noting each bit of perfection.* She searched around for something, anything.

He reached for her hand and rubbed his thumb along her knuckles. His hand was so large compared to her own. His fingers were warm, sheltering. She never wanted to let him go.

"I never know what you're thinking," he said.

"You're not so easy to read yourself." She wanted to reach out and run her fingers along his jaw, his cheek, across his lips. The corner was dark, and the fire crackled merrily a few feet away. Every detail, from the wisp of smoke from the logs to the exposed timbers in the lodge, Evie wanted to catalogue for later. Soon, she would have to admit her part in Allison's downfall, and she was sure there wasn't going to be another day like this for them. Not together, holding hands near the fireplace on a perfect, snowy day. She sighed and looked out the window—and gasped.

Jack was holding Sean's ski mask in one hand and pumping a fist into the air with the other. Sean was zooming down the bunny hill, small feet planted perfectly on the snowboard. He was heading directly for the wedge-shaped jump, and his miniature figure was gaining speed with every second. Evie stood up, arms raised, as if she could warn them through the glass.

The next moment, Sean hit the jump and launched into the air. He floated gracefully for several seconds. Then he crashed to earth with a sound that wasn't audible to them but was to other people on the slope, who came running to his aid.

## Chapter Sixteen

Gavin reached the door before he'd even begun to process what he'd seen. The icy blast of air seemed to knock the breath from his lungs as he sprinted toward Sean. By the time Gavin slid to a kneeling position near his nephew's small body, Jack was already wiping the snow from his face, gently unbuckling the helmet straps.

"I think he just had the wind knocked out of him." Jack's voice was shaking, higher than normal.

"You think?" Gavin growled the sarcastic comment. He was trying to keep his temper in check, but he was torn between wanting to scoop up Sean and strangle Jack. "What were you thinking? He's five!"

"He hit it just right, it was perfect. He just forgot to…land."

"Oh, he landed." Gavin leaned over Sean's face and tried to sound calmer than he felt. "Can you hear me?"

In response Sean screwed up his face and started to cry.

"Does it hurt? Can you tell me where it hurts?" He had never felt so helpless, watching his nephew lying on the hard-packed snow, curious onlookers gathering around.

"My rear end hurts." Sean finally managed to squeak out a few words. Tears leaked out of his eyes and he struggled to sit up.

"Here, sweetie." Evie was there, kneeling next to them, wiping Sean's tears with a soft tissue. "Come on up and let's go sit inside for a second."

He sniffed loudly and stood up. "Why are all these people here?"

Gavin gazed around at the small crowd and felt his stomach knot with alarm. "Where's your ski mask, buddy?"

"It was hot so we took it off…." Jack's voice trailed away as he looked at the mask in his hand.

Evie threw him a look that said he'd get a lecture later and snatched the mask from his hand. "Better let me have it for now."

"I think I want to try it again." Sean sniffed a few times and then grabbed his snowboard, trying to stand in the brackets. Gavin couldn't help but be impressed with the kid's toughness.

"Are you sure? We can take a break."

"I'm sure. Jack, can we go back up?"

He looked at Evie, who seemed to be having a silent conversation with her brother. "Okay, but you better put this back on or you'll get more snow in your face if you biff it."

Sean stepped over to let Evie put on the mask, then the helmet.

"Hi, guys." Gavin turned to see a young woman with brown hair and blue eyes, smiling hugely at them, large camera around her neck. The hair on the back of his neck stood up as she stared openly at Sean's re-treating figure.

"Amy, hi. Aren't you visiting that goat farm today?" Evie had crossed her arms over her chest.

"Oh, sure, it was great. Got lots of pictures. I came up here to see if I can get some good shots for the Sunday sports page." Her gaze flicked between Gavin and Evie.

"The sports page?" Evie's voice held a note of something he couldn't define.

"Sure. You know, in case they wanted some good sledding shots for the front. Is this your boyfriend?" Amy stepped toward Gavin and put out her hand. Gavin had the faint impression of a predator sniffing for prey.

"Yes, I'm Gavin." He took her hand, expression neutral.

"Amy Morket, reporter for *The Chronicle*. Well, nice to meet you. See you at work, boss." Another thorough once-over and Amy turned back to the lodge. The crowd of worried bystanders drifted away, murmuring words of relief at Sean's lack of injury.

Evie blew out a breath. "That girl reminds me of myself ten years ago. And not in a good way. Questions, all the time."

He slipped an arm around her shoulders. "Isn't that usual for reporters?"

She thought about it for a moment. "Journalists are a curious lot, that's for sure. But most of us know not to be annoying about it. It's the way she pops up everywhere. She's supposed to be touring a goat farm today, but instead she's up here. I can't hardly turn around without bumping into her."

Jack let out a whoop as Sean managed a small hill, this time without falling face first into the snow. "He's a natural!" he called toward them.

Evie sent him a thumbs-up and let out a laugh. "My brother should never come off this mountain. He's so happy up here." The smile faded from her face. "And I think if he gets up the nerve, he's going to quit his job and do just that."

"Better now than when he has a family to support."

She watched him adjust the snowboard, settling Sean's boots into the latches. "I want him to be happy, even if he makes almost nothing. He was never made to sit in an office all day. I wish our father could see that."

He understood. He wished for a lot of things, mostly to understand what made his parents act the way they did. How could they possibly reject Sean? How could they refuse to see Allison because she kept her baby? But he still loved them. Strangely, illogically, his heart still ached for their family to be whole.

At the bottom of the hill once more, Sean trudged through the snow toward them, small figure showing obvious signs of tiredness. Jack had the board over one shoulder and was smiling ear to ear.

"He did great! Probably the easiest kid I ever taught."

The little boy lifted his face to his uncle and beamed. "Did you hear that?"

"I sure did, buddy." Gavin sat him on the bench and gave him a hug. "Are you ready to call it a day?"

"Yeah, I bet my mom is really sad without me." His big blue eyes were deadly serious.

"Do you want to call her and tell her we're coming

back? Then she will know you're on your way." Evie held up her cell phone and Sean nodded.

They headed to the car while Sean chattered on her phone.

Gavin looked over at Evie and couldn't help the warmth that spread through his chest. What a perfect morning. He hadn't thought about work once. Maybe that wasn't a good thing, but it sure felt good right now.

She slid him a look. "What are you thinking about?"

He coughed, surprised. "That's my line."

"It's hard for me to read your expression. Like, right now, you seemed happy, but then your eyebrows came down like this." She demonstrated with a fierce scowl.

He couldn't choke back the laughter. "Okay, I look nothing like that."

Evie shrugged a sort of "have it your way" motion and smiled. "Anyway, are you happy? Or mad? Or both?"

"I just…was realizing how little I think about work when I'm with you and wondering if that was good or bad."

She nodded. "The other day I forgot something important at least three times. This probably doesn't bode well for future success in our careers."

He almost tripped over a lump of icy snow in the parking lot as he turned to grin at her. Those bright blue eyes, the sweet smile framed by dimples. She was strong, faithful, funny. She exuded life, grace.

But Gavin had always been the serious science geek, the lab rat who spent his time working instead of socializing. Patrick's memory had consumed him as he fought his solitary battle. She was all about the community and bringing people together. Could they find a place together, meet in the middle? Was he wrong to even think of making room in his life for something other than his scientific work?

She stopped and pointed. "See, right there. You did it again!"

"What? Did what?"

Sean was still describing his every snowboard maneuver to his mom on the phone, and he obligingly stood still next to them.

"You were smiling, then it just faded away." Her face was set in a stubborn frown. "You know, if you're having second thoughts, about this," she waved a hand between them, "it's okay to tell me. I don't want you to hide your reservations because you don't want to hurt me."

She was worried that he might not really like her. Love her.

Sean continued to chatter as Gavin stepped toward Evie, reaching out a hand to her cheek. Her skin was silky soft but hot to the touch. He slipped his hand behind her head, running his fingers up into her hair. Her eyes went half-closed. He could see a pulse jumping at the base of her throat, her lips parted slightly. He leaned in, promising himself just one kiss. Her perfume was clean, light. He felt her hands up against his chest, and he slipped an arm around her waist, drawing her near. Her breath was warm against his mouth. Nothing had ever felt so perfect.

"And they're kissing. No, real kissing. Right now. Uh-huh... Still kissing." Sean's voice cut through the fog that was wrapped around his brain.

A tug on the back of his coat. "Uncle Gavin, my mom says to knock it off."

Evie leaned back with a gasp, her hand to her mouth, eyes wide with laughter.

Gavin kept an arm around her waist and growled back, "Tell your mom she's being bossy."

Sean dutifully repeated the message. Evie shook with laughter, her face pink.

"She says if you can't control yourself," he paused, listening to his mother, "she can get a bucket of ice water ready."

Evie broke down completely, laughing into the front of his coat, her shoulders shaking. He couldn't help grinning. Little sisters. Always getting in the way.

"Uncle Gavin, what does that mean? Why do you need a bucket of ice water? Are you thirsty?"

Gavin felt his face go hot and nodded at Sean. "Sure am. Tell your mom we're being good now."

Sean looked at them, little boy face screwed up in concentration. "He says he's being good, but he's still hugging her." There was a short pause. "My mom says hands off."

He chuckled and released Evie, although he missed her soft figure immediately. Her expression told him she wished he'd held on a bit longer. "Tell her she wins. And we'll be there in about half an hour."

Another messaged delivered and Evie got her phone back. "Let's get going, Mr. Snowboard Champion of the Year."

"Can you call me that all the time?"

"Hmm. Maybe just on Saturdays, okay?"

"Okay." His little face was bright with happiness, and Gavin knew exactly how he felt.

He caught her watching his face as they pulled out of the parking lot. "Yes?"

She blushed, her eyes darting away. "Just waiting for the scowl."

"No more scowling. I promise." And he couldn't imagine being unhappy when he thought of the days ahead, starting with tomorrow. All of his favorite people in one place, around some good food. It just didn't get any better than that.

"If you're trying to convince me to move, it's not working." Allison stood in the doorway to the kitchen and stared, wide-eyed. The enchiladas were just out of the oven, green sauce peeking through the bubbling pepper jack cheese. In a smaller dish, the more kid-friendly penne pasta over simple sauce sat cooling.

Evie snorted, hands deep into the pie dough she was kneading. "If I wanted you to leave, I would put you to work in here."

If she popped it in the moment Gavin and Grandma Lili got here, it would be done and cooled right after brunch was over. It had been tricky, getting to church with her brother and preparing an entire brunch, but Evie was all about the planning. Put together last night, even though her muscles were complaining from the sledding exercise, it had been simple to pop them in this morning and let them cook while she was gone. Allison was still in hiding, so she kept an eye on the food, but Evie could tell the young mom was more than ready to be honest with the world about her past with Senator McHale.

Evie's stomach clenched. Not out of worry for Allison, but in the knowledge that as soon as she was no longer sheltering Gavin's sister, Evie needed to be honest, too. And that step scared her to death.

"But I like cooking, actually. One of the clubs where I used to sing had a nice grill. The owner was one of those guys who liked fusion food. Cuban American, Korean Cuban, Cuban Vegan... Well, anything Cuban."

Evie shrugged off the dark cloud of worry and attempted a bright smile. "Then come on in. Actually, we should get Sean in here to help with the pie. I have leftover dough and he can make shapes and toast them in the oven."

"I don't know if you want my kid in this kitchen," Allison said, gazing around at the bright white cabinets and gleaming floor.

"It's all washable. Bring him on in." Evie hurried to prepare a place for Sean at the counter. Rolling out some foil and taping it on, she grabbed cookie cutters and a little cup of flour.

"Really, Evie? Can I help?" Sean was speeding into the kitchen, not really waiting for an answer, eyes wide with excitement.

"Sure, you'll be over here." She rummaged through a small cabinet and came up with a tiny oak rolling pin. She held it up toward Allison. "I knew this would come in handy. I saw it at a flea market and bought it. Jack thought I was nuts."

Allison grinned. "I see why. It's a bit small."

"I told him it was for small pies." Evie hurried into the living room for a chair and brought it back for Sean. She would miss having the little guy around, rebel yells and all. She hoped they would still come visit after they'd moved back to their own place. Even if she and Gavin weren't together any longer, if he couldn't forgive her for not telling him the truth sooner.

She felt a smothering wave of fear and pushed it back once more. Focus on the moment. God would take care of the rest.

There was a knock at the front door, and Evie looked up, confused. Gavin and his grandmother were more than half an hour early. She didn't bother to wash her hands but trotted to the living room and peered through the peephole.

Evie swung the door open, already talking. "I thought you guys were coming at two. Where's Lili? I was just…" Gavin stepped inside and closed the door, but there was no welcoming hug.

"I need to talk to you." Just a few simple words, but the world seemed to tilt and shift under Evie's feet. "Senator McHale just gave me a call. He said he was checking in on how our office was doing, but the truth is that internet article has got him scrambling to explain why he hasn't supported his kid for five years. He had a lot to say, and it wasn't all about Allison." His voice was cold, cold, cold. "It seems the paper that published those pictures of him got a new editor. One that was more willing to tell him exactly who sold those pictures in the first place."

Oh, no. Not now. Not yet. She'd wanted to tell him her own way, quietly, humbly. But the moment had come in a flurry of accusations.

"Will you listen if I try to explain?" She could barely see through a sudden sheen of tears, but she was desperate. To explain, to go back to the moment she should have told him everything.

He shrugged, brown eyes narrowed, expression tight with anger.

"When I graduated from journalism school, I moved

to Aspen. I worked as a freelance photographer to pay the bills. Mostly I hid in the dark and tried to catch people doing things they shouldn't." She took a quavering breath. It was all coming too fast, like it was rehearsed. She hated herself for feeling fear. It wasn't the guilt that hurt anymore; it was the fear of losing Gavin.

Gavin raised a hand, as if to ward off her words. His face was tight and pale. But when he didn't speak, she went on.

"I'd like to say it wasn't personal, but knowing the person I was then, I don't think that really would have mattered. It was thrilling to be around famous people. I also hated them because they weren't drowning under their college debt, like I was. When I heard Senator McHale was cheating on his wife, I decided to follow him until I got a picture I could sell. I knew there was a lot of money in it for me." Her mouth felt sour, but she swallowed back her emotions. She needed to tell the truth, no matter what came next.

"You did it for the money." His voice had dropped an octave.

Evie felt the hair on the back of her neck stand up. Some small part of her realized she'd never seen Gavin angry. Not really. Not like this.

Evie stared up at him, emotions warring within her heart. No matter what good thing they might have had, it ended here. "I did sell those pictures of Allison. I didn't know who she was, but I knew the senator was running for President."

She felt her eyes start to burn and angrily brushed them with the palms of her hands. She wasn't crying because of what she'd lost. She was angry at the person she had been so long ago. She would never be able to really get away from her past. It would always be lurking there, somewhere in the dark. She would be punished for her actions over and over.

"Once I realized how wrong it all was, I took the money and tried to do something better, something good for the world. It doesn't excuse my behavior. And I understand how it must feel, as Allison's brother—"

"No, you can't understand." His head was bowed, as if he were carrying a terrible weight. "There is no way you could know what it's like to watch a person you love walk away from God, to live a lifestyle that only leads to disaster. I watched her throw everything away for a man who wasn't worth a second glance. And then she was shamed publically and abandoned by our parents."

The pain in his face was like a physical blow. Evie felt her stomach roll. She didn't know what that was like, but she did know what it was to carry the guilt of that on her shoulders.

"I talked to Allison. We've made peace with it. And for what it's worth, I didn't know who she was before…" Her voice trailed off. *Before I met you.*

"I'm glad she knows."

Evie knew what he meant. He'd been afraid that Allison would feel the betrayal all over again, being sheltered in the home of the person who had ruined her life the first time around.

"But that makes me the last to know. You didn't feel like you could be honest. Even after we talked about truth and not hiding from each other."

Evie put a hand to her chest, as if to keep her heart in its place, as if she could protect herself from his words. The resignation in his face was like the final nail in the coffin. It was over. "I wanted to explain at the right time, in the right way."

"Any time would have been a good time." His face was heavy with misery. "I never liked journalists."

Evie was silent for a beat. "I'm sorry for who I was, but not for who I am."

Gavin shook his head. As if there wasn't any difference between the two. And since her past was always with her, maybe there wasn't.

She forced herself to look him in the eye, to stand firm when all she wanted to do was walk into his arms and ask him to forget everything she'd said, to kiss her like he had before he'd known all her secrets. She had never felt so safe in her whole life, and she ached to be there again. But right now, it seemed like they were separated by an entire ocean, all because of the person she used to be.

Allison came into the living room, speaking into the tense atmosphere. "Sean's got flour on every inch of your kitchen." She looked from Evie to Gavin. "What's up with you guys? Should I go back in the kitchen?"

"No, I have no secrets from you. Unlike you two." He watched Allison stop, consider his words, her gaze flashing to Evie and back to him.

Allison paused, choosing her words carefully. "I thought she told you."

"No." That one word held barely concealed hurt. If Evie hadn't known him, she would have thought he was shrugging it off. But the line of his mouth and the tightness around his eyes told her he was taking the news personally. "Maybe you shouldn't have assumed she was being honest, either."

His gaze raked over Evie and she wanted to weep,

wanted to beg him to understand. But if there was something she had learned recently, it was that mistakes can't be unmade.

"I'm going back in the kitchen. You two need to talk this out." Allison turned on her heel and left them in the stinging silence.

Evie wanted it to be over, for the conversation to end so she could find somewhere quiet to let out her grief. But he was still there, standing stiff with anger.

"There was another article today on the gossip website."

His words were so casual it took Evie a few seconds to process them. Her head came up with a snap, eyes widening.

"It was from our trip to the mountain. Isn't it strange how they got pictures of Sean snowboarding without his mask? Right when I was lured inside with you?"

"Lured inside?" Anger finally surpassed her shock. She planted her hands on her hips, spitting the words now, so angry she could hardly talk.

"I think these articles aren't ending up at *The Daily* because it's *The Chronicle*'s rival and that would have hurt your sales. Why on the internet? Because they paid the most, and we all know your paper is in trouble. You and Amy found a way to make some easy money."

"First of all, our internet site has been up since this Wednesday and has already tripled our subscribers. I even have a little celebrity section that will be clean and upbeat." She spoke clearly but her voice wavered, and she forced her trembling hands into fists.

She hauled in a breath and went on. "I don't care who told you I was involved. I wouldn't be surprised if Amy was part of it, but I didn't sell this. And I can't believe you thought, for even one moment, that I did." Tears of anger sprang to her eyes and she blinked them away. She would not cry. Not here.

"Something Lili said last week stuck with me. She told me I had a God-given purpose. She said 'I believe in you.'" Hearing those words felt like air when she'd been drowning. They traveled deep inside and filled up the empty spaces where fear and doubt lived.

She was more than the sum of her mistakes.

"I'm sorry I didn't tell you sooner about the past. I wasn't sure how you would react, and I didn't want it to be awkward with Allison staying here. I was afraid to lose you." Her face went hot, but she could be honest now. It didn't matter what she said.

His eyes were shadowed with pain, and she felt sick, knowing she was the one who had caused it. "From the moment we met, I knew that I would have to tell you what I had done. I imagined a thousand times the expression you would have, the disappointment I'd see in your eyes. It should have happened long before now. But I was weak. It was harder and harder to tell you the truth, the deeper I fell—" *In love with you.*

She couldn't finish. She walked back to the kitchen, choking back tears.

Allison looked up, face taut with worry. She squeezed Evie on the shoulder and left for the living room.

"Do you have any sprinkles?" Sean was busy pressing odd shapes onto the cookie sheet, his hands covered in flour.

"Sure, sweetie." She grabbed the red and green sugar sprinkles by feel from the cabinet. "Remember this is pie dough. It won't be as sweet as a cookie." Her voice was rough, but he didn't seem to notice.

"This is fun! Isn't this fun? You should finish your pie."

"Yes, I should." Evie went back to the pie dough, her eyes blurred with tears. Who knew if anyone was staying for brunch. She wasn't sure she could sit across the table from Gavin as her heart broke into a thousand small pieces. But she would make this pie.

A few moments later, Allison came in. She stood in the doorway. "I'm sorry."

"For what? I'm sorry your life is splattered all over an internet gossip site." She waved a floury hand. "Don't worry about me."

Allison was quiet a moment, watching Evie lace the lattice crust over the blackberries. "But I am worried. I think what just happened…was wrong. He was wrong to accuse you."

Evie nodded, swallowing the lump that threatened to choke her.

The young mom smiled, but it was a strained and tight smile. "Well, I can't keep putting the statement off. It will have to happen now, no matter if—" she glanced at Sean, sprinkling what looked like a pound of sugar on his dough "—anyone else objects."

"I sure wish this had never happened. I know Jack will be so upset. He wanted everything to go well that day."

"It did!" Allison reached forward and hugged Evie. "It was a wonderful day. Sean had so much fun. Don't regret it now."

But the day would always be touched with bitterness for Evie. The kisses she and Gavin had shared, standing in the snow. Based in nothing but simple attraction. There was no faith, no trust.

She felt as if her heart was being caught in a clamp with teeth. "Do you think your grandma is still coming?"

"Let me call her and see." Allison left the room and went down the hallway. Evie tried to finish her lattice work, but she kept pulling too hard, the pie crust tearing into small strips.

"You need me to help you." Sean got down and scooted his chair over to Evie's work space.

"I sure do." She had to smile at his confidence. This was not a child who'd been emotionally stunted. He knew love, knew he had worth and value.

"I'll hold this one and you put that one there." He picked up a strip and pointed with his other hand. Evie followed his instructions, even though the crust was crooked. They worked together for a few minutes, creating a lattice that was more tangled than crosshatch. He beamed at the finished product. "There, see? That's how you do it."

"Thanks, buddy," she said, glad to be reminded of innocence in a world that was full to the brim of betrayal and suspicion.

Allison popped back into the kitchen. "Wow, nice pie." She grinned at Evie, but her eyes were sad. "Grandma's headed over in a little bit. She's getting the salad ready. Come on, Sean, let's go play with the trampoline."

She didn't say anything about Gavin, and Evie didn't ask. They would just concentrate on the brunch. And each other. Not the missing person who should be with them today.

Evie slid the pie into the oven and set the timer. She could do this. Her shoulders straightened. He was just a man she'd thought she'd known. A few kisses, some confidences. It wasn't anything to call a relationship. He'd gotten the city through the pertussis epidemic. That's what she would focus on, the noble part of him she always admired. It didn't matter that he had completely misjudged her, accused her of betraying his family.

Evie wiped down the counters and put away the sprinkles. God had told her in very clear terms what she was supposed to do. And she did it. That was all. Nothing else was promised. But as much as she told herself these things, as hard as she tried to believe them, Evie's heart still ached with every new resolution to be grateful. She had glimpsed something wonderful with Gavin. It was only a glimpse, but she would never be the same woman she had been before.

Pausing at the sink, her hands in the running water and eyes squeezed shut, Evie let the tears flow down her cheeks. One minute to grieve for what might have been, and then she would go on. Allison needed support, and Sean needed them all to put aside the drama so he could be a little boy. She wiped her cheeks and straightened up. God was faithful, ever merciful. That she would rely on, no matter what else was crashing down around them.

## Chapter Seventeen

Gavin stood up and paced his office. He had come here to calm down, but he felt like he was going to jump out of his skin. It had been two days since he'd walked into Evie's apartment, and the look on her face still haunted him. Grief, hurt and deep resignation.

He'd been so sure he was in the right. But when he'd called Grandma Lili to explain about the brunch, all his sureness started to unravel.

She could have been angry with Evie, shocked at hiding a lie, defensive of Allison and her grandson. But instead Grandma Lili had gently exclaimed over Evie's past and even admired her refusal to give up.

He groaned, rubbing his eyes. It was as if she liked Evie even more, now that she knew how far she had come from the person she was once, only five years ago.

He was the same old Gavin, always doing the right thing, never tolerating any mistake. How could that be any better? His chest ached with the suspicion that he had acted unjustly, and to someone braver than he was. The idea shook him to his core. She was a woman who had the strength to walk away from wealth and fame and bitterness, a woman who devoted her time to building up instead of tearing down. He sucked in a shuddering breath, pain coursing through him. He had been so wrong, and he didn't know how to make it right.

Grabbing his coat, he shoved his arms through the sleeves. When all else failed, there was always more work to be done. Baby Gabriel was almost ready to go home. Nothing like an infant on the mend to make him forget what a mess he'd made.

Minutes later Gavin suited up at the door of Gabriel's hospital room. He knocked lightly and a soft answer prompted him to enter.

"Hey, it's our superhero." Calista cradled her newborn in one arm, a book in her other hand, and flashed a huge grin.

His shoulders slumped, but he rallied with a smile. "That's me." He aimed for lighthearted, but his tone was bitter even to his own ears.

"Uh-oh. Come sit. Even superheroes have bad days." Calista patted the chair next to her.

"I came to see Gabriel. Grant said he's doing really well." Gavin tried to deflect Calista's sharp gaze by flipping through the pages on the chart.

"Thanks to you and Evie." She touched his sleeve. "Without that article I wouldn't have known to bring him in right away." She cleared her throat, struggling for control. "I'm sure you've saved more lives than my baby's, many more."

She went on. "If that doesn't make you smile, there's always the thought of the Christmas pageant. The kids are thrilled. Grant's not too calm about it, either. He loves Christmas. We both do. It's a special holiday for us." She gazed down at Gabriel, a small smile touching her lips.

"So, tell me what makes a superhero look so defeated."

Gavin lowered himself into the standard-issue hospital chair and gazed up at the tiled ceiling. "I'm an idiot," he said simply.

To his surprise, Calista laughed, a bright sound that filled the room. "I know that look. Did Evie discover your secret identity?"

He snapped his gaze to her, shock silencing him.

She waved a hand. "How did *I* know it was about Evie? Easy guess. Now, you don't have to give me any details, and I can tell you exactly how to fix whatever you've done."

Resting his elbows on his knees, he shook his head. "You're assuming it can be fixed."

"If you're the man I think you are, what you've done is probably very stupid, but not unforgivable." Calista's voice still held a note of mirth, but her green eyes were serious.

"So, what's your advice?" He was sure it would never work, whatever it was.

"Grovel."

"What?"

"I said you need to grovel. Not just apologize. Don't send flowers. Go over there and grovel. Show her what you feel."

Gavin stared, trying to wrap his mind around the idea of a gesture being big enough to make Evie forget his cruel words. He had misjudged her so badly, he didn't know if there was anything that could change it. Grandma Lili said she believed in her, in a God-given purpose, but what could he say that wasn't just parroting the words?

"Here, hold Gabriel for a second." Calista passed him the tiny bundle, dark hair peeking from the top of the blankets. "He'll help you sort it all out."

Gavin snorted softly, cradling the warmth of the little boy in his arms. "He must be pretty smart already." He could feel his muscles relaxing as he gazed into the baby's serene countenance.

"Just try it." She patted him on the shoulder and leaned back in her chair, eyes falling closed. "I'll be right here if you need me. But you can't look at that sweet face and tell me there is anything impossible with God's help."

His lips tugged up as he watched Gabriel sleep. Maybe she was right. Maybe life wasn't as predictable as he thought, and love sometimes got a second chance. His heart thudded loudly in his ears. *Love.* He didn't know when it had happened, couldn't point to a moment it began, but he loved Evie. He loved her quiet strength and her tenacity that somehow translated to gentleness with every other being. He loved her ability to accept forgiveness. He loved how she grabbed for grace and held on with both hands, how she lived her life with such vibrant hope.

He wanted a life like that, not the one he had that was filled with fear and dread. Since Patrick's death he had always prepared for every disaster and been surprised when it didn't arrive. His hands tightened around the little baby as realization struck him. Years had gone by, full of pessimistic anxiety, and although he said he trusted God, he expected the very worst at any moment. Evie knew that true faith was hopeful.

Gavin straightened up with a deep breath. He knew what he needed to do. And it spoke louder than any apology he could ever say.

Ten feet down the sidewalk, Evie could already hear the caroling coming from the Mission. Her bright red Christmas dress and a delicately woven braid covered in crystal snowflakes announced she was ready to celebrate. The snow drifted down in lazy clumps, but the weather wasn't bitterly cold. The lights shone through the glass front, displaying brightly colored decorations and the twinkling tree.

Jack flashed a grin and pointed to the crowd inside. "This is going to be some party. I think I see Allison and Sean already."

She nodded, pasting on a bright smile. She hadn't heard from Gavin since Sunday. The pain was still so fresh it took her breath away. On the outside, she was fine, maybe a little sad. On the inside, she felt as if her whole life had turned to dust.

Jack paused, his usual cheer fading away. "I wish you and Gavin could…"

"I know. Me, too." She shrugged, hoping she looked nonchalant.

It should be clear now that Gavin had been wrong. Amy Morket quit the day after the photos came out on the gossip site. Evie had heard she'd moved to California, bragged about getting an absurd amount of money for a few pictures. She was going to join the celebrity chasers. Evie's heart ached for the girl. She knew sometime, somehow, she was going to see her life had been wasted. And she knew just how that felt.

The first few days after Allison's announcement,

they had been overrun with photographers. Allison's phone rang and rang, reporters and TV interviewers and even a few tabloid shows wanting to "reunite" the senator and his son. The only call that had mattered to Allison was the one from her parents. It would be rough and take time, but reconciliation was beginning between them.

"I'm just happy Allison's getting a new start. A real one, this time." She meant it. Nobody deserved a clean slate more than Allison and Sean.

Jack slung an arm over her shoulders and hugged her close. "I'm a big fan of new starts."

Evie smiled, wishing there would be one for her and Gavin. But life didn't always work that way. "Let's head in. We don't want to miss the pageant."

The lobby was filled with the sound of excited kids lining up to talk to Santa. Evie snorted as she recognized Jose behind the bushy white beard. Grant listened intently to a small boy telling what seemed to be a very long story. Lissa walked through the crowd of kids with a tray of cookies, an oversize Santa hat on her head.

"Evie!" Sean's little voice cut through the noise. She turned just in time to feel his arms wrap around her waist. "You came."

"Of course I did." She laughed a little, but the truth was she really hadn't wanted to come. If there had been any way to stay home, she would have.

Allison came toward them, dark hair curled and tied back with a green ribbon, her face alight with happiness. "There you two are." She reached out and hugged them both, with Sean an awkward lump in the middle.

"You and Jack are coming to Grandma Lili's for

Christmas brunch tomorrow as my guests. Don't even try to say no."

Evie nodded, not trusting herself to speak. She couldn't sit there, across from the man who had made her dream of a husband and marriage for the first time in her life.

"Gavin, tell them to be on time or else," Allison said.

Evie whirled around, eyes going wide. He was achingly familiar, hair brushed back, a few waves still showing up the professional haircut. He smelled wonderful, like soap and sandalwood, and was freshly shaved. But the thing that really threw her was his tie. It was perfectly straight.

"I came to see if I could talk to you for a few minutes." His voice was soft, as if the lobby weren't full to bursting. Evie glanced at Allison and realized his sister was already turning away, Jack on one side, Sean on the other. Sneaky girl.

"All right." She didn't want to be rude. It felt like her heart had slammed shut and there was no key to unlock it.

"Do you mind if we step outside? It's so hard to talk in here." He looked nervous but determined.

She nodded and followed him through the glass double doors onto the sidewalk. The strains of the Christmas carols echoed faintly, and the snow fell softly from the black sky.

"Evie, what I said was wrong." He stopped, looking at his hands.

"But you thought it. Even for a little while, you really believed it could be me." Her voice cracked on the last word.

He nodded. "I'm sorry. And I'm asking you to for-give me. You probably feel like I never knew you at all, to even consider the possibility. I was so wrong. About a lot of things." She didn't want to look in his eyes but couldn't help herself. The warmth in his gaze made her feel valued and respected. She tried to push away the overwhelming feelings and recognize the cold fact of it: he had believed the worst about her.

"When we worked on the article together, we saved lives. Gabriel's coming home. The Mission's Christ-mas party and caroling is happening, just like the kids needed. We made a difference, Evie, you and me."

She was silent, wishing she knew what to say. Some-times sorry wasn't good enough.

"Since Patrick died, I've lived like the sky was al-ways seconds away from falling." He drew in a ragged breath. "I had no faith that God would care for us. It was a hopeless situation, and all I could do was fight a losing battle. You opened my eyes to how wrong it was."

He reached in his jacket breast pocket.

"I have something for you. I hope it helps you un-derstand how much you've changed my life, how much I believe in you." It was an envelope, with a tiny bow and "Merry Christmas" written on the front.

She opened it, shooting him a curious glance. The folded paper opened up to show a flyer for a small, brick building on the northeast side, not far from down-town, right off the main boulevard.

"I saw this little place. It's in the right area, the right size. I talked to the Realtor today and made an offer. If you'll let me help, I want to be part of your dream for the thrift shop you wanted to open for the no-cost baby supplies." He pulled out another sheet.

"There are so many people in my area of work who want to help but don't really know how. I spent most of yesterday on the phone. This is a list of people who work with the county and state who said they'd be willing to lend a hand and give advice as needed, pro bono."

"How did you know—" Evie felt her throat close up around the words she yearned to speak. Her hand was still clutching the flyer, eyes filled with tears.

"Allison told us that day Grandma Lili came to cook dinner." His face was creased with anxiety, his eyes pleading with her. "You're not the kind of person to prey on the vulnerable. I was so wrong to accuse you. This thrift shop is the perfect example of all the ways you try to lift others up."

He took a breath, as if steadying himself. "I'm begging you to forgive me, Evie. I'll never be at peace until you do." She wanted to agree, say how it felt to have him beside her. But that's not what he was asking. He only wanted forgiveness, which she could never deny him. Her heart had made its own decision the moment he'd asked.

She smiled, her heart in her throat. "I do forgive you."

He nodded and took a deep breath. "I need to tell you something else."

Her brows went up, wondering what else there could be, besides the wonderful little shop and their new-found peace.

"I love you, Evie, for a hundred different reasons."

He loved her. Her heart began to pound so hard she could barely hear him.

"You're brave and smart and gentle and always root for the underdog. You've grown past a huge mistake. You showed me what real hope means."

Snow drifted around them, but she didn't feel the cold. He paused, eyes bright with deep emotion. "Do you think, Evie, that if we both kept our focus on our God-given purpose, that we could find happiness together? That would be the only way because, you and me, we're bound to get into all sorts of trouble."

His brown eyes were crinkled in laughter, and she felt a giggle rising up in her throat. What a time to be laughing, but she knew exactly what he meant. Loads and heaps of trouble were in their future. Two stubborn, intelligent people who thought they knew it all. What a recipe for disaster.

"Yes, Gavin." In the end, she settled for showing him what she felt because getting words past the ache in her throat was too much. The flyer crumpled against his chest as she put all of the love and gratitude she felt into her kiss.

She never wanted to move, to let him go an inch away from her. She felt the world shrinking to the space of two people gloriously in love.

His hand was warm in hers, and she gripped it tightly, letting her heart feel hope for the first time in a long while. She was laughing in earnest now, not quite believing that they were getting yet another chance.

He was pulling her close, arms wrapped around her waist. Evie let herself fall into his kiss in a way she never had before, with complete trust and abandon. No fear, only hope.

"Evie? Didn't my mom tell you guys to stop that?" A small voice sounded right near her elbow, and she looked down into the face of Gavin's godson.

"Sean!" Allison's horrified voice came from the doorway.

"I thought you were waiting to talk to Santa." Gavin's face was serious, but his voice was full of laughter. He pulled away from her, eyes bright with happiness.

"My mom had to go to the bathroom. She said to stand in line and not come out here." He stated it as naturally as if he had actually obeyed his mother, not the other way around.

Allison's face flushed deep pink. "Sorry you guys." She grabbed Sean's hand and started tugging him back to the party.

"You don't have to leave." Gavin looked up at Evie and she nodded. She felt herself glowing with pure happiness. "We've worked it out."

Allison burst into tears and ran to hug them both, shoulders shaking with sobs, her green ribbon squashed against Gavin's jacket.

"Whoa! Overreaction," Gavin said, laughing.

"No… I'm just so happy. I couldn't stand two of my favorite people not speaking." She stood back, wiping her eyes with her sleeve.

Sean cocked his blond head. "Does this mean you're going to be kissing more?"

"Come on, buddy. Let's get back inside." Allison grabbed Sean's hand and walked him to the Mission doors. "You guys have exactly five minutes. You don't want to miss the pageant."

Evie felt her face go hot, and Gavin chuckled in her ear, his warm breath sending shivers down her spine.

"One thing, Evie…" His arms were strong around her and she leaned into him, inhaling the familiar scent of him. "Can you put some airbags in that old car? The worry is just about killing me."

Laughter bubbled up from inside and she nodded. Some things wouldn't change, and she wouldn't have it any other way. Her heart felt as if it was unfolding, second by second. She was so thankful, so amazingly grateful for second chances. And thirds. And fourths.

Evie looked up into his face, laying a hand on his cheek, feeling as if it all wasn't quite real. His lips moved, whispering words she couldn't quite catch over the sound of the party and the beat of her heart. But she knew what he'd said, felt it deep in her bones.

His words were just a reassurance, an echo of the faith he'd shown in her. She stretched up on tiptoe and pressed a kiss to his lips.

"I love you, Gavin." The words came from that unfolding place inside and came out sounding like a breath of pure hope.

\* \* \* \* \*

Dear Reader,

The idea for Evie's story came to me in early spring about two years ago. A close friend had just explained why she didn't read any news articles about celebrities. She didn't want to be part of the culture of gossip. Well, I sure wasn't a gossip in person, but I did click those fun links to see what famous people were doing, good and bad. I'd never considered that I might be fueling our country's thirst for tabloid articles. What an eye-opener!

*Season of Hope* starts years after Evie changes her life. She clings to God's grace and His promises for a fresh start, but still carries guilt and feelings of never being good enough to balance out all the bad she's done to other people.

Gavin is the kind of man who wants to protect the world, but he also carries hurts from his childhood. Later, when his sister is embroiled in a very public scandal, Gavin's dislike for reporters grows even stronger. His fear of the unknown stands in the way of his growing faith.

Evie and Gavin are searching for forgiveness, in themselves and from others. Evie's freedom from guilt can happen only when she decides to stop looking back on her past, and Gavin has to move forward from his fear to become the man God wants him to be.

I love all social media! But my friend inspired me that spring day to avoid wasting time on even the silliest "news" sites about famous people and instead invest my words in something better. Building up, shoring up and lifting up the people around me. To be less "social" and more "community of faith."

I would love to hear about the special times in your life when someone's words lifted you out of a dark place! You can reach me on Facebook at Virginia Carmichael, my blog, virginiacarmichael.blogspot.com, or at the cyber recipe site Yankee-Belle Café. You can also write me a letter c/o Love Inspired Books, 195 Broadway, 24th floor, New York, NY 10007.

*Virginia Carmichael*

WE HOPE YOU
ENJOYED THIS

# LOVE
# INSPIRED®
## BOOK.

If you were **inspired** by this

**uplifting**, **heartwarming** romance,

be sure to look for all six Love

Inspired® books every month.

*Love Inspired*®

www.LoveInspired.com

SPECIAL EXCERPT FROM

*With her family in danger of being separated,
could marriage to a newcomer in town
keep them together for the holidays?*

*Read on for a sneak preview of*
An Amish Wife for Christmas *by Patricia Davids,
available in November 2018 from Love Inspired!*

"I've got trouble, Clarabelle."

The cow didn't answer her. Bethany pitched a forkful of hay to the family's placid brown-and-white Guernsey. "The bishop has decided to send Ivan to Bird-in-Hand to live with Onkel Harvey. It's not right. It's not fair. I can't bear the idea of sending my little brother away. We belong together."

Clarabelle munched a mouthful of hay as she regarded Bethany with soulful deep brown eyes.

"Advice is what I need, Clarabelle. The bishop said Ivan could stay if I had a husband. Someone to discipline and guide the boy. Any idea where I can get a husband before Christmas?"

"I doubt your cow has the answers you seek, but if she does I have a few questions for her about my own problems," a man said.

Bethany spun around. A stranger stood in the open barn door. He wore a black Amish hat pulled low on his forehead and a dark blue woolen coat with the collar turned up against the cold.

LIEXP1018

The mirth sparkling in his eyes sent a flush of heat to her cheeks. How humiliating. To be caught talking to a cow about matrimonial prospects made her look ridiculous.

She struggled to hide her embarrassment. "It's rude to eavesdrop on a private conversation."

"I'm not sure talking to a cow qualifies as a private conversation, but I am sorry to intrude."

He didn't look sorry. He looked like he was struggling not to laugh at her.

"I'm Michael Shetler."

She considered not giving him her name. The less he knew to repeat the better.

"I am Bethany Martin," she admitted, hoping she wasn't making a mistake.

"Nice to meet you, Bethany. Once I've had a rest I'll step outside if you want to finish your private conversation." He winked. One corner of his mouth twitched, revealing a dimple in his cheek.

"I'm glad I could supply you with some amusement today."

"It's been a long time since I've had something to smile about."

*Don't miss*
An Amish Wife for Christmas *by Patricia Davids,*
*available November 2018 wherever*
*Love Inspired® books and ebooks are sold.*

www.LoveInspired.com

# Love Inspired

## Save $1.00

on the purchase of any
Love Inspired® or Love Inspired®
Suspense book.

Available wherever books are sold,
including most bookstores, supermarkets,
drugstores and discount stores.

---

# Save $1.00

### on the purchase of any Love Inspired® or
### Love Inspired® Suspense book.

Coupon valid until April 30, 2019. Redeemable at participating retail outlets in the
U.S. and Canada only. Limit one coupon per customer.

52616033

5 65373 00076 2     (8100)0 12391

Canyon Air Force Base was silent. Houses shuttered, lights off. Streets quiet. Just the way it should be in the darkest hours of the morning. Captain Justin Blackwood didn't let the quiet make him complacent. Seven months ago, an enemy had infiltrated the base. Boyd Sullivan, aka the Red Rose Killer—a man who'd murdered five people in his hometown before he'd been caught—had escaped from prison and continued his crime spree, murdering several more people and wreaking havoc on the base.

"What are your thoughts, Captain?" Captain Gretchen Hill asked as he sped through the quiet community.

"I don't think we're going to find him at the house," he responded. "But when it comes to Boyd Sullivan, I believe in checking out every lead."

"The witness reported lights? She didn't actually see Boyd?"

"She didn't see him, but the family who lived in the house left for a new post two days ago. Lots of moving trucks and activity. She's worried Sullivan might have noticed and decided to squat in the empty property."

"Based on how easily Boyd has slipped through our fingers these past few months, I'd say he's too smart to squat in base housing," Gretchen said.

"I agree," Justin responded. He'd been surprised at how much he enjoyed working with Gretchen. He'd expected her presence to feel like a burden, one more person to worry about and protect. But she had razor-sharp intellect and a calm, focused demeanor that had been an asset to the team.

"Even if he decided to spend a few nights in an empty house, why turn on lights?"

"If he's there, he wants us to know it," Justin responded. It was the only explanation that made sense. And it was the kind of game Sullivan liked to play—taunting his intended victims, letting them know that he was closing in.

He needed to be stopped.

Tonight.

For the sake of the people on base and for his daughter Portia's sake.

*Don't miss*
*Valiant Defender by Shirlee McCoy,*
*available November 2018 wherever*
*Love Inspired® Suspense books and ebooks are sold.*

www.LoveInspired.com

Looking for inspiration in tales
of hope, faith and heartfelt romance?

Check out **Love Inspired**® and
**Love Inspired**® **Suspense** books!

**New books available every month!**

---

**CONNECT WITH US AT:**

Facebook.com/groups/HarlequinConnection

 Facebook.com/HarlequinBooks

 Twitter.com/HarlequinBooks

 Instagram.com/HarlequinBooks

Pinterest.com/HarlequinBooks

ReaderService.com

# *Love Inspired*®

## Inspirational Romance to Warm Your Heart and Soul

Join our social communities to connect with other readers who share your love!

Sign up for the Love Inspired newsletter at **www.LoveInspired.com** to be the first to find out about upcoming titles, special promotions and exclusive content.

### CONNECT WITH US AT:

Facebook.com/groups/HarlequinConnection

 Facebook.com/LoveInspiredBooks

Twitter.com/LoveInspiredBks

LISOCIAL2018